TRUTH

THE STR
WITHIN

DI Hamilton Book Four

Tara Lyons

Also By Tara Lyons

DI Hamilton Series
In The Shadows (Book 1)
No Safe Home (Book 2)
Deadly Friendship (Book 3)

Praise for Tara Lyons

"All I could say when I finished this book was OMG!!! I thought I was being pretty smart and has guessed the identity of the murderer boy was I wrong, I did not see that coming – what an excellent debut it is from Tara Lyons." **Donna Maguire - Donna's Book Blog**

"This is a must read for crime thriller fans!!" **Claire Knight - A Knight's Reads**

"An exciting chase for an unknown killer that takes the reveal to the very last pages and leaves you holding your breath. A fantastic read." **Emma Welton - Damppebbles**

"As a debut novel all I can say if the author has left herself a lot to live up to but given the quality of the writing and her ability to keep you on the edge of your seat I am sure she will rise to the challenge." **Amazon Reviewer**

"Tara Lyons has nailed it with this superb thriller." **Amazon Reviewer**

"Full of thrills and unexpected plot revelations, I found myself not wanting it to end." **Amazon Reviewer**

"Excellent characterisation and a brilliant plotline made this a five star read from beginning to end." **Anita Waller - Best selling author**

"I fell in love with DI Hamilton from the start, what a hero! I promise you this story will keep you on the edge of your seat. I WANT MORE!!" **Gemma Myers - Between The Pages Book Club**

"Despite the grimness of the topic in this novel, it is an easy and enjoyable read, a fast-paced excellently written thriller." **Caroline Vincent - Bits About Books**

"No Safe Home ticked all the boxes for me It is fast paced and gritty and definitely a must read I cannot recommend it enough giving it 5 massive gold stars." **Shell Baker - Chelle's Book Reviews**

"Tara Lyons has brought yet another cracking story to the table." **Susan Hampson - Books from Dusk Till Dawn**

"From the brilliant writing that flows throughout, to the intricate plotting that kept me guessing to the very end, this book had me hooked." **J A Baker - Author**

"Some real surprises and all wrapped up so well at the end. A thoroughly enjoyable read!" **Amazon Reviewer**

"A well written novel that holds you to the end. A nice twist and well observed characters, I couldn't put it down." **Amazon Reviewer**

"This book has a great prologue with that #killerhook right from the start and an awesome build up of suspense and anticipation that kept me wanting to turn those pages!" **Noelle Holten - Crimebookjunkie**

For Nan and Grandad
Reunited

Prologue

She sliced the razor blade across his throat with the confidence of an expert assassin. It wasn't her usual method, but improvisation was needed as he had stared up at her, lovingly and unknowing. He gasped, his dark brooding eyes widening as he thrashed on the bed, his shackled hands powerless to help. A choking gurgle reverberated from deep within his chest and a splattering of blood gushed from his mouth. His face fell to the side, the continual wheezing and giant gasps of breath infuriated her, while the crimson liquid streamed down his cheek and chin, joining the river flowing from his neck.

With his brain quickly starved of oxygen, the man's eyes rolled into the back of his head, unconsciousness taking over. She intently watched his every twitch and shudder, wishing she could actually witness the last breath escape from his already blue tainted lips. But time was against her. If permitted, she would happily stay rooted there on top of his naked body; his arms bound to the black iron headrest in expectation of pleasure. She would feel his skin turn cold underneath her and watch the light fade from his eyes. He deserved it. But time wouldn't allow such luxuries, and she jumped from her superior position.

She stood in front of the small mirrored tiles above the sink in the corner of the room and inspected the splashes of blood decorating her face, neck, chest and arms. Time wouldn't allow for a shower, either. She grabbed the white flannel from its place on the taps, ran it under the water and scrubbed the man's stains from her skin. The plan had been set in motion. This chapter of her life had finally ended and she needed to move on.

The woman rushed, brushing her hair into a sleek bun and then pulling a small box from underneath the bed. She slipped the cropped, black wig into place over her head and collected the man's clothes from the floor. Dressing in his black shirt and trousers, she finished the outfit with her own black trainers and bomber jacket. She paused briefly to roll the waistband up and over a few more times; already trying to push the image of the dying fat bastard from her mind. Inside the pockets she found keys, an access card and a decent sized wallet.

She inhaled deeply and unlocked the bedroom door. Now, it was time.

The silent hallway, illuminated only by the dim spotlights running along the ceiling, greeted her. All the doors along the corridor were shut, some locked, and the occupants inside fast asleep. The darkness that surrounded her wasn't an issue; she could walk these halls blindfolded and still find her way. Plus, the man visited her at the same inactive time every night, so as not to be found and caught — and she would do exactly the same.

Her fingers glided along the magnolia walls in an attempt to stop her from racing down the corridor. Her heart drummed double-time and her chest heaved with her short, sharp breaths. She felt as though she stood at the beginning of a marathon, itching to hear the sound of the klaxon — the sound that would set her feet free and catapulting over the starting line. Whispering to herself to keep calm, knowing her mind and body needed to work together, she stopped at her first obstacle and reached inside her pocket. The badge holder now sat firmly on her waistband and she gripped the huge collection of keys in her hand.

She pulled at the badge holder's chain and rested the access card against the black box situated next to the door handle. The light flashed from red to green. She stepped over the threshold into the main room and held her breath while her eyes scanned the area. The large TV stood idle in the corner of the room while the industrial wall clock seemed to cheer her on.

Tick.

You've got to get out of here.

Tock.

Almost there, not far to go.

Tick.

You've waited long enough.

Tock.

Although the CCTV camera focused on the main seating area, she took no chances and slowly closed the heavy door before flattening her back against the wall and sliding along it. She edged towards the lifts, willing her body and heart to slow down. A whistling tune from somewhere in the distance made her halt and close her eyes.

Tick. Tock. Tick. Tock.

The sound repeated, louder and louder, until it was the only thing drumming in her ears. Sucking in a lungful of air before opening her eyes, she continued slithering down her path. The cold wall came to an end and another CCTV camera was in place above her, monitoring access to the lifts and emergency exit. The other man, the one she had never seen, could peer at the CCTV screens at any moment. The cold bricks of the wall had offered some comfort, some security, and now, suddenly, she was too afraid to move from them. But the fear was fleeting as she thought about the naked bastard who could be found at any moment and what was waiting for her beyond this building. It was a gamble, but it was a gamble she had to take. Pushing herself from the wall and stroking the access card over the second black box, she fled through the door leading to the stairway. Panting, and without taking a moment to check her surroundings or if she was even alone, she descended the stairs two at a time; the thud of her heavy footprints and the beating of her heart deafened her.

On the ground floor, she took a moment to catch her breath and stared at the main door — her goal. As expected, her path wasn't clear; a bald muscular man sat in a cubicle surrounded by Perspex partitions. She couldn't keep the grin from tugging at her lips; the fat monster upstairs had violated her but, ultimately, had been her escape route and had inadvertently set her up with all she needed to know. Now, she watched the muscular man sitting with his feet on the table, leaning back in the chair, his eyes not on the camera screens but on his phone — gambling, she had been told.

To stay out of sight, she crouched and crawled closer to the main door. The thought of slicing his throat, too, had crossed her mind, but he was double her size — as was his weapon compared to hers. She needed to be clever. Calling on her inner logical self, she looked around, searching every inch of the area, and within seconds she was back on her feet. After racing across the corridor, she smashed the glass covering the red box with her elbow and pressed the emergency button, before dashing behind an adjacent machine.

'Shit!' the man screeched, barely audible over the siren, despite her now being so close to him that she could make out the tribal swirls of a tattoo snaking up from his shirt collar and around his thick neck.

The alarm shrilled throughout the building and the man was on his feet, thundering into the centre of the room. He used his radio, calling out to the fat bastard, but no reply came.

Tick.

You've only got seconds.

Tock.

He's going to find you.

Tick.

The others will be coming any moment.

Tock.

Muscle Man walked further away from her, towards the corridor she had just come from and reached for his access card. Chatter came over the radio; a woman's voice that she didn't recognise. But then, she'd seen so many people and heard so many voices.

'What's going on?' the mystery woman squealed.

'It's the fire alarm. I'm checking it now.'

'We have to get everyone out of here.'

'Hang on…' His voice was distant.

It had to be now. She took flight from her hiding spot, darting towards the door like a soldier at war. The siren was a mere drone in the background as she slipped between the metal detectors.

Access card swiped at the third and final machine, her hand steady and balanced, she then outstretched her hand holding the keys. She had five to choose from, but the decision was easy. The gold key slid in and turned the main lock with ease. She slipped out of the door and exhaled.

The night sky was black; not one star glistened down as a beacon of hope, but at this point, hope was insignificant. The cameras no longer mattered. The keys dug into her flesh as she ran towards the iron gates — the largest silver key holding her freedom. The whistling wind mingled with her short and erratic breaths as she slammed her free hand against the cold steel.

No one expects you to escape through the front door.

Like a wild dog, she sprinted down Lambeth Palace Road towards Albert Embankment; the River Thames sang to her, the city she grew up in calling her home, away from her prison. For ten minutes she ran, never looking back, but her ears pricked for the slightest hint that someone was following her. She stopped at Lambeth Bridge, not to catch her breath — she could run for miles after preparing her body — but instead to appreciate her victory. She gulped in the cool air and groaned while releasing it slowly. Closing her eyes, she titled her head back and allowed the breeze to wash over her face.

She was free.

Chapter One

Denis slid the blade across his cheek and flicked the excess foam peppered with fine, black stubble into the sink. Despite only approaching his fortieth birthday, Denis was old-school and preferred the traditional cut-throat shaving razor with its wooden flip-style handle and snapped-in-half razors over the modern electronic tools advertised everywhere for men these days.

The single beep from his mobile phone did nothing to disturb his concentration as he whisked away the last few strands of stubble with military precision. Tilting his face from side to side, checking the short beard was as perfect as he could manage, Denis then wiped a towel over his face and stared at his reflection. He hated to admit it, but he knew his features mirrored those of his estranged father — the big dark eyes, the chiselled jawline and the light-brown complexion of his skin. He shook his head, discarding the image of the man he had to remind himself had no impact on his life, and instead pictured his mother, Philippa, the born and bred Londoner now enjoying retirement in the picturesque Lake District. Philippa had raised Denis single-handedly, guiding him along the crossroads of life — never forcing his direction, but always encouraging him to do his best and help others whenever he could. It was one of the reasons he had decided to join the Metropolitan Police. His mother was an inspiration to him, and one of the strongest women he knew. With the exception, of course, of his wife Elizabeth. And with the faces of the two women in his life staring back at him in his mind's eye, his thoughts naturally wandered to Maggie, his daughter.

A hollow pain attacked his chest, and he sucked in a lungful of air as though he'd just narrowly escaped the overwhelming aggression of a tidal wave. Flashbacks of that night assaulted his brain, causing him to grip onto the cold steadiness of the bathroom sink in the hope of keeping himself grounded. A heartache that never dulled or subsided, never healed with time or became a distant memory. His one demon in life, the shadow that followed and haunted him every single day, was that he hadn't saved his only child. He was forced to live with an injustice that he would never be able to forget or move on from. Heartbreaking, he thought, how the simple task of shaving brought Maggie to his mind — how so many menial tasks did every day — and yet how, before she died, he was a stranger to the life-changing experiences taking place in her life.

Denis's mobile sprung to life again, this time, two text messages and a phone call in quick succession succeeded in piercing his thoughts. He grabbed it from where it sat on the closed toilet seat and, recognising the station's number, swiped at the green bar on his phone.

'Detective Inspector Hamilton.'

'Guv, it's me,' replied the voice on the other end.

'Clarke, what are you doing in the office this early?'

'My car's gone in for a service, thought I might as well come straight in, although I haven't had breakfast yet—'

'I'm assuming you didn't call to update me on your eating schedule,' Hamilton interrupted as he walked out of the bathroom and downstairs.

Detective Sergeant Lewis Clarke, the suave bachelor of Hamilton's Murder Investigation Team, had been his partner for four, coming up five, years. Although polar opposites in personality, looks and character, they worked well together, sharing a balanced bond between conventional and quirky. Recently, however, Hamilton had made more of an effort to work closely with the two newer members of his team, Detective Constable Robbie "Rocky" O'Conner and DS Yasmine Dixon; but, he had to admit, he missed his partner's laid-back attitude in the face of tragedy — something they were presented with on a daily basis.

'Hardly, guv,' Clarke chuckled. 'New case. DCI Allen was about to phone you himself, but found me—'

'I'm leaving the house now, give me twenty minutes and I'll be at the station for the briefing.'

Hamilton supported the phone between his cheek and shoulder as he slipped each arm into a thick wool, long-line black coat, wrapped a scarf around his neck and pulled a black woollen hat over his close-shaven head. He tapped his pockets, making sure he had his keys and wallet, set the alarm and left the house. While Clarke continued talking, Hamilton double-locked the front door as, for a change, his wife had left for work before him.

'Limited details at this time, guv. It's straight to the crime scene for us.' Clarke proceeded to give Hamilton the address while he climbed in the car and entered the postcode into his satnav. 'A wine bar in Soho … you'll probably have to pass the station.'

'I'll collect you on en route.' Hamilton rolled his eyes as he ended the call and reversed out of the driveway.

Twenty minutes later, the pair turned off Shaftesbury Avenue — down the wrong way of a one-way street — and onto Greek Street, parking near The Palace Theatre. Usually a hive of activity, the area was understandably quiet at 7.30am on a Friday morning; except for the inquisitive people who had wandered out onto the street, or those stopping on their way to work in an attempt to uncover why a police cordon had been erected.

Hamilton instructed the uniformed police on duty to keep the civilians as far back as possible. His biggest pet hate was social media, due to its instant power in sharing people's most intimate, terrifying or private moments with the world. He and Clarke walked away from the crowd, along the side of the theatre — its red-brick facade dominating the road — and towards The Empress wine bar.

Another uniformed officer greeted them at the entrance — a petite, tanned woman with blonde hair pulled back so tightly her eyebrows seemed to stretch up. The Empress was a small black building with a large neon sign spelling the words "cocktails and dreams" on the tinted windows. Hamilton couldn't see inside, but the officer informed him it was the flat upstairs he wanted.

'I think SOCO are almost finished, sir,' she said, pointing out the silver case packed with obligatory gloves and shoe covers. 'But take that front door and head up the stairs.'

He nodded his thanks and followed the officer's directions, Clarke in tow. Reaching the narrow landing, they were met with a howling screech and gushing cries just as pathologist Audrey Gibson stepped out of the room in front of them.

'Morning, Inspector, morning, Sergeant,' she said, pushing wisps of fiery red hair from her face and nodding over Hamilton's shoulder. 'That's the wife in the kitchen. She found her husband about an hour ago when she came home.'

'Have a chat with her, Clarke,' Hamilton instructed before returning his attention to Audrey — flushed cheeks glowing from her otherwise pale-white skin. 'May I?' He gestured to the room she stood in the doorway of.

A tall and slender man lay face down on the spotless cream carpet — spotless, that is, except for the claret stain made by the river of blood flowing from the gaping hole in his head.

'I'd estimate time of death was less than four hours ago,' Audrey informed him; another wail from the kitchen sent a shiver down Hamilton's spine.

'Is that the murder weapon?' he asked, pointing at the solid bronze sculpture of an embracing couple, already packed into a clear evidence bag.

'There's brain matter all over the base of that statue, so with this answer I don't feel like I need to estimate…' She smiled. 'Yes, it's the murder weapon, Inspector.'

He peered around the room and surmised that nothing seemed to be disturbed; a large flat-screen TV, Xbox console and laptop had been left behind in, what seemed, their rightful places. He thanked Audrey, who was ready to leave for the mortuary, and joined Clarke in the kitchen.

'Guv, this is Maureen Kane,' his partner said while walking the small length of the kitchen to meet him at the threshold. 'She came home about an hour ago and found her husband, Henry Kane, dead in the living room.'

Maureen bawled at the reality of the word "dead", and Hamilton walked further into the room, pulling a chair from underneath the small oval table to join the distraught woman. She made no attempt to look at him, kept her face down, black hair hanging loosely forward, reminding him of something from a horror movie.

'Mrs Kane,' he spoke softly and lightly touched her shoulder.

When she finally looked up, Hamilton's breath hitched at the sight of her beauty. Despite the sadness in her bloodshot and watery eyes, he couldn't ignore the woman's porcelain skin, smooth and blemish-free, which was accentuated by her full red lips.

'I shouldn't have left him alone,' she said, shaking her head.

'Where were you, Mrs Kane? And what time did you arrive home?'

She sighed. 'I visited a friend last night … had a few too many glasses of wine and … it was Henry who said I should stay over, safer than jumping on the tube. But … I don't like being away from him, so I got the first train home. And then …' Maureen covered her face as the tears fell.

'I understand this is difficult, Mrs Kane,' Hamilton said in a low voice, bending slightly to try and see her face through her hands. 'But the more information we can ascertain now the better.'

Maureen lifted her head again, her eyes closed while she inhaled deeply before fluttering her long lashes, blinking away the tears. 'I got home about six-fifteen … and it was so quiet in the flat, I thought Henry was still asleep. I hated the thought of disturbing him, so thought I'd lie on the couch … you know, watch some TV while I waited for him.' She paused to wipe the silent tears falling. 'And then … then … I saw the blood. I saw Henry.'

'Did you move your husband, or touch anything?' Hamilton asked.

She shook her head. 'No. Yes … I picked up the statue. We bought it on our honeymoon in Hawaii, we used to say it was the two of us hugging, but then … then I saw all that … stuff on it. I screamed. Dropped it and ran in here.'

'Is that when you called 999?'

'Yes. And I haven't been able to go back in that room since. That's awful of me, isn't it? I'm a coward, leaving my Henry all on his own.'

'It's totally reasonable, Mrs Kane, and probably the best thing you could have done. It means the crime scene won't have been contaminated too much, hopefully. Do you have any idea who would have done this?' The beautiful face frowned. 'I mean, nothing seems to have been stolen from the living room — though we'll need you to confirm that — so I'm doubtful this is a robbery gone wrong.'

Maureen gasped. 'No.'

'Is there access from the wine bar to your flat?'

'Yes,' she said, pointing to a black door behind her, which Hamilton had noticed and already assumed would lead back downstairs. 'Those stairs take you to the office behind the bar.'

Hamilton stood up, walked around Maureen and twisted the handle. The door swung open to reveal a dark staircase, equally as narrow as the one he and Clarke had just climbed.

'Oh my god,' Maureen exclaimed. 'That should have been locked. Henry *always* locks that door. He hates the idea of opportunists from the bar wandering up here.'

Hamilton murmured to himself and eased around the kitchen, looking for any signs of disturbance, though he didn't expect to find much.

'Clarke, make sure that door and this room is dusted for prints, too, if it hasn't been done already. Mrs Kane, in addition to checking your flat, we'll need you to confirm if anything is missing from the wine bar — which will need to stay closed for the time-being.'

'Yes, of course, I … I guess I'll need to contact the staff. We don't own the bar, we just manage it … about a year now. The flat came with the job.'

'You'll be appointed a Family Liaison Officer shortly, and they'll be more than happy to help with the task of informing people. But what I will need from you before I leave is any surveillance footage from outside the building, from the bar itself and if you have any up here.'

Maureen's eyes widened, the bloodshot vessels highlighted further. 'I never dealt with any of that stuff … I mean, I didn't t-think …' she stuttered.

Hamilton sat back in front of her and cupped her shaking hands in his own. 'It's okay, don't let this side of things worry you, that's my job. Are there cameras in the office downstairs?'

'Yes. But there's no cameras in the flat.'

Clarke reappeared, reassuring him SOCO had already collected evidence from the kitchen, and a team had already been sent downstairs to the office and bar area. Hamilton requested his partner join them, retrieve the CCTV footage when possible and meet him outside at the car.

'Okay, Mrs Kane, you've been very helpful, but just to clarify, there was no one your husband had any trouble or issues with? Maybe someone he'd thrown out of the bar recently that you can remember?'

Maureen frowned and shook her head. 'No. No, it's not like that in here. We don't run a tacky, boozy place. We serve people who want a few drinks with colleagues after work and those catching a show at The Palace. Being in central London, but running a calm establishment, is exactly what drew Henry and me to The Empress. He loves it here … loved. I mean loved.'

'And the name of your friend?'

'Pardon?'

'The friend you stayed with last night. We'll need that person to collaborate.'

The crying woman flinched. 'I don't understand … am I suspect? You couldn't possibly think I would hurt Henry?'

Hamilton stood and raised both hands outwards in front of him. 'It's procedure, Mrs Kane, and something that needs to be done. I'm sure you understand?'

Nodding, she said, 'Yes, of course. Susie Richmond. She lives in Paddington … Sussex Gardens. Number forty-two.'

'Okay, thank you, I'll send an officer to speak to Susie at some point. Unless you want us to contact her sooner, perhaps you'd like her to come and sit with you, once I've had an officer take an official statement from you—'

'What do you mean sit with me? I can't stay here. Are you all leaving now? What about Henry?' the woman said without taking a breath.

'Yes, I'm leaving, but uniformed officers will be here for a while. As I said, to take your statement and then shortly after that a Family Liaison Officer will arrive. As for your husband, he will be taken to the mortuary now for the post-mortem.'

Maureen nodded quietly, her entire body shivering as her focus returned to the floor once again, and Hamilton couldn't be sure if she had taken in all that he had said.

Chapter Two

When Hamilton and Clarke arrived in the incident room at Charing Cross Police Station over an hour later, the team were waiting to be briefed. All except Rocky, who seemed glued to his computer screen and oblivious to the fact they'd walked in, until Clarke not so subtly cleared his throat.

'Sorry, guv,' Rocky said, and swung his chair around the desk to join them. 'I was just tying up those loose ends from the last case that you requested.'

The young lad, as Hamilton saw him — although at the mature age of twenty-eight and currently finalising a divorce, Rocky was anything but a "lad" — ran a hand over his head, through the long, unruly, brunette hair and nodded at his superior. The team had just closed a triple-murder investigation involving a group of friends from Brunel University, but Hamilton understood from the look on Rocky's face that was not the case he had been referring to. Rocky joined Hamilton's team a couple of months ago and had worked two cases with a passion and eagerness that never faltered — as well as alerting him to a possible issue within his own team. Although the rookie had transferred from Hertfordshire, he was born in Ireland and left Drogheda as a teenager with dreams of joining the force and working in London.

'We'll catch up later regarding that,' Hamilton replied to Rocky before addressing the team as a whole. 'Let me update you all about this morning.'

He stood in front of a clear white board, where each new investigation began with little to no clues, but a lot of speculation. As frustrating as this period sometimes was, it could also be one of the most beneficial times in a case, Hamilton thought. With no obvious suspects at this point, his team's ideas usually went off in different directions, with each of them thinking independently about the murder case. It was then up to him to bring that all together and make them work — and think — as one.

'Clarke secured the CCTV footage, so I want the first priority to be someone looking over them,' Hamilton said.

'You think it could be a disgruntled punter?' Rocky asked, his mind clearly refocused on the new investigation.

He shrugged. 'I don't know if I'm convinced on that, but we can't discount it — it's not like it would be the first time a drunken customer has wanted to dish out some revenge.'

'I'll trawl over the CCTV with Clarke,' Rocky said. 'It might be worth going back at least a week or so to try and identify anything that would confirm or deny that theory.'

'Also, if the Kanes were only managing the bar, it could be a case of mistaken identity,' Dixon offered. 'Perhaps the killer was actually looking for the owner of The Empress.'

Hamilton nodded in agreement. It wasn't a hypothesis that had crossed his mind, and he liked her way of thinking. The newest member of his Murder Investigation Team, joining them at the beginning of their last case, Dixon was the one person Hamilton hadn't fully clicked with. But despite setting off on the wrong foot — thanks to an off-the-cuff joke from Dixon about throttling her children — they had worked together well on the previous investigation, and he found she offered fresh ideas with a straight-to-the-point approach.

'Yes,' he said. 'Dixon, I want you to find out everything you can about The Empress and the owner of the building. Also look into the last person to manage the wine bar — it could be them with the grudge.'

Lastly, he turned to his computer wizard of a sergeant, Kerry Fraser. After Clarke, Fraser was the longest serving member of the team and more efficient than all of them put together when it came to digging into the lives of victims and criminals. She had the potential to make one hell of an inspector one day, Hamilton felt.

'Fraser, I want you to find out who the Kanes are. Where did they come from before managing this wine bar? Who are their family? Are they in debt? Also, before I left the crime scene, I instructed PCs Goldberg and Williams to visit a Miss Susie Richmond. I'd like you to liaise with them at some point this afternoon and check that the woman confirms Mrs Kane's whereabouts.'

Satisfied that the team were busy with their assigned duties, Hamilton entered his office, sat down at the desk, and pulled out a thin file from his top drawer before studying its contents. Although it wasn't much — a still CCTV image, information regarding the arrest of a Pete Campbell and a single sheet of paper — it was all he had. It wasn't the arrest that troubled him — he'd added it purely for timeline purposes — but rather the image of Fraser collapsed on the ground on Stratford High Street and a man stepping over her. It had been due to this mystery man knocking her out as to why they nearly let Pete Campbell slip through their fingers just over a month ago. The picture was grainy, and only showed the man from behind, but it was clear to Hamilton that the unidentified male was tall, muscular — weighing at least fourteen stone — and had a razor-short haircut. The paper contained his own handwritten notes: *Johnny* and *drug-addict friend*.

All this information had been given to him by Rocky, who had found Fraser crying in her home after an anonymous delivery of rotten flowers. And although the lad hadn't wanted to break his colleague's confidence, Hamilton was glad he had. Hard work from his team is something Hamilton expected, and a trait Fraser had in abundance. Despite the fact she hung back in the office more than being out in the field, her work was imperative to making arrests, and he knew that many of them wouldn't have happened without her — and her computer skills. However, over the past month, Hamilton had seen a change in Fraser; she hadn't been making many witty remarks or contributing her opinion to cases as much. It was one of the reasons he hadn't approached her yet about the information Rocky had gathered together. Guilt gnawed at his insides like a rat, the feeling of betraying a colleague almost overwhelmed him, but he told himself he needed more information before he could confront Fraser.

Rocky had agreed with Hamilton's way of thinking, and the pair decided to look into Fraser's friend, Johnny, with the hope of giving her peace of mind regarding his whereabouts. However, due to their mammoth case load, it had been almost a week since he had discussed the situation with Rocky; though he knew these were the *loose ends* the constable had referred to in the incident room.

A knock at the door pulled Hamilton from his thoughts and he slipped the folder back into the drawer before inviting Dixon into his office.

She smoothed her long, jet-black hair behind her ears as she stepped into the room. Born in Marrakesh, Dixon's all-year-round sun-kissed glow made Hamilton shiver for a holiday; the countdown to his fortieth birthday and Christmas looming meant the temperature had dropped considerably in London. She stood tall and slender — an athlete's figure — with boundless amounts of energy, as though she was ready to give chase to a suspect at any second. Dixon's family had left Morocco when she was only two years old, and she had explained to Hamilton that she rarely visited her extended family. London was her home; Amersham to be exact — where she lived with Warren, her husband of ten years, and their two children, Sabrina and Ali. At the moment, everything Hamilton knew read like a background check on a stranger — he was still to uncover a deep knowledge of the person behind the sergeant title.

'Guv, I've tracked down the owner of The Empress wine bar … Joseph Wilde. I've just spoken to him on the phone, he was shocked but grateful that I'd told him about the break-in and murder, said he's going to head over there to see Mrs Kane, but it will take him about an hour.'

'Anything suspicious?'

Dixon turned down her mouth and shook her head. 'He sounded genuinely shocked over the phone, said he got on well with Henry Kane. The couple started working for him a year ago, managing the bar and renting the apartment upstairs. Said he'd even met up with them socially a few times. His record is clean, a legit businessman, owns a few wine bars dotted around the capital but doesn't manage any of them. He lives in Surbiton with his wife.'

'Okay, head over to The Empress anyway and have a chat with him. Find out just how *social* he was with them. Perhaps he had a thing for the wife and wanted Henry out of the way.'

'Surely he would have at least staged a robbery to throw us off his scent,' Dixon replied.

Hamilton shrugged with a wry smile. 'Hey, if we're offered amateur criminals, take it happily, because Lord knows it doesn't happen every bloody day. Sometimes the most obvious answer is the one staring us in the face.'

Dixon nodded while Hamilton stood up and the pair left his office to join the rest of the team in the incident room — just as Fraser ended a call.

'Boss, that was Audrey Gibson,' she informed him. 'Said she has something of interest for you and that you should phone or pop in to see her as soon as you have a chance.'

'I'll scoot over to the mortuary now. Rocky ... you join me.'

He also decided Dixon would visit The Empress alone — there were officers and the FLO at the scene to question the wine bar owner with her — while Clarke and Fraser stayed behind to continue with the CCTV viewing.

Hamilton waited until they were in the car and pulling away from the station before he asked Rocky what he'd uncovered so far. Rocky sighed heavily, causing Hamilton to take his attention off the road for a few seconds — focusing on the sergeant as he turned in his seat. It was then that Hamilton noticed the lack of brightness in the lad's hazel eyes, and the dark circles beneath them.

'Well ... spit it out,' he said.

'Johnny Tanner — Fraser's childhood friend and drug-addict — has been located.'

'That's a good thing, now we can—'

'No, it's not good,' Rocky interrupted, and Hamilton piped down to hear him explain. 'I found Johnny in The Wellness Rehabilitation Centre in Fraser's hometown of Kent. He didn't send her those rotting flowers ... they were hand delivered.'

'And he was in rehab at the time?'

'Yes.'

'What about the incident on Stratford High Street?'

'He was in rehab then, too,' Rocky continued. 'In another attempt to kick the drug habit, Johnny tried to take his own life about four months ago. He's on suicide watch and receiving daily therapy and care. It wasn't him.'

Hamilton drove over the roundabout while drumming his fingers on the steering wheel. 'What if you've found the wrong Johnny Tanner?'

'I haven't. It's him. I saw a photograph at Fraser's house and I visited The Wellness Centre over the weekend ... I didn't speak to Johnny, just a member of staff.'

Hamilton raised his eyebrows as they pulled into the mortuary car park. He'd been unaware of just how far Rocky had taken this after-hours investigation and was impressed with his forward-thinking. He parked the car and sat back with a sigh.

'Okay, so Fraser has assumed Johnny sent the maggot-infested flowers because she disowned him, and what happened in Stratford was just someone helping our suspect get away while she gave chase ...' Hamilton summarised.

'Yes.'

He turned to face Rocky. 'But we now know different. While these could be unrelated incidents, we can't ignore the fact that we don't have the answers for them, and we can't leave our colleague, and our friend, in the dark.'

'Remember her cat went missing?' Rocky remarked. 'Well, what if it hasn't gone missing at all, but this same man who struck her from behind and sent the flowers also took her cat?'

'The facts you're putting together point to a possible stalker, you do realise that, don't you?'

Rocky turned away, facing forwards out of the window and silently watched the hospital staff enter and exit the building. He just nodded as an answer to Hamilton's question.

'Then even more reason we have a duty of care to inform Fraser what you've found.'

'I know,' the sergeant said as he hung his head. 'She'll be disappointed that I betrayed her trust though, guv.'

Hamilton inhaled deeply and slowly released the puff of hot air. 'Probably … but in the long run, it's the right thing to do.'

'Nothing's even happened … I mean, those flowers were delivered weeks ago.' Rocky lifted his head, a look of childish hope etched on his face.

'Exactly, so no harm telling Fraser because it's probably all blown over now. We'll do it together once we've closed this case. How about that?'

Rocky agreed, and although the hope had been squashed, the sergeant still seemed a fraction more positive than he first did, Hamilton felt. They both exited the car, heading towards the mortuary entrance of the hospital in silence. Hamilton wasn't sure what he believed; whether Rocky had blown everything out of proportion or if indeed Fraser was being followed by the man in the CCTV image. But what he did know was that she was the type of woman who would not appreciate being kept in the dark, and that was something he could rectify.

Hamilton sped up, the sharp wind whipping against his skin, and pulled the scarf higher around his cheeks. 'Come on,' he said. 'Let's see what Audrey thinks will interest us.'

Chapter Three

Eighteen years ago

She sat in her room, snuggled up in the single bed with her new duvet — covered with an image of her favourite boyband, Five — pulled up as far as it could go while still allowing both arms to rest on top to hold her book. Half way through *Romeo and Juliet* — reading for pleasure, not yet on her school syllabus — it was quickly becoming one of her all-time favourite books, and she had quite a few, because she had fallen in love with the *idea* of love. She was infatuated with how, despite being teenagers, both Romeo and Juliet *knew* they belonged together.

No one will ever love me like that.

Not with the gap in the middle of her two front teeth, her lank hair which was neither brown nor blonde. It was that ridiculous colour everyone referred to as "mousy" — a word no one in their second year of high school wanted to be referred to as — and it couldn't be styled thanks to its lifelessness. She hated the endless number of freckles on her face and neck and arms, which seemed to have multiplied like rabbits over the summer holidays. She had what her mother continually referred to as "puppy fat", which her mother also said was "totally normal with all the hormones flying around."

The summer holidays had not only brought with it extra freckles and her thirteenth birthday, but also her first period. She wondered if her mate T — who was tall and slim with a headful of bouncy curls as bright as the sun —

has started her period. T had no "puppy fat" and Devon, *the coolest boy in school,* always wanted to talk to *her*.

He never wants to talk to me.

She heard the light creak of the floorboard outside her room and ducked down to a lying position, throwing the book under the duvet as she did. Her mother had told her to go to sleep hours ago, but she'd been busy secretly scribbling in her diary about the joke Devon had made in class that day before picking up a book to read. The house had gone quiet about an hour previously, and she knew that meant they had all gone to bed. So she'd switched the light on, thinking she would be safe to finish the book.

As her bedroom door slowly opened, she realised she'd been busted, that her mother must have spotted the glimmer of light under the door while passing. So she was surprised to actually see the figure of a man peering into her room.

'Everything okay?' she asked.

He placed his finger over his lips as he stepped inside the room and gently closed the door behind him. *Too gently.* He sat down at the end of the bed, his weight pulling the duvet tight over her feet, and smiled.

'Is Mum okay?' she asked, frowning as to why he had come into her room at this time of night. He never had before.

'She's fine,' he whispered. 'Actually, she's asleep, so we better keep it down.'

'Oh.'

He smiled again and then looked around her room, stroking the duvet as he did. He focused on its image for a few moments and then asked if she liked Five.

'Yeah, of course, you know they're my favourite.'

'I love their song … you know, that one about in the dark, I'll show you my love. It's always playing on the radio,' he said and moved closer, his voice still a soft hush.

'Yes, "When the Lights Go Out." I love it too. I know all the words.'

'I bet you fancy one of them, too, don't you?'

She felt her cheeks flush with heat.

'Come on, tell me which one it is.'

She giggled. 'I think Scott Robinson is really cute.'

'No way. My friend knows Scott … yeah, he's a Londoner, isn't he? I'm sure if I ask my mate, he'd arrange for you to meet him.'

'Seriously? That would be amazing … I mean, wow, really? Could you really do that?'

He smiled. 'I've got the connections, and for you … well, for you I'd do anything.'

She squealed and sat up in the bed, but he placed his finger over her lips and reminded her that her mother was sleeping. Apparently, she had a migraine, and it would be unfair to wake her at such a late hour, he had added.

He moved closer again, this time so much so that she had to move her hand away so he didn't sit on it or so it didn't end up on his thigh. She swallowed hard.

'Your mum told me what happened to you this summer … you're a woman now, you know? You'd need to be careful … meeting pop stars and hanging around with boys at school.'

Her eyes widened. 'My mum told you that? I thought it was just between us… I mean, it's girl stuff.'

'I know, sweetie, but she tells me everything. She trusts me and so should you. I'd keep your secrets … if you wanted me to, of course.'

But Mum said that would be our *secret — girls together. Yes, it means I'm becoming a woman, she also said that, but that it was my decision who I told. I haven't even told my friends yet.*

He lightly stroked her face with the tips of his fingers, dragging her thoughts away from her mother. Opening and closing her mouth again, she wanted to tell him to stop, but the word wouldn't come. She focused on the creases of the duvet cover, Scott Robinson now looking disfigured with the folds in his face, anything to not look at *him*.

'I bet you're surprised your mum told me, aren't you?' he asked.

She looked at him and nodded.

'It's because she loves me. She told me I'm the best thing that has ever happened to her. Also, mummies do lie, sweetie. Your mum doesn't want you to grow up and have all the fun, she probably told you that you didn't have to tell anyone that you had your first period, if you didn't want to. But I see it … I see the woman you're blossoming into.'

His hand trailed down her neck, his fingers resting on her collarbone, his palm on her chest. She gasped but didn't have the chance to say anything before his lips briefly touched hers.

'I don't want … no … don't,' she mumbled and pulled back her head.

He followed her movement. With their faces still just inches apart, she could smell his warm breath mixed with a hint of stale beer. The hand on her chest felt heavier, as if he were pushing her to lie back down, and his free hand pulled back her Five boyband duvet.

'I'll show you I can keep your secrets,' he said. 'I'll show you the woman you've become.'

Chapter Four

Audrey Gibson was in her office when Hamilton and Rocky arrived. She greeted them with a smile and jumped into conversation immediately. Hamilton couldn't decide if this was purely down to a chatty nature or if it were more the desperate *need* to speak. The prospect of spending most of your day with the dead would certainly entice as much conversation as possible with the living, he thought.

'We could have done this over the phone,' she said, 'but I'm glad you're here. Please, both of you take a seat. It's rare I have the time to chat to you in here.'

While Audrey rooted through her files and folders, the two men did as they were instructed — each pulling a chair from the large table. Hamilton watched as the red-headed woman hummed unwittingly to herself until she found what she was looking for, then she struck her index finger in the air and took a seat herself.

'Yes, so, Mr Kane,' she said, thumbing through a folder. 'As we said, cause of death was the blow to the back of the head. However, during the post-mortem, I discovered quite a few wounds.'

'He was tortured?' Hamilton asked.

She smiled and shook her head. 'No, forgive me. What I mean is much older wounds … healing wounds.'

'Such as?'

Audrey cast an eye over her files and filled her lungs. 'Bruising on the left thigh, ribs two to five on his left side were also broken, as well as what look like burn marks on his right forearm. All at different stages of the healing process.'

'So, Mr Kane could have been in a fight recently and sustained these injuries?' Rocky asked, peering up from his notebook.

'Hmmm, it would have been more like a few fights,' Audrey replied. 'As I said, they're at different stages, so the broken ribs for example probably happened well over a month ago, but the burn marks — which appear to be from something like a cigarette or a cigar — are much more recent.'

Hamilton leant forward, pressing his fingers into a steeple and balancing his chin on them as he listened to Audrey and Rocky volley their thoughts back and forth across the table. Something bugged him — an itch he couldn't reach at the corner of his mind; something begging to be remembered.

'I could give Clarke a call, guv,' Rocky said, disturbing his thoughts. 'Limit the amount of CCTV he's looking at … although, of course, a fight might not necessarily have happened at the wine bar. Perhaps the wife could shed more light on the brawl.'

'Yes …' Hamilton agreed and stood. 'Is that all?'

'For now, yes, Inspector,' Audrey said, and brushed her hair away from her face.

Hamilton thanked her and left the room, instructing Rocky to call Clarke, requesting he study a specific time frame of the CCTV — his own assumptions now coming to the fore — and then to contact Dixon and inform her of their imminent arrival.

London's streets were crowded — no longer due to the police cordon — just a few hours later. Greek Street and the surrounding Soho area was filled with commuters, tourists, shoppers and theatre-goers out in droves. The city was used to it.

Dixon stood outside The Empress wine bar, her jet-black hair now pulled back in a clip, rubbing her gloved hands together and hopping from foot to foot in the cold.

'Got the information you needed, boss?' she asked.

'Yes, I think so. Who's upstairs?'

'The family liaison officer was already here when I arrived — Susan ... something, I can't remember. And Joseph Wilde just showed up, he's talking to Mrs Kane now. She gave me a list of employees, so uniform are in the process of tracking them down to interview.'

Hamilton nodded and brushed past Dixon, motioning with his head that she and Rocky should follow him up the stairs. He wasn't surprised to find Mrs Kane still sitting in the exact spot he had left her in at the kitchen table. Though her husband's body had been removed, the sight of his blood on the carpet would be upsetting. He briefly cast his eyes over Joseph Wilde, a heavy-set man — double the size of Mr Kane — with a head full of dark hair, peppered grey at the temples, and wearing dark-rimmed glasses. The man sat opposite Mrs Kane, gripping the woman's hand as it rested on the table.

'Maureen, hello. I'm Detective Inspector Hamilton. I spoke with you this morning.'

'I remember,' she mumbled, and watched as he sat next to her — face and eyes as swollen, and yet still as beautiful, as before.

'I had a few more questions I'd like to ask you.' He took her silence as permission to continue and explained about the wounds found on her husband.

The woman turned down her mouth. 'Henry didn't tell me about any fights.'

'And you didn't ask?'

'What do you mean?'

Hamilton folded his arms. 'Surely you would have noticed the bruising on his thigh, and Mr Kane would have been in some discomfort for a while … I mean, you wouldn't have even been able to hug him without him crying out in pain, I'm sure.'

The woman licked her dry lips and sighed. 'We … hadn't been intimate for a while … So, no, I wouldn't have noticed.'

'Was the lack of affection due to problems in your marriage?' Hamilton probed, noticing the twitch along Mrs Kane's jawline.

'No.' She frowned and looked across to Joseph who smiled and rubbed his thumb across her hand. She pulled her hand away and reached for the packet of cigarettes on the table. Tears sprung from her eyes but she said nothing.

'I'd been wondering if those were yours,' Hamilton said, and then sighed loudly. 'You see, when I discovered Mr Kane had burn marks along his forearm, I thought of that packet of fags I'd seen in here earlier, but couldn't remember if I'd actually seen you smoking.'

'It was self-defence,' Mrs Kane suddenly screamed, her eyes wide as she scanned the room. 'He dragged me home from Susie's house … said I wasn't allowed any friends … said he was going to kill me.' She wiped the tears now gushing down her face and chucked the cigarette in the ashtray. 'I have bruises too … he hit me all the time. For years. I finally found the strength to fight back this morning, after hours of him bullying me and not letting me sleep. I just lost it and hit back. I kicked him in the ribs and reached for the statue after he punched me.'

Mrs Kane moved to the edge of the seat, her right leg bouncing up and down, wringing her hands together as she looked around the room again.

'But the damage to your husband's ribs happened much earlier than just this morning,' Hamilton said, pulling himself to the edge of his own chair. 'Nevertheless, let's move on from there for just a second, as you've already mentioned your friend … Susie Richmond, wasn't it? You see, I've spoken to my colleagues in the office, and the police officers who went to her home this morning discovered Susie wasn't there. And she hasn't been there for over a week; she's on holiday, a neighbour confirmed. We've also checked the CCTV footage — namely the camera focusing on the main entrance — and no one left or entered this building after midnight. So, when exactly did your husband drag you home?'

'N-no… You've got it wrong,' Mrs Kane stuttered, but a darkness had overshadowed her face, the porcelain skin now looking ghost-like, the tears and sorrow disappearing.

Hamilton leaned forward and stared the woman directly in her eyes. 'And while I believe that you did, in fact, kick your husband in the ribs, leg and thigh, and even stubbed out your ciggies on him, our pathologist has confirmed that these happened at different intervals over the past month or so — one hundred per cent not last night or this morning. It was *you* who bullied your husband. Did *he* finally try to stand up to *you* this morning and you lashed out at him again? Only this time, it wasn't with your foot but with a brass statue.'

Mrs Kane screeched as she leaped from the chair, running for the door leading to the wine bar, only to be met by two police officers.

'Maureen Kane, you are under arrest for the murder of Henry Kane—'

'No!' she screamed, as Hamilton continued to read the woman her rights, lashing out like a wild beast. 'This is all wrong. It … it's self-defence. I was protecting myself. What weasel husband lets their wife beat them up? Joseph, help me out.'

As Dixon escorted Mrs Kane from the kitchen, with the woman's arms flailing in the air and her protests echoing in their wake, Hamilton turned to the owner — his face now as white as the ceramic floor tiles.

Joseph shook his head. 'I can't believe it. Are you sure?'

'Mrs Kane has continually lied since I met her this morning; about her alibi, her husband's wounds and now she's just shown that lovely temper of hers. Of course, further investigation will be needed, and my officers will continue to talk to the other employees to gauge if they noticed anything about the couple's relationship, but I think it's clear what Mrs Kane was doing,' Hamilton explained.

'They looked so happy. I mean, Henry was a bit quiet, but … but I never would have imagined it was because he was … what … being abused by his wife? Really?'

'Sadly, domestic abuse can happen to anyone, Mr Wilde. Bullying and mistreatment doesn't discriminate against gender.'

The man shook his head. 'That saying really is true; you just never know what happens behind closed doors … or the strangers you classed as friends and employees who are living within those bricked walls.'

Once the team had returned to the station, Hamilton requested Dixon and Rocky lead the interrogation with Mrs Kane after the woman's solicitor had arrived. It wasn't often a murder suspect was arrested on the same day the body was found, Hamilton thought, and was pleased with how efficiently his team had worked, as well as how swiftly Audrey Gibson had informed him about the post-mortem findings … another rarity. Hamilton climbed the stairs to the incident room, knowing if he could make a start on his notes, or at least update DCI Allen, he'd have ended the week on a high.

'Alright, guv,' Clarke greeted him. 'I'm just processing the exact frames of the CCTV we need to prove Mrs Kane's story was completely fabricated.'

'Brilliant. Let's get the full reports from the officers who visited Susie Richmond's house in there also,' Hamilton replied, gazing around the room. 'Where's Fraser?'

'She popped home. A neighbour messaged her about a window being left wide open and, because she's heading out tonight after work, she wanted to dash back and lock-up properly.'

He looked at his watch and shrugged. 'Not much point coming back to the office, not when we can finish up here.'

'Well, she's only having a drink across the road at The Duke and Duchess with that red-head pathologist.'

'Audrey.'

'Yeah, her. She's a bit of alright, don't you think?' Hamilton didn't comment but pulled his mobile from his coat pocket. 'Fraser invited us along, but I've already got a hot date. Do you fancy a few pints with them?'

'Not tonight, I'd—'

'Rather get home to the missus and watch a film?'

Hamilton caught the teasing tone and looked up — a wicked smile evident on Clarke's face. He rolled his eyes and light-heartedly grunted.

'Oh, how well you know me, partner.'

Clarke laughed. 'How is Elizabeth? Planning a surprise party for the big four zero, I bet?'

Hamilton peered back at his phone. 'Well, if I knew, it wouldn't be much of a surprise … but she bloody better not be. I've sent Fraser a text and told her not to bother coming back to the office. I'll update the chief and then clock off for the evening.'

'Sure thing, guv, I'll catch-up with Dixon and Rocky … make sure we've collated all the evidence. Have a good weekend.'

'And you, mate,' Hamilton said as he walked away, planning for nothing more than a few chilled days with Elizabeth.

Chapter Five

Nightfall and its unwelcome collage of thoughts and feelings came all too soon for Hamilton. Although he and Elizabeth had begun the weekend with the peace and quiet he had yearned for, something … something he couldn't quite put his finger on, was missing. He suddenly realised this wasn't the first time in the last few months he had felt this way; whether it was due to the cases he had recently worked involving children or his old friend, Billy, coming back into his life with his young daughter, Amelia. After sighing deeply, Hamilton rubbed his eyes, then crossed his hands around the back of his head and stared up at the plain white ceiling.

Maggie's face filled the void, filled his thoughts; the wild brunette curls that bounced around her oval, olive-skinned face, framing her huge brown eyes … those eyes were impossible to forget. She could speak to him with those vibrant eyes. They had always told him so much — whether she was happy or sad, or excited. And yet, when she needed him the most, he hadn't heard her. Had the sparkle faded long before that night? Had she smiled and laughed as often as before? Did her eyes really speak to him, or was it just something he consoled himself with now … because how could he have missed all the signs?

He wondered what Maggie would look like now, on the verge of her twenty-first birthday. Would she smell the same, from the coconut scent of her face cream and strawberries from her shampoo? He smiled, thinking of how she might be enjoying her fresher's year at university; she'd always had a passion for animals, and cared about them dearly. He had imagined her becoming a vet and, someday, owning her own practice. How could someone so pure and beautiful and innocent be bullied and pushed to—

'Penny for them?' Elizabeth's smooth voice burst his thoughts as she slipped into the bed next to him.

He propped himself up, resting his head on his hand and focused on his wife's emerald green eyes. He smiled but shook his head.

'What did the counsellor say?' she asked, eyebrows raised.

'I wouldn't know. I've never seen one.' He attempted to sound light-hearted and jokey, but he knew she could see right through him, she always could — they had been together since they were seventeen.

'When we think about Maggie, we should share those thoughts and memories with each other … we should talk about her together.'

'How did you know?'

Elizabeth's pink lips drew a knowing smile. 'I know that face. That far-away, reminiscing look you get when you want to smile and be happy at the memories, but yet, it's also the last thing you want to do because you feel so guilty. We shouldn't feel guilty for thinking about her—'

'But I should feel guilty about not saving her.'

She sighed. 'Oh, Denis. You can't blame yourself for that forever. How many times are you going to make me say that? And you can't continue to use the word *I* … like you did this on your own. I mean, I'm a teacher for heaven's sake, I should know the warning signs of bullying. It was something our beautiful daughter kept from us both.' Elizabeth's voiced pitched, causing her to pause for a moment. '*We,* the two of us as a mother and father, didn't save her.'

He took a moment to study his wife; the firm-but-fair school headmistress who loved the idea of having a laugh, but, somehow, never managed to fully partake in it. Just like him. The way she always offered a smile to other people's joy or celebrations, yet that happiness never reached her eyes. Just like him. They carried their sorrowful past into every waking moment, into their present choices and their future dreams.

'There isn't a word for losing a child,' she said softly. 'You can be a widow or an orphan, but …'

He brushed away the strands of wavy, auburn hair that had fallen over Elizabeth's face, tucked them behind her ear and pulled her closer to him. There were no words, Hamilton thought — no words to comfort the heart-wrenching statement she'd just made. But, for once, he wasn't going to feel guilty about it. He couldn't always make things appear better by saying the right words, he summarised — not for what they have both been through. It wouldn't be the end of that particular conversation, whatever it was or wherever it was headed, but for tonight it didn't matter. He held Elizabeth in a loving embrace.

Hours later, under a blanket of total darkness, Hamilton's phone came to life with an urgent message he couldn't ignore. He gently slipped his arm from under his wife and tip-toed as quickly — and as quietly — as he could around the bedroom grabbing at everything he needed.

***

Hamilton marched into the incident room just after 4am, surprised to find Clarke already there — and already half a cup of coffee into the morning.

'For Christ's sake, why weren't we sent straight to the crime scene?' Hamilton bellowed. 'What the hell is going on?'

Clarke shrugged. 'I know as little as you do. Urgent briefing for everyone, that's all.'

'I don't see the need for all the cloak and dagger stuff. Where's everyone else?'

'Dixon's gone looking for the chief. She's as impatient as you.'

Hamilton frowned and made his way to the alcove in the corner of the office, a kitchenette-type area the team had cobbled together, and switched the kettle on to make tea. Hamilton couldn't function without at least three cups of the strong, sugary stuff, especially if it was before six in the morning. He sighed and wrapped his fingers around the warm mug, hating the wait in the dark but clearly having no choice in the matter.

'So, you were out last night, weren't you?' he attempted a conversation to stave off his impatience. 'Hope you didn't down too many pints.'

'Not a one.' His partner grumbled a noise — an all most half-hearted laugh — and shrugged nonchalantly.

Hamilton perched on the edge of Clarke's desk. When he received nothing further, which was very unlike his chatty partner, he simply raised his eyebrows.

Clarke chuckled and rubbed a hand up and down his face. 'Ah, I don't know, it's nothing really. Can't really sleep lately and I've lost my appetite, but it's probably just … I'm so busy. You get it, we're all bloody busy here.'

Hamilton said nothing, but eyed Clarke; his partner took pride in his appearance, and was always well turned out, but today there was more to it. A new crisp pinstriped suit, a sparkle in those tired eyes and an over-powering aroma of expensive aftershave.

'Don't tell me it's a woman, mate?' Hamilton stood and clapped a hand across Clarke's shoulder. 'It bloody is, isn't it? Has someone finally got their claws into the bachelor of the station, our very own Lewis Clarke?'

The colour rose from his partner's neck, a red rash had snaked itself along his cheeks and reached his ears like wildfire. 'Shut up, Denis.'

Hamilton's eyes widened. Clarke never called him by his first name. 'Whoa, this must be serious. So, who is she? That hot date from last night, eh?'

It was rare for Hamilton to get involved with any type of gossip, but this wasn't just his partner of nearly five years. This was "I'll-never-be-tied-down-by-a-woman" Clarke.

'Well, yes. No, not exactly.' Clarke gazed around the room and hunched his head down, as if the computer screen would shield his words. 'It's Audrey.'

'Audrey Gibson?' Hamilton roared. The look of horror on Clarke's face encouraged him to tone down the volume. 'How could you have a date with Audrey? I thought she was going to the pub with Fraser?'

Clarke rolled his eyes. 'Jesus, I feel like a flaming teenager talking to you like this. But … I don't know. This is weird. I'm weird. I didn't have a date last night, but when they said they were heading to The Duke for a few, I didn't want them to think I'd been waiting for an invite from them … so, I just made the date up. I planned to join them about an hour later and say the woman wasn't my cuppa, and maybe turn my charm on to the red vixen from pathology, but …'

Far more interested than he ever thought he would be — perhaps it was the early morning start or lack of free time for his own life, he thought — Hamilton pressed Clarke to continue.

'Well, Fraser and Audrey had already left by the time I got to the pub. I could hardly text them to see where they were 'cos they'd think I crashed and burned with my date—'

'Heaven forbid.'

'And what if they'd gone off with a pair of geezers themselves; I'd look like a right prat and—'

'That's not your style.'

'So, I had one pint and went home. It's all a bit …' Clarke glanced around the office again and whispered, 'Fucked up.'

Hamilton couldn't contain the laughter escaping his lips. 'I'm sorry to inform you, partner, but I think you're in *love.*'

'Don't talk wet, guv,' Clarke replied, and pulled his suit jacket straight. 'And, actually, no more talking about this again, full stop. I shouldn't have bloody mentioned it.'

The conversation was abandoned when Dixon barged through the door.

'The chief's ready for this briefing,' she said.

Her golden skin appeared paler today, as if the years of witnessing unthinkable crimes had finally caught up with her — or perhaps she just wasn't an early riser — and Hamilton noticed the deep furrows in her brow.

'Have you been told anything yet?'

'Erm … a bit. Murder case, guv.'

Hamilton bit his tongue on a snide remark and instead rolled his eyes at the sergeant's weak answer. However, she'd clearly understood his frustrated look and attempted to shake away her tiredness before continuing.

'Sorry, guv, it's a bit of a complex one … and I'm not fully up to speed with everything yet. I really should leave it to the chief to update you on this one. But I can tell you that we need to get over to Manor Hall Hospital, it's on the Thames. And we need to get there as soon as we bloody can.'

The change in Dixon's tone intrigued Hamilton, but he attempted to keep his countenance calm and asked where the rest of his team were. All the while, however, his thoughts were as busy as a worker bee in a hive … and he couldn't focus on one single thing.

'Rocky's in the briefing room already, but the chief said he's not waiting any longer for the rest of the team … he said we work with who we have here now, and that's final. We have to get over to that hospital, guv.'

He nodded as he followed Dixon's marching figure through the door. 'Sounds ominous. Okay, let's go, we can catch Fraser up when she finally makes an appearance.'

Chapter Six

Eighteen years ago

A week had passed since he had sneaked into her bedroom. She had stripped the sheets, the Five boyband duvet thrown into the bin — much to her mother's surprise — and she'd made up a story about growing too old to have pop stars on her bed and posters on her walls. It felt as though everything in her life had changed, yet everything was exactly the same. Her mother woke her every morning for school with breakfast waiting downstairs and waved her off when she left the house; her friends at school gossiped about the new girl in class and talked about the latest storyline in *Hollyoaks*. She felt nothing. Numb.

Every night she sat up, in the corner of her bed, knees pulled up under her chin and stared at the door. She watched for any silhouettes passing, blocking the light from the hallway that creeped under the bottom of the door. Her mother couldn't understand why she now insisted on that light being left on at night, and she wasn't prepared to tell her the real reason. Instead, she shrugged it off, hoping her mother wouldn't push the issue and quietly prayed her demand was listened to. It was, and so she waited. She waited for the light to be blocked for more time than it took for someone to walk past to use the bathroom or to go downstairs. She waited for the door to quietly swing open again. She waited for him.

Her copy of *Romeo and Juliet* had slipped down the side of her bed that night, a week ago, and that's where she left it. Her longing to read of star-crossed lovers now made her stomach turn. Her images of love and romance had decayed like a poisonous apple, and she now understood why some people choose to write about evil witches and demons — far more truth than make-believe when it came to mirroring her reality.

Tonight, she sat in the position that had become normal and squeezed her hands together in prayer. She formed a new nightly routine of whispering to God, or the angels, or to anyone who would listen, asking to be left alone. She opened her eyes, noticed her knuckles turning white with the pressure, loosened the grip on her own hands and tried to steady her breathing.

She peeked out of her window, too afraid to have the curtains closed and her room be propelled into complete darkness, and looked up at the clear black sky. Not a star twinkled, but the moon shone in a cloudless sky and she took that as some kind of offering of hope.

Sleep beckoned her, as it always did at this late hour, but she brushed it off. The wall clock said midnight, and it had been twelve thirty when he'd come into her room last week, so she told herself that she only had to last another half hour. It was starting to catch up with her, the lack of sleep, and it was showing in her day-to-day activities. Her English teacher had been shocked to find her napping in class yesterday and threatened to call her mother. She'd promised it was a one-off, not sleeping the night before due to an upset stomach, and breathed a sigh of relief when the teacher chose to believe her. Luckily, with no school tomorrow, it wouldn't matter if she only got a few hours of rest ... just until her mother woke up in the morning at least.

With the claws of sleep dragging down her heavy eyelids, it became more and more difficult to ignore the call of dreamland; a place where T curled her hair before their Saturday trip to the cinema, where she laughed at a joke Devon interrupted the class with, where her grandparents visited for a Sunday roast, and where she hugged and kissed her mother each morning before leaving the house.

A song played in the background; a gentle melody that she knew well but couldn't find the words to sing along to. She was at the beach and realised, right there in that tranquil moment, that it was her most favourite place to be. She smiled. Although she'd only been to this particular seaside once, it felt like home. It felt safe. She walked across the sand slowly, so the soft warm grains could find the groves of her toes and nestle in there … until the shore became harder and wetter, and the white peaks of the waves crashed down and ran across her skin. She looked out to the ocean, to the endless rhythm of the waves, until it finally met the turquoise of the never-ending sky. The sea sparkled in the sun. She closed her eyes, committing that image to her memory, begging herself never to forget it, and tilted her head to the sunshine. The heat soaked into her skin, giving her the energy she needed, an uninterrupted boost her soul craved. Until the waves grew higher and splashed her hands and stomach. She stepped back, looked down and frowned; the ebbing tide crawled further away from her. Another splash to her hand made her spin around.

She gasped, the shining sun had been stolen by the gloom of the night. Her eyes blinked rapidly as she tried to focus, and her mind screamed at her to come back from the glistening water's edge. There was no need for her eyes to wander, to decipher where she now was. Her breaths came fast and shallow as his fingertips lightly grazed her stomach and hand. On her back, in her bed, she stared into his demonic expression.

Chapter Seven

Hamilton stood with the iron gates in front of him and the sound of the crashing Thames behind him. Pellets of rain beat against his head and, despite Dixon offering shelter under her umbrella, he allowed the increasing downpour to wash over him. His heart felt as heavy as an anchor, pulling down with it his ability to breathe and swallow at ease, and causing a pain to spread throughout his entire body.

Behind the bars, a new build stood tall and proud. The freshly painted bricks seemed to shine through the drizzle, like a beacon of hope to all who stepped foot inside, but now, Hamilton knew different. The outside was a mask for the horridness behind its walls. A ball of anger erupted from the pit of his stomach, cremating the anchor, and he drew in a lungful of cold air before wiping his face.

Stepping forward, with Dixon mirroring his movement, he wondered why she hadn't broken through his trance. Instead, she had stood in silence next to him — for what felt like hours but could have only been minutes — and allowed him to contemplate the circumstances of the crime they were about to face. Although she asked no questions, he had asked himself plenty, but the one question screaming louder than them all was, *are you to blame for all this?*

Together they entered the gates, passing security and SOCO teams who were as oblivious to the heavy rain as he was, and entered the building. He went through the motions of ID badges, signing in with an officer, placing protective footwear over shoes and slipping on latex gloves, but his mind was trapped in a goldfish bowl and everyone around him was stuck in a slow-motion movie. He caught Dixon staring at him, her lips were moving but he could hear no sound. He shook his head from his personal vacuum.

'… Because you look a bit pale, sir.'

He caught the tale-end of her sentence and nodded in agreement. 'A bit shocked, to say the least, Dixon. I can't quite comprehend how I didn't know this place existed.'

'Well, the chief did explain in the briefing that—'

'I'm well aware of what he explained,' Hamilton snapped. 'But that doesn't mean I'm okay with this … *place*, and it certainly doesn't mean that *I* shouldn't have known about it, for Christ's sake.'

Hamilton rubbed a hand back and forth over his head. He didn't want to take his frustration out on Dixon, but the fury bubbled like boiling water inside him. As she turned to speak to a young uniformed officer, Hamilton steadied his breathing, intent on calming down and facing this investigation with a clear head.

'Okay, guv, there's a doctor at the end of the corridor waiting to escort us to the crime scene,' Dixon said and led the way.

'I didn't mean to bite your head off, it's just …'

She dismissed his words with a wave of her hand. 'I'm just surprised you asked me to join you. What with Clarke's history and knowledge, he seemed the obvious choice over me or Rocky, not that I'm complaining, of course.'

Hamilton nodded. 'It crossed my mind. However, I need Clarke to compile a comprehensive list of everyone who was involved in the first investigation—'

'What if it's not related to this murder?' Dixon asked.

'It will be, and you'll be a fresh pair of unbiased eyes at this scene, which is what I need this morning.'

A slim woman wearing ripped jeans and bright red Converse paced back and forth between the small space at the end of the corridor. Her short, curly hair bounced as if it had a life of its own. Hamilton frowned, looking for the doctor in charge that he had been promised. As he slowed, the woman turned and marched the few steps towards him with her hand held out to shake his.

'Hi, I'm Doctor Emine Inamdar, I'm the hospital's head physician.'

'Ah … I see.'

She laughed. 'What were you expecting, a long white coat and stethoscope?'

'Well, not the stethoscope.' He paused before introducing himself and Dixon.

Her jade eyes shone brightly against her light brown skin. 'It was my night off, but I was called when the fire alarm went off, so excuse the casual attire. Although, we are more informal here, anyway — first name terms and all that — it helps the patients trust us if we don't actually look like doctors,' she explained while placing an access card over a black box and opening the door for them.

'But you are a doctor, correct?'

Emine stopped to peer at him briefly, one eyebrow raised slightly, though she gave a small smile and continued walking through a maze of doors and corridors.

'Yes, Inspector Hamilton, I'm a *real* doctor. This facility—'

'Is a joke,' he interrupted.

He heard the woman's deep sigh and surmised it wasn't the first time she had faced such scepticism about Manor Hall Hospital.

'This facility, Inspector, started off as a trial, but I'm proud to say we've already had some success stories.'

'I'm guessing you won't be adding murder and an escaped convict to that list.'

She stopped in the middle of an upstairs corridor, the SOCO team passing in and out of a room behind her. Although she had folded her arms across her chest, one corner of her mouth tugged upwards, a slight smile threatening to break out. Not out of amusement or joviality, however, Hamilton thought.

'I won't pretend to be anything but devastated about last night's events.' She held up her hand to stop Hamilton interrupting her again. 'And I can assure you, I will be conducting a full investigation myself into the staff and the security of this hospital. I've worked here for nearly a year, since the first day this building opened, and not once has a patient tried to escape. They're here to seek medical care and help for their mental health.'

Hamilton shook his head as a bead of sweat dripped down his forehead. 'Doctor Inamdar, the people in this building are *criminals*, not patients, and should be treated as such. I — and many other police officers in this city — worked tirelessly to make the arrests we made, but it seems someone only has to scream the term "mental health issues" and they get put into this cushy looking place.'

'I fully understand your concerns, Inspector, but you have to understand not everything is as black and white as it seems. Yes, the people in our care have committed crimes but, for them, making the distinction between right and wrong can be very difficult sometimes. They all have their own demons—'

'And are literally given a get out of prison free card for murdering innocent people because of their personal *demons*, Doctor.'

Emine lowered her arms and fiddled with the thick white watch-strap on her left wrist. The ball of fury had returned to Hamilton's stomach, but he realised they could argue about this for days … *Would it really matter? It wouldn't change the events of last night.* A debate wasn't what he was here for.

'I can see we're not going to have a meeting of minds today, Inspector.' Emine ironically agreed with his internal thoughts. 'But the use of this hospital and the way the police system is using it is something you'll have to take up with your superior. I'm here to answer any questions you may have about my pa … about your suspect.' She offered him another smile.

Hamilton gazed over her shoulder again and, for a moment, watched the people milling in and out; the rustling of their all-in-one white suits echoed like thunder in his ears, the constant camera clicks adding a gun-fire backing track.

Dixon cleared her throat. 'Where are the other patients?'

'Most are in their bedrooms,' Emine replied. 'We moved the patients from this floor into another part of the hospital for now. I appreciate you need to collect your evidence, but we'd really like to get them back to their own rooms as soon as possible. For some of them, it's the routine that keeps them safe and content.'

'Patients and staff will need to be interviewed,' Hamilton informed the doctor.

She nodded, and he saw a look of sympathy flash in her eyes. 'Of course, as I said, I'm here to help and … although you may not agree with what we're doing here, I would never want to endanger the general public. I'm fully aware of the previous crimes committed.'

This time, Hamilton returned the doctor's smile. After all, the woman was only doing her job, as they all were. He stood tall, marched towards the room and spotted a blaze of red hair in the midst of all the activity, hunched over the bed.

Hamilton glanced around the room. A pool of wet blood glistened as a ray of sunshine broke through the window and brightened the room; the bare walls, void of personality and character, except for the small bedside table which was stacked with books by James Patterson, Conrad Jones and Truman Capote. His eyes widened as a feeling of utter disbelief took hold of him. *Are there really no boundaries in this place? Let's give a murderer various crime novels to indulge in during her free time.*

Audrey sprung up, pushed the hair from her face and looked up at Hamilton who towered over her petite frame. It gave him a moment to scan the lifeless naked body, but his eyes stopped and hovered over the man's large chest.

'No stab wound to the heart?' he asked.

Audrey frowned and shook her head. 'No, a blade to the victim's neck, and the murder weapon was left here for us. I assume a knife was weapon of choice in the past?'

Hamilton nodded and remained quiet as he turned slowly in the room. The furniture scarce, no personal photographs were pinned to the walls and he saw no diary or journal to glean some intelligence from. He drummed his fingers against his thigh, thinking of the court session he'd briefly attended. It wasn't something he usually did, but this criminal had perplexed him at the time and he needed to understand more. However, a new investigation began for his team, and he resorted to reading the newspaper articles of the trial instead — though he felt they never painted a completely true picture. They always had their own agenda to sensationalise, just to help with their sales. He re-joined Dixon in the corridor, still in conversation with the doctor.

'Doctor Inamdar,' he interrupted.

'Please, call me Emine.'

'I've noticed the various cameras and locked doors around the hospital, but you said this was the first time someone had escaped from this hospital, is that correct?'

'Oh, yes, this has never happened before. Despite being a fairly new hospital, and still undergoing development, Manor Hall is a secure facility. Our goal is to encourage recovery and understanding … however, I fully understand we're dealing with a sensitive case here and—'

'Sensitive,' Hamilton echoed. 'This woman murdered six people by the time we arrested her last year, and your security guard is the seventh victim to die in cold blood.'

'Our staff and security system—'

'Is flawed,' Hamilton interrupted again. 'Especially if a criminal can get their hands on keys and access cards that are designed to keep this psychiatric hospital safe.' Hamilton raised both hands, fully aware he'd taken his frustration out on the wrong person. 'Doctor … Emine, I'm a man of procedure and have spent most of my life hunting down vile and evil creatures that stalk this city. While the whys and reasonings of their actions are important, and have lead me to capturing them many times, my ultimately goal is to stop them harming anyone else.'

Emine ran a hand through her brown curls and sighed. 'Not only do I understand, Inspector, but I thank you and all the emergency services in London for everything you do. However, the whys and reasonings of a person's actions are the exact things I need to uncover if I'm to succeed in helping them.'

The largest smile Hamilton had ever seen, showing off a full set of snow-white teeth, appeared on Emine's face. He knew this wasn't a time for jovial expressions — a confused criminal was on the loose and another innocent body lay in the room behind him — but she was infectious and he couldn't help but allow the corners of his mouth to turn upright. Ever so slightly.

Emine continued, 'And that's why I've given DS Dixon some files that will hopefully help your case. I'm sure you'll send the warrant over for these immediately, however, with the confidential information they contain.' He saw the twinkle in her eye and tipped his head. 'They're not my full notes from all our sessions, of course, but rather an outline of them.'

'Plus a very small visitor's log,' Dixon added.

Hamilton held his hand out, particularly interested in that list. As he read the three names, his heart quickened. With a deep frown, he launched down the corridor, storming to the locked door, waiting for the doctor to catch up with him.

As the trio walked back through the maze of the hospital back towards the entrance, Emine explained her thoughts on the situation. Her continual reference to the "patient", rather than the "cold-blooded killer", grated on Hamilton's nerves.

'I had actually been really impressed with her behaviour and openness of late, except—'

'So you thought she was cured?'

The doctor huffed, crossed her arms in front of her, and Hamilton spied a thick paperback grasped in her hands. 'There is no cure for this disorder, Inspector. She was on medication for her depression and anxiety, but I focused, and worked closely with her, on a talk therapy treatment. Sadly, I hadn't had the breakthrough yet.'

Hamilton raised an eyebrow. 'I'm afraid you're going to have to give it to me in layman's terms. What breakthrough, exactly?'

Emine inched herself closer. 'Dissociative identity disorder, or multiple personality disorder as it's more commonly known, is a severe form of dissociation. The patient literally disconnects themselves from their thoughts, memories, feelings and even their identity. The host personality will feel very confused and forgetful and be totally unaware of other personalities, but they are all very real.'

'How many personalities can there be?' Dixon asked.

The doctor whistled. 'That's some question, Sergeant. The medical explanation for the disorder is when a personality becomes dissociated into two or more distinct characters, who, in turn, control and dominate. However, throughout treatment, an average of thirteen or fifteen personalities can be identified and, though uncommon, instances have been documented of patients with over one hundred personalities.'

Hamilton rolled his eyes and pulled at his shirt collar. He couldn't say he didn't believe what the doctor was saying, but he also couldn't admit to accepting her thesis, either.

'What can cause the change in personalities?' Dixon asked. 'I mean, you said you'd been pleased with her behaviour.'

Emine nodded. 'Environmental triggers, life events or perhaps it was a memory we unravelled during treatment. All of these things would have easily caused the sudden shift from one personality to another.'

Hamilton sighed. 'And the breakthrough you said you'd been waiting for?'

'Many factors are linked to the reason for a patient developing dissociative identity disorder, such as severe emotional, physical or sexual abuse or accidents and natural disasters, loss of a parent or periods of isolation. A person's identity becomes fragmented. The two or five or fifty distinct personalities become a coping mechanism, because that experience is too violent or traumatic or painful for the patient to face. During the course of treatment, I wanted to identify what that experience was for her, but so far, we haven't.' Emine extended her hand and offered Hamilton the book she'd been holding. 'I wrote this book over a year ago. It focuses on this very subject … which I can tell you're having some trouble with. I hope it will be a useful source for you.'

He thought about refusing her offer, but the constant jerk of her hand towards him convinced him she wouldn't take no for an answer. He accepted the book while remaining eye contact with Emine. He had heard her explanation — just as he had heard and read those key words and phrases during the trial — but he was unsure how the medical diagnosis could actually help him catch a killer.

Again, as if she read his mind, Emine answered. 'Like I said, there would have been a trigger, recently, to cause the shift in personalities. Uncover that, Inspector, and you'll find the woman you're looking for. Uncover the suppressed trauma and you'll find Grace Murphy.'

Chapter Eight

Hamilton picked up speed, jogging from Manor Hall's entrance to his Vauxhall parked on the main road outside the gates. Dixon kept pace while he called over to her — the early morning wind taking his breath away — about the visitor list for Grace Murphy.

'I didn't read it, guv,' she shouted back as they reached the car. 'The doc told me more about the last treatment session—'

'You drive,' he interrupted, throwing the keys towards her.

From the passenger's seat, Hamilton tossed the thick paperback onto the backseat and pulled his mobile from the inside pocket of his coat. Dixon started the engine but her hands hesitated over the steering wheel. She looked at Hamilton and, with a deep frown set on her forehead, shrugged.

Hamilton held a finger up as the call connected; he knew Dixon was waiting for directions, but even he wasn't sure if they were returning to the station or not.

'Damn voicemail,' he roared, and tapped the screen, selecting the second person on his favourites contact list. 'Clarke, where are you?'

'Same place you left me, where else? I've got a list of—'

'And Fraser? Is she there yet?'

'No, guv. Rocky's tried her a couple of times, but he's had no answer.'

'Me and Dixon are heading over there now.' He turned to his waiting driver and reeled off Fraser's address before continuing with Clarke. 'I want you to get a squad car round there immediately.'

'What's happened?'

Hamilton looked out the window and glanced up at the London Eye in the distance through the raindrops pelting the glass.

'Did Fraser tell you that she had visited Grace Murphy in that psychiatric unit about four months ago?'

Dixon's hair swung mid-air as she snapped her head in his direction, before concentrating on the road again.

'No … no, she didn't. You don't think Fraser had anything to do with this…'

Hamilton sighed. He didn't want his thoughts to go there, to think that Fraser could have betrayed them, but the fact that his partner wondered the same thing, made him doubt everything he thought he knew about the sergeant. 'I don't know, Clarke, but it's a bit too much of a coincidence — and you know how I feel about those. Look, get uniform over there now and tell them not to let Fraser out of their sight until I arrive. Also, make sure that Rocky is fully up to speed about this entire case. We don't have time to dwindle on catch-ups.'

'Will do, guv.'

As he slipped the phone back into his pocket, Dixon said, 'We've got about a twenty-minute drive, guv. Tell me everything I need to know.'

He shuffled in his seat and mirrored Dixon's line of sight directly ahead of them. The sound of passing traffic, beeping horns and torrential rain slipped away, replaced by the memory of that first body.

'It was about this time last year we found the first body,' Hamilton begun. 'A naked woman in the River Thames, her clothes and ID left for us to find, with a single stab wound to the heart. At first, it was a single case, but it soon became clear, when another five victims were found murdered in the same way, we had a serial killer loose in the city.'

'All women victims?' Dixon asked.

'Yes. So, our initial instincts pointed us to a male suspect, and we thought we had someone but … no, and after four months of murders, it went quiet. We launched social media appeals, TV appeals, newspapers articles … but nothing came from them. The chief forced my hand and moved us on to the next investigation. Luckily, due to the alert set in place, Fraser followed up the murder of a Maria Lee, the killer's sixth victim. She had been Grace Murphy's therapist and murdered because she had uncovered Grace's erm dissociative … personality, erm, disorder.'

'Doctor Inamdar said it's easier to refer to dissociative *identity* disorder as DID.'

Hamilton exhaled heavily. 'Anyway, Fraser tracked down Grace Murphy — who, by this point, was referring to herself as Carly — and we arrested her moments before she boarded a plane to Alicante.'

'Yes, the doctor mentioned the dominant alter Carly, and that it would have been this personality committing the murders. Grace would have been completely unaware … though, the doctor also said that during the treatment, Grace spoke of haunting nightmares she'd suffered during the period of the murders.'

'I met Grace on many occasions, she was the assistant manager of a theatre in Central London, and we discovered, at some point in her life, she had known some of the victims,' Hamilton said, sliding his hands under his thighs to stop him from clawing at the skin around his nails. 'To me, Grace was a woman surrounded by grief and death and was struggling to deal with it, but she seemed ... I don't know, a genuinely nice person. Respectable. Honest. When we arrested her at Luton Airport, you could see the evil in her eyes, hear the menace in her voice. I had been completely fooled by her.'

'Guv, she wasn't trying to fool you. The disorder meant—'

'She had no recollection of the crimes. Her *alter ego,* Carly, was the hard, cold-blooded killer. Yes, I'm well aware of the medical crap that comes with this disorder, but it's not something I can come to terms with as easily as you seem to have done. You know, I woke up in an awful mood this morning, can I blame *that* side of me if I lash out and whack someone in the face today?'

Dixon made a noise between a sigh and a laugh, and Hamilton was thankful for the light-hearted way she had taken his comment. A niggling feeling in the corner of his mind scratched away so hard that he felt the tension rise through his neck and pitch up camp in his temples; almost as if warning him not to make jokes about this case, or this criminal.

'I know it's more complicated than that,' he backtracked. 'I did try to keep up with the trial, find out more about this Grace — and Carly, I suppose — Murphy, but it became difficult, what with the usual workload, and I soon lost touch with it.'

'Apart from the therapist, did you uncover why she had killed the other five women?' Dixon asked as she indicated left onto Fraser's road.

'We knew that her grandfather passed away before the first murder, and her lawyers used that as the trigger for the disorder—'

'Given what the doctor just explained to us, I'd think the triggering experience was more than that.'

Hamilton shrugged. 'It's obvious that's what got Grace Murphy transferred to Manor Hall Hospital. Anyway, she never confessed. Said she *couldn't* confess to something she didn't remember. Her mother explained how Grace had been heavily drinking since the grandfather's passing, and any changes to her daughter's character or moods or … personality, even, she had attributed to the alcohol.'

Dixon parked behind the squad vehicle and the pair exited the car. 'Well, considering everything you've just told me, why in God's name would Fraser visit the woman in hospital?'

'That'll be my first question,' he replied, and marched towards the open front door of Fraser's apartment.

Hamilton was surprised to find a uniformed officer standing guard just inside the front door. He peered further down the corridor to find a second officer on the phone, and he took a slow step forward. The first officer threw an arm up, halting Hamilton to the spot, and explained to him that SOCO were currently being informed.

'Informed of what?' Hamilton retorted, and stepped away from the officer's arm. 'Where the hell is DS Kerry Fraser?'

The young officer's face flushed. 'The house is empty, sir. DS Fraser isn't here.'

'So what the hell are you calling the scenes of crime team for?'

'That would have been my call, sir,' said the other officer, now off the phone and just feet away from Hamilton. 'PC Shand, sir. After receiving no reply, I went around the building and found the back door unlocked and the glass smashed. The kitchen isn't a pretty sight, and I rang the station to update them on the case. I knew you were on your way … and there's a letter addressed to you.'

Hamilton lunged forwards, wondering if Fraser had left an explanation of her actions, but stopped abruptly at the kitchen table.

'Holy shit.' Dixon gasped behind him. 'Is that Fraser's pet?'

A grey tabby cat lay in the middle of the table, pinned to the wood with a kitchen knife impaled through its chest. Through its heart. The blow to Hamilton's head felt like it had been delivered by a heavy-weight boxing champion. He knew it was no boxing champion, but rather his own common sense coming into play and mocking him for his immediate — and unjustified — assumptions of Fraser. He shook his head while reaching for the blood-stained paper bearing his name.

'Sir, fingerprints—'

'I know who wrote the damn thing,' Hamilton replied to Shand's objections, who continued to implore that he wait for the forensics team.

With one hand, Hamilton held the single sheet of lined paper and unfolded it with his thumb. His eyes quickly roved over the short sentences, the scribbled writing as manic and rushed as the message itself.

When Dixon called his name, Hamilton sharply inhaled a lungful of air, the tension spreading from his temples like a dark cloud eclipsing the sun. His hand stood firm, but he cleared his throat twice before he read the note aloud.

'*I have something of yours, Inspector. I'll fuck with your life. Just like you and your team fucked with mine. I won't be silenced and you will not win. I am not some stranger to be ignored.*'

Chapter Nine

Fraser closed her eyes and continued to control her breathing; slowly in through the nose, hold for three seconds and then out through the mouth, while attempting to empty her mind of the nightmarish visions attacking it. She'd been in the confines of the coffin for more than an hour, at least, and the desire to scream and bang against the dark wood had begun to overwhelm her. A vice-like grip squashed her chest, daring her to panic, daring her to lose control.

She rounded her shoulders and flexed her fingers and ankles. Every inch of her body on fire with pins and needles, demanding she move from the horizontal position keeping her hostage, arms invisibly strapped to her sides. Her knees craved to be bent, in a way she'd never felt before, and her mouth so desperately wanted to drink in lung-satisfying gulps of air. But this was all a test.

After Fraser had received the text from her neighbour on Friday, she'd driven home and debated cancelling meeting Audrey. While it was nice to go out for a few drinks with her new friend and colleague, she had to admit the idea of snuggling up in front of the TV with a bottle of wine was a more welcoming one. Perhaps it had been fate she had left a window open; a Freudian slip, she thought. She placed her mobile phone in her coat pocket and locked the front door behind her.

A gush of wind blew in from the kitchen and Fraser followed the cold air. Just as she'd stepped onto the grey

Lino flooring, she spotted the open window above the sink and cursed herself. Although it was unlike her to be so careless, she had come to leaving the windows open a little longer than usual every day in the hope that Felix, her missing cat, would surprise her and return home. The sun had already set on a long shift and the night's shadows danced across the garden. Deciding she needed to tune out and switch off, Fraser dumped her bag and coat in the kitchen, grabbed a bottle of red wine from the cupboard and headed up to the bathroom for a long soak in the tub to prepare her for a good night's sleep.

Thinking about that now, she cursed herself. *Why hadn't I taken my phone upstairs with me? Because you hadn't expected on being ambushed in your own kitchen*, she argued with herself.

Her sleep had been disturbed. A noise from the kitchen woke her. An even sharper gust of cold air brought goosebumps to her bare arms as she stepped into the kitchen and frowned at the shadowy object lying statue-still on the middle of the dining table.

When she woke up, she was no longer at home. The shooting pain in her head merged with the discomfort in her shoulders, as her arms were pulled around the back of her body, and her wrists tied to the wooden chair she sat on. Despite the darkness, Fraser immediately knew her location and searched until she spotted the white face peering back at her from within the shadows.

She had so desperately wanted to speak to Grace Murphy, but the rag in her mouth ended any hope of that. Thankfully, after forcing Fraser to climb into the coffin at knifepoint, Grace had removed all the bindings.

'Now you'll know what it feels like to be trapped,' Grace said — her eyes as dark and bottomless as the night sky — and she scratched her palm with the tip of the knife. It was then that Fraser realised which personality was in control of the situation.

'Carly, please, I can—'

The knife had been jabbed into her cheek, and the small release of blood dribbled down her face and landed on her earlobe. Clearly her attempts to thaw Carly had no chance of saving her from what was about to happen.

'Don't waste the air in your lungs making idle promises of what you can do, Sergeant Fraser. You'll only waste the small supply you'll have in that box once the lid is closed.' The brunette leaned in, so close she could feel Grace's warm breath on her face. 'Let's find out how *crazy* you become when you only have yourself to talk to.'

The sneer on the woman's face forced Fraser's body to shiver, and it was then that she noticed the cold mist of air escaping from both their lips. The theatre felt like an ice box. The lid of the coffin had crashed down and Fraser was left with the echoing sound of brass clicking against brass.

Padlocks, she thought.

Now, with her mind focusing back on the current moment, she wondered how long Grace would leave her here, and if, in fact, the woman was still in the building. The dark, dank smell of the theatre told her no one had been there for some time, so any screams for help would go unheard. Although unsure if the coffin was merely a stage prop, Fraser thought the wood had looked thick and hefty as she'd climbed in; therefore, she believed, any small kicks she could give to it wouldn't inflict enough force to bust through the locks.

She thought about her team and, with it now being Saturday, whether they would even notice she was missing? But most importantly, how the hell did Grace Murphy get out of hospital? If she escaped, surely Hamilton would have been notified by now. Fraser groaned at the realisation of her superior discovering her visit to the hospital. While it would be an uncomfortable conversation to have with him, explaining it would mean she had survived this awful nightmare, and that was something she could live with.

Fraser thought of her mobile phone again, abandoned in the kitchen, and she hated herself. She hadn't even waited to read Audrey's reply about bailing on their night out. If only she'd gone to the pub … if only she'd made a different decision …

Silent tears trickled down her face and tickled her ears where they landed. As hard as she tried to stop them from coming, they wouldn't, and despite no one there to witness her crumbling to pieces, she felt like a failure. But, even more than a failure, the fear tightening her chest — restricting the little air that remained — forced any hope of being found to be buried in the coffin with her.

Chapter Ten

Happy with the security of the coffin, I snatch up the vodka bottle and sink to the floor, tucking my knees into my chest for warmth … for comfort. I can't let the coldness shake my resolve or the tiredness to push me out of control. Last year, I had to embrace the haziness that the alcohol offered because it helped keep Grace's mouth shut — which is also what I need to happen now — but I can't pretend that I don't also need some semblance of a clear head to see my plan through to the end.

Fuck me, my stomach feels like a pin-ball machine. I don't know if it's nerves or excitement.

The search would have already started. My own bloody fault, really, what with setting off the fire alarm and alerting them to a problem sooner than I had anticipated. I should have had at least two hours before anyone even noticed that monster wasn't doing his job. I should have just slit the other guy's throat too. Stupid idea, smashing the alarm.

Why didn't you just wave right in their fucking faces and shout, 'I'm trying to escape, why don't you chase me now?'

It's okay. The universe is on my side … They know why I'm doing all this. It's not right that I should be trapped — in my body or in prison — when none of this is my fault. I had been given just the amount of time I needed to grab the woman I wanted … the woman I needed … to make this work. I've slain the main monster, but there's others out there who need to pay.

Just a little patience.

Patience can make you a winner. The cops will be running all over the place now looking for me and her — their super computer genius. Whatever will they do without her? They'll fuck up by underestimating me. Patience is a quality. A quality I mastered a long time ago — with *no* room for compassion. That's not my style.

Have another drink. Have another drink.

I love the trail of fire the vodka leaves, coursing from my throat to my stomach. I can literally feel it scorching my insides, reminding me I'm alive. Sit up. Don't huddle in the corner. Own this stage and take the lead role once again. Own the role forever.

Perhaps Manor Hall had been a blessing after all. I mean, without that place I would never have found him again or had Doctor Emine shine her knowledge on me. A cruel past met a bright future and it woke something deep inside me.

That bitch in the coffin almost drowned me under Grace's weak and remorseful confusion. I very nearly lost myself, thanks to DETECTIVE SERGEANT KERRY FRASER!

Calm down. Have another drink. Have another drink.

It's time to stand tall again. I feel invincible. I feel stronger. Despite every bad thing, the limelight is calling me.

I felt as though I was underwater, struggling to reach the surface and gulp in the fresh air. Every single time I tried, my lungs were filled with salty sea water. But during the hospital treatments with Emine I gained so much help and guidance. She's taught me so much about myself. About who Carly really is.

I had prayed that Emine wouldn't be working a shift last night. And my prayers were answered. The doctor would have sussed my plan and tried to stop me. She's an impressive woman: smart, independent, sassy. These are the types of women that vulnerable teenagers need in their lives to look up to … to call out for help. I wouldn't have wanted to hurt the doc, but no doubt I would have done what I needed to do. Just as I had to silence Maria Lee last year. A few weeks with Grace was all it took for Maria to uncover the truth and, therefore, she knew too much.

Emine helped me in a way that Maria couldn't help Grace.

Funnily enough, the urge to silence those who know too much, or frankly just kill the wankers who don't deserve the life they've been given, is no longer my ultimate goal. Not now I've ended *his* life. But the urge to pierce the tip of a cold blade into the heart of someone who's wronged me … well, I can't completely deny that urge has been extinguished.

Have another drink. Have another drink.

I can't let my thoughts get diluted. I can't be drowned ever again. You see, I'm not as weak as Grace. Yes, the fury still burns in me, as real as the fiery liquid mapping its way through my body. There will be further suffering, that fact is inevitable.

I hate myself.

Everything is supposed to be better now.

Why am I still in the darkness? She assured me, for so long, that this act would guide me out of the shadows and I wouldn't be a stranger to the world any more.

I'm back in the corner. Lying on the floor and pounding it with my fists this time. It's all flooding back, the waves of pain and fear are smashing against the rocks of rage and threatening to rise above them, take the control away from me.

The escape had been a victory after months of planning and endurance, but it had come at a price. The worst. I can't stop the bile rising from my stomach. I let myself rock back and forth … back and forth … back and forth. It's quieter when I do.

For fuck's sake, now you do *look like you should be in a mental home.*

Okay, I need to breathe. Calming breaths. Deep breaths. Just like during my sessions with Emine. Even she didn't notice the change. Just breathe.

Keep your shit together and you might just pull this off.

Chapter Eleven

'We need to be out there looking for her,' Rocky demanded, and Hamilton wondered if the constable's agitation was born more from guilt than fear … a feeling he himself had been battling with since reading the note.

'And we will, but we need to do this first, just as we do at the beginning of every investigation.'

'But this isn't a norm—'

Hamilton raised a hand. 'I get it, Rocky. Now, looking at the timeline of events we know Grace Murphy escaped from the prison just after midnight. Clever to use the fire alarm, it brought her some time while the snoozing security team ran around with their heads stuck up their arses.'

'Who was the security guard in Murphy's room? And why was he there?' Clarke asked.

'Gabe Hardy,' Dixon said, writing the victim's name on the white board. 'From what Doctor Inamdar told me, once the patients were locked in their rooms at night, there was no need for the night-time security staff to open the door, unless—'

'Unless they thought a patient was in danger,' Clarke finished her sentence.

Dixon nodded. 'However, if that was the case, the protocol would be to radio through to inform a colleague of the door opening.'

'The doors weren't centrally locked?' Rocky asked with a frown.

'No,' Hamilton grunted. 'This place isn't like a prison. Apparently, this hospital is all about rehabilitation without the "barbed wire and tight security", or so I'm told.'

Dixon smirked. 'Yes, well, anyway … all members of staff are in the process are being interviewed. The ones on duty — who were still in the building — first, so hopefully we'll get more of an idea about specifics from them soon.'

'Back to the timeline,' Hamilton said. 'Due to the commotion and head counts, our local officers weren't informed of the escape or even the damn murder until about 2am.'

Rocky pounded the table. 'And then the instruction to come here first put us back even further.'

Hamilton nodded. He agreed with the chief's reasoning for a briefing, what with Grace Murphy being his team's arrest last year and the subsequent background information the station needed as a whole — a media blackout had also needed to be put in place — but he also felt Rocky's anger at the set-back it had caused.

'Yes, if we'd known sooner that Fraser had visited the hospital, we could have possibly intercepted the kidnapping. However, what we do know is the window of time we're working with, and thankfully, that's not a very large window.'

'But Murphy is a step ahead of us,' Rocky continued. 'Even if we only missed her taking Kerry by one hour, we don't know where she's gone.' Rocky's voice hitched at the end, his Irish accent broader than ever.

Hamilton's head and heart pulled him in polar opposite directions. Rocky's emotions burst to the surface, referring to his colleague by her first name, and he couldn't help but wonder if the new constable would be able to cope with the uncertainty that lay ahead of them all. Those same regretful sentiments filled his chest, but he knew the only way to save Fraser was to push them down and ignore them. For now, at least.

'Yes, Murphy is ahead of us, but only one step. We can catch up. The question is …' Hamilton paused. 'Can you keep it together?'

Rocky looked away and sighed. While Clarke and Dixon nodded — a look of pure determination and strength on their faces and in their body language — Hamilton was pleased they had assumed he was questioning them all. Rocky finally looked him square in the eyes, puffed out his chest and nodded silently.

'Okay, here's where I want us to start.' An invisible kick of purpose had Hamilton on his feet. 'Dixon, get round to the mother's address—'

'Surely Murphy wouldn't be stupid enough to go home,' she interrupted.

'No, I wouldn't think so, but can we be so sure? Also, the mother and daughter were close, so I want to know why Valerie hasn't visited the hospital in the past five months. Try and use your motherly instincts to get her to open up to you. Plus, we need to have a chat with that solicitor friend of Murphy's …' He clicked his fingers. '… Natasha Holten.'

'Where are you headed?' Clarke asked.

'I want a have a chat with Audrey Gibson … she was due to meet Fraser Friday night. I want to know what happened.'

'Guv, I'd like to question the friend personally, rather than uniform,' said Clarke. 'She's another person in Murphy's life who hasn't bothered to give her the time of day. I think there could be something more to this … maybe we can work out her plan.'

Hamilton pursed his lips and considered Clarke's request. He had to admit, the lack of visitors to Manor

Hall Hospital since Fraser's recorded visit was strange, and perhaps Murphy had let something slip about her intentions. His partner could be on to something here, he thought. 'Okay, but bring a PC with you. You too, Dixon.'

He looked at Rocky, and for a moment, his heart went out to him. Had they, together, allowed Fraser's kidnapping to happen? His mind raced with scenarios of telling Fraser, and even the rest of the team, about the suspicions they'd had of her missing cat and possible stalker. If they'd spoken out on Friday, not leaving yet another thing to wait until after the weekend, would Fraser be safe now?

'Rocky, I need you to hang back in the office and work on the computer.'

The corner of the constable's lip twitched upwards. 'Big shoes to fill, guv.'

'I know, but SOCO confirmed Fraser's car was not at her home address. Therefore, I'm inclined to believe that's how Murphy got off with our girl …' He paused to clear his throat. 'Check any and all ANPR cameras in the area surrounding Fraser's home and find that car. If we can at least narrow down their direction of travel, we might just make it impossible for that woman to stay a step ahead of us.'

***

At the mortuary, Hamilton glared at the clock on the office wall. Midday … on Saturday, he thought, almost needing to realign his bearings. He should be with Elizabeth, deciding if they'd brave the rain and head out for a pub lunch, or just cook for themselves and snuggle up on the sofa watching a film. He regretted not leaving her a note to find this morning, but his wife of over twenty years was no stranger to waking up to an empty bed.

He drummed his fingers on Audrey's desk, silently praying the post-mortem would end soon — and not for reasons about wanting to know more about the dead, like he usually did.

Audrey breezed into the room, loose flame-red curls bouncing around her shoulders, and launched a beige folder on the table. She slid into the chair opposite Hamilton and her brown eyes met his.

'Gabriel Hardy—'

'Yes, we know," Hamilton cut her off, immediately regretting his snappy tone but struggling to curve his lips into a smile. 'I mean, Manor Hall informed us of his identity ... well, they called him Gabe. I've got officers contacting his next of kin.'

'Sounds like a cool nickname. I guess Gabriel is a bit old-school, I've never met anyone with that name—'

'Audrey,' Hamilton interrupted again. Although he tolerated her chatty nature, warmed to it even, he was in no mood for nattering this afternoon. 'The post-mortem isn't the reason I'm here to talk to you, Audrey.'

'Oh, well, that's disappointing. There's me gearing up with all my extra notes; signs of possible sexual activity prior to death, a curry and beer for dinner and a large angel tattooed between his shoulder blades — more than likely a homage to himself, given the biblical namesake — and it's not even what you want from me.'

Hamilton smiled slightly but it quickly transformed into a sigh. 'And that's where my investigations always start, with the victim, but it's just ...'

Audrey frowned. 'It's just what?'

'I feel guilty saying the victim isn't where my concern lies right now,' he blurted out and instantly regretted it. 'Of course, I'm devastated for this man and his family, and it's the dead who usually point us in the direction of their killer—'

'But this time you have that information already,' Audrey finished.

Hamilton tipped his head. 'Yes, and even more worrying reasons to find our murderer as soon as possible. Which is why you're actually still the person I need to speak to.'

He saw the flash of confusion in Audrey's eyes as she leaned back in her chair — away from her medical notes and findings, away from her security blanket — while he updated her on Fraser's situation.

'Oh my god,' she whispered, and ran both hands through her hair, stopping mid-way as though she might pull the strands from their roots.

'What with you being the last to see Fraser, I need to know everything you can tell me about Friday night.'

Audrey's eyebrows pinched together, and her mouth turned down while she shook her head. 'No, I never saw Kerry.'

'But Clarke said—'

'Yes, we were meant to meet in the pub, but she never showed. Well, no, that's wrong …'

'What's wrong, Audrey? She bloody came to the pub or she didn't, which is it?'

'Sorry, I mean …' Her cheeks burned as brightly as her hair as she took a few calming breaths. 'I was minutes from leaving here to meet Kerry when she sent me a text saying that she had a migraine and could she take a rain check on the evening.'

'What time was that?' Hamilton's words rushed out as quickly as his mind began updating the timeline of events.

Audrey's eyes flickered around the room. 'Erm … I'm not sure, probably about nine.' Hamilton jumped to his feet. 'I have the message on my phone, if you need to see it. It's the reason why I was at the crime scene this morning …

as I hadn't been out … I could be on call…' She lowered her face into her palms.

Hamilton lingered at the door before turning to ask one final question. 'Did you reply?'

Her tear-filled eyes met his and she nodded. 'I told her to snuggle up in a dark room and get some sleep. When I've suffered with migraines in the past, the darkness has always helped me.'

Chapter Twelve

The darkness is my ally. I never lurked in the shadows, I was reborn in them. So many people fear the closing of the day. They fear the shadows invading their homes, their streets, their lives; fear the suffocation of a black abyss and, even when a light is shone, they fear the twilight silhouettes who dance on their bedroom walls and mock their panic of the darkness. But it is in these moments, cloaked in that very same darkness, you have the opportunity to grow.

It is the light I fear. I never feel safe in the brightness; I have nowhere to hide. There are those who dance and rejoice in the sun; the innocent who are yet to be burnt and the monsters wearing their masks. In the harsh beam of light, people choose a role and hide behind their chosen disguise: mother, father, friend, teacher, police officer. But who are they really? Enemy, adulterer, abuser, liar, stranger. You can't know. In the darkness, there are no masks, you're unprotected to the truth.

I don't yet know the sergeant's fate … I think I do, because I have a plan in mind, but people always have a way of surprising you, and you end up taking the second door or path or backup plan. But for now, she needs to experience the darkness so I know what kind of a person she really is. It's fascinating to watch people … not "people watching" in a café while you're sipping on a cup of coffee trying to distract yourself from your own problems, but *really* watch them. From the shadows, when they think there's no chance of them being observed, when they've stripped themselves of their masks.

My thoughts quickly jump to Doctor Emine and I can't help but wonder what's hiding behind her mask. At the hospital she took a real interest in Grace, giving her extra talk therapy sessions and offering help. Eventually, the woman had stirred the memories Grace had fought so hard to bury, her suppressed pain and anger welcomed me back. I no longer needed the alcohol to take control of Grace's body. I found the footway to be in control again, though, of course, that seems to have thrown up more problems than I was expecting.

You never want to share.

A tingle slithers down my back when I think of the doctor. Her confidence and sex appeal, and the ability to command the people in a room as soon as she stepped inside it, blows me away. I'm in awe of Doctor Em. I can't remember the last woman I've met who could radiate that strength and encouragement; a woman who made tough decisions and took ownership of them; a woman who makes me want to accomplish that … to accomplish my goals.

Ultimately, I had to lie to Em. Hell, I thought the woman was inspirational, but I wasn't going to miss out on my opportunity — *this* opportunity — for no quack. I thought faking Grace's progress would have been more of a challenge, I mean, isn't it the hospital's job to recognise *the signs*. But it was during the therapy I found the doctor's flaw — her need to believe in people. Em's belief in second chances, rehabilitation and the need for perpetual hope meant she couldn't see that I, Carly, had become more powerful than all of them. Grace was the mask we wore in the light.

Doctor Em placed blame in the past. She explained that an awful, unthinkable evil lurked in Grace's subconscious and rather than remember it, face it and deal with it, she had created our alter personalities to escape the pain.

The doctor was right, there was an evil, and it was Manor Hall Hospital that brought the wickedness back into our lives, more than the doctor will ever understand.

That face. The face that haunted and sneered and smiled. Carefree and living while we were merely existing. Grace had given up. In order to survive, I stepped up and saved us. Why should I pay for my actions? It's not my fault I'm here … that I've become this person. It's who I have to be … who I was *made* to be.

'Then this bitch comes along and rubs it in further,' I shout out and kick the silent coffin. 'It wasn't my fault I was caught, it was yours … and then I was sent to *that* place. To that hell hole, to be forced to live out that pain over and over again with nowhere to hide.'

You see, it wasn't my fault, it was theirs, and they'll all have to pay now. I just need to wait a little bit longer. This building may be my latest prison, but it's a prison I've chosen for myself, for now, and it will serve me well until the time is right … not long to go. It's time I played with a few more people's lives before I end this. Just the way they've played with mine.

Baby, when the lights go out …

Chapter Thirteen

Clarke, accompanied by PC Goldberg, drove from the Charing Cross station to Natasha Holten's office on Bond Street. He had telephoned her home address before leaving to discover — from her boyfriend — that she was working today. What should have taken a twenty-minute drive doubled due to the weekend shopping hordes in Soho. Despite there being still over a month until Christmas, the city was already alive with winter wonderland attractions, fairy lights and frantic shoppers.

'That mental hospital is so close to a number of underground train stations,' Goldberg commented. 'She could have gone anywhere. She literally slipped right through our fingers.'

'Tell me about it, mate,' Clarke replied while peering through the front window.

A group of screeching teenagers zig-zagged through the slow-moving traffic and he wondered where Murphy could be. And, more importantly, if Fraser was still with her. A sea of faces swam past the car now, he could barely single one person out. What if she were walking alongside them right this minute? What if Murphy had had her way with his colleague and was in the process of fleeing again? The questions spun through Clarke's mind like whirlwind.

The sudden blast of a car horn behind him pulled Clarke from his internal conundrums and kicked him into gear. *I'm no good to Kerry in this state*, he thought while turning on to Noel Street and stretching his neck — clicking his bones in an attempt to relieve some tension. PC Goldberg became a faraway backing track to his own thoughts, planning the questions he wanted to ask — jabbering on about beautiful passers-by, long shift patterns and his plans to move up the ranks of the Met police. Gobsmacked by how many topics the officer could cover in a short car journey, Clarke finally understood Hamilton's short-temper when it came to his own frivolous conversations.

When Clarke finally parked on Bond Street, Goldberg blew a high-pitched whistle. 'Nice area, though not really my cuppa ... no greasy spoon to pop into for lunch.'

While heading towards Forde and Partners across the street, Clarke warned the PC to keep quiet and instructed him to take notes only. He spotted Natasha as she stepped out from under the shelter of a near-by bus stop; her long straight blonde hair rested just above the cleavage-accentuating black shirt, and her tanned legs were complimented by a short tight skirt — despite the cold weather. She flicked a cigarette into the drain and stopped frozen in her tracks, raising her perfectly shaped eyebrows.

'Miss Holten, I'm DS Cla—'

'I know who you are,' she sneered. 'What do you want?'

'We need to have a word with you,' he replied.

Her flared nostrils gave away her feelings of frustration to being collared at work unexpectedly, but the patter of rain water on her sleek hair — which she fruitlessly tried to protect with her hands — seemed to infuriate her more.

'Inside, quickly,' she spat in their direction and turned on her stiletto heels.

Natasha led them through a small reception area where a young ginger lad, no older than eighteen, sat with his eyes glued to a computer screen, and past a few Perspex divided desks. Everything gleamed bright white — the walls, the tiled floors, the intrusive lights — until she opened a door to a back office and, despite its grand ceiling to wall glass windows, it somehow felt softer that its outside counterpart.

'Thanks for giving us your time, Miss Holten,' Clarke said, standing next to the large oak table.

'It's fine, but it won't be long as my boss will be back soon and this is her office.'

'I understand. We just have a few questions about Grace Murphy and—'

'I'm not the solicitor in charge of her case any more,' Natasha interrupted and folded her arms across her chest.

Clarke paused. 'And why is that, Miss Holten?'

She shrugged and looked away briefly. 'Said she didn't want me involved any longer ... not entirely sure why.' Her voice softened for the first time. 'Perhaps she's angry with me.'

'Why would she be angry at you? Aren't you her oldest and closest friend?'

'Yes, but I couldn't stop her from being arrested, from being sentenced and then from being thrown in that ... in that *hospital*.' The fire had returned to her tone and her eyes.

'You don't think she should have been hospitalised?' Clarke continued, his line of questioning now being determined by Natasha.

'No. Well, I don't know, but the picture you all painted of her is not ... it couldn't have been true. That's not my friend, not the Grace I know ... knew.'

'How can you know who she is?'

'What do you mean?' Natasha replied, before pinching her lips together.

Clarke pulled a sheet of paper from his pocket; he didn't need it — he knew the information written on it — but used it for effect. 'The hospital records show you only visited your friend once, just after she was admitted to Manor Hall ... just the once, Miss Holten?'

Natasha's blue eyes darkened. 'Grace refused all visitors shortly after being transferred to the hospital.'

'Why do you think that was?'

'I don't know.' She paused, lowering her gaze to the magnolia carpeted floor for a few moments before staring back at Clarke and continuing, 'I was just as shocked as anyone when you arrested her. She was, I mean is, my best friend and I had absolutely no idea she was suffering with this condition. That she was … murdering people. Perhaps, if I hadn't been so wrapped up in my own life, I could have helped her. How could I not have known?'

'But it wasn't just you who Grace had refused to see?'

'No, it was everyone. Even her mum … that was the shocker for me. But I don't know, it could have just all been too hard for Grace. Maybe she finally felt guilty, even though she couldn't admit what she had done to all those people. Valerie was … *is* distraught. They were so close. Way closer than me and my mother, I always envied Grace that.' Natasha shook her head. 'Wait, what is this all about?'

'Last night, Grace Murphy escaped from Manor Hall Hospital.'

'What the fuck?' Natasha yelped, and threw her hand up to cover her mouth. 'How? I thought the hospital was an extension of her prison sentence … that it was as secure as—'

'Yes,' Clarke interrupted abruptly. 'That side of things is also being investigated. However, what we need to know is, has Grace been in touch with you since midnight?'

Natasha's head jerked back. 'What? No, of course not, this is the first I've heard of it. Christ! Does her mum know?'

'Officers are with her now, Miss Holten. We're trying to ascertain if she's with any close friends or if any relatives might have supported her escape. Do you know of anyone?'

Natasha pouted and shook her head. 'No, but she has family in Ireland … I don't know anything about them. We have the same friends, and they would have told me if … anything. She doesn't have any siblings and her father only ever popped into her life every now and then.'

Clarke thumbed through his memory bank like he was flicking through a magazine. He had no recollection of Grace Murphy's father during their interaction with her last year and wondered why the man hadn't been present after his daughter's arrest.

'What do you know about Mr Murphy?'

'Oh, that's not his surname. Valerie was never married to him,' Natasha replied.

'What's his name?'

'Tom …' Her eyes widened and she puffed air into her cheeks. 'My mind's gone blank.'

'Miss Holten, I'm sure I don't have to tell you, but preventing the course of justice is an arrestable offence.'

She barked a laugh and threw her hands up. 'Seriously, Sergeant? I don't think I'd be any good at my job if I didn't know what constitutes as an arrestable offence.'

'You've also said Grace Murphy is your best friend,' Clarke finally snapped. 'Do you really expect me to believe that you don't know her father's surname?'

'Grace referred to him as Dad. Valerie called him Tom. Why would I ask what his surname is?' Natasha glared at him, but her petite features soon softened. 'Listen, I'm sure I do actually know it, but I swear to you, I have drawn a blank. He was barely around when Grace was growing up, drove around the country or something like that. At school, she didn't mention him too much, and as we got older, it was a topic I didn't approach unless she did first. But he did get in contact with her … I can't remember how long ago exactly, very apologetic, wanting to be involved in her life again. As far as I knew, everything was going fine … it just wasn't something she spoke about in too much detail.'

'But Grace and Valerie are in contact with him again now?'

Her bottom lip jerked forward and she nodded. 'Apparently. From what I gathered, his job kept him busy and ultimately still came first, but they have a number for him for emergencies. Do they use it? I don't know, before you ask, but I guess when you've gone years without someone in your life, there's no emergency you can't face without them.'

'I see.' Clarke gazed over to Goldberg to ensure he'd recorded all the information. 'Anyone else in Grace's life, or Valerie's, that she might reach out to at a time like this … someone who would help her? Protect her?'

Natasha's arms folded once again. 'I know what you're getting at here, Sergeant, and I can save you some time. I'm not harbouring a criminal on the run, nor do I know where she is or who she's with.'

'This is a very serious matter, Miss Holten.'

'Yes, I'm fully aware of that, and I want you to find my friend before anything awful happens … but I'm not sure how I can help you. Neither Grace nor Valerie had much time in their lives for relationships.'

'Why?'

'Grace's grandfather lived with them … gosh, as far back as I can remember, but he died last year after battling cancer for … oh, I don't know how long for … years. Valerie was his full-time carer and Grace spent most of her free time with him. When his health really deteriorated, she accompanied him to nearly all of his oncology appointments. Other than her work, her grandfather took up most of her time.' She glanced out through the glass into the main office. 'I'm sorry, I really have to get back to work.'

'Yes, of course, thank you for your time,' Clarke replied before walking out of the office while Natasha held the door open. 'Just one more thing: did Grace have any love interests or ex-boyfriends she stayed friends with?'

Natasha rolled her eyes. 'Other than Eric Dexter, who met his untimely death last year, she only had one other long-term boyfriend, but that was in our first year of uni. Despite all my encouragement, Grace really didn't have much interest in men.'

'And she wasn't one for flings?' Clarke continued.

'I didn't say she was a nun, Sergeant. Just picky about who she invested her time in.' Natasha slid past Clarke and walked back towards the reception area. 'But I think it is safe to say she hasn't hunted down a previous one-night-stand and made a runner for it with him.'

He grimaced at her sarcasm. 'Well, thanks again for your time, Miss Holten.'

Outside the building, Clarke gazed at the grey-tinged sun on its descent over London — the rain clouds having finally floated away. Tourists, commuters and shoppers whizzed past him like flies — his own thoughts mirroring their incessant buzzing. Helplessness gripped him by the neck; an overwhelming amount of new information had presented itself. Why did it feel like they would need to start from scratch where Grace Murphy was concerned? Clarke thought.

Chapter Fourteen

Eighteen years ago

I sat at the table in the kitchen and sloshed my spoon from one side of the bowl to the other. My eyes were transfixed on the small crisped rice pieces becoming soggier and soggier as the waves of milk turned mud brown. It was Saturday morning, and the thought of eating after … after what happened the night before made my stomach turn, and I retched over the bowl.

'Everything okay, sweetie?' Mum asked, without turning around from the cooker to look at me.

I mumbled something about being fine, that a coco pop had got stuck in my throat, and threw down the spoon. I swallowed hard, unsure of what I could say … what I *should* say. I so desperately want to speak to Mum, but where to start … Do I just blurt out that I had been attacked in my bedroom last night, and the weekend before that, and the weekend before that? Should I start crying to get Mum's attention? I try to force the tears to come, but my brain ignores the request. Maybe I cried so much after that first night that I've dried up any reserves left. Am I so numb and helpless that I can't even summon any emotion?

'Mum,' I say, knowing that I needed to start somewhere.

She hums a reply and just as I'm about to say something, *anything*, he walks in and knocks the wind right out of me.

'Morning, babe,' he grabs hold of my mother's waist, but his eyes pierce into mine. Just before he swings my mum around from the oven, he winks at me.

'I'm cooking your fry-up,' Mum says, and pretends to protest at his hug, but she wraps her arms around his neck anyway, her back still to me.

He leans his head on her shoulder and stares at me while slowly moving his hands down to Mum's bum and, when he pinches it, he licks his lips. I want to scream. I want to run out of the room. But most of all, I want to grab the knife lying on the counter next to the cooker and ram it so far into his eyeball that he'll never be able to look at me again. But, yet again, my body has given up on me and I'm left frozen, sitting on an uncomfortable wooden chair watching the man of my nightmares grope my mother.

'Stop that, honey, Grace is in the room,' Mum says, pulling away from his grasp.

'Oh, she doesn't mind. She loves to see you so happy. Isn't that right, Gracie?' Then, he twirls my mother around and, with his free hand, cranks up the volume on the radio perched on the counter top. 'I love this song.'

I don't know what tune is playing; I can't hear it. I can't hear anything but his low, rough voice repeating my name over and over and over again. *Gracie, Gracie, Gracie, come out to play.* I thrust my hands over my ears, trying to deafen the voices in my own head, but it doesn't work, and they keep singing — almost in sync with the way he spins my mother around and around the kitchen. *Gracie, Gracie, Gracie, come out to play.*

'Stop it.' I hear the scream, but it takes a few seconds to realise the shrill voice is mine.

The two of them pull apart and stare at me; his eyes dark and evil — just how I would imagine Lucifer's to look — but my mum's are sad and welling with tears. I stopped her happiness. I took away her smile.

'I'm sorry, Mum, I don't think I'm feeling too well, that's all. I'm going to go back to bed for a while.'

Her face lights up again and she comes over to me at the table, her hands on my arms give me the strength to stand up. 'Ah, sweetie, I'm sorry. Get yourself upstairs and I'll bring you up a cup of warm sweet tea.'

Although I'm looking at Mum, my eyes are really focused on the devil behind her. The darkness remains on his face, but there's a smirk dancing on his thin lips as he raises his index finger to them…silencing me again.

As though a hand guides me from the kitchen, I push my way out of the door and release a sigh when I'm on the other side of it. As my foot touches the bottom stair, the radio is silenced and I hear his grating voice sing out, "Baby, when the lights go out." I take the steps two at a time, the tears gushing down my face involuntary, and stumble into my bedroom. I close the door and sit on the floor with my back against it.

Through the tears, I draw my nails along my palm — the sharpness of the pain temporarily alleviating some of my sadness. That feeling soon morphs into anger as I think of myself saying 'sorry' in the kitchen moments before. Why am I sorry? What have I done? Who has he turned me into? I can't even talk to my mum now … the person I'm closest to in all the world. He's ripped her away from me. My eyes are drawn to a picture on my cork-board collage — one of me and my grandfather standing on the South Pier in Blackpool — and I stop clawing at myself, ignore the droplets of blood running down my fingers and take a deep breath.

I stand up, switch on my CD player and select Eminem and Dido's version of "Stan" while rooting through my drawers and wardrobe. I grab some spare clothes and my boots and shove them into the duffle bag. I'll need some snacks and water, but I can get those things later tonight when *he's* out of the kitchen — out of the house. I reach over and turn the volume up; I've always loved this song. I don't know why. It's so dark, but I think I finally understand it now: Stan just needed someone to save him.

I've made my mind up. I need to get out of here. I won't be in my bed when the devil comes crawling in here tonight.

Chapter Fifteen

After Dixon had informed Valerie Murphy of her daughter's escape, she and PC Williams took a seat in the living room. The walls were decorated with family photographs, mainly of Grace growing from a chocolate-covered toddler to hat-and-gown graduating woman, with all the rites of passage in-between.

'Ms Murphy, please sit down,' Dixon requested as the woman marched back and forth over the blue carpet; her hair had lost the bright blondness shown in the surrounding photographs. Now, streaks of grey grew unevenly and wild from the roots like trees in a forest, and her skin wrinkled like the trunk. The woman looked a decade older than her fifty-five years.

Dixon sighed. 'Ms Murphy—'

'That makes me feel old. Call me Valerie,' the woman finally replied and sat in the armchair opposite Dixon. 'I know everything there is to know about dissociative identity disorder now. Go on, try me, ask me anything you want to know.'

'Where's your daughter?'

Valerie flapped her hands in the air and rolled her eyes. 'No, that's not what I mean. I've spent the last year of my life trying to understand what multiple personalities means, how a person develops it — how *my* baby developed it — and, most importantly, why the hell I didn't realise what was going on. But I'm stumped with all of those questions. Since the day I became a mother, I made that role my life.

Forfeited nights out, relationships with friends and lovers, gave up the chance on my dream job. Those were my choices, I wanted to live like that because I wanted my baby girl to have all of me. And it paid off because she turned out to be my best friend. When she started working at the theatre, my heart burst with pride. I knew how much she wanted it, and she had gone for it with all she had. I just …'

Dixon moved forward on the sofa, closing the gap between herself and Valerie. 'I understand how you're feeling, but—'

'Is your daughter a murderer?'

She shook her head, locked in on Valerie's expressionless eyes — despite the interruption — and continued. 'I do have a daughter, and can only *imagine* what you've been through and what you're going through again now.'

'How can I know every single detail about the disorder that stole my daughter, yet still know so little about the reasoning behind why she did what she did? You know, I didn't believe it for months after Grace had been arrested … assumed your lot had made a huge mistake. But there was one day in court.' Valerie turned her head and gazed out of the window. 'Something about the way she continually scratched her palm, like a twitch, and then I remembered reading how these alter personalities literally become a different person with their own ways, their own habits, even their own accents and sexuality and gender. And that's when I heard it too, the sweetness of Grace's voice laced with … with evil.'

Dixon waited until Valerie's focus returned to the present. 'That was something you'd never noticed before?'

A deep grumble escaped Valerie's lips and silent tears fell as she spoke. 'I don't know, it's just so difficult to look back, to try and remember … remember when and why. All those people, who the police say Grace … you know … well, all those people who were murdered around the time my father passed away.'

'It was cancer, wasn't it?'

Valerie nodded. 'Grace and I watched the man we loved, a fighter who taught us both to be strong and independent, fade away to someone who needed help going to the toilet. Where's the dignity? Fucking cancer.' She paused to wipe her jumper across her cheeks. 'Grace said that a lot after he died. She was as close to my father as if he were her own. So, you're asking me to examine my daughter's behaviour at a time of utter grief. Yes, she had changed; mood swings, heavy drinking, undeniable anger at everyone and everything. But, throughout that time, there were also the familiar warm hugs, laughter, reminiscing together and gentle tears. Anything out of the ordinary, I attributed to grief. We all grieve in different ways, Sergeant.'

'Yes, you're right, Valerie, but I'm afraid we're not here today to discuss last year's events. We're here because last night your daughter escaped Manor Hall Hospital.'

'And killed another person, you say?'

'Yes, one of the night shift security guards.'

Valerie inhaled sharply and asked for his name.

'I'm sorry, I can't share that information with you at this time. The family are being informed and it wouldn't be right—'

'Why hasn't it been on the news?'

Dixon wondered briefly if the questions were a stalling technique, but when she looked into Valerie's tear-rimmed blue eyes, the pain tugged at her heart. Sabrina and Ali, her own children, flashed in her mind, and she could imagine herself asking as many questions or attempting to decipher her muddled memories just as Valerie did now. Whether a mechanism to deal with the inconceivable pain or the hope that knowledge would shield the oncoming blows, Dixon couldn't decide which, but she did empathise with the lost mother sat in front of her.

'A media embargo, for now, has been put in place,' Dixon explained. 'However, we realise it won't take long at all for a journalist to get wind of the escape and the hospital grounds will become a circus. Names will be protected until our say so is given and then, at that time, I'm sure there'll be a press conference because … we have reason to believe Grace has kidnapped one of our colleagues.'

Dixon ignored Valerie's wide eyes and open mouth and continued blowing the punches; not a job she relished, but if the mother had any information whatsoever, she'd do anything necessary to get the woman to talk. Valerie stood and paced the room, shaking her head the entire time Dixon informed her about Fraser, the slaughtered cat and the handwritten note.

Valerie finally flew back into the armchair, hunched her back and rested her elbows on her knees. Clasping her hands together, in an imitation of prayer, she exhaled between pursed lips. 'I can't believe this … that she would …'

'When did you last see Grace?' Dixon asked.

'It's been months.' Valerie sucked in her cheeks and over-blinked her eyelashes in a bid to hold more tears at bay, Dixon surmised. 'Before the hospital, I saw Grace as often as I was allowed, trying to comfort her however I could. Then, after she transferred to Manor Hall, I had to wait until she was *settled* … or something like that. The first time I visited, she told me not to come back until she requested I did.'

'Why do you think that was?'

Valerie shrugged, looking everywhere but Dixon's eyes. 'She said it was to do with her treatment. That distractions from the outside world wouldn't help her process everything, but …'

'You didn't believe that?'

'She looked so sad, and angry, and confused … all those emotions, all at once, I could see it all in her eyes. I could see the pain … I … I don't know, I hadn't seen it before. Grace wasn't herself when I visited her there, but the doctors were no help. At the end of the day, my daughter was serving a sentence and if I had no visiting order, I couldn't get in the place.'

'You may not have seen Grace, but in the past five months, have you had any phone conversations with her or letters sent between the two of you?'

Valerie shook her head and folded her arms, leaning back in the chair once again. 'Nothing from Grace. I've written a letter every week, just to tell her how much I love her and that I'm here for her, but there's been no replies.'

'I'm sorry,' Dixon said, and she truly meant it. However, as much as she felt Valerie's parental pain, she couldn't let it cloud the job expected of her — and, therefore, she didn't share details about the officers stationed outside surveilling the woman's house. 'Is there anyone you can contact? Someone who could come and be with you, perhaps?'

'I had just got off the phone to Grace's father before you turned up. He'll be over shortly.'

Dixon rose from the sofa and handed Valerie her card, asking her to call immediately if she heard from Grace, or if she remembered anything significant that could help the police find her daughter.

'She isn't an evil person,' Valerie whispered.

Dixon peered over her shoulder before leaving the room. *But she is a murderer*, she thought with a pinch to her heart.

Chapter Sixteen

Hamilton turned in his office chair and glanced out of the window. The rain has finally passed and left a clear, inky-blue night sky to cover London. Street lamps and office lights from the surrounding buildings illuminated his high view of the city. A city that never sleeps — he thinks of how well that old saying describes his home town.

He can't quite believe how the day has escaped in a flash; now Saturday night and not much further along than what they were at the beginning of the day. A text message beep from his phone distracts him and he suddenly thinks of Elizabeth, who he hasn't replied to since before he visited the mortuary. With Clarke and Dixon returning to the station any minute, he takes a moment to call his wife.

After the usual apologies and mumblings about the importance of his latest case, Hamilton paused, confused by Elizabeth's uncharacteristic silence.

'So, how are you?'

'Fine.'

'What are you plans for tonight?'

'Nothing.'

He sighed. After all this time, he knew Elizabeth understood the reasons he fled from the house at a moment's notice so often, but must she guilt trip him with silence and short answers? On the other hand, he thought, how would he feel if the shoe was on the other foot?

'Look, I can't keep apologising.'

'I really needed to speak to you this weekend, Denis. It was important,' she blurted, and he heard her voice catch in her throat.

'Oh, love. It's just—'

'I thought I was late.'

He frowned, thrown by his wife's interruption. 'Late for what?'

Elizabeth sighed heavily, and he could picture her rolling her eyes. 'Denis, I thought my period was late. I thought I was pregnant.'

Hamilton's own eyes grew wider with every word she said. He tried to speak, but his lips ended up mirroring that of a tropical fish sucking oxygen through the water. To call this unexpected would have been an understatement, he thought. Granted, he panged to once again have that father-daughter relationship, perhaps even more so recently after watching his friend Billy with young Amelia. But to admit that out loud, to Elizabeth, felt like a betrayal to Maggie, and so he never spoke of them adding to their family.

When he said nothing, Elizabeth cleared her throat. 'Anyway, I went to see the GP—'

'What?' he blurted; his wife had his attention again. 'How could you not tell me, but you had time to get to the doctors?'

'It's not me who doesn't have the time to talk, Denis.' The fact he heard no menace in Elizabeth's voice was the real slap to the face.

'You're right, I'm sorry, love. Work still takes priority, doesn't it? No matter how much I like to think I've changed since Maggie left us … But, anyway, you've been now. To the doctors. What did he say? Are you?'

'No,' Elizabeth replied abruptly. 'I'm not pregnant, Denis.'

'Oh.' He didn't know how he felt, but there was a swishing sensation whirling in his stomach.

'It's premature menopause.'

Hamilton's mind turned another corner in this maze of a conversation. 'Well, that can't be right. We'll get a second opinion. You're not even forty yet, for crying out loud.'

'Yes, therein lies the premature part of the diagnosis, Denis. It's not very common, one in a hundred women, the doctor said, and there's varying reasons as to why this happens ...' Elizabeth trailed off and matched her husband's silence.

Uncharacteristically, Hamilton was speechless, and he hated himself for it. A pin-like prick continually jabbed his head, urging him to say something to his wife, but what could he say? He was sorry. But what exactly was he sorry for — what Elizabeth now had to go through or the fact that the possibility of more children had now come to an end? He hated himself again, this wasn't about him. His selfishness irritated his mind.

'Adoption is always an option,' she blurted out again and took him by surprise. For a second, he wondered if he had uttered his own thoughts out loud.

'What?' he replied, managing to sound rude and abrupt.

Elizabeth released a long sigh into his ear, a sad and exhausted sounding one. 'Oh, Denis, I don't know what I'm saying. It's just, maybe this has finally made me realise I do want another child. No, that's a lie, I think I've always known, but I couldn't say it out loud. How could I? It would have felt like I was trying to replace Maggie, and I couldn't have ...'

Hamilton's mind shattered into a million thoughts; how could he not have known his wife had always wanted another child? Had his guilt over losing Maggie been the reason Elizabeth hadn't told him? Could they seriously consider raising a child, who wasn't biologically theirs, after everything they'd been through?

'Denis.'

His wife's melodic voice brought him back into focus, but the image of his daughter's face never faded from his mind. Right now, he couldn't confess that the idea of more children had indeed crossed his mind in recent weeks.

'Elizabeth, I…I'm—'

'Denis, don't.' He heard the smile in her voice. 'Listen, I'm fine, and anything else we need to discuss can be done another time. This really isn't a conversation to have over the phone, and I probably shouldn't have said anything … but I couldn't go another day without you at least knowing.'

'Do you need me to come home?' he asked while peering into the main incident room to find his team forming a group around the white board. 'I'll come if you need me.'

'No, you won't.' She paused, but there was no deep sigh, malice or blame. Instead, she continued with a softness in her tone. 'I'm fine, Denis, I promise. You're needed there more than here, so go do what you do and stop that woman from hurting anyone else and make sure you bring Kerry back safe and sound.'

Hamilton had never wanted to hug his wife more than he did in that moment. He could have argued her point about not needing him at home, but it would have been fruitless, they both knew that. So, he agreed, told Elizabeth he loved her and ended the call before her sweet voice hammered another hole into his heart.

***

Once Hamilton had joined his team in the office — as well as the many officers who had now been added to the investigation — Clarke and Dixon gave updates about their questioning with Valerie Murphy and Natasha Holten.

Information and action points, including interviewing Grace's father, were posted on the white board, and Hamilton confirmed he wanted surveillance to stay on the two women. He found it hard to believe Murphy wouldn't reach out to them. Hamilton then updated the team about a possible press conference scheduled for first thing tomorrow morning.

'There appears to be some outrage from the victim's family about a cover up,' he explained.

Dixon was the first with a question. 'Are the family aware Manor Hall Hospital homed criminals who were serving a custodial sentence?'

Hamilton shrugged. 'How much they know is unclear. But they're not impressed with Mr Hardy's name being glanced over, which is prompting them to ask questions.'

'Understandable. So how much information will be given to the press?'

'DCI Allen is in a meeting about all of that right now. We'll know more shortly, but the feeling is we'll launch a search appeal for Grace Murphy.'

Rocky bolted up in his chair. 'Won't that put Kerry in jeopardy? What if Murphy runs, and we haven't found her yet, or what if she …' Though the constable's sentence trailed off, it was clear to Hamilton what he had meant. Fraser's life could very well be in danger if Murphy's mug-shot was plastered all over the news.

'Well, we have tonight to do as much digging as possible and hopefully find their location,' Hamilton said, hoping he had subtly side-stepped Rocky's question. 'The desk sergeant has already ordered in some food, but don't think that's opportunity to sit on your laurels. Eat and work. Comb through the old case files and see if there's anything we have missed so far, maybe another friend Murphy could have turned to for support. And I don't care what time it is, get her father brought in ASAP.'

While Rocky was handed the baton to update the room on his findings, Hamilton took a seat at a nearby table. He steepled his fingers and blew a long puff of air through them, his heartbeat quickening at the impending situation.

The young sergeant placed a map of Central London on an empty white board — a map he had clearly been working on. Various circles graffitied the paper and Rocky explained they contained ANPR cameras that had captured Fraser's car in the past twenty-four hours.

'Christ, she's been busy?' PC Shand shouted from the back of the room.

'Why do you think she's driving all over town?' PC Goldberg added.

'She's not,' Rocky snapped. 'It's Murphy.'

This time, Shand raised a hand before speaking. 'To put us off the scent, perhaps?'

Rocky nodded. 'Exactly that. The car has been driven within a mile of this bloody station. Covent Garden, Hyde Park, Soho. All over, really. Murphy isn't stupid; if we went by these sightings, we'd be chasing our own tails for hours, days even.'

'So what's the plan?' Another officer asked.

'I've focused on the very last sighting I could find of the car, about two hours ago, just here …' Rocky pointed to the map. 'And I'm looking into possible directions of travel.'

'What if it's not Murphy at all?' Dixon threw in. 'What if she paid some kid to joyride the car around for the day while she's been making a run for it in the opposite direction?'

Rocky's eyebrows flew upwards. 'Well … I don't know … I guess that's a possibility I hadn't thought of,' he stuttered, as the room came alive with mumblings and theories from the other officers.

Hamilton pulled himself up from the chair. Whether it was his six-foot stature or his contorted expression that silenced them again, he didn't know, but he was pleased for the respect nonetheless.

'While it's an excellent observation, Dixon, I don't think it's the correct one.' He raised a hand to cut off her counterargument and continued with his thoughts. 'Rocky, I also think we're wasting time looking at where Murphy *could* have possibly travelled to from the last sighting.'

'Why?' a lone voice called from the sea of officers.

Hamilton glanced at Clarke, who simply answered the question with, 'Because she's still in London.'

Glad his partner had jumped on the same train of thought, an internal buzz of hope spread through Hamilton like the first rays of sunshine warming his face on a summer's morning. He unclasped his hands and bounded over to the white board.

'In her note, Murphy made it quite clear that she wanted revenge. She wants to play with me, with all of us, for arresting her. She's bloody well driven right past this very station, knowing that eventually we'd look at the cameras. Covent Garden, Hyde Park and Soho are places where she has killed before. And the fact that she's taken Fraser tells me she's not about to skip town.'

'Okay ... so where does that leave us?' PC Shand bellowed in a monotonous tone. 'What are we supposed to do, run around London hoping we'll bump into this crazy woman?'

Hamilton narrowed his eyes, staring at Shand until the officer finally looked away, and sucked the air between his teeth. 'As I was about to say. Rocky, the sighting of the car in Covent Garden, when was that?'

Rocky's finger trailed over a piece of paper in his hand. 'This morning, one of the first sightings, so—'

'So that's exactly where Murphy is. The London Theatre in Covent Garden, to be exact. It's where Grace Murphy worked before we arrested her.' He thumped the desk, cursing himself for not thinking of it sooner. 'She felt comfortable at the theatre, safe even, it was like a second home to her. Of course, that was until we arrested the manager for murder ...' he trailed off, fearing at the moment he could muddle the prospect of finding Fraser with insignificant details of the previous investigation. 'I want to know what's been happening with that building in the past twelve months, who owns it and if we can get eyes on it immediately.' Then, facing the room, Hamilton advised the officers to prepare for a raid.

Chapter Seventeen

A swift kick to Fraser's lower back sent her rolling across the wooden floor, but she didn't care. Instead, she welcomed the crouching position and sucked in the cold air as if she was drinking through a straw. Dizziness took over and forced Fraser to sit with her back against the wall and her knees tucked up under her chin.

It was dark; the stage lit only by a few church candles surrounding them in a circle, as though she was about to be offered up as a human sacrifice. Finally, Fraser made out Grace Murphy's figure when the woman took a step towards her. The woman's body was a shadow, an outline with her hands behind her back, and the face dark and contorted. Fraser wanted to utilise her training, entice a conversation between herself and her attacker, but the goosebumps spreading over her skin as well as her chattering teeth made her realise her mind was as frozen as her body.

Murphy plunged forward, wrapping thick and battered bell rope around Fraser's wrists and then her ankles. Within a matter of minutes she was hog-tied and hating herself. Why hadn't she kicked out? Why wasn't the adrenaline coursing through her veins, urging her to fight? Had her job taught her nothing about these situations? No, she answered herself, thinking of how her training had focused on her rescuing the gagged and bound victims, and always with a team behind her.

While wondering if she should actually say something, Murphy stood and looked down at her like a piece of shit she'd walked in and dragged through the house. A gun hanging limply in her hand.

'I thought a knife was your weapon of choice.' Fraser heard her own voice but frowned at the hint of sarcasm staining it — *what am I thinking, antagonising her further?*

Murphy cackled, reached her arm around her waist and untucked a large blade from the waistband of her trousers. The woman's dark eyes flicked from one weapon to the other, as her hands bobbed slowly up and down, before flashing her evil glare at Fraser again. 'For you, I haven't decided which is best to use.'

Fraser looked away while Murphy bent over and lowered the tip of the knife into one of the candle's flames. The woman was toying with her, and she couldn't yet decide which emotion had taken control of her senses: fear or anger.

Murphy roared laughing again, twirling the handle of the poker-hot blade in her hand, and paced around the stage. Dramatically weaving around the candles with large steps and swaying near the naked flame, Murphy hummed a tune.

'How did you know where I lived?' Fraser blurted, again not recognising her own voice.

The figure stopped prancing around the stage and stood right in front of her, making Fraser strain her neck to look up, the rope pulling tighter on her wrists as she did. Murphy's eyes were as black as coal and she had dropped her head to one side. Fraser's mind couldn't persuade her throat to swallow the thick saliva.

'I was watching you,' Murphy replied. 'Well, not me personally, of course … you made sure that wasn't possible, didn't you? But, this time, I wasn't working alone.'

Unsure if it was the question she had asked, Fraser wondered what had made Murphy purse her lips together so tightly that they turned white with fury, and why she had contorted her face into a scowl after finishing her sentence. Regardless of her expression, the woman was talking, and Fraser tried to keep the flow going.

'Why me?' she continued.

'Because it's your fucking fault I was arrested. Your fucking fault I was sent to that hell hole. Your fucking fault that I had to—' Murphy stopped abruptly and scratched her scalp with the tip of the knife.

The grating sound sent a shiver down Fraser's spine.

'I really had you wrong, lady.' Murphy continued with a snarl.

'How do you mean?'

Murphy leaned back slightly and ran her eyes of stone over Fraser. 'Well, you're pretty and obviously good at your fucking job, yet … yet you're so lonely. You work and you go home. All alone. You have no one to go home to, except that daft cat.' Murphy paused and smiled deviously. 'Well, you *did* have a cat to go home to.'

An image of a shadowed figure on her dining room table, before she was knocked out in her kitchen, flashed through her mind — only this time, her mind allowed the shadows to clear, and she saw the blood and fur. She gagged, the saliva mixing with bile as it made its return up from her stomach, the manic woman's laughter echoing in her ears the entire time.

Fraser suppressed her screams of rage and anger and sadness. Though the coarse ropes chaffed against her skin, the dizziness skated on the edge of taking control and her heart ached when she thought of her fur baby Felix, she refused to let Murphy feel victorious. She pulled a deep breath in through her nose, pushed back her shoulders and looked her captor square in the eyes.

'Perhaps I should feel honoured.'

Murphy flinched. 'What?'

'All this …' Fraser looked around with wide eyes … 'This theatrical performance, risking your life to escape from the hospital and taking another victim's life because of me. Your desperate need for revenge has brought us here, hasn't it?'

'Victim,' Murphy screeched. 'Far from it, he …' she trailed off, her attention unfocused as she paced back and forth and scratched the back of the hand which gripped the gun. 'And yes, if it wasn't for you, I'd be in Spain now, enjoying my life and … and I've said all this. Why are you making me repeat myself?'

'You can't keep running away from what you've done, Grace …' Fraser cringed, shook her head slightly and tried to correct herself. '…Carly, the crimes you've committed—'

'Why did you come to the hospital to visit me?'

Fraser paused at the interruption and found Murphy's eyes glaring at her. 'My mother suffered from bipolar—'

'I don't have bipolar.'

Fraser shook her head again. 'No, I know … I thought maybe I could help—'

'Help? Help? You fucking put me back into my nightmare.'

Fraser sighed, the constant cutting in and wandering around from Murphy made her feel nauseous. She couldn't remember the last time she'd had a sip of water, or a bite to eat, and manoeuvred her tongue around her mouth and teeth to unlock an ounce of spittle.

'Carly, listen to me, what you're doing is wrong and you need help. You're hurting the wrong people. I'm not the source of your pain.'

Murphy bared her teeth like a dog. 'I was less safe in that hospital than anywhere I've ever been in the last twenty years. *You* condemned me to that. My body was imprisoned as well as my mind. I just want to be free.' The last word hung in the air, like the sombre note at the end of a heart-wrenching ballad, and the woman's head fell back.

Fraser, terrified about the uncertainty of Murphy's character, soothed her voice. 'I spoke with your doctor … Emine, I think her name was, and she told me how well you were doing.'

'And I bet you believed everything the good doctor told you.' Murphy fell to her knees and shoved her face into Fraser's. She sniffed a few times before whispering, 'You smell of sex. Are you shagging your boss?'

Fraser recoiled, remembering Murphy's accusations when she and Hamilton had arrested her at Luton airport. Back then, Murphy had seemed hooked on the idea that the pair were having an affair because Hamilton had brought her, instead of Clarke, with him. She saw now that Murphy used this as a distraction to not answer the vital questions. Murphy licked Fraser's cheek and swiftly jumped back onto her feet.

'Stop this,' Fraser shouted. 'I know what you're trying to do, but I won't stop. I'm not the person you're mad at. Your pain runs deeper than this. Something happened to you, and you need to open up and accept the help before it's too late.'

Murphy's head tilted from one side to the other. 'Too late for you, you mean?'

Fraser gritted her teeth, determined to get through to Murphy. 'Grace, I know you're in there, just listen to my voice. Yes, I arrest criminals and help send them to prison, but I truly want to help you. I want to get to the root of why you're angry, why these murders had to happen. If we can do that together, no one else needs to be hurt and we have a chance of ending all of this. You can see your family and—'

Murphy's fist connected with Fraser's cheek, causing her to topple over onto her side, a gush of blood fired from her mouth.

'Shut up. Shut up. Shut up!' Murphy screamed. 'You have no fucking clue what you're talking about. You're—'

Murphy spun around as if she had heard something and Fraser used the disturbance to try to pull herself back up into a sitting position. The angle of the body wrapped in rope made it impossible. Suddenly, the woman was behind her, the knife against her throat, whispering in her ear to stay quiet.

'Who hurt you?' Fraser whispered back, wanting to make a connection with Murphy. But a forceful reply came in the form of Fraser's hair being yanked back. The pressure it caused on her interlocking wrists and ankles made her whimper. The blade pushed further into her skin and she silently nodded.

'We need to leave,' Murphy said before lowering the weapon.

'Where are we going?' A strip of duct tape passed Fraser's eyes and her heartbeat doubled.

'No more fucking questions from you.' Murphy kneeled in front of her; her breath once again warming Fraser's face. The woman sat back on her hunches, stared at Fraser and dug her nails into the palm of her own hand, scratching until she drew blood. After letting out a long sigh, she said, 'If there's so much as a peep from you, the next person's blood you see will be on your hands.'

Chapter Eighteen

As the convoy of police cars and vans drove along Victoria Embankment from New Scotland Yard, Hamilton glanced back out of the window at the sixteen-storey Gothic clocktower surrounded by scaffolding. Both hands on Big Ben's illumined face ticked along to midnight and yet despite the bell's silence, due to renovation work until 2021, the familiar bongs sounded out of habit in Hamilton's ears. As Clarke navigated along the Thames towards Covent Garden, and the night-time view of London sped by, the imaginary sound vibrated deep within Hamilton's mind. He frowned, the tension squashing his head down as he turned back around in his seat, the bells ringing just for him, reminding him of precious time slipping away.

The bongs bounced from flashback to flashback: Hamilton meeting Fraser for the first time over three years ago as a young and eager sergeant; she had told him swapping Kent for London was something she needed to do for personal reasons — no more was said, and Hamilton didn't pry; he fully understood the need for privacy. Natural blonde hair, usually swinging in a long pony-tail, and the little, if any, make-up on her porcelain face always made her appear younger than her twenty-nine years. Fraser glued to the computer in the morning, the afternoon and well into the evening during most of the team's cases; her patience for research, attention to detail and the ability to pick out a suspicious transaction on a bank statement in under thirty seconds. The man stepping over Fraser's body in the street. Her dead cat on the dining table. The note.

Screeching tyres shook Hamilton from his thoughts and he automatically flew into action with the rest of the officers. Deploying the Police Firearms Unit had been a necessity after Hamilton's own team had been unable to get their sights inside The London Theatre. The venue had been closed and the front entrance barricaded for over a year. However, with the location being their only lead for a possible whereabouts of Grace Murphy — and potentially Fraser — Hamilton took a step back after the armed officers gave the team a briefing.

While different teams scattered themselves outside the theatre to disrupt any escape plan Murphy may have and protect any pedestrians that could pass by — despite being midnight, the streets were never fully empty — Hamilton and his team followed a group of armed officers down a side alley which led to a back entrance of the theatre. Utilising earpieces as their method of communication with the officer leading the raid, Hamilton hand-signalled for Clarke, Rocky and Dixon to stay crouched behind him.

With an order finally shouted into their ears, the officers sprung forward, smashing through the back door and into the darkness of the building. Hamilton and team filed behind the armed officers, their torch beams leading the way along what Hamilton knew to be the corridors leading to the theatre's offices, green room and costume area. He strained his ear through the noise of doors opening and closing, boots thudding on the floor and the repetition of the word 'clear' being shouted. Frustration bubbled inside Hamilton's gut, he desperately wanted to run around the armed officer and check the next room, wanting to move things on faster, his eyes finally adjusting to the dimness.

'Activity on stage … main arena,' a voice echoed through the earpiece.

A beam of light spread out in front of him and Hamilton identified the hallway that would lead him to the backstage area. He hot-footed along the corridor, aware of feet following him, but the commotion and chaos making him unsure who it actually was. The area in front of him glowed brightly for a few moments and smoke snaked up his nostrils.

'Blaze extinguished,' the voice came again in his ear. 'Theatre is clear.'

Hamilton stepped out onto the stage and his eyes scanned the open space — an officer releasing a fire extinguisher next to the burnt ends of the huge black curtains; large church candles dotted around the stage, their fiery wicks coming to an end; helmeted colleagues checking each row of seats. He turned to thump the wall, but instead landed his fist into a stage prop, and his hand punched directly through the brick-effect cardboard.

'How the hell have we missed her again?' Hamilton yelled.

'Guv,' Clarke called out from his hunched over position at the front of the stage. 'There's traces of blood here. It's fresh.'

Hamilton clicked his fingers, preparing to give an order to call SOCO immediately, but found Dixon reaching for her phone and giving him the thumbs up as she walked away from the thudding footsteps of officers still checking the dress circle and upper circle seats. Hamilton looked over at them and shook his head.

'What are you thinking, guv?' Clarke asked, stepping up next to him. The deep frown lines in his partner's forehead looked as though they had been carved by the Egyptians; stubble grew wild and patchy over Clarke's usually clean-shaven face and his skin looked tinged with a dull greyness.

'I'm wondering why Murphy would come here,' Hamilton replied, and released a long sigh, assuming he himself looked as disheartened as his partner.

'Well, she worked here.'

'No, Grace did.'

Clarke's furrows etched further into his skin and he made a noise, a grumble or a sigh, Hamilton could not decipher. 'Yes, guv, but Grace and Carly are the same person. So, effectively, it's the same thing. This was *their* place of work.'

'No, it's not the same thing at all.' Hamilton rubbed a hand back and forth over his head. 'I'm with you, Clarke. I don't get this whole split personality thing, but the fact of the matter is, we need to get our heads around it.'

'It's weird—'

'It's real and we need to deal with it,' he lashed out. 'I just can't help but think that this place was important to Grace and not her alter personality Carly … so why come here?'

Clarke shrugged his shoulders. 'In that case, perhaps she was hoping we wouldn't connect this place to her.'

'Or maybe she actually did want us to find her,' Rocky interjected. 'Think about it, today she's driven that car all around our vicinity. Look here.' He pointed to the blood staining the wooden floor. 'If that's Fraser's, there's a chance she's been within a ten-minute walking distance of us the whole bloody day.'

Before he could sympathise with Rocky's frustration, a uniformed officer interrupted them by calling Hamilton's name from the last row of seats in the stalls. He dashed down the sides steps with both men, and now Dixon too, hot on his trial.

'Sir, we discovered a letter addressed to you here.' PC Goldberg pointed to the end chair and handed the envelope to Hamilton.

He snatched the paper and ripped the envelope opening. His team continued to discuss the whys and maybes of Murphy's plan, but Hamilton zoned out from their voices as his eyes once again hungrily read the hand-written note. A shiver corkscrewed up his back.

'Well, come on,' Rocky snapped, 'what does it say this time?'

One by one, Hamilton looked at each of his team in their eyes and then focused back on the paper. He exhaled a deep sigh before mustering the energy to read out loud. '*If you're reading this, Inspector and friends, you made it in time before this godforsaken place burnt to a crisp. Shame, really. But even still, once again, you were too late, but I'll give you a round of applause for good effort. Sadly, a good effort won't save your friend. Don't you want to see her alive? Have you not worked all of this out yet? I'll give you one more chance. Just one. For now, this means you're too close to me and the curtain hasn't risen on the final act just yet, so I've had to move on. Yes, your precious sergeant is still alive … I can't promise how long that will last with the amount of fucking questions she asks, though. However, it's almost Sunday. A day of rest. I mean, even God rested on the seventh day, right? But it's more important than that; it's the day I've been waiting for. So that's the only time we have left. Tomorrow, Inspector.*'

Despite the crashing and banging of the firearms unit and other officers, the four of them remained silent. The piece of paper, gripped in Hamilton's fingers, took centre stage in front of all of them.

'What does that mean?' Rocky asked, his tone no more than a whisper.

'If we don't find Fraser tomorrow, there's a chance we never will.' Hamilton clenched his teeth, screwed the paper into a ball and stormed out of the auditorium.

Chapter Nineteen

Hamilton threw a folder on the office table, ignoring it as it continued to skid along, sending papers flying into the air and onto the floor. The noise in the incident room hitched up a level as the officers piled back in, all preparing for a debrief of the raid and all disappointed with their wasted efforts. Though he stood like a statue watching his exhausted team, his feet unsure where to take him, Hamilton's mind whizzed like an aircraft propeller; each question and image and thought spinning and merging with the next, his mind unable to settle on one.

DCI Allen shouted Hamilton's name and tipped his head in the direction of the corridor before leaving the office as swiftly as he'd entered it. A lifebuoy had been thrown and Hamilton grabbed it with both hands. Saying nothing to the officers crowding the incident room, Hamilton followed his superior and welcomed the coolness of the empty space.

'This is a shambles, Denis,' Allen fired off as soon as the pair had walked out of ear shot of the office. 'How in God's name did this happen? Didn't you cover all your bases before sending teams of officers into that building? Had you no intelligence of whether your suspect was in the theatre or not?'

The two men, similar in six-foot stature, stopped and glared at each other. The questions continued. Hamilton's hovercraft mind finally came to a stop and he focused on Allen's round face growing redder and redder the more he spoke. He threw his hand up and watched the horror cloud Allen's face as the interruption froze him mid-sentence. Although Allen was a fair boss, hardly ever poking into Hamilton's decision and always allowing him to guide his team as he saw fit, the entire station knew you never interrupted the stout and stubborn DCI from Cork.

But it was too late for Hamilton. He lowered his hand and let it shake beside him, his chest rose and fell furiously in front of him and he snorted a puff of air before he spoke. 'Yes, sir, how in God's name did this happen?'

Allen frowned. 'What—?'

'I'll tell you how it started, and then you can tell me why you think my team are to blame.'

'Now you wait one minute, Denis—'

Hamilton's hand reacted again, this time a steady palm flying up to Allen's face. 'A convicted murderer's lawyer uses the disguise of mental health issues to get her a pass at a safe-haven where she could enjoy nice chats with a chilled out doctor, be free to wander around a stately home and—'

'You hold on one second, Denis.' Allen wagged his finger in the direction of Hamilton's hand. 'Manor Hall Hospital is not a *safe-haven* as you so blasé put it. It is a government institution for … for … ill criminals to serve their sentences in a protected environment.'

Hamilton threw both hands in the air now. 'A *trial* government institution, that no one seems to have known about … certainly no one I've spoken to … and it sounds like not even you're sure what or who that place is for. Sir.'

'I'm well aware—'

'Of the key cards and small access points?' Hamilton snapped. 'Don't label something as a secure institution for criminals and then have inexperienced security guards chilling out on the night shift and informal doctors prancing around in their trainers. Whoever set this up might like to think that mental health issues or disabilities or illnesses make these criminals less of a threat, but the truth of the matter is that building, filled with murderers, rapists, drug dealers and paedophiles, is not conducting itself under the Prison Service Instructions. Jesus Christ, at the very least, where are the officers and actual keys to lock the damn doors? And because of that … Grace Murphy killed a man, escaped and is now driving round London with her middle finger up at us for kicks. And that, *sir*, is how in God's name this all happened.'

'Denis, I understand your frustrations, but with job cuts and the like …' Allen sighed, stopped defending the situation and looked Hamilton square in the eyes. 'Yes, it was still a trial and Manor Hall Hospital is a facility that … and I hate to say this because it sounds like a huge cliché … was on a strictly need-to-know basis.'

'I think I, and every officer who makes an arrest, have the right to know where that criminal is held. Although, I'm no fool, so please don't treat me as one, sir. Manor Hall Hospital has continued to slip under the radar because of the press and community. The uproar it would cause from the locals would be problematic, shall we say, for the force. Correct?'

Allen tipped his head once more, and the pair walked along to the end of the corridor and stopped at the small square window overlooking London's Charing Cross. Allen puffed his cheeks and wrought his hands together. 'Whether you're correct or not, Denis, is neither here nor there.'

'What do you mean?'

'A press conference is taking place at 7am in the hunt for Grace Murphy.'

Hamilton glanced at his watch: five hours. 'Full disclosure?'

'The press team are working on the wording and logistics about what to share regarding Manor Hall Hospital,' Allen said, a seriousness darkening his face as he leaned closer into Hamilton's personal space. 'But, Denis, whatever qualms you have about this place, put it to one side for now and concentrate on catching that woman.'

Hamilton flinched. '*That* woman has kidnapped a member of my team. Of your bloody team, sir. Don't for one moment think that is not my top priority.'

Allen held his hands up in surrender for a moment before nodding his head. 'Yes, yes, I know. I've requested a couple of officers from Kent Constabulary visit Fraser's parents at the crack of dawn. They'll stay with them during the press conference. I suggest you and your team get some shut eye and refuel in the next few hours too.'

DCI Allen patted Hamilton's shoulder as he walked away, with the gait of a professional soldier, and climbed the stairs to his own office. Hamilton stared into the void, his mind turned from propeller to black abyss in moments. It was the flash of Fraser's face that pulled him from the wreckage.

While he knew conferences and appeals aided so many investigations, Hamilton worried that all this press could have come too late. Thinking over the words on Murphy's last note, he knew they didn't have time to be chasing down hundreds of possible sightings or taking calls from the public. He rushed back to the incident room, his brain in full circulation once again, and split the officers into teams, telling them to get a couple hours of rest in the interim. His own team of three, like him, refused to slowed down.

'Right, guv,' Dixon said when the four of them had regrouped at the white board. 'Before the raid, you said you wanted Murphy's father brought in.'

'Damn it, yes, I—'

Dixon shot her hand up and stopped his flow; he light-heartedly grunted at life's karma. 'Well, I remembered that after questioning Valerie Murphy she said Grace's father was on his way to her house.'

'Brilliant, let's get over there.'

'No need,' the DS continued, 'while you were with the DCI, I contacted the surveillance team outside the Murphy residence and they're bringing him in now.'

'Right, I want some background on this guy before I have a chat with him.'

Rocky hunched over a near-by keyboard and spoke to the computer screen. 'I'm already on top of that, boss.'

'Good work.' Hamilton beamed, impressed with the initiative of his team. 'What do we know?'

'Not too much, but still more than what we had a few hours ago,' Rocky replied, and once comfortable in his chair, he continued to read. 'Thomas Billows, now a driver technician for Crawford Limited, one of the largest vehicle logistics companies that services the UK, he's actually worked for them for almost thirty years in different roles.'

Hamilton nodded. 'So that confirms what Natasha Holten said about the father being on the road a lot, worked more than he was at home. Okay, what else?'

'No parking fines, no arrests, no county court judgements.'

'A law-abiding citizen … they still exist, then,' Clarke quipped.

'Apparently so,' Rocky continued. 'The man owns no properties and his last known address is still documented as Valerie Murphy's home. The newspapers barely commented on his presence during his daughter's trial last year, focusing more on the mother who Grace actually lived with. I guess the press assumed he wasn't on the family scene.'

Hamilton's eyes ran over the white board for a few moments, his team silently watching him, until he asked, 'Any social media presence?'

'A Facebook account, but it's slim on updates and postings. I couldn't find anything of interest at a quick glance.'

'Dig a bit deeper,' Hamilton requested. 'Check out his list of friends and see if any of those match up with Murphy's, then thoroughly look at any of his photos … I'm not sure what for, but …'

'Anything suspicious. I get it, boss.'

Hamilton turned around, nodding his head to Rocky's comment and folding his arms over his chest. 'Clarke, check out the financial side of things, will you?'

'What do you mean?'

'Grace Murphy isn't stupid, and it seems even less so when her alter personality is running things. We don't know what her plan is, but we're concluding we've got twenty-four hours until Fraser stops becoming useful to her. Why is that? Is she leaving the country? We know she wanted to escape to Spain before. Perhaps holding Fraser hostage has been to keep us focused on that, rather than the bigger picture of her fleeing London. But, whatever it is, she'll need money.'

'You think someone's helping her?' Clarke asked.

'It's the only explanation,' he replied with a heavy sigh. 'Check for any abnormalities in withdrawals, purchases or transfers. Her father, mother, friends … anyone at this point. Murphy must have received funds somehow, and I want to know from who. We've been duped by this woman before, I won't let it happen again. I won't let her take another innocent life … especially not when she's messing with one of our own.'

Chapter Twenty

Half an hour later, Hamilton and Dixon were sitting across from Thomas Billows in the interview room. The man's forehead etched into a deep frown, and his small dark eyes were a stark contrast to his pale oblong face. He drummed his fingers on the table rhythmically, drawing the attention of the two officers to his dirty fingernails. He kept eye-contact with Hamilton during the initial few moments of silence.

'Are you going to tell me why on earth you've dragged me in at this ridiculous time?' the man blurted. 'Have you found Grace?'

Hamilton smiled internally, the silence had broken Thomas Billows in less than two minutes, and he believed that said a lot about a person. The tone in which he spoke only piqued Hamilton's interest further in this man. *Why does Mr Billows sound so irate?*

'Strange your daughter was your second thought,' Hamilton replied.

Thomas's frown burrowed further. 'What are you talking about?'

'You seem … annoyed, Mr Billows, why is that?'

'Well, your lot dragged me in here, with no explanation, away from Valerie when our daughter is missing. Yes, I'm a little annoyed and want to know what the blazing hell is going on.'

Hamilton turned down his lips and cocked his head from one side to the other. 'Missing … that's a strange word to use.'

'What the fuck are you on about? Stop talking in riddles and tell me why I'm here.' Thomas's fingers stopped drumming, his face flushed red and his small eyes grew wide.

Hamilton eased forward, his arms resting on the table, and spoke gently. 'Yes, I suppose, technically, your daughter is *missing*, in that we don't know where she is. But she's a criminal on the run, escaped from prison—'

'Hospital,' Thomas interrupted.

'An institution where she was serving a prison sentence, Mr Billows.'

'But she needed help … she still needs help. Can't you see that? You have to find her.' A change in the man's voice, almost like a desperate whinge, made Hamilton sit back and fold his arms. He studied the man's face; the redness had subsided, but the wrinkles and creases remained.

'Do you know where your daughter is?'

Thomas shook his head. 'Of course I don't.'

'Why do you think she needs help?'

'Are you joking? It's you who says she's murdered people.'

'You don't believe she has?'

The man sighed. 'No one wants to believe that of their own child.'

'Why do you think she's doing it?'

Thomas broke eye contact with Hamilton, stared at the table and rubbed his hand over his white bald head; back and forth, back and forth. 'I don't know,' he finally murmured.

'You haven't been around much.' Hamilton decided to change tack. 'I mean, you and Valerie aren't together, are you?'

The man's eyes shot up. 'No, we're not, haven't been for some time. What's that got to do with anything?'

'We're trying to find your daughter, Mr Billows, who not only murdered someone on Friday night, but who also kidnapped my sergeant. Everything has an importance. So, if I ask a question you'll answer it, because, after all, I'm doing all this to find your *missing* daughter.'

Thomas flinched momentarily, but nodded and slumped backwards in the hard, plastic chair. 'Okay … no, I haven't been around much since Grace was a teenager.'

'Why?'

'A combination of reasons.'

Hamilton raised his eyebrows and extended his hand out and around, gesturing for Thomas to elaborate.

The man cleared his throat. 'Valerie and I … we … had some issues. I guess, if I'm honest, I stopped finding her attractive. I was offered a promotion, it meant more time on the road, and … well … I couldn't get out of that house quick enough.'

'What about your only daughter? Did she play no part in your decision making?'

Thomas shrugged his shoulders and looked away again. 'Fatherhood … I don't know … wasn't for me.'

Hamilton edged closer again, steepled his fingers and rested his chin on his knuckles, glaring at the man in front of him. An unexpected emotion coursed through his veins: hate. Here sat a man with every chance of watching his daughter turn from child to woman, but who chose to abandon her because he no longer fancied her mother. Hamilton took a deep breath, remembering there was more than one side to every story, and exhaled slowly.

'Why were you and Valerie Murphy never married, Mr Billows?'

'We met young. She got pregnant pretty much straight away. I guess we didn't really know each other … we thought it was love, but what do teenagers really know?'

He briefly thought of his own relationship with Elizabeth, and how their situation sounded so similar to this one … yet, theirs worked. *Why?* he thought. *The difference in people's relationships is fascinating.*

'But Grace Murphy is your child?' Hamilton asked.

The crimson patched reappeared on Thomas's cheeks and neck. 'How fucking dare you? Because I never married Valerie, it must mean she was shagging every man in town, so she couldn't possibly know who the father was.'

Hamilton raised his palms. 'It was just a question, Mr Billows. You said she got pregnant straight away and that Grace doesn't have the same surname as you—'

'That means nothing.'

'It's just strange that you never came up before. I mean, last year, I had quite a lot of interaction with Grace, even before she was arrested. Then, during her trial, where were you? No one seems to remember you, Mr Billows.'

'Like I said, my job took me away a lot. I don't really have a place to call home, and Valerie calls me when she needs me. If I'm in London, I've sometimes kipped on her sofa, but mostly I'd stay with a friend or in a bedsit.' Thomas paused and wiped a hand along his thigh. 'Valerie didn't tell me … or couldn't get in contact with me straight away. I came when I could.'

Hamilton raised his eyebrows and looked to his side. He tipped his head, silently asking Dixon if she had anything to ask Thomas. She puckered her lips, nodded and made a humming noise as she turned away.

'Mr Billows, what do you do with all your money?'

He shook his head once again. 'Now what are you on about?'

'Well, from what I know, driver technicians of your experience get paid quite well. Travelling the country, working through the night and being away from your family … for those who have families, of course. It's strange that you choose to sleep in bedsits or on your ex's sofa.'

Thomas's fingers silently drummed the table again. 'There's no point in buying a home that I'm hardly ever going to live in and I don't like to be tied down. I take myself off abroad every now and then. I still help Valerie out with the bills and the rest is saved.' He smirked at Dixon, and Hamilton realised it was the first time the man's face had lit up. 'I'm a simple man, detective.'

'Any of your wages given to your daughter?' Dixon raised her hand. 'And I mean recently, not while she was growing up.'

'No, Grace refused point blank to take any money from me.'

'Why is that, Mr Billows?'

The man's smile slipped from his face and his nostrils flared. 'Said she didn't need me … didn't need my help.'

Dixon sat back and tapped the table lightly as she did so. Hamilton knew it was a signal that she had no further questions.

'Okay, well, thank you for coming in, Mr Billows,' he said and stood up from the table. 'An officer will escort you out, but we may need to speak to you again.'

'Of course.'

'Do you have the address of where you'll be staying?'

'With Valerie, of course.'

Hamilton shook the man's clammy hand and then left the room. He waited until they had gained some distance from the interview room before asking Dixon what she thought of the man.

'He sees himself as a let-down. I guess that's obvious,' she said. 'But then, some people just aren't built to be parents.'

Hamilton grumbled as he climbed the stairs to the incident room, unconvinced that was Thomas's problem. He wanted to see if Rocky had found out anything more about the man. There was something more to Mr Billows, but he couldn't quite put his finger on it.

In the office, Rocky waved Hamilton and Dixon over to his computer station before drumming his fingers over a few buttons on the keyboard.

'Boss, I don't know if this is anything, but have a look at these pictures,' Rocky said.

Hamilton stood behind the sergeant and his eyes gazed over the myriad of photographs on the screen. Despite hating the social media site, and staying away from a personal account, he knew the blue background colour meant he was staring at a Facebook account.

'That's Thomas Billows,' he said.

'Yes,' Rocky confirmed, 'not his own photos, but I've found he's tagged in quite a few on a number of nights out around the country.

'And?' Hamilton asked as Dixon and Clarke joined them.

'Well, as I said, I don't know if it's anything significant, but he tends to like the younger woman,' Rocky continued, and scrolled through more images. 'They're obviously in pubs and clubs, but most of the women he's with can't be older than eighteen or nineteen. Twenty, at a push.'

'There's nothing wrong with having a type,' Clarke added. 'Even if they are young enough to be your daughter.'

Dixon perched on the table. 'He also just admitted that one of the reasons he left Valerie Murphy was because he didn't find her attractive. Obviously, the younger model is his type.'

Clarke guffawed. 'Not exactly a criminal offence, Dixon.'

Hamilton's mind wandered while his team batted their opinions between each other. He agreed with Clarke; it wasn't a crime to enjoy the pleasure of women's company thirty years your junior, but it added to his feelings of uncertainty about Thomas Billows.

'Let's just keep an eye on him,' Hamilton finally said. 'I'm going to organise for a family liaison officer to head over to the Murphy household.'

Rocky spun around and frowned. 'Aren't FLOs reserved for victims and their families?'

He nodded. 'But this is an exceptional case, and we don't really know the family. At least if we have a FLO present in the morning when the press conference is aired, they'll be able to capture their reactions, see if they make any phone calls and who gets in touch with them. It can only enhance the investigation.'

'I'll get that actioned now, guv,' Dixon said, and darted out of the room.

Hamilton retreated to the whiteboard, his mouth drier than sandpaper and the ticking hands of the wall clock drumming in his ears. His feeling of utter helplessness was slightly outweighed by the hope that Fraser was safe.

Chapter Twenty-One

Fraser blinked rapidly, her eyes trying to focus through the darkness, hoping to make sense of the shapes in front of her. She squinted and pulled her head down into her shoulders, the fracturing headache like a heavy weight. The pain caused her eyelids to flicker much slower now, craving her to shut them tight and curl her body into a foetal position. But it was then she realised she was no longer bound and gagged and pushed through agony to come up onto her knees. Her hands fell to the floor, keeping her steady on all fours as she glanced around the dark, cold room, her eyes finally adjusting to the shadows. Old beams and brickwork were exposed, pews lined up in rows like soldiers and dusty, metal plaques adorned the walls. Her eyes stopped on curled up figure in the corner opposite her.

Fraser tried to speak, but the air caught in her dry throat. She cleared it and tried again. 'Grace?'

When no answer came, her weak body crawled forward towards the figure; long hair falling down over the woman's face. Fraser stopped, peering over her shoulder she could just make out the outline of a door in the distance.

'That's not my name,' a female voice whispered, and Fraser wondered if Murphy had kidnapped someone else.

Knowing she couldn't leave a vulnerable person behind, Fraser suppressed her pain and crawled closer again. She reached out a hand but the stranger flinched further into the corner as though her fingers blazed like hot-pokers.

'I'm not going to hurt you.' Fraser coughed, sucking in more dust as she did so. 'I'm here to help you. What's your name?'

Sobs echoed from underneath the mass of hair, and Fraser impatiently bobbed her left foot on the cold stone floor. She wondered if she had enough time to build a relationship with this woman; form a bond of trust so they could both get out before Murphy returned. Fraser looked back at the door, a heart-wrenching urge to run towards it was extinguished the moment she heard the word help whispered. Her head flicked back to the shaking figure.

'I'm a police officer, I'm here to help,' Fraser said in a voice that sounded much stronger than she felt. 'What's your name?'

The woman finally turned her head and Fraser gasped, falling flat on her arse as her hand flew to her mouth. Fraser stared at the familiar face that now looked so pale, weak and scared.

'I'm Livia. Are you really here to help?' said the woman, but the tone of the voice made her sound like a child.

'Who-who-w—' Fraser choked on her own words, her dry windpipe strangling her as she struggled to speak.

'Here, I have this,' Livia said, and handed her a bottle of water, while her eyes scanned behind them furiously. 'I stole it from Carly, so don't let her catch you with it.'

Fraser nodded and accepted the bottle, with robotic motions she felt she had no control over, as though she were caught in a daze. She unscrewed the lid and gulped the cold liquid. Her hand trembled as droplets of water escaped the bottle and ran down her chin and neck. When she finally pulled it away from her lips, she sighed loudly.

'Thank you,' she said, and handed it back to Livia. 'I'm sorry. I was trying to ask who you are.'

The woman huffed, like a child at the early stages of a tantrum, and her eyes scanned the darkness behind them once again. 'I told you. I'm Livia.'

That stroppy voice again, Fraser thought. 'How old are you, Livia?'

'I'm thirteen,' she whispered. 'I ran away from home, but now … now I don't know how to get back.' Her eyes widened and she placed her index finger over her lips. 'Shh … she's coming.'

Livia pulled her body back into a ball, her head resting on her knees and the long strands of hair falling back over her, like some kind of safe cocoon. Fraser heard no noise of anyone else. They were alone.

Fraser froze, the cold chill in the room attacking her fingers and snaking itself up her arm and neck. Her eyes wandered over Livia's body, and she noticed the black trainers, black trousers and black bomber jacket Murphy had been wearing in the theatre. She was sure she had just been introduced to another of Murphy's alter-personalities, one she and her team had known nothing about. The tears caught in her throat, but she refused to let them fall, adamant that if this young girl was a ruse to lead her to her death, she wouldn't show her fear. But, even as she held on to that last shred of strength, Fraser wondered if she actually believed it herself. Because, right there in that moment, was the first time she believed she wouldn't get out of this situation alive.

While she tried to determine if now would be the best time to make a run for the door behind her, while Murphy's defences seemed to be down, Fraser's mind clouded. The headache dulled to a point where she felt like her brain was swimming around her skull, making her rock from side to side. She soon realised she was on her back and the room itself was spinning around her. The grand mural painted on the ceiling above her made her smile.

'Angels,' she slurred, as her eyes flickered opened and closed.

'You might meet them soon,' said the voice from the corner, but it no longer whined liked a teenager.

She watched helplessly as the balled-up figure uncurled itself, dropping the water bottle to the floor, and slithered towards her. Silent tears slid down Fraser's cheeks while a fist came plummeting to her face — as if she were watching a slow-motion video — and she just had enough time to call out for her mum before the darkness swallowed her completely.

Chapter Twenty-Two

As Hamilton entered his office, the lamp on the desk offering the only light in the room, he reached for the switch on the wall. The worries and frustrations of the past twenty-four hours washed over him, and his brain played a ping-pong match between Fraser and Elizabeth; their faces flashing in front of his mind's eye, his guilt intensifying with each serve.

He perched on the desk and pulled his mobile from his trouser pocket. Regardless of the time, he needed to check in on his wife, or at least let her know he was thinking of her and the unease she must be feeling right now. Had he really wanted another child? Could he bring another life into this world when he classed himself as such a failure the first time round? The questions took over the rally, accompanied by memories of Maggie, and his breath hitched in his throat.

'Guv.' Clarke bulldozed into the office and rescued him from his thoughts.

He slipped the mobile back in his pocket, without having sent the text message, and frowned at his partner's aghast expression. 'What is it?'

'They've found a body,' Clarke blurted.

'I think the DI on call should take this one, we—'

'No, guv, it could be Fraser.'

Hamilton was on his feet and racing from the room. Clarke continued to reel off the information about the crime scene and location while he motioned for Dixon and Rocky to follow. In unison, the four of them darted through the office to the car park. Silence in the car remained while Clarke continued to pass on the attending officer's report, which had been shared by the desk sergeant.

'Wait,' Dixon interrupted, 'I've been reading over Murphy's original case files … Wasn't her first victim last year found at Hyde Park?'

Clarke nodded. 'That's what first rang alarm bells with me. But Fras …' he hesitated and shook his head. 'This victim wasn't murdered in the manner Murphy used before.'

'What do you mean?' Rocky called from the back seat.

'Previously, she stripped her victims of their clothes, as a way of humiliating them and leaving them vulnerable, and then killed them with a knife to the heart.'

'That wasn't the MO for Gabriel Hardy at Manor Hall Hospital.'

Clarke shrugged. 'No, but that could have more to do with what weapons were available to her and the fact she was trying to escape.'

Dixon peered between the two front seats. 'Okay, so how does this victim … I mean, why do they *think* it could be Fraser?'

The momentarily silence buzzed in Hamilton's ears, and he took his eyes off the road for a second to look over at his partner. Clarke had turned in his seat, staring absently through the passenger window, and his cheeks puffed as he exhaled.

'The victim has been beaten beyond recognition,' Clarke finally answered.

Despite Hamilton's vehicle sudden screeching halt in a bus stop on Park Lane, there was a slowness in the way the four of them exited the car. Although a new day was in the preparation stages of setting on London, there would evidently be no dawn sunshine and the dark, brooding clouds mirrored Hamilton's mood. The harsh fresh air slapped his cheeks and he sped off again, on foot this time, and hurdled himself over the railings into Hyde Park, running past the Joy of Life Fountain and towards the Serpentine. The irony of the location wasn't lost on him, and though his legs were leaden with bitterness, he trudged on.

He diverted course when he saw a white tent and forensic activity taking shape at the Bandstand and, as his breathing became laboured, Rocky jogged past him effortlessly. Hamilton stopped, not too far from the crime scene but far enough to not be able to hear or see anything that would answer the burning question in his heart, and just for a moment he didn't want to take another step.

He watched SOCO halt his team in their tracks. Rocky's arms flying in anger, his speech sounding all dramatic. Hamilton knew he should be able to work out what was being said, but his ears had cut off all sound around him. He had become a mere observer to a silent film. Audrey ran from the tent and attempted to placate the situation, her hands surrendering and her face … what was that look in her eyes? Hamilton wondered.

A droplet of rain smacked down on Hamilton's forehead. He drew in a breath, as deep and lung-filling as if he'd just emerged from an angry rip current, and sound finally returned; a pathologist shouting about protective clothing, Rocky demanding to see the victim, Audrey telling them she's sorry and that they had to calm down.

Once again, Hamilton's feet were on the move and he joined his team within seconds. He pushed Rocky back, demanding the sergeant compose himself and step aside, he would be the one to identify Fraser.

'I'm afraid you can't, Inspector,' Audrey said, her palm still hovering over his chest.

He briefly glanced down at her hand, which she moved simultaneously, and then narrowed his gaze back on her. 'Give me the damn shoe covers, then.' He put a hand out to the tall pathologist stood next to her. 'And let me pass.'

Audrey scraped her long fingers through her ruby red hair and slumped her shoulders. It was sadness, Hamilton thought, that was the look in her eyes.

'I mean you won't be able to identify—'

'That is a member of my team in there, Audrey, you'll let me in there this second.' He didn't intend on using his height over her petite frame as a weapon, but as he glowered down at her, she edged backwards.

'By all means, Inspector,' Audrey replied in a hard tone. 'But I can tell you now that you won't find who you're looking for in there.'

Hamilton spun round and held his breath, hoping the head pathologist would continue. She did, and he exhaled slowly as she uttered the words, 'The victim isn't Kerry Fraser.'

He refused to let the haziness fill his mind, he'd been given a warning here — a wake-up call — and time was fast slipping away.

'We were told the victim was badly beaten. How can you tell it's not her?' Clarke called out over Hamilton's shoulder.

Audrey took a few steps away from the crime scene and waited until all four members of the team had surrounded her before she continued, 'Yes, there are similarities in that the victim is blonde and probably the same height. The lacerations and injuries to her face are so intense that we're unable to make out any features. However, I checked the victim's left wrist and she *doesn't* have a tattoo.'

'And Fraser does?' Dixon asked.

'Yes, a semicolon.' Audrey frowned. 'You didn't know that, I take from the bewildered expression on your face.'

Hamilton swallowed the ball of saliva that had built up in his mouth while listening to Audrey. 'No, I didn't know, but I'm bloody glad you did.'

'I've heard about the semicolon tattoo,' Dixon said. 'It's a project aimed at empowering people who have suffered from depression, addiction, mental illness and suicidal thoughts. The semicolon is a symbol of hope.'

Rocky twisted his lips. 'I don't get it.'

'In literature, the semicolon is used when an author decides they don't want to end a sentence,' Dixon continued. 'Therefore, the punctuation mark symbolises to the wearer that they are the author, and the sentence is their life. A few famous people have come forward with this tattoo, and the project is a really important one.'

Clarke whistled. 'Wow, that's deep. I never knew she had one, either.'

'So … so, you're saying,' Rocky stuttered, 'Fraser has struggled with depression or mental illness or …'

'The tattoo is for her mother,' Audrey interjected, 'who suffers from bipolar. She attempted to commit suicide when Kerry was a teenager, and so Kerry chose to get the tattoo to celebrate how far her mother has come since that day.'

'Christ! One of us should have at least known that,' Rocky barked as he turned and walked back in the direction of the car.

'She's a private person … never really spoke about her past,' Hamilton said to Rocky's fading figure.

He nodded for Clarke to follow the constable before turning back to Audrey and asking, 'I don't suppose you know if this was actually a murder committed by Murphy?'

'Well, that was the other reason the attending officer assumed this was Kerry,' Audrey replied. 'The victim's jumper had been raised, leaving her torso bare, meaning they discovered something written in what we assume is her own blood. Would you like to see the body now, Inspector?'

He nodded, asked Dixon to accompany him and together they placed the protective shoe covers on and followed the pathologist inside the forensic tent. He groaned and looked away from the victim's blood-soaked and swollen face.

'Fuck's sake, that's brutal,' Dixon whispered; the first time he had heard her use profanity, but it was warranted, thanks to the victim's red and blue skin, broken blood vessels and eyelids the size of golf balls.

Hamilton's eyes flashed back to the victim, this time resting on her naked stomach, and he read the small words which had been scrawled over her white flesh like a child's finger-painting:

Tick tock,
Hamilton.

Chapter Twenty-Three

Back in the incident room, Hamilton — along with Clarke and Rocky — delivered the news to the officers who had stayed back. There was obvious relief in the room that the body they'd found wasn't Fraser's. Hamilton went on to explain that Dixon would remain at the crime scene with DI Daly to update them all as and when new evidence came to light. He wondered if the Hyde Park victim had been chosen simply because of her similarities to Fraser; had it been a gruesome twist of fate because she was in the wrong place at the wrong time, or had Murphy stalked this woman too? His mind clicked to a thought and he summoned Rocky to his side.

'We never did find a lot of information about the mystery figure who attacked Fraser,' he began, and then hesitated for a few moments. 'Or the dead flowers and missing cat, but what if this has all been connected to Murphy? Perhaps she's been following Fraser all this time.'

Rocky scrunched his face. 'Impossible. Murphy was in Manor Hall Hospital at the time of those events.'

'Yes, but we already know that place wasn't as secure as it should have been.' He hummed while deep in thought. 'It just makes me think, even more so, that someone on the outside was helping Murphy. She could have asked them to keep an eye on Fraser, so she knew her patterns, how to enter her home … how to get to her.'

'Okay, guv, what do you want me to do?'

Hamilton rubbed his index finger deep into his temple. 'Check the dates of the Stratford incident and when the flowers were hand-delivered to Fraser's home. Try and cross reference those with Murphy's father; was he in London? And check them against the best friend, Natasha Holten. One visit from her friend could have been enough to pass all the information they needed. Not seeing her for the past four months could be a cover.'

'Leave it to me,' Rocky replied, before pouncing on his computer.

Hamilton stared at his watch. It was just shy of forty-eight hours since Murphy had escaped, since two people had lost their lives, since Kerry had been taken. His stomach clenched when he realised he had now began thinking of Fraser as Kerry; no longer just a colleague, but a victim. The sun had refused to rise on Sunday morning, grey clouds casting a shadow on the entire building, but the time had come for the press conference. Extra constables and sergeants had been assigned to the case, and they now waited in the incident room in the anticipation of numerous phone calls — hoax and, hopefully, otherwise.

Hamilton entered his office. The imminent inclusion of the press into this case worried him; would it actually hinder the investigation, possibly sending Murphy into a further rage and therefore placing Kerry in further danger? Or would they finally catch the break they needed with a sighting of this woman? Despite the thousands of CCTV surveillance cameras covering the capital, London was an easy city to get lost in. The ball of questions bounced back and forth off the wall of Hamilton's brain. He needed to occupy his mind.

As he walked around his desk, he noticed the thick paperback balancing on the edge. Its white background was a stark contrast to the colourful lapel pin on the front cover. Hamilton couldn't remember bringing it up from the car to his office, but he grabbed the book and opened it at the first chapter.

Lost in a world of words, Hamilton didn't notice Clarke approach and lean against the doorframe until he heard his partner's voice. '*The Stranger Within*, by Doctor Emine Inamdar.'

Hamilton looked up, glancing at the wall clock as he did, and was shocked to find he'd been sat there for almost forty-five minutes. He lay the book on the table, careful not to lose his place, and asked Clarke if he had an update.

'Dixon called—'

'About the body?'

'No, the FLO who is stationed at Valerie Murphy's house got in touch with her. Valerie is demanding to see her.'

Hamilton grunted, grabbed a sheet of paper from his tray and slipped it in between the pages as a bookmark. 'No doubt to complain about her ... about Thomas Billows being questioned.'

'Do you want me or Rocky to come?' Clarke asked, and walked with him into the main office; as predicated, the reinforcements were shielding plenty of calls.

'No, I'll meet Dixon there,' Hamilton replied, and stopped in front of the whiteboard. Photographs of the latest victim, including the bloody message addressed to him, stood out more than anything else surrounding them. 'I want you here, Clarke, getting any and all camera footage of the Hyde Park Bandstand and the surrounding area, streets, roads. Murphy has to be travelling around somehow, be it car or train or foot. And if she's got Fraser with her, our girl wouldn't be going along quietly.'

Clarke stood closer to his superior, nodding in acknowledgement of the task set for him, and then released a heavy sigh. 'Why is she after you, guv? Why has she made this so personal?'

An hour ago, Hamilton would have answered that it was revenge — pure and simple cold revenge — for arresting Murphy, but now, his mind played around with other explanations. He peered over his shoulder in the direction of his office, of the book, and then turned back to the blood-stained message etched on the victim's body.

'Maybe it's her way of asking for help, Clarke.'

His partner frowned, confusion contorting his face. 'What the hell does that mean?'

'I'm not entirely sure, but it's something I'm trying to work out.' He sighed and crossed his arms over his chest. 'Remember last year, every time we found a body it was because of an anonymous tip we'd had ... What if Murphy was actually making those calls? I don't know, so the bodies didn't go undiscovered, so that we'd finally find who was committing the murders ... so we'd finally find her.'

'Yeah, we found her at the airport about to make a run for it. With, what ... more than five dead bodies in her wake. Hardly a cry for help.'

'I think that's exactly what this victim was,' he said, drumming his index finger on the image of the petite blonde, unrecognisable from the beating. 'Someone crying out for help before it's too late.'

***

Valerie Murphy sat on the sofa, her knee bouncing as if it were a separate limb to the rest of her body, unable to control the twitching and jerking. Thomas lay a hand on her thigh, but she pushed it away and stood up, listening to Susan, the family liaison officer, usher more officers into her home.

When Susan led the new comers into the living room, Valerie was pleased to see the Mediterranean-looking detective had returned, as she had asked. She had felt a warmth from this woman the last time they had spoken, almost a telepathic understanding from one mother to another, and Valerie knew she would try to help her daughter. She was surprised, however, to see the male mixed-race inspector again. His name slipped her memory now, but she remembered meeting him last year when he had treated Grace as a victim and witness, rather than a cold-hearted murderer.

'I'm sure you're both aware,' Susan said to Valerie and Thomas, 'but just in case … this is DI Hamilton and DS Dixon. Please, everyone, take a seat. Valerie has some important information she needs to share with you. I'll get the kettle on.'

Ah, yes — Hamilton — that was it, Valerie thought, and she clocked the look of confusion etched on his face. She waited until they had both sat down before she joined Thomas on the sofa again. He gripped her hand as soon as she did and her entire body tensed. She didn't want his dramatic sympathy, she hated him. She hated herself.

'So, Ms Murphy, what is this about?' Hamilton spoke, his tone low and gentle, but his tight jaw and clasped hands told her he was in no mood for playing games. Luckily for him, she wasn't either, but as much as she wanted to speak, she continually choked on her own words.

'When you're ready, sweetie.' Thomas's whispered words propelled her from the sofa again, and she stood in front of the two officers, wringing her hands once again.

Hamilton cleared his throat, taking his gaze off her for a few minutes and focusing on her ex. 'I'm sorry, Mr Billows, do you not know why we're here?'

'No. Valerie only spoke to Susan. Then she advised that it was best to wait until you were here to take an official statement before any—'

'I watched the news,' Valerie interrupted. 'I knew Gabe.'

She didn't miss the look the two officers shared. The woman threw her long dark hair over her shoulder and reached for a notepad in her handbag. The man dropped his praying hands and inched forward on the sofa. Susan entered the room and efficiently worked around them to put cups of coffee and tea and milk and sugar on the table. Thomas kept repeating the word *who*, over and over, making her want to slap him even more. Valerie watched everything whizz around her, as if she wasn't really in control of her body or tongue and couldn't do or say anything further. *This is what an out-of-body experience must feel like*, she thought.

'Valerie.'

'Ms Murphy.'

'Valerie.'

The repetition of her name rose like a foghorn, and Valerie glanced around the room, four sets of expectant eyes watching her.

'Ms Murphy, you said—'

She held up her hand to stop Hamilton from speaking any further. 'I know exactly what I said, Inspector.'

'Just give her a moment, please,' Susan added. 'Valerie, sit here on this chair and take your time.'

Valerie did as instructed, taking a deep breath, and launched into her memory before she could stop herself. 'About eighteen or nineteen years ago, I started dated a guy called Gabe Hardy.' She paused and looked at Thomas before continuing. 'We weren't together then, Tom, and it was the first time I had dated anyone since you left. Anyway, I think I got a bit carried away with the attention and I let

Gabe stay over as and when he wanted. Which was more often than not, especially over the weekends when he didn't have much work.'

'Did you know he worked at Manor Hall Hospital?'

'No, of course not.' She shook her head furiously. 'He wasn't there the time I visited Grace, but that's my point … You see, Grace was only about thirteen when I was dating Gabe, but she would have remembered him. The picture they showed on the TV … he hadn't changed that much, a few more wrinkles and grey hairs, put on a bit of weight … but I think she would have known him, still. So, you must be mistaken, she didn't kill him. She's been framed and she ran away because she's scared, she—'

Valerie stopped abruptly when she noticed the detectives share that look again. She wanted to ask what it meant, but she realised her hands were trembling, as was her chin. The tears fell silently down her cheeks, choking any words on the verge of being released.

'Ms Murphy, how long were you and Mr Hardy dating?' Hamilton asked, his dark brown eyes glaring into her.

She stuttered through her sobs. 'Not too long, about six months, but it was weird …'

'What was weird?' The inspector continued to badger her while Susan offered her a tissue. Thomas stayed completely quiet.

'I thought … we were enjoying ourselves. We really got on, and he made me laugh, and feel good about myself again. But then, I don't know, I felt like he lost interest in me. Grace had started acting up about the same time, mood swings and temper tantrums and she even ran away one weekend, so maybe it was me who stopped giving him the attention he was used to. He finished things with me and I never saw him again.'

Dixon cocked her head to one side. 'Did Grace tell you why she had run away?'

'She said she wasn't happy.' Valerie paused and looked down, watching her nails pull at the skin around her fingertips. 'It was about the same time I stopped calling her Gracie. She'd shout that it wasn't her name and get very upset, and she wanted to stay at her grandparents' house a lot more. I figured it was built up pain and anger due to our split ...' She wagged her finger between herself and Thomas. 'And then the confusion of seeing me with another man, maybe, I'm not sure ... she was still a young girl. So, my dad took her to Blackpool for a second time. She had loved it there when he first took her, and when she came back I told her Gabe was gone and I promised her that there would be no more dating. Things got better again soon enough.'

'When Grace ran away, did you notify the police?' Dixon asked, and Valerie looked up; she saw an unexpected sadness in the woman's eyes — much like how she imagined her own tear-stained eyes looked.

'There was no need to call the police, although I nearly did.' She remembered those few horrific hours when she rang all of Grace's friends after she missed dinner and wasn't home by eight in the evening. 'I know that's not too late, but she was only thirteen and it was so unlike her. My father phoned at about nine o'clock, just as I was ready to dial 999. He had found Grace hiding in his shed in the garden, so she hadn't gone far, but she stayed there that weekend and he said he would have a chat with her. I don't know what it was about, but like I said, they organised their seaside trip and ... normality returned.'

Hamilton's dark eyes found hers again, but this time when he spoke, his jaw and lips and shoulders all looked more relaxed. 'It was your father who then moved in with you and Grace, isn't that right?'

Valerie nodded. 'About four years ago, yes. We nursed him through his cancer treatment, but he lost his battle.' She puffed her cheeks and exhaled. 'Wow, two years today. I can't believe I didn't realise it was his anniversary today. It's just … everything that's going on with Grace … and you know … Christ, I feel awful. How could I forget that?' She paused and took a few moments to control the overwhelming urge to cry and scream and crumble to the floor; there would be plenty of time to remember her father, but right now she had to help her daughter. 'Anyway, when my father did pass away, Grace was devastated. She shared a very special bond with him.'

'Of course.' Hamilton spoke softly but got to his feet like a spring pinched his arse. 'Thank you for calling us so soon, Susan, Ms Murphy. We have to leave now and I must ask you not to speak to the press in the meantime, because I'm sure they'll be camping outside your house soon enough.'

A sickness built in Valerie's stomach as she stood to face the inspector. It was the last thing she wanted outside her home, but if they could help shed light on the fact that her daughter isn't a cold-blooded killer, she didn't care.

'Susan will help ward them off,' Hamilton continued, 'but if you and Mr Billows could stay in the house for the time being.'

She tugged at his sleeve, her fingers wrapping themselves around his wrist. 'Grace isn't a monster. She's been framed and she needs help. Please find my little girl, please help her.'

His eyes wavered between her and Thomas, but his voice was strong and confident when he uttered, 'I will.' And Valerie knew DI Hamilton was telling the truth.

Chapter Twenty-Four

When Fraser opened her eyes again, the taste of iron tarnished her mouth. She spat on the tiled floor and wasn't surprised to see a glob of blood fly from her mouth. Still in the same place as before, this time her wrists and ankles bound again by thick rope, the light of day was now shining through the high stained-glass windows. Now, she could clearly make out the plaques of names and dates ranging back from the early nineteen-hundreds; the large candles covered in cobwebs stood neglected on an iron candelabrum; a discoloured Virgin Mary stood high — almost floating — in an arched devotional area. Fraser shivered when she couldn't tear her eyes from the blank expression of the virgin mother, but was brought back to her senses when a floorboard creaked to the left of her.

She spun her head around — the only body part she could move — and saw Murphy's blank expression also staring at her from where she sat in the pews. The look was a far cry from the one she'd last seen before passing out, but it still worried her. She had lowered her guard with Livia, only to be tricked and beaten again. But now, looking at Murphy, a wave of fear took hold of her neck and a trail of goosebumps ran down her spine and arms.

'I'm sorry,' Murphy said; the voice was not the childish one of Livia or the angry one of Carly, there was a sadness in this tone.

'Grace?' Fraser replied. 'Is that you?'

Murphy nodded but refused to make eye contact with Fraser. A sprinkling of hope burst the bubble of panic that had been threatening to erupt and she knew this would be her chance to get through to Murphy ... her last chance at breaking free.

'There's no need to apologise, Grace. I know you can't remember anything that's happened while your alter-personalities are in control.' At that, Murphy raised her head and looked in the direction of the altar, where Fraser sat uncomfortably tied-up. 'It's not like forgetting to buy the milk or what you went into another room for. You completely black-out, aren't present, suffer from amnesia.'

'How do you know all this?' Grace said, barely louder than a whisper.

Breakthrough, Fraser thought. 'After we arrested you, I researched dissociative identity disorder. If I don't understand a certain subject, I'll invest a lot of time reading and researching until I get it. That's just the type of person I am.'

'H-have I hurt you badly?'

'No, not really,' Fraser lied. The rope had torn the skin from her wrist. She stopped wiggling and concentrated on keeping her voice calm and level. 'But everyone who has been hurt ... well, I know that wasn't you. I know you're not dangerous or evil. The fact that you have this disorder means you've been hurt in the past. Something has made you suffer, you've been hurt by someone in your life, and so I know you don't want to be the cause of anyone's suffering.'

'But *she* does,' Grace replied an octave higher.

'Yes, and it's understandable that a different personality will show different traits.' Fraser paused, calling to the forefront of her memory all she'd read about the disorder earlier that year. 'There are common personality types and ... and that includes a *perpetrator* alter and an *avenger* alter.

142

Carly is using the trauma to express that pain and anger and hostility to others … probably just as the person who hurt you did, Grace. Who? Who hurt you?'

'I … it's not fair, I was j-just a child … He said he loved me and I trusted h-him,' Murphy stuttered through her whimpering.

Fraser scooted her bum forward, digging her heels down and trying to pull herself along, all the while ignoring the burning pain in her shoulders and stomach. She knew if she could get closer to Murphy, let the woman open up about her trauma, that she could persuade her to untie the rope.

'I tried, you know,' Murphy added as Fraser struggled with her movement. 'It wasn't my fault. I told him to stop every time he came into my room. I wanted to tell my mum but I didn't think she'd believe me. Well, he told me she wouldn't believe me and I guess I … I believed him.' She barked a low grumbling laugh that made Fraser stop in her tracks. 'If any of that even makes sense.'

'But you didn't suffer with the disorder then?' Fraser encouraged Murphy to continue to speak so she could work on moving to the stairs at the edge of the alter.

'Maybe. I'm not sure. But then, Livia is only thirteen, so maybe I did. Maybe I trapped her at that age so as not to forget what happened. I'm still not one hundred per cent sure how all these personalities, or the *system* as Doctor Emine calls them, works and fits together. It helped, talking to the doctor at Manor Hall, but part of me doesn't want to understand. I don't want any of this to be real … and how can it be real if I don't remember it happening. I just want to go back to normal.'

Murphy was on her feet, charging towards Fraser, but the officer didn't feel afraid; a softer look in the woman's eyes told her it would be okay. She watched with wide eyes as Murphy knelt on the stairs and started pulling at the thick rope knotted around Fraser's ankles.

'This isn't right. You shouldn't be here,' Murphy blurted. 'You have to get away from here now. Don't tell anyone I'm here and I won't hurt another person.'

Desperate to keep the calm woman on side, she nodded in agreement. 'Of course, I won't tell a soul. I'll keep your secret.'

Murphy's fingers instantly stopped fiddling with the cords, despite all the knots not yet untangled. She raised her head slowly and glowered at Fraser; the whites of Murphy's eyes dulled and a blackness overtook. Fraser swallowed hard as she watched the woman drop her hands to her knees and scratch her palm, abandoning the escape plan.

'W-what did I—' Fraser choked on her words and felt a bead of sweat run down her temple as Murphy rolled her head around and cracked her neck.

'What the fuck did you just say to me?'

Fraser wracked her brain to remember the words she'd just uttered, registering now that whatever they were, they had triggered Carly to take control.

Chapter Twenty-Five

O utside the Murphy household, Hamilton hesitated at his car while his mind segmented all his thoughts into separate compartments. Right now, he needed to be in two places at the same time as his assumptions jumped a mile ahead of him; could he be right with what he was thinking? He needed the words of an expert, and so he turned to Dixon, deciding to trust her with the second priority on his list.

'Take your car and head back to the station,' he instructed. 'Update the team about Gabe Hardy and find out everything you can about him. Tell Rocky to include him in the search he's doing too. We could have made a mistake thinking this man was a complete victim.'

Dixon frowned, her long hair swished as she doubled-paced to her own car parked behind his. 'Okay, dating the mother means that Murphy knew him, but why does that make him any less of a victim? Reading over last year's case files, it seems pretty obvious Murphy targeted people she knew, or had a least some dealings with.'

'Yes, people that Murphy deemed weren't worth the life they had been given,' Hamilton drummed his fingers on the roof of his car. 'A nurse who worked at the hospital where her grandfather had treatment, an old friend battling with alcoholism, a colleague who stole the man she loved … the list goes on.'

'What are you saying, guv?'

His hand stopped mid-air and he clenched it. 'To Murphy, they all hurt her in some way and her murder of choice, the stab wound to the heart, perhaps it was more symbolic of how she was feeling. I'm not sure, yet … that's what I need to go find out.'

'But they're old murders, over a year ago, guv,' Dixon called out. 'How does that have anything to do with what she's doing now? The killings have been brutal and she's kidnapped a police officer.'

'She hasn't had the help she needed,' Hamilton shouted as he pulled open the car door. 'I'll meet you back at the office.' And with that, he jumped in the driver's seat before Dixon could reply.

He shocked himself with the way his thoughts were changing towards Murphy; not that he no longer saw her as a murderer, that remained the same, but the idea that perhaps this criminal had been asking for his help all along. Hamilton knew the way he worked and that, yes, he could be stubborn and headstrong, but only because he was clear on his perception of the world — one of right and wrong, black and white, yes and no. However, the last twenty-four hours had seen a diluting of those beliefs; his mind showed them merging, creating a grey world of things that he had ignored in the past, most probably because he didn't understand them. Adamant to rectify that, and hopefully use it to save Kerry, Hamilton switched the siren on in his car, the front grill now ablaze with blue flashing lights. He pressed at the accelerator as much as he could.

He pulled up outside Manor Hall Hospital, blocking the iron gates where he parked, and locked the car door as he ran into the open gravel space in front of the building. He saw the doctor approaching her own car, oblivious to his presence.

'Emine,' he yelled, and ran in her direction.

The doctor spun around, her soft curls bouncy as before in the wind, and flashed her gleaming white team with a huge smile. 'Detective Inspector Hamilton, this is a surprise. I wasn't expecting to see you again so soon.'

'I read a lot of your book,' he replied in bursts as he tried to catch his breath.

Emine cocked her head to the side and raised her eyebrows, her smile growing even wider; Hamilton couldn't think of anyone whose grin lit up their face with such happiness as it did on the doctor's. 'Well, that's made my day, Inspector.'

'We've also uncovered more information about Grace Murphy, and I'd really appreciate your opinion on a theory I have.'

She played with her lips and groaned, as if toying with him. 'I was just going for something to eat. I've just come off a night shift and—'

'I won't take up too much of your time.'

'Very well,' she said with a serious tone, but Hamilton was sure he spied a glint of excitement in her eyes. 'But on the condition that we walk around the corner to the local Wetherspoon's. I can eat and you can share your theory.'

Hamilton gazed around. 'I don't think that's very appropriate. This is urgent.'

'It's close,' she said as she pressed the button on her keys to lock her car and headed towards the gate. 'It would take the same time to walk back inside the building to my office.'

With little choice, Hamilton followed the doctor and, true to her word, within five minutes they were sitting at a small corner table in the local pub. With it not even being midday, there was only four other people there, and they were all sitting far enough away from Hamilton so that he could speak freely. While Emine's eyes scanned the menu, he updated her about what he'd learned about Valerie Murphy and Gabe Hardy.

'So, couple that with what you read in my book, and you think you have a hypothesis about Grace's dissociative identity disorder?' Emine asked as she lightly brushed a few stray curls away from her face. 'Tell me, Inspector.'

Hamilton took a deep breath before speaking, 'You wrote that this disorder could be born from many factors, but the most significant and studied is that of severe trauma such as abuse.'

She nodded. 'Yes, extreme and repetitive physical, sexual or emotional abuse, particular in early childhood and adolescent.'

'And what if that's exactly what Gabe Hardy done to Grace?' he blurted. 'I mean, I have no concrete evidence right now, that's why it's a theory. And after speaking to the mother, I don't think this idea has even entered her mind. But Grace was thirteen and refused to be called Gracie, she exhibited mood swings and forgetfulness and she ran away from home. All these things occurred while that man stayed at her home. During her trip to Blackpool, Hardy had left the home and things returned to some semblance of normality after her return. So, what do you think?'

Emine sat back and held eye contact with Hamilton for a few moments. The smile had been replaced with a serious and troubled expression. 'You could be right.' She held up her hand when Hamilton bolted up right in his seat. 'But like you said, with no evidence, it's just a theory. However, let's run with it for now. If, as you say, her grandfather took her away from an abusive environment, and then when she returned her abuser had left, Grace would have seen her grandfather as a saviour. Her protector, even. When the original murders started two years ago, it was just after his death, so that would have been the trigger for Grace's dissociative identity disorder.'

'The thing that bothers me is the timeframe. If this is what happened to Grace Murphy, that was over eighteen years ago, can the disorder really have been dormant all that time?'

Emine sat forward, her hands resting on the table and her fingers entwined. 'The brain is an amazing organ, Inspector, and we really don't give it enough credit. You see, this mental disorder is a defence mechanism for the trauma a person has faced. There are many cases profiling people who suffered as a child and only began dealing with it some thirty years later. I would imagine that for Grace, her grandfather was a safety net — she couldn't be harmed when he was around because, as a child, he had fought off the bad man — and when he died, she needed the security and protection of the "system" … her alter personalities. Then, finding her abuser actually working at the hospital?' Emine paused, sniffed deeply and swallowed the threatening tears. 'It triggered the reaction of Carly again.'

Hamilton moved in closer to the doctor, aware that a few more punters had entered the bar. 'Your book talks of so many cases of this disorder, but there's barely any mention of those who suffer with it turning to murder.'

'Because it's so rare.' She held his gaze again, her soft brown eyes showing an understanding for a mental disorder that he was finally beginning to get his head around. 'Dissociative identity disorder isn't how it's portrayed in films, which add the murder and monster traits for cinematic effect. The patients I've worked with are more likely to self-harm then hurt someone else. You see, they know how it feels to be scared, to be tortured, to be abused and fear for their lives, that they wouldn't inflict that on anyone else.'

He nodded, understanding exactly what the doctor meant as he'd read over that very paragraph in her book more than once. But he still couldn't help asking, 'So what makes Grace Murphy so different? Why has she used her alter personality to murder and kidnap?'

Emine left her hands and shrugged, then sighed and smiled slightly. 'The brain may be an amazing organ, Inspector, but it's also a very complicated organ. I'm telling you this mental disorder doesn't make killers, just the same way as growing up in the system doesn't. But each person is different. Grace's *evil* or *bad* alter of Carly is clearly the personality carrying the rage and pain and sadness that is associated with the abuse and therefore using that to exact revenge and pain.'

'How do I use all this information to get Kerry back before she's hurt ... if she hasn't been already?' He heard the desperation in his voice as he clenched his hand into a ball.

Emine reached out and gently covered his fist with her own smooth hand. 'You've been working so hard to figure out who Grace Murphy is, and why she developed these personalities ... But maybe it's now time you looked past the mental disorder and viewed Carly as a murderer as you would any other criminal you've come across. Perhaps then you can save your colleague.'

Chapter Twenty-Six

'Mum, is that you? What are you doing here?' Fraser called out.

She squinted, trying to make out where she was but everything seemed blurred, fogged-up as if she were sailing a ship through the mist. She stepped forward and reached out her hand, desperate for her mother to turn around and rescue her. But, looking down slowly, Fraser realised she no longer needed rescuing, her wrists and ankles were no longer bound, and she moved forward freely. She turned her hands over, moving in slow motion as if they had a mind of their own, and noticed the burn marks from the ropes were no longer scorching her skin.

Fraser didn't understand if she was still stationed at the altar, at the mercy of Murphy's personalities, her surroundings now completely out of focus and closing in around her. But the woman stood in front of her like a beacon dressed in white was now undoubtedly her mum; she couldn't mistake the long blonde hair peppered with streaks of grey and the kink at the bottom which flicked the strands into small curls.

'Mum,' Fraser called again.

This time, her mother turned around and walked towards her. A blazing light trailed behind the moving figure, but it only made everything harder for Fraser to see; it was all out-of-focus and clouded. She couldn't make out her mother's face, couldn't see the features of her small lips wrinkled from years of smoking or the blue eyes that used to shine as bright as sapphires before the diagnosis. It was more a feeling she felt deep in her stomach that it was in actual fact her mother standing in front of her.

She swallowed the lump in her voice, her throat as dry as sand, and stuttered, 'Am I dead?'

No answer came, but she felt her mother's eyes bore into her own — though she still couldn't actually see anything. But she knew it was the same stare she received after the doctor explained the diagnosis of bipolar; as if, once her mother knew the reasoning behind her depression and extreme highs and lows, it changed her. Ignorance protected her mother, and she could deal with her bouts of hormonal mood swings, as her mother referred to them, as long as it meant nothing; as long as it was nothing serious — despite the suicide attempt. But once their doctor had prescribed the medication, her mother couldn't ignore the disorder any longer, and neither could Fraser. She spent weeks in the library and on the Internet finding out absolutely everything she could about bipolar and the drugs her mother was on. She was determined to know everything and help things appear smooth at home.

Things progressed, and with the help of the medication and therapy, Fraser felt like she had her mother back. There was a deep sense of pride that filled her; especially as her mother now had no reservations for asking for help — that had seemed to be the hardest hurdle to jump. Fraser could never understand why that had been so hard for her mother to do.

She frowned at the bright figure now in front of her; wondering why it was this particular image of her mother she pictured in her mind.

Suddenly, she was lying on the floor, her body being moved by a force she couldn't stop. She called out, but the sound of her voice echoed in the darkness; her mother had gone.

'Don't worry, my flower, I have you now.' A deep Irish accent pierced through the shadows of Fraser's mind, confusing her even further. This wasn't a voice she knew.

It sounded nothing like Rocky's diluted tone, but carried a musical intonation, as though she could have been far across the Irish Sea right at that very moment. Fraser opened her mouth to speak again, but she had been silenced, her body tied-up once more.

'I have you, no need to fret.' The voice spoke directly to her again; she could feel the warm breath on her face. 'I'll save you from this place, flower.'

The voice was deep and hushed, and Fraser knew it had to be a man, but there was also something light and soft about it — almost high-pitched at the end of each sentence.

Her head lulled back and she fought to open her eyes, but whatever message her brain was sending to her body, it wasn't listening. Fraser had no control over her movements and she saw no objects or figures any longer, just blackness. She soon realised the lack of support to her head was because she was moving, being carried away by the arms placed around her back and underneath her knees. Despite feeling petite, the hands felt strong and in control of her entire body, carrying her away with confidence. Yet, with each step taken, Fraser's head continued to bob around, until she felt the crook of the man's armpit and nestled in to stop the wave of nausea attacking her. A smell of jasmine hit her nose with full force and she swam in the familiar aroma.

Where do I know that smell from?
Why can't I open my eyes?
Mum, are you still here?

The waves crashing against her face did nothing to wake her senses, but rather the tide tugged at her unconsciousness and dragged her further under the current of the ocean; those unanswered questioned lapping around her helpless brain. All she could do now was pray that the man was in fact here to save her.

Chapter Twenty-Seven

Hamilton walked back to his car parked outside Manor Hall Hospital with an extra weight on his shoulders. Although he was pleased the doctor hadn't laughed at his theory, and had in fact backed-up his ideas further, a continued itch niggled at the back of all his thoughts. But he couldn't reach it to relieve it.

He mulled over Emine's words; Murphy as a person who chose to commit murder, rather than the disorder forcing her to. He knew this was a train of thought that would work better for him. An abused teenager is protected through life by her loving grandfather; cancer snatches him — her saviour — from her life and the past suffering, pain and fear returns, causing rage and fury to take over, and break her down. Then, just when she thinks she's free, she's arrested and potentially subjected to the abuse again once imprisoned. The woman wants revenge on everyone, but part of her still wants help.

After turning the corner onto Lambeth Palace Road, Hamilton was surprised to see a woman in uniform standing next to his car. As he walked closer, he cursed when the peaked cap and starched navy uniform made him realise the woman was in fact a traffic warden, and she was busy writing him a penalty notice.

He cleared his throat, attracting her attention and held his warrant card in her face. 'There's no need to attach that to my windscreen. I'm DI Hamilton and I'm on police business at the moment.'

The woman finished jotting down the car number plate and ripped the piece of paper from her pad. The fierce action made Hamilton flinch, but he refused to move his ID before she'd cast an eye on it.

She shrugged. 'Sorry, sir, but this is an unmarked vehicle. You can't park on double yellow lines or outside private property.'

He followed her index finger, which pointed at the hospital, and he groaned with a half-laugh; he hated that building since he first laid eyes on it. The traffic warden slipped the penalty notice under his wiper blade, took a photo of the car and shrugged before walking off in the direction he'd just come from. He whipped the yellow plastic from the window, intent on not letting it affect him — after all, something like this, something that would usually anger him, was a blip in the ocean considering what Fraser was facing, he thought — jumped in his car and switched on the engine. As he pulled away from his illegal parking space, with the intention of returning to the incident room, his mobile phone buzzed in his pocket. The Corsa's Bluetooth picked up the call and Rocky's voice fill the car through the radio speakers.

'Nothing on the father or best friend, guv, but I quickly turned my attentions to Gabe Hardy,' the constable explained. 'And you'll never bloody guess what, but there's a transaction for a bouquet of flowers the evening before Fraser's delivery.'

Hamilton thumped the steering wheel. 'Damn it. What about Stratford?'

'I can't confirm anything yet, but I can use the train station's cameras now to identify if he came and went that day. Now I know who I'm looking for.'

'Do, just to confirm my suspicions,' Hamilton replied as he came to a stop and parked on another set of double yellow lines — this time turning on his hazard lights. He instructed Rocky to put him on speaker phone so he could relay to the team his theory as well as the conversation he'd just had with Doctor Emine.

'I don't understand.' Rocky's loud but diluted Irish tones echoed in the confined space. 'If Gabe Hardy did in fact abuse Grace Murphy, why in heaven's name would she use him to help her get revenge on Fraser?'

Hamilton opened his mouth to speak, but Dixon's voice was the next to be heard. 'Survival.'

'What do you mean?' Rocky replied.

'As a child, Murphy was vulnerable to do what Hardy forced on her. She had no allies, no one she could trust, but perhaps here, she saw a way out. Hardy was her key to escaping the hospital, prison, and seeking revenge of the people who put her there. The fact it also meant she could finally slay the demon of her nightmare must have felt like a reward.'

Hamilton nodded in silent agreement, forgetting his team couldn't see him, but before he had the chance to contribute to the conversation, his partner's voice broke through the speakers.

'Well, here's what I don't understand,' Clarke said. 'Audrey has sent through more details from Gabe Hardy's post-mortem and not only did he have a high quantity of cocaine in his system, but he also had sex shortly before he was murdered. So, are you trying to tell me that Murphy would really have had sex with the man who *possibly* abused her as a child?'

'How can Audrey be so sure intercourse occurred shortly before he died? Does it mention that on the pathology report?'

Clarke hummed for a few moments before reply, 'Yes, prostate-specific antigen is a glycoprotein produced in the prostate and secreted into the seminal fluid. There was traces of the fluid found on Mr Hardy's groin and upper thighs.'

'That proves he ejaculated, not that the pair had sex,' Dixon argued.

'Murphy could have been promising sex in order to get Hardy to do her biddings,' Rocky added. 'He could have given her drugs and money, followed and attacked Fraser in the months leading up to Murphy's escape … all because she was using him. If he really did abuse her, she would know what a creep he was, what sex meant to him, and she could ultimately use that to seek her vengeance.'

'It's a working theory,' Hamilton murmured, but his thoughts had begun to wander again — listening to the volley of ideas from his team, his own mind raced ahead.

'And if this theory is correct, then it's absolutely devastating, no child should have to endure any form of abuse,' Rocky's voice filled the car again. 'But how does this help us now? How does this help us find Fraser? It just means that Murphy had eyes on her for a while, so this was premeditated. One hundred per cent she knew what she was doing.'

'Well, the alter-personality of Carly knew what she was doing, Grace wouldn't actually be able to remember—'

'Oh, please, Dixon,' Rocky interrupted an octave higher than before. 'Jesus, the woman is a murderer, regardless of what name or personality she uses.'

'Rocky, come on—' Clarke tried to mediate, but Rocky spoke over him too.

'No, I won't. Sure, I feel for the woman, I told you this is devastating and disgusting, but if we got emotionally attached to every murderer's back story, we'd never arrest anyone. I couldn't find much on the CCTV. Once she left Hyde Park I couldn't track her. We need to know where she is now so we can rescue Fraser before she turns up dead in another one of Murphy's special places.'

Silence followed the constable's speech, and other than the crackling of the phone connection, no sound came through the radio. But Rocky's words had struck a chord with Hamilton. 'What do you mean one of Murphy's *special places*?' he asked.

Rocky exhaled loudly. 'Well, I mean she's bloody messing around with us, isn't she? Running around central London, hitting all the spots where she had murdered someone previously, then having us descend on her old place of work — she loved the theatre by all accounts of the trial — and finally punching someone to a pulp in Hyde Park, where you found the first dead body after her grandfather died—'

'Hold up, something's come through,' Clarke interrupted.

Hamilton's frustration mounted as the mumble of voices and snatches of sentences cracked through the speakers and into his car. He tapped the button on the door to lower the window slightly, welcoming the cold breeze on his clammy face. 'What's going on?' he barked.

'Sorry, guv,' his partner replied. 'A few things we're just confirming here with the team, but a call has been taken; a member of the public thinks she may have seen Murphy but can't be one hundred per cent as she said the woman was wearing a baseball cap, and she didn't get a good look at her face. But it was picked up by the officer because the sighting was on Hyde Park Corner, the caller had just finished her shift at a local casino at about 4am.'

'Did she mention if Murphy was alone?'

'The woman can't be sure of that, but she said the suspect did jump into a black Ford Focus and managed to remember the last three letters of the registration plate.'

'That won't help us now. We don't have the time to—'

'No need, guv,' Clarke cut in. 'After Ms Murphy's revelation about her ex, Rocky's quick investigation showed that Gabe Hardy is the owner of a Ford Focus, and yes, the letters gave by the caller match those of Hardy's plate. The caller said the car raced down Park Lane in the direction of Marble Arch.'

Hamilton turned the ignition on. 'I'm at Lambeth Bridge. I'm heading over that way now.'

'Rocky's running an ANPR check now to see where—'

The car's sirens sparked to life, drowning out Clarke's voice, and Hamilton indicated right before slamming into first gear. 'I can be at Hyde Park Corner in ten minutes. The roads aren't gridlocked yet,' he yelled over the noise. 'Tell me any locations that have spotted that car and I'll follow the route.'

The light traffic cleared a path in front of him, yet panic filled his gut as he manoeuvred the car around a double-decker bus and honked the horn at carefree pedestrians about to step out into the road.

'Okay, boss, listen to me.' Rocky's voice returned. 'The database shows the car heading northwest on the Harrow Road.'

'Jesus Christ, that road is miles long, narrow it down further,' Clarke snapped. 'Guv, let's try and avoid the traffic, so follow Hyde Park round to Lancaster Gate station and then turn on to Gloucester Terrace. That'll bring you onto the Harrow Road.'

'I'm sorry,' Dixon piped-up, her voice full of impatience rather than apology, 'are we seriously leaving the boss out there alone to follow the murderer who seems to have it in for him and Fraser?'

Hamilton sensed a touch of annoyance in Dixon's voice, and he knew she'd want nothing more than to be in the car giving chase with him right now — even if he was chasing a tail of smoke hours behind time.

'Well, no … obviously not.' Clarke replied. 'But we can't be sure this will even lead to anything. It's the second car Murphy's used and it could be another wild-goose chase.'

'*Could* be.' The sarcasm in her tone blared through the speakers. 'But it's also the first sighting we've had of Murphy — using Hardy's car, no less — I think it's the best lead we've had since she escaped the hospital. I'm not comfortable leaving the boss out there alone.'

'Okay …' Clarke hesitated. 'No, you're right. Get on top of that now, Dixon, so we're ready for when we have a final location. Then, the two of us can head off to meet Hamilton and Rocky can deploy the back-up and a firearms team, if needed.'

'There's nothing further on the Ford after Queen's Park Library,' Rocky roared over the other two, his fine Irish brogue now filling the car loud and clear.

Hamilton zoned out, their voices fading further into the distance, as he pumped into third gear and sped along the busy road, expertly zig-zagging and weaving along the road. He mentally soaked up everything Rocky and Clarke had explained, processing every detail on the back and forth conversation they'd had since he stopped the car, and his heart-rate doubled in speed. 'I think I know where they could be,' Hamilton shouted. 'I need you to contact Valerie Murphy immediately.'

Chapter Twenty-Eight

Fraser felt the freezing wind chill her bones before her unconsciousness finally surrendered and permitted her eyes to flutter open. She gasped when she focused on Murphy crouched in front of her; the woman's face inches from her own, dark eyes glaring with a smirk dancing on her lips. She hated the way Murphy's head slowly moved from side to side; appraising her like a lamb being offered to a pride of lions for slaughter.

Her heart pounded inside her chest as she allowed her eyes to flicker beyond Murphy's brooding stare; they were outside. She felt the cold stone against her back, which kept her sitting upright, and observed the numerous headstones surrounding them. They may have left the confines of the chapel, but it was clear they hadn't gone far. Fraser peered as far and wide as her restraints would let her, seeking out the man who had transported her to this grave, but the two women were alone.

'No point looking for help. No one is here,' Murphy snarled and dragged her nails back and forth over her palm. 'This cemetery might as well be abandoned for all the use people make of it these days. I mean, how can they not want to visit their loved ones any more? Is it not *cool* enough to come and pay your respects, perhaps leave a fresh bunch of flowers?'

Spittle landed on Fraser's cheek, but despite the venom in Murphy's voice, the image of flowers sprang to her mind and she remembered the notes of jasmine she'd smelt earlier.

It lingered in the air, still, and she realised the familiarity of it had been from Murphy — it was *her* perfume. The realisation of no strong Irish man having come to her rescue brought tears to her tired eyes.

'Your grandfather was from Ireland, wasn't he?' Fraser whispered, her voice conveying the fear torturing her. 'I remember from … before.' She stopped speaking, scared to mention the previous investigation and resulting arrest against Murphy.

The woman frowned, statue still for a few moments, and Fraser blanched in anticipation of another whack to the head. Although risky to try and engage Murphy in conversation, Fraser felt she had been brought to her dying spot and therefore had nothing left to lose. She inhaled deeply, reigning the tears back and refusing to crumble right at the end.

Surprisingly, Murphy lowered herself to the ground and looked comfortable with legs bent and wide and her arms dangling over her knees. She indicated with her head in the direction behind her, then looked to the grey-black sky and exhaled loudly.

'That's his grave, my grandad's, I mean … my saviour.'

Fraser peeked over the woman's shoulder at the gleaming black granite headstone. Though blocked, she could easily read the top of the gold lettering.

Patrick Murphy loving father and grandfather.

'Was he your saviour because he rescued you from the man who hurt you as a child?' Fraser asked then cleared her throat; she craved a drink of water, but the last time she had accepted a bottle, she'd passed out. The light drizzles of rain spiked her face and she furiously licked her lips to welcome any kind of moisture. Murphy's glare returned and growled with bare teeth like a dog. 'You don't have to be angry because I'm asking questions … I mean, isn't that why I'm here? To explain everything to me and then … to kill me.'

Fraser heard the quiver in her last words and hated herself for fuelling Murphy's menace; the woman reciprocated with a terrifying grin.

'Are you trying to be brave?' Murphy patronised with a cackling laugh. 'Grace tried to be brave, but she was fucking useless.'

Fraser attempted to steady her breathing, not wanting to miss anything that was said. She'd noticed the different personalities rarely mentioned the other — especially by name — but from her research knew that they were more than likely very aware of each other. The angry tone Murphy used now was clearly aimed at the host personality.

'Grace allowed that monster to come into her bedroom week after week while Mum was in the next room. Why didn't she stop him? Why didn't she scream out for help?' Murphy stopped and panted as though she had been running a race with her own memories.

'She said she was scared your mother wouldn't believe her,' Fraser spoke softly, remembering the conversation they'd had in the chapel.

'Ha,' Murphy barked, the words travelling on the wind and echoing around the vast space. 'Like your own mother wouldn't bloody believe you over some nasty, disgusting, vile creature she'd only been dating for a few fucking weeks. He was a rebound from Dad, someone to give her attention but no one important or special to Mum. Of course she would have believed us. Grace should have been stronger, stood up to him and saved us from … from … from the *things* he did to us.'

Murphy was on her feet, pacing around her grandfather's headstone before stopping abruptly and picking up a bottle of vodka Fraser hadn't noticed lying on the grass. She didn't want the woman to fade into a drunken oblivion, worried where that could lead them both, so Fraser attempted to keep Murphy talking.

'But your grandfather, he believed you … he believed Grace?' she asked.

'That man … my grandfather … he was amazing. He just knew things, without needing to be told, without needing to have things spelt out to him. After I ran away, he found me in his shed and he hugged me — not for too long, of course, old Irish men don't — but he wrapped me in a protective bubble and I knew he'd make it right. And he did. He took me on holiday and sent that devil packing; when we came home, he had already left. Oh, and don't be tricked by his name. He was no fucking angel,' Murphy spat and clawed at her palm once again.

Fraser thought about the different types of personalities that were common with this disorder, information she'd discovered through her research, and remembered the protector or rescuer alters that could be adopted. Once Murphy had been sentenced, Fraser assumed it had been Carly filling the role of being the tougher and braver personality, but she could see now it was the grandfather who fit the protector alter. It also had to be him who lifted her from the chapel to this grave.

'Did he used to call you flower?'

Murphy launched towards Fraser, but stopped short and fell to her knees. She held her breath, fearing for certain she'd get at least a slap for speaking so freely of the man Murphy held on a pedestal. But, instead, the woman sobbed loudly, nodding her head in response to Fraser's question. She noticed a change; there was a softness in Murphy's tearful eyes, her shoulders slumped forward and she lightly held Fraser's hands.

'I'm sorry I can't help you,' Murphy whispered, and just by the sing-song tone, Fraser knew Grace now spoke to her. 'Things have gone too far and … I just can't … I mean, I'm not in control of anything. I'm sorry.'

A fire of hope ignited in Fraser's stomach and she tried to sit up, to look into Murphy's eyes. 'Grace, don't be sorry. You've done nothing wrong. Of course you have control, you have control right now, Grace. There's still time to do the right thing; untie these ropes from my hands and feet, Grace.' Fraser hoped the repetition of the woman's name would help keep her focused long enough to free the shackles.

Murphy turned down her lips and shook her head from side to side. 'It's too late. For both of us. I'm so sorry. None of this was supposed to happen, and my dear, dear grandad would be turning in his grave to know she's killing people and connecting his name to it. Yes, he was my saviour, and he pulled me from the darkest ditch of my life … I never knew his own death could awaken a monster within me. I-I never knew she was there.'

'Grace, you just need some help. The doctor … at the hospital … there was progress. Just let me help you now. We can do this together,' Fraser desperately reasoned.

Murphy sighed and reached into her jeans pocket. 'I managed to swipe this from the chapel. It's not much, I know, but perhaps you could leave a note … I don't know … for someone special in your life, for someone you love.'

Fraser looked at the crumpled piece of blank paper and small biro, like the kind she'd seen in the betting shop when she would pop in to back a horse in the annual Grand National. She frowned, her chin trembling. 'I don't understand.'

Murphy smoothed the wrinkles out of the paper and rested it on Fraser's knee before slipping the biro into her right hand and angling her constrained wrists into a writing pose. 'I'm sorry, I'm just not … I'm not strong enough. This is all I can do for you,' Murphy whispered. 'Use this to say goodbye to your family and friends.'

Chapter Twenty-Nine

As Hamilton's car whizzed along the Harrow Road, passing Queen's Park Library while he impatiently waited for his team to call him back, he ran a red light with a honk of his horn. With Kensal Green station now on the horizon, he continued to head in the direction he assumed to be their final destination — the place they'd find Murphy — and he knew he couldn't be wrong; he would be gambling with Fraser's life if he was.

His mind raced as fast as the vehicle he drove, while contemplating the lead-up to Murphy's arrest last year. When he had first met the young woman after the New Year celebrations, she had been grieving the loss of her grandfather and then a colleague who had been murdered. She had openly told Hamilton and Clarke she feared for her own life, that she felt convinced someone had been watching her from the shadows. Then, when an old school friend of Murphy's had also been murdered, Hamilton immediately put her on the possible victim list … rather than potential suspect; a decision which had plagued him ever since. But, to him at the time, Grace Murphy felt no more a murderer than his own mother could be; and Hamilton had always prided himself on his ability to successfully judge a character. After he and Fraser had arrested Murphy, and following the trial, Hamilton felt he had been tricked; she had a dark and disturbing personality unseen to the world. And although he found that secrecy in many abusers and murderers and psychopaths he had arrested in the past, he had felt — at the time — that the diagnosis of dissociative identity disorder had been a ploy by the woman's defence team to get her a reduced sentence.

The short, sharp ringtone pierced through Hamilton's memories and Rocky's docile tones soon filled the car. The constable quickly confirmed that he had spoken to Valerie Murphy and Hamilton had been right about where the grandfather's grave was situated.

'How did you know?' Rocky asked.

'I couldn't be one hundred per cent sure it was Kensal Green cemetery,' Hamilton admitted, 'but when you said Murphy's direction of travel was along the Harrow Road, I made an educated guess. It's the Murphy's hometown, and I know the area well enough. If it had been one of the other two catholic cemeteries I can think of, she would have been driving a different route to the one she had been on.'

'It doesn't mean she's still there,' Clarke's voice came from a distance, and Hamilton assumed he was driving the car his team now travelled in to meet him.

Hamilton nodded in agreement to himself before saying, 'You're right, it doesn't, but what else do we have at the moment? The team in the incident room are still fielding calls from the press conference, so we have that as back-up. If anything else, we might find another clue or note—'

'Hopefully not another body,' Clarke interrupted, throwing a blanket of awkward silence over them. A shiver snaked down Hamilton's back because, while he understood it hadn't been his partner's intention, they were now all clearly thinking of Fraser — and if her cold body could be hidden somewhere in a mass of graves.

Dixon cleared her throat, the noise grating through the car's sound system. 'How far out are you, boss?'

'I'm here, just pulled up at the Saint Mary's Catholic Cemetery entrance, but I can't take the car any further past these gates. I'll run the rest of the way. Any idea where—'

'Ms Murphy said her father's grave was located at the back of the cemetery, at the top of a raised hill and slightly concealed by a large tree,' Rocky answered before the question had been asked.

'Okay, I'm disconnecting now but will have my phone with me.'

'We're about twenty minutes behind you and a firearms team have been deployed also,' Dixon explained. 'But, boss, hold back as much as possible until you have the back-up. Just in case it's a trap.'

Hamilton mumbled something about having everything covered, grabbed the keys from the ignition and clicked the lock button as he jogged away from the car and through the single rusted iron gate. Although he knew the location of the cemetery, he was unfamiliar with the actual grounds, and once he'd run along a gravelled track with a few headstones on either side, he was surprised to come to a huge opening. In front of him stood row after row of different coloured and conditioned headstones; white and black with beautiful gold lettering as well as large statues weather-beaten and unloved. The memorials lined up further than he could see and narrow walkways leading to his left and right and down the centre called to him like a challenging maze.

He scanned the area, desperate to choose the correct direction, when a building caught his attention. Hamilton jogged down the path to his right until he stood dwarfed by a tall-but-tapered chapel. Although the structure looked out of place, its faded brick work and dark windows gave the impression that it had, in fact, been there since time began. It just felt …unexpected, he thought. If he'd chosen the left path, he could have missed the chapel completely, and he'd not noticed any signs of its existence on his sprint into the cemetery. Suddenly, a light flickered from behind the window furthest from him and it was then Hamilton noticed the large wooden door slightly ajar. He stepped forward and lifted his hand to the brass doorknob, but hesitated for a few moments.

What if Murphy is luring me into a trap? Although there's no way she could have known I would have connected her grandfather to all this ... or is there? Surely, she knew her mother would have recognised Gabe Hardy and reported that information to us; the rest would have been a gamble whether or not we would have spoken to Doctor Emine and learned about the possible trauma in Murphy's life. Had she been relying on me to connect the dots?

Hamilton's internal speech persuaded him to reach for his mobile and text his team — who, from what they told him on the phone, he hoped wouldn't be more than fifteen minutes away by now — with details of his location and plans to enter the chapel. The last thing he wanted to do was join his captive colleague rather than freeing her.

***

Fraser handed back the piece of paper, bile rising from her stomach as she thought about the final words she had just written for her mother, and by the look in Murphy's eyes, she knew that Carly's sadistic personality was in control once again. She found it difficult to understand, considering all she'd learnt about dissociative identity disorder, that Murphy had such a sinister alter. From what she had read, people with the disorder weren't the monsters, but were rather the victims of monstrous abusers and events. However, from the things Fraser had seen in her life — from her own best friend's drug addiction, the cheating and lying from the many criminals she'd arrested — she knew only too well that you can never truly understand individual people. Even those you think you know so well, there can so easily be a side to them you've never seen, a stranger within the person you think you know, a side that they keep hidden from absolutely everyone … until something breaks, and they unleash it on the world. Fraser thought about how Murphy must have pushed her demons so far to the back of her mind, so deep down into her subconscious, that the woman unintentionally created an evil side to herself that demanded revenge and retribution for what she'd had to face when she was an innocent child.

After Murphy took the farewell letter, Fraser lowered her head and blew on her shackled hands, hoping her breath would go some way to warming her numb fingers. As though it had sparked an opposite reaction, her whole body trembled and she had to open her mouth to stop her teeth chattering against each other. The cold bit at her skin as though it contained broken shards of glass. The heavy, grey clouds above whizzed past — her eyes couldn't focus on which direction they were headed in — as if they were in a race to get away from the horrors about to unfold. Although confident it must be Sunday now, she didn't have a clue what time it was. For a moment, Fraser thought of asking Murphy, but the question was slammed out of her head by more pressing matters — questions she had the right to know the answers to.

'You know, I had Felix for three years before he went missing—'

'Who the fuck is Felix?' Murphy spat.

'My cat,' Fraser replied, and as she gazed up at the woman, saw an evil grin tug at Murphy's lips. 'I thought that maybe he'd just got lost and some kind person decided to feed him and then … well, you know, cats become attached to that sort of thing. He was happy in another home ... that's what I had hoped, anyway. But you, you had him, didn't you? How? You would have been in Manor Hall Hospital then.'

Murphy sighed heavily and moved from one foot to the other as though agitated with the situation, and possibly the conversation, but Fraser couldn't care less; it was she who had been forced to write a farewell letter on the brink of being murdered.

'You owe me answers.'

Murphy roared laughing and scratched the palm of her hand. 'I owe you nothing. You arrested me, remember, and—'

'And now you're free! About to get the freedom you've been so desperate for while I ... well, you're taking my life ... aren't you?'

Murphy pouted in contemplation and then tipped an imaginary hat in Fraser's direction. 'I get it. You want things all tied up neatly in your head before you meet your maker. Obviously, you're talking to the right person when it comes to feeling confused in here ...' She jabbed her index finger on her temple repeatedly. 'So, I'll grant your request. Another ten minutes or so won't hurt. It's still the twenty-sixth of November after all.'

The woman pulled a gun from the waistband of her jeans, rested it on the top of her grandfather's headstone and sat cross-legged opposite Fraser, as if the two were about to light a bonfire and share spooky tales. Fraser snorted at the thought — there were no tales, only real-life nightmares the pair were about to discuss.

'So, Felix?'

'You became a project to me, Kerry ... it's okay if I call you by your first name, isn't it? Detective Sergeant just doesn't seem fitting for someone sitting on a cold, wet grave bound by thick ropes.' Murphy paused and waited for Fraser to nod in agreement before she continued. 'You see, when Grace first saw *him* working at the hospital, it spun her back into the fear and pain she had felt when she was thirteen. Then, when you came along trying to visit, it sparked an anger inside that only I could fulfil. Grace was surrounded by people who had abused her, tortured her and captured her — I had to get us out of there. And, as difficult as I knew it would be, I also knew I had no choice.'

Fraser frowned, but decided against posing any further questions. Although it seemed confusing, hearing Murphy talk about Grace and Carly as two completely different people, she felt confident enough she could keep up.

'Anyway.' Murphy exhaled deeply and theatrically. 'I formulated a plan, and one day, I made sure that as he was coming off his shift at 7am, I was being escorted to Doctor Emine's office. I had fed the doctor some spiel about needing to see her first thing, even before breakfast, because that's when my mind felt the clearest ... she bought it.

'His eyes flashed when I walked past him coming out of the staff office. I knew all I had to do was wait ... and sure enough, the following night, the monster found his way to my room and let himself in. Just like he had before ... when I was young and ... that first night he had come into my bedroom. The lies and the soft voice and the roaming hands.'

Murphy lowered her head and looked to the side, as if her eyes only need her grandfather's name to give her the strength and courage to continue. Fraser mirrored the action, but only to rub away an unexpected tear falling down her cheek.

'But this time, he wasn't dealing with a scared and vulnerable child, like before.' Murphy's dark eyes focused on Fraser, and it brought goosebumps to her already pimply, cold skin. 'I used him. Told him if he wanted anything from me this time, he had to do a few tasks for me first … and he liked it, the fucking bastard. He actually enjoyed it. The thought of rewards and treats for doing as I instructed—' Fraser watched the woman heave and spit phlegm on the grass. Murphy's gaze didn't return to her but stayed fixed on the ground as she continued. 'You had the audacity to stroll into the hospital, wanting a chat … who did you think you fucking were? So, after that, I gave him your name and told him where you worked and made him follow you, find out everything he could about you. He broke into your home one day while you were at work. That same night, when he told me everything, I ordered him to return and take your cat. *Felix* was looked after, so you were right, but only until I could escape from Manor Hall. I had the keys to his flat, so I went there first, before coming to your house.

'The bastard seemed to take a liking to you … it must be your youthful, girly looks. And, after a month or so, he started telling me things you were doing and places you visited without me even asking.' Murphy drew her knees up and wrapped her arms around them. 'He told me about a time he had followed you while you were working with your team, but that, for some reason, you'd been left on your own to chase a guy … he saw an opportunity and took it. He knocked you out. How he laughed about it; the sick fuck told me how it filled him with a sense of power he hadn't felt in ages, to leave you helpless in the street, admitting he would have raped you if the area hadn't been filled with people. But instead, he stepped over you like a piece of rubbish, leaving you vulnerable … You see, that's what he likes, to feel in control and powerful. He's an animal. *Was* an animal. But I didn't like where things were going, and I had to put a stop to it.'

Murphy paused and looked at Fraser — the frightened woman's eyes widened with obvious anticipation of what she could possibly say next. Murphy sighed long and hard while dragging her long nails back and forth over her red palm until spots of blood appeared.

'I didn't touch him, you bitch,' Murphy yelled. 'Just having him in the same room as me, sitting on my bed again, revolted me. I threw up every time he left, but I knew he was the key to me getting out of that prison. I just had to learn everything about the cameras and the exits and other night security staff. It took some strength not to slit his throat straight away ... but there was an end goal, and I had to play the game. I knew I had to do it just right, just like this, to get rid of you both and be free—'

'How the hell will you be free? You've killed people, escaped from a criminal institution and have threatened to kill an office—'

'It's no threat.'

Fraser flinched, mad at herself for letting her emotions get the better of her and blurting out her thoughts. But fear, with its vice-like grip, quickly strangled any other emotion from her body and left only trepidation in its place. She watched Murphy's face; the contorted way her skinny, brown eyebrows knitted together, her eyes scrunched into small, black holes, and her lips pulled back to bare clenched teeth.

She shifted from one numb buttocks cheek to the other and swallowed the saliva in her throat with some difficulty as Murphy stood up and rested her right hand on the gun. She closed her eyes momentarily, faces whizzed past in her mind; her mother, Johnny, Audrey, Hamilton — people who meant something to her but who she would never see again. Slowly, she blinked her eyes open and peered up at Murphy, the first drizzle of rain making her squint.

'Who?' Fraser asked. 'Who did this to you?'

Murphy relaxed her face and a distant, far-away look took hold of her features. 'Gabe,' she replied. 'Gabriel Hardy.'

***

Hamilton held the door and gently closed it behind him, careful not to disturb the silence within the chapel. He took a step forward and then stood still in the darkness, his ears straining for any sound — a creak from a floorboard, a whisper carried through the shadows or a person breathing. But nothing came. Convinced he was alone, Hamilton fiddled inside his pocket, grabbed his mobile and blindly turned on the phone's torch.

He shined the beam around, quickly taking in the derelict building; cobwebs and broken pews as well as dusty statues and candle holders. Something caught his eye and he walked along the filthy dark carpet towards the altar. He stopped short at the stairs and crouched down, letting the light beam hover over a particular area of the wooden floor. The wet, ruby blood glistened in the light, and he was under no illusions that it wasn't fresh. He shot up, quickly scanned the area for another door or office, but he could see nothing other than a few empty water bottles and cables of rope.

With the phone held high, Hamilton ran back the way he came out the chapel door. His heart-rate had doubled in speed, not from the quick jog but from a tension squeezing his chest, and his breathing became laboured. He looked around the eerie quiet cemetery, begging himself to choose a direction, but his feet froze to the spot. Despite it only being Sunday afternoon, the dark, moody clouds threatened to bring nightfall early, and as he looked to the sky hoping for an answer, a rain drop smacked him on the forehead.

As Hamilton's eyes drew back down on the burial ground surrounding him, he noticed a small incline to the pathway up further to his right. He thought back to Rocky's explanation of where Murphy's grandfather's grave was situated and took off in that direction before his brain could try and rationale his actions.

The drizzle of rain mixed with the sweat beads on Hamilton's forehead, the deceiving slight incline actually much steeper than it had looked from afar. He clocked a large oak tree up ahead and used that as his focus while bypassing memorial headstones and weaving over flowers as best he could. A pink teddy bear briefly caught his attention and he thought of the many children buried beneath the earth he now sprinted over — just like his own daughter was in another cemetery not a million miles from there. His thoughts gained momentum as his legs climbed higher and higher.

Thanks to the words he had read in the book by Doctor Emine, he couldn't shake the idea of Maggie suffering from a mental illness. *Well, the possibility*, he thought to himself — it was something he found hard to believe. Could he really have been so blind to his daughter's traumatic experiences? Could there really be any similarities between his sweet, kind-hearted only child and the woman who used her past as an excuse to kill innocent people?

His internal questions went unanswered as he came to a halt behind the tree which he had used as his goal. He scanned through the heavy drizzle and around the numerous headstones until his eyes finally settled on two women about a hundred yards in front of him. Fraser's tethered ankles and wrists sparked a range of emotion in Hamilton. While relief that she was still alive flooded him, a ball of anxiety made him wonder what she had already been through.

Just as he tried to formulate a plan in his mind, unable to hear the words Murphy uttered, he saw the unstable woman snatch a gun off a near-by headstone and casually point it in Fraser's direction.

Chapter Thirty

The beep from the mobile phone in Rocky's hand startled Clarke, and he took his eyes off the road for a moment to watch his colleague read the message. He refocused his attention and indicted left to exit the Harrow Road and drive onto the narrow path leading into the cemetery.

'For crying out loud, what does it say?' he snapped as the silent seconds began to feel like suffocating minutes.

'It's from the boss.'

'And?' Dixon piped up from the back seat and Clarke clocked the roll of her eyes in the rear-view mirror.

'Give me a sec,' Rocky replied slowly while continuing to read.

Clarke tutted and twisted his body slightly to try to snatch the phone from Rocky, but before he had a chance to reach out, Dixon screamed for him to stop. Simultaneously, Clarke whipped his head back to the road and slammed his right foot on the brake. The car stopped inches from Valerie Murphy's knee caps.

'Fuck's sake,' Clarke panted and cut the engine.

'I'll go to her,' Dixon said and dashed out of the car.

'Rocky, what the hell does the message say?' he demanded.

'Sorry. Okay, the boss says that Murphy has a gun and Fraser is tied up.'

'Are they in the chapel?'

'No, the grave … the grandfather's grave.'

'Shit. Quickly reply; tell Hamilton to stay put and that we're here. Then, get on to the armed team in transit and update them.'

Clarke jumped out of the driver's seat and left the car door open behind him. He came face to face with a hysterical Valerie Murphy — tears streaming down her red and puffy face, and the skin on her arms a tinge of blue, the white T-shirt doing nothing to fend off the winter chill — and Dixon, who seemed to be having trouble placating the woman. He slipped off his coat and wrapped it around Valerie's shoulders, telling her to put her arms into it. Although the woman continued to cry and mutter something incomprehensible, she did as she was told. His black Superdry Camden overcoat hung from her small frame, but it went some way in calming her, as if the mere touch of wool on cold skin awoke her from the crazed trance she'd been in.

'Ms Murphy, what are you doing here?' Clarke asked as he clocked Hamilton's car parked a few yards ahead of them by the gates to the catholic cemetery.

The woman inhaled deeply and pulled the coat closer against her body. 'Well … well, when you rang … not you personally, I don't think, b-b-but—'

'Calm down, Ms Murphy,' Dixon said softly, but Clarke tapped his foot in annoyance — there was no time for this, he thought.

Valerie sniffed back her tears and cleared her throat. 'When I was asked about my father's grave, it suddenly dawned on me that I hadn't even looked for Grace here … and of course, this is where she would be. I found her here many times after her grandfather died. A few times, she … she drank too much and passed out at his grave and—'

'Ms Murphy, I'm going to need you to sit in the car and wait,' Clarke interrupted, and turned to Rocky who had now joined them.

'The armed response unit gave an ETA of ten minutes,' the constable explained. 'A protest of some kind is scheduled for this evening in Marble Arch, but the traffic and crowds are building in the street already.'

'Great,' Clarke moaned. 'That's all we flaming well need.'

'Armed response unit,' Valerie echoed Rocky's words, her blue eyes wide with terror.

'Ms Murphy, please remain calm and stay in the vehicle,' Clarke reiterated his command to the woman, but he could see the frenzy return as she dragged a skinny hand through her wild hair, her eyes darting from him to Rocky and back again. 'Ms Murphy, your daughter is armed and—'

'No, no, no, no,' Valerie repeated the word over and over again, but Clarke saw a shift in her — there was now a look of determination and strength as she stopped shaking, her eyes stopped wandering and her body visibly stood straighter. 'My daughter is not dangerous. You have to let me see her.'

'That's not a good idea,' Clarke said, and peered at his watch; he knew anything could happen in the next three minutes in that graveyard, let alone ten minutes.

'Perhaps …' Dixon hesitated and stared at Clarke briefly. 'Perhaps it wouldn't be such a bad idea to have Ms Murphy talk to her daughter.'

He felt torn. It wasn't procedure to bring a civilian into the line of fire — whether it was a family relative or not — but he also knew Hamilton would not be up there sitting tight as requested. With the backup team still too far out to offer any assistance, he knew he couldn't leave his colleague and boss in the hands of an unbalanced criminal.

Could this mother be our only chance of making sure no more blood is shed today? Is she the answer to saving Fraser … and Hamilton?

Clarke had made a decision. He pushed the car door shut, clicked the lock button and told everyone to follow his lead as he turned and darted into the catholic cemetery.

***

Murphy aimed the gun towards Fraser and stood still, listening to the rain grow louder with a backing track of wind whistling through the large trees around them. The cold crept to her bones, seeping through the man's clothing that still clung to her body, and although the combination of those two things should make her skin crawl, a rare calmness washed over her. But, just as quickly as it had come, the tranquillity was snatched away again. She frowned and brought her left hand up to the side of her head, pushing her palm into her temple in an attempt to alleviate the pressure. Murphy felt her skull shattering under her fingertips, her throbbing head demanding her to drop to her knees as a kaleidoscope of memories whirled inside her mind.

'Why does the peace never last?' she yelled, succumbing to the pain and falling to the ground. 'Why do they have to show me over and over again? I don't want to see this in my head any more. I-I-I …'

'He's gone now … he can't hurt you any more, Grace,' Fraser whispered.

Tick. Tock. Tick. Tock.

Murphy raised her head slowly, the crushing weight subsiding slightly, and she looked into the sergeant's kind eyes.

Am I Grace? Or Carly … or Livia … or Stan? Help me.

The internal questions repeated over and over again until the voices in her head — demanding to know who she was — deafened her. She frantically shook her head from side to side and let a blood-curdling scream escape.

'Grace, please don't do this,' the detective sergeant continued to whisper, the soft tone of the woman's voice now grating on her as it fought to be heard over so many others in her head. 'You can get the help you need. I can help you … I want to help you. Will you let me help you, Grace?'

Who am I? Am I really still Grace? The little girl who wanted to be on stage, who wanted to be an actress … who, even back then, wanted to be someone else. Play a different role.

Murphy slumped her shoulders and lowered her arm slightly, the gun now pointing to the wet grass by Fraser's feet. The heavy drizzle came fast, scratching her body like shards of glass falling from the sky.

Why can't I remember what I've done? Why am I here?

'Grace, let me help you,' Fraser repeated. 'You're not alone. You don't have to do this alone. You don't need to keep trying to get revenge … the monster who hurt you is gone.'

Am I Grace?

Murphy looked up to the sky and let the rain pelt against her face, washing her skin clean, looking for answers to her questions that wouldn't come. She thought of her grandfather, and completely understood why she was in fact at his grave. He had saved her as a child, taken her away from the monster who stole her childhood, but she couldn't understand why it was now her passing on the pain and fear to someone else. She gazed down, staring at the cold metal in her hand: *Where the hell did I get a gun from?*

A twig snapped, not too far in the distance, and broke her concentration. Murphy raised the weapon again.

***

Hamilton crouched down and moved away from the security of the large oak tree. With nothing to hide him, he moved slowly from one headstone to the next, hoping the memorials of the dead would shield him from Murphy's sight until he could get closer to Fraser.

His eyes never faltered from the two women. As he slinked closer, he heard Murphy roar; a chilling scream that sent the birds fleeing from the safety of the trees, their squawks of panic mingled with her shrieks of instability. He paused and lowered his body behind a white headstone, the rain making it harder to see exactly what was happening in front of him. He squinted, watching Murphy fall to the ground and wail. This was his chance.

Hamilton's heart thumped, despite him moving at a snail's pace, and he wiped a hand over his face in hope of removing the droplets of water falling from his eyebrows and nose, but they were replaced with fresh ones as soon as he did. The rain soaked through his clothes and his brogues squelched in mud that made the grass underneath feel unstable. He moved forward, Fraser's quavering voice pulling him along. His crouched strides grew wider as Murphy lowered the weapon to the ground. With the woman's attention elsewhere, Hamilton decided to take a giant leap forward; his plan to knock the gun from Murphy's hand.

The mud squelched underfoot again, sending Hamilton's left knee to the ground. He cursed as he landed directly on a mound of fallen sticks, the edges prickling his shin and the noise alerting Murphy to his presence. He pulled himself back up, not wanting to give the woman a height advantage as she raised the gun again. Her nostrils flared when she caught sight of him and he took a few steps closer to her and Fraser.

'Grace Murphy, put your weapon down.'

The woman pointed the weapon at Hamilton's chest and, with her free hand, yanked Fraser by the hair, dragging his colleague onto her knees and using her as a human shield between them. When she had Fraser in place, Murphy then turned the gun and rammed it into the side of Fraser's head with such force, the sergeant almost toppled sideways. Hamilton saw the fear in Fraser's eyes and stopped in his tracks. He wiped the rain from his face again and then made a surrender gesture with his hands.

'Okay, okay, I'm not coming any further,' he said.

'How nice of you to join us, Inspector,' Murphy said with a half-smile. 'Front row seats for the final act of the show ... only right, really.'

Hamilton lowered his hands and tried to steady his breathing; it had been a long time since he'd seen Murphy, and yet despite the vicious actions in front of him, he couldn't shake the image of the fragile, grieving woman he'd first met.

'Put the gun down, Grace,' he repeated.

'I'm sorry, she's not here at the moment, please leave a message.' Murphy laughed at her own joke while tugging harder on her prisoner's hair and peering over Hamilton's shoulder. 'I see you're alone, Inspector. Couldn't get the backup this time, eh?'

'They're on their way, Grace. So why don't you just put down the gun now before this gets out of hand,' Hamilton said, and slowly inched one foot forward. 'Harming DS Fraser will only make things worse for you. Stop this now and we can still help you.'

'What is it with you two wanting to help me,' Murphy yelled, her voice carried with the wind and echoed in the distance. 'I don't want your fucking help. Maybe if Grace had been given a bit of help when she needed it, we wouldn't all be here right now.'

Hamilton slid the other foot forward. 'We know what happened. We know all about Gabe Hardy and your grandfather. I understand,' he said, and outstretched his hand. 'Just give me the gun.'

Murphy applied more pressure to the gun, forcing Fraser's head even further to the side and exposing the straining veins and muscles in her neck. 'I. Don't. Want. Your. Help. I want to fucking finish this. I feel like I'm going to explode. It *has* to end here.'

Chapter Thirty-One

Hamilton jumped when he heard commotion from behind him, but felt thankful it had also startled Murphy enough to freeze her to the spot. As the women looked over his shoulder again, he took the opportunity to peer around. Relief and panic flooded him simultaneously; grateful to have the support of his team but frustrated the noise hadn't come from the armed response unit he'd been expecting. He was also surprised to see Valerie Murphy leading his team towards the grave. He mopped the rain from his face again — his wet hand adding rather than taking away — and the heavy downpour made the world around him look like an old black and white movie.

He cast his eyes back to Murphy. The woman's focus now on the four people approaching them. He took a risk by taking another step towards her. Fraser tightened her jaw and slightly shook her head, but he ignored her warning and attempted another move.

'I wouldn't if I were you,' Murphy hissed while dragging Fraser a few steps back in the mud; this time, the detective sergeant couldn't mask the pain and yelped like a wounded puppy. 'And you lot can all stop right there too.'

Hamilton didn't need to turn around again, obvious that Murphy had directed her last sentence to his team and her own mother. He knew they would do as instructed. But as he heard the voices of Clarke and Dixon yell out, he saw a figure move past him in his peripheral vision. He instinctively threw out his arm and turned to block the oncoming threat.

'Ms Murphy, stop right there,' he yelled, and fumbled with the woman in a soaking coat at least four times too big for her, as she attempted to push past him. 'Stop.'

'No,' she screamed. 'Let me get to my daughter. She needs me.'

'I don't need you,' Murphy yelled. 'You're too late, Mother.'

Valerie stopped squirming, giving Hamilton a chance to lock his arms around her body — in case the woman decided to sprint off again. Right now, Murphy was in charge on the situation, and he wouldn't let anything endanger Fraser's life any further. Again he thought back to his first encounter of Grace and Valerie, and what a tight mother-daughter relationship they had — a bond similar to that of his own wife and daughter — yet now, the pair looked like complete strangers to one another.

'Don't antagonise her,' Hamilton whispered in Valerie's ear, who now slightly blocked his view of Fraser and Murphy. 'Your daughter is very confused right now.'

She nodded slightly, took a deep breath and called out to her daughter, 'I want to help you, darling.'

Murphy's eye roll was not subtle, and for the first time, Hamilton could understand why the woman was so furious. In the last year, everyone who spoke to Murphy promised they wanted to help her, promised they *could* help her, Hamilton thought. But that was only because now Murphy was the wrongdoer … who offered to help her when she truly needed it? Who put out their hand when she was an abused child and vowed to rescue her, vowed to stop her pain? When Murphy was alone and frightened, with obviously no one to turn to or talk to, she only had herself to rely on. And that's exactly who she was relying on now, today, and in her moments of fear and uncertainty. Watching the look of pure disbelief on Murphy's face, Hamilton finally got it.

'Don't tell her you can help her,' Hamilton whispered again. 'You can't understand what she's going through now. But explain you're here for her now and you're sorry.'

He heard Valerie inhale loudly, as though new air would give her the strength she needed to talk to her daughter. Could two people who were so close really have lost the ability to understand each other? *Is that what happened between me and Maggie?*

'Grace, darling.' Valerie fell over her own words and paused for a few seconds. 'I heard about what happened to Gabe and I ... I'm sorry—'

'Sorry for what? Letting that creature into our lives ... into my bed? Or for this?' she said, gesturing the gun to her grandfather's grave before ramming it back into the side of Fraser's head. 'I thought you would have waited for me, Mum.'

Valerie's breath hitched in her chest like a newborn baby who'd just had a marathon crying session; Hamilton loosened his grip on her. 'W-what do you mean?'

'Grandad's headstone.'

'I-I ... but you stopped me from visiting you. I—'

'So it's my fault,' Murphy hissed and turned the gun on her mother and Hamilton. 'You went ahead and chose the headstone and the words and ... and everything without me because I wouldn't let you visit the fucking mental hospital.'

'I didn't know—'

'What? That *your* boyfriend tiptoed from your bed to mine in the middle of the night. Stinking of beer ... it made me gag. You didn't know that he would pull back my covers ... that he would touch me.' Murphy sucked in a lungful of air and Hamilton felt Valerie's body shake under his body — though the cold and rain had obviously become oblivious to them all now. 'Can you believe that a man like that could end up working in a psychiatric hospital. Full of vulnerable women ... and you all say it's me who needs help. This whole fucking world is messed up.'

'B-b-but where is this coming from?' Valerie's croaky words called out. 'I mean ... why didn't you tell me this before? Why have you never said nothing in all the years—'

'I didn't know,' Murphy screamed, the gun shaking in her outstretched hand. 'I didn't remember.'

'Grandad,' Valerie whispered and sobbed.

'He saved me ... he was the only person I trusted. Then, the fucking cancer ... We weren't safe any more and Grace completely crumpled like the weakling she always was. She needed me.' Murphy's wide eyes roamed in various directions behind Hamilton, but he daren't follow her gaze as the gun never faltered from its position on him and Valerie. 'A good man was taken from this world, a man who truly protected me. You people don't deserve the lives you were gifted with. Selfish, vile and vain ... that's what you all are. You hide behind this *I want to help you* line but do nothing. Nothing!'

'Please, Gracie—'

'Don't. Call. Me. That.'

Peering around Valerie's head, Hamilton witnessed the look of evil on Murphy's face: the clenched teeth and twitching jaw and her unblinking wide, black eyes. They were losing any grip on the situation they might have had, and it seemed Valerie could well be pushing Murphy further. As he forced his brain to think of a plan, various sounds disrupted the eeriness around them and brought the area to life; vehicles screeching their brakes in the near-by distance, feet squishing in the wet mud, the rustle of clothes he knew only too well were that of bullet-proof vests and thick black attire. Even the rain fell back to a light drizzle.

'Grace Murphy, lower your weapon to the ground.' The booming order came from a deep male voice behind him, but Hamilton kept visual on Murphy, preparing himself to move towards Fraser when the time came.

'Darling, please ...' Valerie whispered, and moved a foot forward. Hamilton tightened his hold around her once again and told her to be quiet. 'Just listen to me, darling. Listen only to my voice. I'm sorry. I'm so very, very sorry. I'm sorry I didn't protect you, and I'm sorry you couldn't talk to me, but I *promise* you I will do absolutely everything I can to protect you now. Let me prove it to you, Grace. I would do anything for you. You're my daughter and I love you. Give me a second chance to show you.'

'You loved that man, that evil monster, and you wouldn't have believed me. I was just a little girl ... telling tales.'

Hamilton heard the change in Murphy's voice; an octave lower and no longer dripping with venom towards her mother. He slowly slid more to Valerie's side, no longer blocked by the woman, and tapped her back to encourage her to keep talking. For the first time, he felt confident Valerie could calm her daughter and he could reach for the weapon. But he was aware of the noises around them growing closer and knew he'd have to make a move soon, before the armed unit rallied Murphy's fury again.

Valerie sighed. 'Oh, sweetheart, is that what that evil bastard told you? Of course I would have believed you. You will always be my little girl, no matter how old you get or what you do ... You're my Gracie and I hate myself for putting you here. This is my fault and I'm so sorry.'

'It's not your fault, Mum. It's his ... and mine and his—' She aimed the gun fully on Hamilton and gritted her teeth again. 'He sprouts on about help and justice, but it was him! He locked me up with that monster again. I just want to finish this now. I want to be free, Mum. From him, from you, from her … from Grace.'

'Darling,' Valerie said, inching forward again, 'you're right, this has to stop. But not like this. You're not mad at this woman who you've dragged here, and you're not mad at the police; they're guilty of doing nothing but their jobs. You're mad at me, and I understand that … but take it out on me, not them.'

'Mum, stop.'

'But I didn't do my job, darling, my job as a mother, and I'm so sorry. I should have protected you. I should have been there for you and I should have noticed what was happening to you. I hate myself and you should hate me too. You are my only baby, all I ever wanted from this life is you. When I held you in my arms for the first time, any worry or panic I felt about being a mother just vanished. When you looked at me, with all that pure innocence and dependence, I knew I would fight against the world for you. I failed, Grace, and I'll never be able to tell you how sorry I am, but don't do this. Don't do this here … here at your grandfather's grave … shielding yourself behind him and some kind of mental illness. I'll step up now. I'll protect you from everything and everyone in our own bubble. No one will ever hurt you again … not while I'm around.'

Hamilton heard the crunch of twigs and metal machinery expertly moved in the hands of the armed response team. He knew they wouldn't give Valerie much longer to talk her daughter down. They were only using it as a cover to get themselves into place, and he suddenly felt helpless in the middle of it all. Right in that moment, Hamilton understood his own daughter might have felt as torn and lonely as Murphy did as a teenager and the pain crushed him. He could only hope now that the parent who clung to his forearm could save her child in a way he couldn't, and before anyone else lost their life.

'You think I'm hiding behind some kind of illness?' Murphy hissed. 'You've understood nothing about what I've told you, have you? About me ... about what I want. About the people who have to pay for this.'

'But you can put all that behind you now, Grace.' Valerie's voice hitched in her throat. 'We need to move past what's happened. Of course I know how hard that will be, and we'll work on a brighter future together ... no evil monsters or fake personalities.'

Although Hamilton thought the promise of a bright future was a futile one, given the circumstances, he sighed with relief as Murphy smiled at her mother and nodded in agreement to the image she'd just painted. But just as he lowered his guard and signalled for an officer to the right of him to advance on the situation, Murphy turned the gun. Before he had the chance to shout out or move closer to stop her, she pulled the trigger.

Chapter Thirty-Two

Lack of sleep had finally zapped away all of Hamilton's remaining energy, and the past forty-eight hours had completely drained his emotional reserve. He so desperately wanted to get home to his wife, but there was one person he had to see before that could happen. He pushed open the door and walked into the room, his wet brogues squeaking on the polished tiles. He then gently eased himself on to the edge of the hospital bed and puffed out a lungful of air.

'How are you?' he asked when his presence didn't entice the attention he'd hoped for.

Fraser stared absently out of the window. 'There's nothing wrong with me. I just want to go home.'

'They had to check you over, you can understand that surely, but you've made your feelings clear and the discharge papers are being sorted now.' He paused and lightly touched Fraser's arm. 'But that wasn't exactly what I meant.'

She sighed heavily but finally turned her head and met his gaze. 'I'm numb … no, I'm not! I'm angry and disappointed and …' She shook her head. 'I don't know how I am.'

'That's pretty understandable at the moment, considering what you've been through,' he replied, worried that the tears bubbling in his colleague's eyes were about to unleash themselves. Not that Hamilton had a problem with that, he'd seen his fair share of breakdowns, but he felt guilty for the pain Fraser harboured. 'You know, none of this was your fault—'

'Murphy took her own life,' Fraser blurted. 'I contributed to that. But I also felt relieved … when I felt her grip on me loosen and saw her fall to the ground. It wasn't me. I hadn't been shot and I felt happy. How evil is that?'

'Jesus Christ, Fraser, that's hardly ev—'

'A young woman killed herself today and I felt relief. Relief, for crying out loud. I'm in a position where I'm supposed to help these people.'

'Fraser, you tried your best.'

'No, I only pushed her further away from getting help. I'm just as much to blame as …' She paused and looked away again, but to the shadowy night sky outside the window. 'Don't you want to know why I visited Murphy?'

'Yes. Why did you?'

'I needed to understand her mental illness. Understand if it was anything similar to my mother's bipolar. Understand what made her choose to kill people.'

Hamilton turned down his mouth and nodded. 'I get that. You needed—'

'Who cares what I needed?' Fraser faced him again, her eyes red and puffy, her blonde hair — still dirty from the mud and rain — fell around her face. 'Because I needed to understand something that was none of my business, I triggered a reaction in a woman who needed to be in that hospital receiving treatment and help. Because I so desperately needed to be in the know … it set her on a path that saw her turn the gun on herself. I feel so mad.'

Fraser's tears finally fell, silently but furiously, and Hamilton reached over to the bedside cabinet and grabbed the box of tissues. He placed them on the bed and waited for Fraser's breathing to steady.

'Is that why you're mad? Because you think it's your fault Murphy killed herself?'

She brought the tissue to her face and wiped her eyes, the dirt under her fingernails showing and the dried blood on her cut arms still evident. 'Yes, I'm so mad. I'm furious. I added to her pain and rage. We're in a position where we're supposed to stop the bad guys … but Murphy began all this as a victim. I mean, a paedophile was allowed to walk the streets, was allowed to work in an environment with vulnerable women. And yes, while he's also dead now … look what had to happen. Look at how many people had to die before we even knew he existed.'

'It's not a totally awful way to be.'

'What isn't?'

'To be mad. To be emotional.'

'Grace Murphy was furious too.'

Hamilton sighed deeply. 'Grace Murphy had a mental illness. It's very different to how you're feeling now. I can't say anything that will take that away, but I mean, it's not all bad because you can use that to push you further in this job. In the next investigation, you'll evaluate things differently, see people differently … be a different person.'

'What if I'm not the right person for this job?' Fraser wiped her eyes again.

Hamilton shrugged. 'I can't answer that for you, Kerry. But what I will say is that you're a good copper. What we do every day is difficult, and what we see is even worse … human beings being the worst possible sides of themselves. But we all do this job for our own reasons. We all have that fire inside of us that makes us get up every morning and face the terrors and Godawful shit that happens in this world every day. We investigate, and sometimes we get it wrong, but we learn from it so that next time we're a bit quicker in catching those bastards out there. And yes, we'll offer help, but sometimes … well, sometimes, that's not enough. Yes, Grace Murphy was a victim, but she was also a murderer. But you can't blame yourself every time. All you can do is your best.'

'Well … when you put things like, I feel like a bit of a moaning mini right now, boss.'

Fraser hinted at a smile, and Hamilton held her hand and squeezed it tightly, knowing that everything he'd just said to her still remained true to himself. The pair sat quietly for a few moments, both lost in their own thoughts. He hoped his words really would have an effect on Fraser, but he understood the MIT wasn't for everyone; after all, he'd almost left the Metropolitan Police after Maggie committed suicide. He understood the frustration and guilt that came with not saving someone, but he'd learnt a long time ago that sadly not everyone could be saved, because not everyone accepted help. He cleared his throat, let go of Fraser's hand and stood up.

'So, the doctors checked me out,' Fraser said, straightening herself in the bed and regaining her usual profession attitude. 'They found traces of Rohypnol in my system. It must have been in all those bottles of water Murphy gave me. Explains how she kept moving me from place to place.'

'I know. The doctors updated us. Rocky also uncovered the identity of the dead woman in Hyde Park.'

'The woman who resembled me?'

'Yes, but we're thinking that's just a coincidence now. It turns out the woman was a well-known drug dealer. Possibly a contact through Gabe Hardy. Cocaine was present in his system and it would seem Murphy got quite a bit of information from him, and so it's the likely source of the Rohypnol.'

Fraser frowned. 'Murphy always seemed to have a reason for killing, though. Why would she murder this dealer contact?'

'I'm not one hundred per cent confident, obviously, but perhaps the drug dealer had seen the press conference and wanted more for her silence. Or it could just be that Murphy needed to tie up loose ends … worried the deal would lead us to you too soon. Anyway, the drugs are exactly the reason the doctors want you to at least stay one night in the hospital.'

'I want to go home. Wait, is it—'

'Your house has been taken care of, Kerry. You're free to return when you want. But if you think you won't feel safe there, I can arrange something for you.'

She smiled. 'There's no longer a threat to me, boss. I'll be fine. But thanks. Anyway, I'm sure Chief Allan is fed-up of me using police resources.'

'Oh yeah, everyone's overtime will need to come out of your wages this month, you understand? Cut backs are a bitch, and really, I think you would have been fine without us.'

Fraser let out a small laugh and quickly wrapped an arm around her ribs. 'Don't make me laugh, boss. Everything hurts.'

'Well, be sure to know you have all our support, and we're instructing you to take as much time as you need before coming back to work. Have some leave before you start again.'

'How do we start again?'

Hamilton puckered his lips and inhaled deeply through his nose. 'We move on to the next case and help the next person as best we can.'

'Is that enough, boss?'

'Well—'

'I mean, how do you just carry on when a victim — because like you said, that's what Murphy was — takes their own life and you could have prevented that. How do you just move on?'

Obviously not realising the implications of her words, Hamilton struggled to keep the emotion rising in his throat at bay. He swallowed hard and said, 'You can only hope that you learn something from each tragedy and take it forward to do better for someone. Someone who can accept your help.'

Fraser nodded and turned back to the window. Hamilton had planned on feeling sensitive in this enormous scale, and knew it was time to head home. He said goodbye to Fraser, making her promise to call him if she needed anything, and walked to the door of her private room. Just as his hand twisted the handle, she called his name, and he turned to look at her sad, pale face once again.

'Why, boss? Why didn't she turn the gun on me? It had been her plan … to kill me on the anniversary of her grandfather's death. Why did she kill herself instead?'

Hamilton let the silence sit between them for a few moments; it didn't feel awkward, it felt enlightening. 'She was struggling to find peace, you heard her say that yourself, and she didn't know who she was any more. But I also think it had something to do with what Murphy's mother said … about not letting anyone hurt her while she was around.'

'I thought that was a good thing,' Fraser replied, and bit her bottom lip. 'Her mum was getting through to her.'

'No,' Hamilton said with a sadness in his heart. 'It just reminded Grace that one day her mother wouldn't be around, just as it happened with her grandfather, and there'd be no one to protect her but herself. She'd be all alone, in a world she viewed as evil, with only the strangers within herself for company.'

Epilogue

Denis Hamilton tilted his head back and gazed up at the ninety-five-storey skyscraper and still couldn't manage to see the top of the building. The Shard, covered with eleven thousand glass panels, stood in all its glory dominating the Southwark skyline as if its knife-like tip were about to penetrate the dull clouds circling above it.

'Happy birthday,' Elizabeth said, and extended her arms skywards.

'But it's not my birthday until next month,' he replied with a smile.

His wife punched him on the arm. 'Well, it wouldn't have been a surprise if I brought you here on your exact birthday. Are you surprised?'

'Yes, it's a great treat. I just don't understand why we need to celebrate me turning forty … like it's a good thing.' He smiled again, not wanting to dishearten Elizabeth's kind gesture, but he'd wanted to stop celebrating his birthday many years ago. It wasn't an age-related issue, but more because it reminded him of what he'd lost.

Elizabeth slipped her arm through his and led him to the entrance of the building. 'I know you've been through a lot at work, and we still haven't managed to have *that* chat, but sometimes, you just need to slow down and enjoy what you've got … and that includes celebrating birthdays, mister.'

His wife made him smile and he vowed to himself that he wouldn't complain or scold today. He would enjoy himself — just as he'd been told to. Hamilton was usually the one giving the orders, but in his personal life, he was happy to be led for a change. He pecked her on the cheek and continued to follow her.

Elizabeth flashed their printed tickets to the woman standing at the glass door, who instructed them to take the stairs and turn right. His wife was surprised to find security and metal detectors awaiting them, and the fact they had to shed their coats and empty their pockets into a tray, just like at an airport. But Hamilton knew only too well the precautions tourist attractions like these needed to take against terrorists. Once they'd collected their belongings and posed for the obligatory photo in front of a green screen — he wondered what image they'd magic-up behind them in time for their expensive exit — they headed to the first of two lifts which would soar them to floor sixty-eight.

After exiting the lift, walking around and then taking the stairs to seventy-two, Hamilton and Elizabeth gazed out of the windows to point out Wembley Stadium in the distance and The Gherkin building much closer. Despite the cloudy November day, tourists filled the floor of London's highest viewing platform to take in the panoramic sights of the city.

Elizabeth waved a piece of paper in front of him. 'This trip comes with a couple of glasses of bubbly. Let's order them now and grab that table by the window.'

Once seated, they talked about the beauty of The Shard's architecture and how, as Londoners, they so often missed out on the beauties it had to offer; it wasn't the done thing to act like tourists in your own home. They chatted and skirted around the subject until they had run out of things to say, and Hamilton suddenly felt awkward.

'I don't like this, love,' he admitted. 'It's not like us to bother with small talk. Jesus, we've been together way too long for that crap.'

Elizabeth sighed and took a sip of her drink before she spoke. 'I know, you're right, but now really isn't the time.'

'And if we keep saying that, we'll never say what we really want to say.' She looked around, as if worried the people around them would be eavesdropping on their conversation, but it soon became clear the Thames had hold of their attention more than anything else. 'Talk to me.'

'I don't want to be a childless family any more,' she finally blurted out. 'I don't know if it's because I've been told I can no longer get pregnant, or if it's something I've always wanted, but I just couldn't tell you—'

'Hey, what do you mean you couldn't tell me?' Hamilton asked, put his champagne flute on the table and pulled his chair closer to his wife's.

'We lost our daughter, Denis,' she said, placing her finger under his chin to force him to look at her again. 'I haven't even mentioned her name yet and you look away from me. Why can't you talk about her?'

'I talk about Maggie all the time,' Hamilton said, and took his wife's hand from his face, but kept it entwined with this own.

'Yes, we talk about Maggie in the comfort of our own home, in the privacy and security, but you never talk about her with other people. It's as though you're still ashamed or … guilty that you didn't save her.'

'Of course I am, Elizabeth,' he whispered, though he didn't care about the people milling around them now; they had all blurred into white noise. 'I always will be.'

She smiled, but it was a sad smile which didn't reach her eyes. 'So will I, but Denis, we'll have no life if we continue to live it like this. We couldn't help Maggie, our daughter, but we can't blame ourselves for that forever.'

Hamilton looked out the window to London Bridge and inhaled deeply. In his wife's words, he heard the same piece of advice he had tried to give Fraser just a few days ago in the hospital. He thought over the case they'd finally closed, and the book he'd read by Doctor Emine, and wondered if his own daughter had faced a stranger within. He couldn't deny his thoughts constantly went back and forth to Maggie during the investigation, and he wondered if it was because he saw elements of her in Grace Murphy. He didn't save either of them, but then, did they want to be saved? Could they have been saved? Hamilton asked himself.

He downed the remaining bubbles in his glass and squeezed his wife's hand. While tracking down Murphy, he had let his mind wander to the idea that Maggie had also suffered with mental health problems, and now he knew that was a certainty, not a possibility. She *had* suffered, *had* felt alone and *had* felt she had no one to turn to — just as Murphy did — and while the way they dealt with their pain was polar opposites, they ultimately both took their own lives. Although Murphy developed various personalities as a way of coping and his daughter harmed herself in the lead up to her death, was there really a difference when they were tortured as young teenagers?

'What about fostering?' he announced unexpectedly and turned to face Elizabeth.

She drew her head back and frowned. 'Where did that come from?'

'Well, you said you wanted to adopt … but if we're being honest, I don't know if I could replace Maggie.'

'Denis, it's not replacing her, it's—'

'Wait, hear me out.' Elizabeth nodded and he continued, 'Maybe replacement is the wrong word, but I know it would feel that way to me. But, you're right, there are so many kids out there who have faced tragedy in their already young lives; be it bullying, or abuse, or the death of a loved one.

It's those kids who need the most help. It's those kids who grow up to be confused and lost adults in a world that is crying out for them to turn to the dark side.'

A small giggle escaped Elizabeth's lips. 'I feel like I'm speaking to the Detective Inspector now.'

He smiled, a rush of warmth and excitement fluttered in his stomach. 'Maybe you are … but that's only because of what I've seen in my line of work. By the time we get to the criminals, it's too late to help them, either because they don't want to be helped or they literally can't be because of what they've done. It's frightening, the monsters I see every day in my job. But imagine those very people were given more of a chance when they were younger. Christ, not that I'm saying all foster children are potential criminals.'

His wife laughed again. 'Don't worry, I get what you mean … help those who have faced tragedy and maybe you set them up for a smoother ride in this world. You sound very passionate about it, Denis.'

'I actually didn't know I was,' he admitted. 'I'd also need to do a bit of research into the whole process of fostering, but I know the local councils are crying out for foster parents in London, especially for older children. So many couples want to adopt and foster babies, which I can understand, but we can't forget about the teenagers who need a safe place to live and people who can guide them before a permanent home is found for them.'

'I was not expecting this from you, Denis. Where's my sensible, no-nonsense and predictable husband gone? Perhaps the champers has gone to your head.'

Hamilton tutted. 'Less of that. I'm not predictable.'

'Okay, that was below the belt … grouchy is probably a better word.'

His mouth gaped open and closed like a fish out of water until Elizabeth erupted into hysterics that now did attract the attention of the tourists around them.

'Calm down, I'm kidding,' she said and raised her glass. 'Here's to our future, Denis.'

He clinked his empty flute with his wife's and smiled as she delicately sipped the remaining drink. Hamilton would never really understand why his daughter committed suicide, but after everything that had happened this weekend, he finally felt he could find some peace and finally write the next chapter of his story.

THE END

Acknowledgements

Firstly, I would just like to say a huge thank *you* for finishing this book. I know the themes of alter-personalities and dreamlike states can be difficult for some people to read about, however I've learnt a lot about dissociative identity disorder while writing this book and I wanted to share that with you all. I hope you found something in the story that you could enjoy.

When my grandad passed away, I felt at times that I had become two people. There was the Tara I presented to the world — I smiled at people and told them I was fine, so not to make them feel uncomfortable with my grieving — and there was the Tara who cried at night and grew an unnecessary temper with my family. It was then I started to wonder about our personalities and how fragile our minds really are. And so, the DI Hamilton series began with *In the Shadows*, and I hope this book delivers more answers for you.

Mum, for your support, friendship, time and encouragement, I will never be able to thank you enough.

Acknowledgements are always hard to write, especially as it seems the list of people and groups to thank grows with each book — and I never want to miss anyone. But to all my dear friends who have helped me get here, and to all the online book clubs and readers who have championed what I do, I salute you and thank you from the bottom of my heart. Special mention must be made to all those in Crime Fiction Addict, Crime Book Club, THE Book Club and Book Connectors online Facebook groups.

Bloodhound Books, thank you for continuing to believe in DI Denis Hamilton and publishing the series. The whole team — Betsy, Fred, Sumaira, Alexina, Sarah and Heather, and all the authors in the kennels — are true gems. To my editor, proofreaders, Katherine Everett and Maria Lee, huge thanks for helping to make this book the best it could be.

To my JLBX coffee crew (despite never drinking a cup of coffee in my life!) you are always there when I need you. A fierce group of women who could run this world. Thank you for always believing in me, for the banter and for the good vibes only.

Finally, to Daniel and Leo, who kept themselves entertained, ate without me and stayed quiet when I needed peace to write this book, I love you both.

35970641R00132

Printed in Poland
by Amazon Fulfillment
Poland Sp. z o.o., Wrocław

THE GREAT SECRET

A Time-Twisting Tale

THE GREAT SECRET

A Time-Twisting Tale

Told by

Alex Y. Ferguson

Cover images:
Top: Armada Portrait of Elizabeth I at Woburn Abbey
George Gower - Oil on Panel, circa 1588

Bottom: Queen Elizabeth I at Tilbury, 1588
Alfred Kingsley Lawrence - Oil On Canvas, 1938

ISBN: 9798730769748

PublishNation
www.publishnation.co.uk

*This book is dedicated to
my great-granddaughter Tameeyah.
When she can read well enough,
she'll find herself in her own book.*

BEGINNING

The man and the girl were singing as the motorcycle combo turned into where a gate would've been if the combo hadn't removed it on an earlier occasion. The combo rattled round the Council house to cough into silence by the kitchen door. The couple finished the chorus and applauded themselves. In the neighbouring garden, Mr. Stanley shook his head. In her kitchen, Mrs. Stanley smiled to herself. The young couple tumbled into the house.

The young man set down his saddlebags & guitar case. The girl rattled a biscuit tin triumphantly and set it down on the kitchen table..

"This is the best day we've ever had," the girl announced, "The Saturday market is streets better than Thursday."

The girl filled the kettle and put it to the gas.

"I agree. I was in splendid voice."

"Like Donald Duck you were!"

"I have no idea who this person is, but I very much doubt if he ever sang Memories better than I did this morning. I saw girls with tears in their eyes."

The girl shook her head at him affectionately.

"You really can't take teasing, can you? You are my blackbird, my thrush, my robin redbreast! I too had tears in my eyes. You awoke every broken heart in the market."

"Can't I be your sky lark too?"

"And my ostrich! God, it takes a lot of feathers to soothe your plumage! Content now?"

The young man turned to the biscuit tin, but the girl forestalled him.

"Counting the takings can wait. Though it's a helluva weight."

The kettle whistled and the young man was startled.

"The kettle whistles a dozen times a day and still you jump."

"It's not natural."

1

"It's the great great grandchild of Heron's steam engine. You must know about that. Come on!"

The young man regarded the kettle suspiciously. The girl picked up the tray.

"Hot tea. Loads of sugar. Iced buns. What more would we want?"

They were attacked as they entered the sitting room by two men who threw them to the floor. The tray clattered across the room to strike the paraffin heater, shedding pot, tea, milk, loads of sugar, iced buns and happiness. Both the man and the girl were clubbed to unconsciousness. They were bound, gagged and hooded in less than two minutes. Their assailants waited for instructions from the pearly white bearded man who had planned and watched the attack. His younger companion had flinched at the violence. To the Stanleys the men would've appeared to be dressed for an historical carnival. Lord Francis Walsingham would have been deeply offended. His companion was much celebrated at Court for the shapeliness of his legs.

"What would you suggest is the best measure to ensure loyalty?"

The young man couldn't take his eyes from the blood dripping from the girl's neck.

"You have no answer? The best measure to ensure loyalty, sir, is to separate a man from whomsoever he has a deep attachment."

He poked the unconscious body with a fine calfskin shoe.

"Isn't that so, Master Marlowe? Sometimes known as Kit Marlon. Scribbler of plays. Favoured by the common herd. Loyal agent of her Majesty. I will ensure he carries out the Queen's commission."

"And the girl?"

"To ensure the rascal will behave."

He looked around at the simple, mismatched furniture.

"We have wasted enough time. Let us be away!"

The two retainers picked up the bodies and the party vanished.

ONE

Standing at the window, Mary Prior stared out into the farmyard to say, "I don't see what's so fascinating about our old barn."

Her husband James came from the scullery after washing his hands in anticipation of lunch.

"And he asked if he could look at the barn?"

"Decent enough man. Could do with a haircut. Nice voice. What else could I say, but yes, when my husband comes for his dinner. Mebbes I should've asked why."

"I shall have a chat with him."

"What about your dinner?"

"It won't spoil in the oven for two minutes."

The visitor turned at the sound of the farmer's boots and smiled at him. Jim Prior caught at a memory.

"Father did say you'd turn up one day."

"Is it Jimmy?"

Jim Prior smiled to say, "That's the old man. I prefer Jim.

"I was very fond of your father. A most generous man."

"He told me you saved his life."

"It was nothing."

"It is to me!"

"He's not still with you?"

"Trinity churchyard. But you've weathered well."

The visitor showed an intelligent face, bright eyes, neat beard and a tangle of dark hair.

"All due to wine, women and song."

With some effort, the two of them opened the heavy door and Jim Prior stood aside to allow his visitor to enter. They looked up to marvel at the skilful configuration of local oak that upheld the roof throughout the centuries.

"My father said it must be three, four hundred years old?"

"He's not far out. In sixteen twelve, an actor called Ned Alleyn and his company of London actors played Christopher

3

Marlowe's new play, Downfall of the Tyrant, here in your barn for the Duke of Norfolk and his guests."

"You do surprise me! What was they doing hereabouts?"

"They had become a Travelling Company by necessity of King James issuing warrants threatening to hang, draw and quarter every man jack of the Company."

"Sounds serious. Why would he do that?"

"He believed they were lampooning him. A dangerous thing to do. Gingr Jimmy was easily offended."

"Were they?"

"Who am I to say? There were those who thought King James a tyrant."

"And the Duke of Norfolk?"

"Norfolk was no fan of our Scottish sovereign. When the Duke learnt the Company was here, he demanded the play be performed for him and overpaid in gold. Which gesture saved Alleyn's Company."

"How come?"

"The King accepted the gold. And a disclaimer so cleverly scribed by Marlowe to read either yae or nay. Which further convinced the humble plebeians that Ginger Jimmy was indeed the Tyrant."

Jim Prior laughed and cried, "And this all went on here?"

"If only these walls could talk."

They looked around on the assembled farm machinery.

The two men approached the rear of the great barn where stood a small cottage built of bales of barley straw.

The visitor said, "I'm sorry. This is going to take some shifting."

Jim Prior laughed to say, "Ten minutes."

He walked away and returned riding a forklift. Above the noise of the engine, he called, "Ten minutes. If you want to time it."

The visitor showed empty wrists and the farmer began to rebuild the cottage two bales-width from its present site. The visitor removed the last two bales. They stood together to regard the machine revealed.

It was a battered, shabby 1935 1000 cc BSA 612 motorcycle combination.

4

"Nineteen thirty-five. They don't make them like they used to."

"But that's more than seventy years old!"

His visitor surveyed the bike with joy & reverence. Jim Prior shook his head in disbelief.

"You're not gona ride that?"

"Of course! It's a BSA. Nobody ever built a better engine. HC593. York City Police."

"Better your neck than mine."

They wheeled the machine out into the sunshine and cleaned away the scruff of years and barley straw. Mrs. Prior came out onto the farmhouse doorstep to watch.

"Enough! The wind'll sweep the debris away. I must be on the road."

"If it starts."

"Oh, ye of little faith!"

The visitor tried to kick start the engine. He tried until he could kick no more. Jim Prior dismantled the carburettor and Mrs. Prior provided hot sweet tea. Petrol was siphoned from the Priors' car and the motorcycle combo was run round & around the yard until the men were breathless. Jim Prior tried to kickstart the machine without success.

Mrs. Prior came to have her photograph taken sitting on the bike. She slipped as she dismounted and kicked the starter. The engine burst into life and Mary Prior was awarded a kiss from a stranger. After which he danced around the yard while Jim Prior rode his wife cautiously out from the yard and twice around the paddock without knocking over any bee hives.

The visitor thanked his hosts, mounted Apollo's Chariot and rode out from the farmyard into the wider, wickeder world.

Mary Prior did offer a bed for the night, but the visitor pleaded, "I would wish to do so gladly, but I have somewhere to be."

And left it at that.

The Priors were sorry to hear the old engine fade into the distance.

"That girl who came the other week looking for him.."

"Why didn't you tell him?"

"Slipt my mind, I guess. Never mind. She'll find him."

"What a strange man," mused Mary.

"My father thought the world of him."

"He seems very young."

"Did I ever tell you why?"

"I don't think so."

"These thugs turned up to rob the house. Dad wouldn't give up what they had. They set about to beat him and would've killed him, but luckily our friend was sleeping in the barn. He came to see what was wrong and took on the four of them. He was going to hang them and had the nooses set up. Those bastards were snivelling, weeping, begging for their lives. Dad persuaded him not to execute them That's why he gave him the old bike."

They'd scarcely entered the house before Mary said, "There's two men in the yard, Jim!"

Her husband took a look and said, "What's going on? Some sort of carnival?"

The tall man was dressed in black with tricorn & stockinged legs. The only distinction were the silver buckles on his shoes. Jim Prior's first thought was of a priest. The younger man was dressed in doublet & hose with a cloak and feather in his hat. A silver decorated belt carried a sword in sheath.

Puzzled, Jim said, "Mebbes they're collecting for someat."

"I don't like them. Be careful, Jim."

"Can I help you, gentlemen?" Jim called as he crossed the yard. As he approached he smiled to say, "I like the getup."

The tall man said, "We are looking for a friend."

A tiny voice in Jim's head bade caution.

"Nobody here but us chickens."

"We know he is here. We were told he would be so."

"Only my wife and myself, sir."

To Jim's surprise the tall man said, "You are uttering falsehoods, fellow. He is here. Or he has been here. I have urgent need to speak with him."

"I'm sorry. We haven't seen anybody in the last week, but the egg man. You'd find him at Shaldon Lesser. Everybody knows him."

"I'll ask you once more, fellow. Have you him hidden here? If he is gone, where has he gone?"

Mrs. Prior arrived to seize her husband's hand.

"Come away, Jim! We'll phone the police. So, you'd best be gone."

The older man bowed without a hint of sincerity.

"Madam, I'm trying to persuade your husband to answer a simple question."

"He doesn't have to answer your questions."

"Mary," said Jim urgently, "go back in the house."

"Then perhaps I should ask you the same question.."

Jim Prior interrupted to advise, "Don't answer him, Mary. Go back in the house."

"Take no notice of your husband. It would be better for you both if you answered honestly. You have had a visitor. A man accused of sorcery. Is he in the house? If he has departed where is he bound?"

"The last person we've seen this week is the egg man. He comes to collect our eggs for the packing station. But nobody else has been anywhere near us. Except you, of course."

The sword blade struck faster than a viper and Mary Prior fell slowly, clutching for her husband's hand. Jim Prior cried out in despair and knelt by his dying wife.

"Will you answer my question?"

"Sod you!" cried Jim Prior. He looked down at the rapier blade protruding from his chest, tried to stand up and fell dying over his wife's corpse.

*

Bell Harry was chiming, but the young woman wasn't listening. The night was moonless dark and the rain was spiteful, beating on her hood & cloak. Between flaring torches at rare intervals the street was cellar-black.

She had little sense of time, always working until Noah said, "Ye can go now, Annie." She would fill the empty tankards at the bar before she found her cloak. Marianne would walk away, but Annie kept the good will of the drinkers whereas Marianne didn't care.

Tonight felt different. There was a lessening of footfalls until finally there was only one pair of footsteps behind her.

The night seemed darker & more foreboding. She noticed there were no footmen below the rain-spitting torches at the big houses, awaiting their masters' return. They knew her and bantered with her. She felt safe with their presence. But it was later than she had thought and later was more dangerous. When she stopped to listen the footsteps stopped. Where the walkway was not paved it was difficult to distinguish the footfalls. Thankfully, Annie stepped into the familiar alley and ran to the faithful torch above the boarding house door. She hammered on the heavy oak.

Her follower appeared in the alley mouth. He was not tall, but squat, with heavy shoulders, cloak & hood glistening in the rain. He raised a long blade.

Gathering her courage, Annie cried, "Leave me alone!"

The man shook his head.

"Please! I has done nothing to offend."

"The Father would disagree, Hannah."

Her murderer came at her faster than she could've imagined.

She had barely time to bring the short crossbow up from inside her cloak and tug the trigger. The iron bolt struck her assailant in the neck, burying itself to the fletching. The man looked astonished, opening his mouth to protest when a veritable flood of blood from mouth & neck silenced him. He was dead before his skull rang on the cobbles. Silence screamed. The rain beat on his cloak & hood. The crimson river began to invade the cobbles. Annie cried at the corpse, "I niver meant it. It were Noah give me the bow. I didn't want t'take it!"

She shook her head, staring at the unmoving corpse. Then she heard a car door close and the engine fire.

When she looked down there was no corpse, no flood of blood. Anna was holding her handbag, not a crossbow. The car passed, tyres hissing through the rainwater. The driver flashed her and she raised a hand in response. To calm herself she spoke aloud as her tutors had taught.

"The correct term for cross bow is arbalest. For this useless piece of information we are blessed."

Her frantic heart began to slow: her breathing to relax. With clumsy hands she found her key ring, fumbled to insert the key and opened the door. Anna stepped into the hallway, shutting out night, rain & death. She found she was still trembling and took a deep breath to call up the stairs.

"Only me!"

She dropped her keys on the hallstand, shook and hung up her coat & beret to examine her image in the mirror. She wiped away the rain tears. On shaky legs, Anna mounted the stairs to the landing. In the sitting room, she found Carole enthroned on the couch, propped up with cushions, watching PBS America & eating an apple. Immediately, she felt calmer.

It was Carole's particular talent, creating calm. When they had succeeded in getting a grumpy coach driver to make an unscheduled stop at Houndhough Farm, he had driven off without releasing their luggage. They realised this loss as the coach dwindled to vanish down the valley road. Carole had said, "Oh, dear, I'd planned to feed the chickens in my corduroy breeks. I was to ask you to take a photo to show I'm not frightened of chickens any more. Would you have minded?"

"Not at all! But why the corduroy?"

"To frighten the chickens."

They had both laughed. Frosty February at Houndhough became much less frosty.

Carole switched off the television to ask, "Went the day well?"

Anna took a deep breath.

"Despite Horrible Horace's calamitous handling of the lighting, I shall be Peter Pan again tomorrow. And if I can't find another gig, I'll be the frightful creature forever more."

"How was the delectable McLeich?"

"Fell over his sword, but retained his credentials. Oh! Michael fell from the rigging."

"Ow! That put a dent in the proceedings!"

"No, Wendy covered for him. She was brilliant. One in a million."

"You've never mentioned her before."

"Tameeyah Wells. But she lives and dies as Wendy Darling. When she was at the Barn in Liverpool she lived Jenny, a petty thief. The director had to keep returning stuff to the cast."

"No way!"

9

"Oh, yes! But she's a good kid. Very quick-witted. She adlibbed a little scene with Michael, dusting him down, counting arms, legs, head. 'Til he got his breath back. Very funny. The audience roared."

"Well done!"

"That's our Wendy! Or Tammie. Or Tameeyah."

"And Jenny?"

"God forbid!"

Anna walked to the window to make sure there was no dead thug lying in the roadway with a crossbow bolt through his neck. The street, lined with parked cars, was silent under the fluorescent lighting.

"How'd your day go?"

"Don't ask."

"Bad, eh?"

"Worse! Dry rot. Wormy rafters. Mould. Failed damp course. Staircases that come away from the wall as you walk up. And the owners ignore every sign of distress. By their stupidity, wonderful historic houses that properly maintained would last for generations yet are in danger of being demolished because no one cares enough to save them."

"Wow! I've never heard you angry before."

"You, Anna, know nothing about our city. You're just passing through."

"That's not fair. I saw the board outside Fisk Row. *Under renovation by Truscott & Daughter.* Truscott. A wonderful name. Four hundred years ago the builder would have been Truscott. Are you by any chance?"

"Sorry to disappoint you. Dad borrowed the name. *Truscott & Son, Master Masons.* He thought it sounded trustworthy. At least it doesn't say *and Daughter B.A. Hons. History.* I can plaster a wall. And lay on gold leaf."

"Did you ever think you'd be patching up old houses?"

"I wanted to be an archaeologist. And we don't patch up old houses! We restore and renovate. We save the past for the future. Most people don't care."

They fell silent.

"Have we been having a row?"

10

"No! I apologise. I'm just passionate about what we do. My Dad's the same."

"I'd like to meet him someday."

"I wouldn't advise it. He never stops talking."

Anna laughed.

Carole offered, "Why don't you set the microwave at three minutes. Wait one minute. Take out the box. Eat the box."

"Thanks, Carole! You're too good to me."

Carole switched on the television.

Anna vanished into the kitchen as Carole called, "Did you know there've only been three American presidents you could describe as honest?"

Anna switched on the microwave

"As many as that? Amazing!"

"D'y'want to know who they were?"

"No! Please, no! I've spent the evening entertaining the British Public. I've been punished enough."

"No, you haven't! At least half the house would be Japanese."

Anna confessed, "I must admit they're pretty appreciative."

She brought her supper into the sitting room, hesitated and returned to the kitchen to fetch two bottles of beer from the fridge and then retraced her steps to fetch the bottle opener.

"Are you ever gona settle down?"

Anna plumped into the sofa, opened the bottles, gave one to Carole and drank deeply from her own, declaring, "Never! Like my dearest chum, Peter, I shall never grow old."

"A sure recipe for heartbreak."

"I didn't hear that."

Carole silenced the adverts to say, "When we're working we never know what we might find."

"I vote for a miser's hoard. You know how forgetful some misers are."

"Last month Jimmy called me out into the Elizabethan garden to see what they'd found."

Carole answered the unspoken question.

"A haven of peace where guests will relax, drinking tea in an Elizabethan garden."

11

"Oh, how wonderful! You must invite me one day. That sounds very much me.."

"Jimmy and Alan discovered the remains of a younger man and an old man. And two gardeners, housemen, labourers."

"Really?"

"Dumped in a hole to hide them. Not laid out with any respect. Drop a young gent in the pit. Drop the old gent on top of him. Add two commoners for good measure. Fill in the hole."

"If that's reality, I'll stick to the greasepaint."

"The archaeologists are on it now. Indications are late sixteenth century. Due to the soil some fabrics have survived. Two gentlemen and two labourers."

Anna interrupted to ask, "How do they know?"

"Gold buttons. An early pair of spectacles. Shoe buckles. It would appear they were killed and dumped into the hole where they were found. The young man had been strangled and the skull of the old man had been crushed."

They were both silent until Anna asked, "This was at Fisk Row?"

"No. We're also working on another site. What was once Boxborough Manor."

Anna couldn't resist interrupting.

"A Manor! Did Queen Elizabeth visit there? Sit in her own Elizabethan garden. Drinking tea. Did they have tea then?"

"This is serious stuff, Anna!"

"Sorry. I live in a world of fantasy. Pirates. Red Indians. Vengeful crocodiles. Sorry."

"Boxborough Manor. East of the city. On the bank of the Stour. Set in its own grounds. It's our biggest project ever. The intention is to create a luxury hotel while preserving the Elizabethan setting. But I'll be glad when we're out of it."

"Oh, why?"

"There's an odd feeling to the house. It's not welcoming. You might be working, painting a detail and you have the oddest feeling someone is watching you. But, of course, there isn't. But I'm not the only one who senses what I can only describe as the hostility of the house. The house doesn't want

12

us there. The girls have noticed, but not Jimmy or Alan. They'll work 'til late, but the girls won't."

"But you'll be out of it soon?"

"You look concerned. Don't worry! No monster is going to step out of a closet and eat me."

"I can be your bodyguard. Remember! I have a sword."

The women laughed and Carole brought two fresh bottles of beer from the kitchen.

"Can we forget the Manor and enjoy the Horror Channel, please?"

*

Carole switched off the television and took Anna's supper box and the bottles to the kitchen bin.

"D'y'need waking in the morning?"

"No. First call for noon. Let poor dogs lie."

Carole went down to the front door to push the bolts home.

On her return, Anna asked, "I wonder why they had to die. The hole would've needed to be dug first. It wasn't a quarrel over cards or a woman. They were invited to the house and then, to their surprise, set upon and murdered. Perhaps the elder gentleman was attacked and the young man came to his aid? Such gallantry costing him his life."

Carole offered, "Then you can understand how I won't be accepting any complimentary overnights when the new hotel opens."

*

Anna sat on her bed and listened to Carole singing as she prepared for bed. It was satisfying and real. When she stopped singing, Anna heard voices in the street. From the window she watched an entwined couple walk the pavement towards the river. The rain had stopped. She heard them laugh and felt she was intruding upon their happiness.

In the house almost opposite a light appeared at the bedroom window. Within minutes the light was extinguished as someone found their way back to bed. Much thanks for this relief. As

13

Anna was about to turn away a taxi passed and stopped. A man and woman exited. Anna heard the man say good night to the driver. The couple passed from her vision into the house. The street was silent.

The street lighting illuminated the cars, parked as tightly as sardines in a can. It was a sight Anna much respected. If she owned a car it'd need to be lifted into position by crane every evening and lifted out in the morning. How Carole achieved this without a crane she could only wonder at.

The street was silent, undisturbed, safe. There was no alley, no guttering torches, no shabby boarding house. There was no murderous thug. Anna returned to her bed, propping up the pillows and reaching for the script at her bedside as she lay down. The script was Christopher Marlowe's Midsummer Night's Dream. She began to read, praying to keep sleep at bay. For in that sleep, what dreams may come?

TWO

Dawn on the fresh green trees beckoned a sweet Summer morning. The day was beginning and life was waking. The old man and the youth coaxing the sheep from the pasture to cross the ancient road onto the farther pasture at the woodland edge hesitated. The erratic grumble of an old engine announced the approach of an antique motorcycle combination. The motorcycle slowed to a halt and the rider raised a glove in salute. The old man signalled his thanks.

The sheep began to flow as a woolly brook across the road into the safety of the fresh pasture. The old man and the dogs had their eyes on the sheep, but the boy was more engaged with the motorcycle combo and its rider. The man at the handlebars was tall, dark-eyed with overlong midnight hair spurning a safety helmet. If asked to describe him the boy might've said pirate. The old man called to him.

"Are thee with uzz, John?"

The youth flushed as the dogs rebuked him too, recalling him to the last rebellious ewes that had turned back into the old pasture. If lost it would take the morning to catch them. With Tess and Tops, the youth retrieved them, apologising to the rider on the motorcycle as the old man stood by to close the gate on the last lingerers. They stood together at the latched gate, watching the young man kick the engine into life and slowly move away, gathering speed.

The old man said, "If ye work ya fingers to the bone and save every penny ye earn, thee can buy thasel a flying death trap like yonder and kill theesel within a week. Let's hope one of those days is a Sataday so thee can dazzle the girls riding up and down Ullington High Street, afore ending up in Co-op window."

The youth smiled, watching the progress of the old motorcycle combination up the arrow-straight Roman road and started to say something when the motorcycle vanished.

"God's sake!" the old man cried.

His grandson, John, was already sprinting up the road to where the motorcycle combination had vanished. When the old man reached him, the youth complained, "There's nowt! Nowt at all."

The road was clean. Not a smear of a skidding wheel. The verges and ditches were empty. The trees and hedges were undamaged.

"I don't understand," said the old man.

"Gone."

"If ye say aliens, don't thee come home to breakfast with me."

"I wasn't saying that."

"Then uzz says nowt, 'less somebody else says someat. And then we just lizzen."

"But I won't forget what I saw."

"I weren't asking."

When John drove the quad into Frazer's service station, the old man asked, "What now?"

John didn't answer, but went into the shop. When he returned he said, "The man filled up here."

"So what?"

"I need to know he's real."

The old man shrugged acceptance, but when the youth pulled into the 24/7 Eat Now, he protested, "What's the point, John?"

"There was a motorbike and it vanished."

When he returned, he said, "He ate here. They remember the motorbike."

"Satisfied now?"

"We saw what we saw, Grandad. That's all I needed to know."

*

The open road lay before him. The sun edging above the trees promised a sunny Summer's day. The rugged engine of the motorbike combo was rattling happily with just a hint of arthritis. In the mirror the rider could see the old man and the

16

youth standing at the gate watching his progress. Then the machine hit the invisible barrier, throwing him forward and ending up in the rose bay willow herb. When the man recovered his senses he found it was raining steadily and the sky was sullen grey. As he struggled to pull the machine back onto the road he stopped, sniffed the air and fled into the neighbouring copse. Over the rise, marching towards him, filling the road, was a Roman legion.

"God rot the eccentricities of Time! Forever mindless bloody chaos!"

The ranks marched steadily, oblivious of the rain, each man carrying a mountain on his back. At the head of the column marched the Honour Guard escorting the legion Eagle. A horseman galloped alongside the ranks and stopped to stare at the strange machine lying in the willow herb.

"Please!" begged a desperate rider, loud enough for no more than his own ears, "Please, ride on! The Legion has many a mile yet to march. The boys won't be happy if you keep them standing in the rain."

The horseman dismounted and its biker groaned. The curious officer drew closer. In desperation the rider picked up a stone and threw it at the approaching figure. By mischance, the stone struck the officer's helmet. He cried out, remounted and rode at the trees, shouting his anger. There was nowhere for the unfortunate to hide. When the horse thundered into the willow herb with its rider waving his sword, the man sprang up under a storm of dead leaves, screaming, "I hold the Fates bound fast in iron chains, And with my hand turn Fortune's wheel about and sooner shall the sun fall from his sphere than Tamburlaine be slain or overcome!"

The horse reared, spilling its rider who fell, striking his head on a tree stump. He lay confused and the narrator capered about before him, cursing the poor fellow with violent gestures, crying out, "I know, sir, what it is to kill a man. It works remorse of conscience in me. I take no pleasure to be murderous, nor care for blood when wine will quench my thirst. Therefore, go! Go, I say! Go nurse your sore head and trouble me no more!"

17

With satanic gestures the curse was awesome and the horseman regained his steed and rode away soberly. Kit watched as he joined the endless column. Embarrassed, he spoke to no one. It took hours beyond count for the legion to pass, legionaries, auxiliaries, cavalry, stores in countless wagons, camp followers and finally the cavalry escort as rearguard.

The motorbike rider crouched in the rain under a tree as he dared not approach his machine. Finally he watched the last horses of the rearguard vanish and a shivering figure dragged the combo onto the road.

"And later years they complain of traffic jams!" he complained to the unfeeling sky.

He dispatched an earnest prayer to all the gods of Rome he could remember before trying to start the machine. The engine sprang to life, proving prayer works. He rode forward cautiously. There was no barrier to his progress. To whatever gods might be listening, he complained, "What do I say to excuse my lack of diligence? A Legion en route to confront Boadicea denied me the road? Who would believe that?"

*

Anna was in the pit of the New Theatre, amidst the enchanted groundlings stilled by the magic of the great actor, Ned Alleyn, in full voice. She knew she was watching Kit Marlowe's play, Tamburlaine. She had seen the drama last year at the new Globe. But now she was overwhelmed, watching the original company led by Ned Alleyn.

A dark-bearded man, with a mop of midnight hair, was sitting on the edge of the stage, swinging his legs, watching the audience. Anna knew immediately it was Christopher Marlowe, although she had only ever seen a poor print of the playwright. To Anna's surprise he saw her and varying emotions flooded his face. He dropped from the stage to push his way towards her.

Anna, in fright, turned away to push against the crowd. He was too quick for her and caught her startled arm. He began to say, "Let's find silence where we may." But his voice was lost in the tumult acclaiming Ned Alleyn's performance. With a firm grip of her arm he pulled Anna, struggling, out into the open street.

She protested, crying, "You're hurting my arm!" He did not relax his grip. The playwright held Anna against the theatre wall to demand, "Who are you, girl? Why do you haunt me?"

The explosion that broke his grasp was Carole, thoughtlessly slamming the street door as she departed on her quest to rebuild Elizabethan Canterbury. Anna stared at the shadowed ceiling of her room, struggling to recapture fragments of the dream.

"Why do you haunt me?" she repeated.

Before she showered Anna went down to the front door and tugged bolts, top & bottom, securely home. It was a childish gesture, but she found it reassuring. As she ate breakfast the telephone rang and she jumped as a startled hare.

"This is not true Peter Pan behaviour!"

The telephone had stopped ringing by the time she decided she was brave enough to answer.

"You have to do better. Now you'll worry it was the offer of an audition."

She consulted the framed picture of Carole's grandfather above the telephone table. He had been a sweet-looking boy with a cheery grin. There was something mindful of Carole in that grin.

"Another calming presence?"

And brave. With medals to prove it. He had even jumped out of aeroplanes, which made Anna wince. On the table was the locked glass-faced casket that held his Webley Mark 4 revolver with which he had forced surrender on a vital blockhouse full of over-armed SS soldiers.

"I'm not asking you to jump out of aeroplanes. But I think we need help, girl."

Anna rang the theatre and spoke to Gillian.

"No, I'm absolutely fine. It's a family matter. It's time Melanie had a chance to shine anyway. I've been there. I know what it's like. So, please, let Melanie do the matinee and I'll be in sparkling fresh to play the evening. Thank you! I owe you."

*

19

Anna studied John Hazlitt's degrees & awards that speckled the reception room wall. There was a photograph of him in university robe with a ridiculous mortarboard precariously balanced on auburn hair. There was amusement in the eyes that suggested he was aware of his ridiculous garb. Among his graduating class he didn't appear tall, but there was an air of quiet confidence about him. Anna was turning away when she realised he was standing among the young women; almost as if he'd arrived late for the ceremony or was unconscious of gender.

To his secretary she said, "Is he any good?"

She smiled to say, "Good at what? I understand he plays cricket and enjoys squash. He's kind to his mother and dogs. As to his ability as a psychologist, I can only judge by his appointment book. Where you only appear as you caught his interest and not Mister Baldwin's choice to inject himself with a poisonous substance rather than attend."

"Boy!" cried Anna, "Whatever your salary, it ain't enough."

*

"You're a serving girl called Annie living in the sixteenth or early seventeenth century. The night of the attack did you know where you were?"

"Canterbury."

"How'd you know?"

"Bell Harry was chiming."

"You're a Canterbury girl serving in a tavern. What d'y'do?"

"I serve drinks to customers and clean the bar. And anything Noah tells me t'do, I do."

"What's the name of the tavern?"

"The Ark"

"So, there has to be a Noah."

"The customers call him Noah. I call him Noah."

"Who drinks there?"

"Men. Labourers. Alcoholics. A few craftsmen."

"No women?"

"Only prostitutes. Noah tolerates them because they bring in the men, but any knockabout and they're out."

"Such as?"

"Sally cut another girl."

"What happened to her?"

"Noah sewed her up, fed her and sent her packing."

"And Sally?"

"She was back in a month. I think she got round Noah."

Hazlitt paused to ask, "How long have you worked at the Ark?"

"Don't know. I suppose Annie would say forever."

Hazlitt added a note to his page.

"The landlord. Noah. Can you describe him?"

"About fifty. Grey beard. Strong. Patch on his left eye. Pretty rough. But a kind man. He might have a thing for me, but that happens. He's never said a wrong word or laid a hand on me."

"What's his wife like?"

"Marjorie. She died three years back. A bad summer for cholera."

"Can you think of any reason why that man might wish to kill you last night?"

"Kill me, no. Rape me, yes, I suppose. That's why Noah makes me carry the bow. Just to scare."

"Had you seen him before? Say, in the Ark?"

"No. But he was no different to the men who drink there."

"He said something to you. Tell me again."

"He said, 'The father would disagree, Hannah.' But that's wrong. I'm Annie at the Ark. Who's Hannah? Was he after some other girl?"

John Hazlitt put aside his notebook & pen. He pressed the button on his side table to say, "I think we deserve coffee. Don't you?"

"Please!"

*

As they waited for coffee, Hazlitt asked, "Do you like Canterbury?"

21

"I love it. Canterbury is Marlowe's home town. Where else should an actor be?"

"London?"

"I've been and will be again."

"And you're working?"

"I'm playing Peter Pan at the Queen's. For the tourists."

"That's not Marlowe."

"Peter Pan is a big favourite with the Japanese visitors. They can find Faustus at the Bernhardt, but they fill every seat at every performance for Peter and Wendy."

"You appear so young. The perfect Peter Pan. How old are you, Anna?"

*

The coffee arrived to save Anna from answering. She sipped her coffee and Hazlitt offered, "I have had some experience of people who claim to have travelled in time. A few I believe because there are authenticated cases of time walking, but fantasists' stories change and too often they claim to have met historical figures. There's little kudos to be gained working as a barmaid in a modest inn in Canterbury. Unless our national playwright is a regular."

Anna couldn't resist laughing.

"He'd have to be dragged in."

"If you agree I'd like to investigate your story further."

"I'd like to find out if I'm really walking in Time. I want it to stop. What if one time I can't come back?"

"I can understand your concern. So, is there a pub in Canterbury called the Ark? Has there ever been a pub in Canterbury called the Ark with a Noah at the helm? If there is or has been, that's where we should begin."

THREE

Carole had barely sat down at her desk to open her screen when Joe Randolph appeared smiling before her.

"Carole! Do you know, my dear, whenever something tricky comes up at Truscott, we immediately turn to you?"

"Don't lie to me. You spoke to my father and he said, send Carole."

"Yes."

Carole groaned.

"This is the first time in weeks I've come into the office."

"We've missed you."

"Don't waste the charm. I need to review what Padstone is proposing in stained glass for the landing windows for Fisk Row. I've been promising him for weeks."

"There's a difference of opinion about panelling in the lower passage."

"Let me guess. Boxborough?"

"I know you don't like the house."

"I'll get it over it. When do they want me there?"

*

Ned Alleyn shook the sleeping shoulder of his friend Kit Marlowe who muttered, "Away with you, Ned. I'm dying."

Alleyn sat down heavily on the makeshift cot and pulled down the blanket.

"You may indeed die, Kit. If you do not attend the summons."

Kit opened his eyes and stared at his oppressor.

"You should not be permitted to awaken anyone from their slumber, Ned. You have a face that extinguishes hope on first sight. Leave me be!"

Kit Marlowe tugged up the blanket and turned away. Ned Alleyn stood to take hold of the cot rail and tipped his friend to the floor. Kit kicked at his oppressor who caught an ankle and dragged the unwilling awakened from the tangle of the cot. Kit surrendered and sat up.

"Ned, I have had a very bad night."

"You drink with actors and scribblers. What else may you expect?"

"A cannon has exploded in my head and my belly is a cauldron of fire. Have pity and leave me here to die."

Alleyn took the jug from the washstand and poured cold water over Marlowe. Kit shook his head, spluttered and wiped his face with the bed robe.

"What are you trying to tell me, Ned?",

"You have a missive from the Queen. Are you not close to her, a most cherished adviser?"

Kit Marlowe laughed and shook his head.

"The virgin queen? Ned, you do not know our Elizabeth. She is a sour shrew, a heartless tyrant who will turn on you in an instant if it pleases her. She sends her lovers to the gallows or the axe. Makes her own rules. She will lift her robe to her ankles, piss on a marble floor and smile at those about her. Not because she must, but because she wants to shock."

"I'm not listening. I have climbed the stairs to your stinking chamber because you have a missive from her Majesty."

Ned Alleyn offered the sealed paper and Kit seized it.

"It's from Walsingham."

"It has the Queen's crest."

Kit Marlowe broke the seal and read the message.

"He has a mission for me. I must attend today."

"You must find a clean shirt. A blind man would refuse that rag. And washing your face might help."

"Why cannot I, a simple scribbler be left in peace with ink and quill?"

"Because some time ago you sold your soul to Sir Francis Walsingham, Spymaster to her Majesty. You are kin to your Faustus."

More kindly, he added, "I'll bring you a glass of brandy."

Descending the stairs, Ned Alleyn found Dickie Burbage at the landing window, catching & pulling wings off flies.

24

"I'll have him speak louder, Dickie. I wouldn't want you to miss a word."

"I tell you this most sincerely, Master Alleyn, that man is a danger to this Company."

"That man is the finest playwright in England. There's none to match him. Shall I strike you from the Company? There are many clamouring to be a player."

"I repeat only what is common knowledge. Marlowe is wading ever deeper into dark waters. I fear he will bring us all down."

"Then attend to your own business, Dickie. And spend less time in Gomorrah. Your breath would stun a bear."

*

The long table in the Historic Documents boardroom was spread with maps, paper and vellum scraps. Hazlitt sat at one end with magnifying glass and reading lamp, scanning a faded vellum. Anna was working her way through a stack of documents the custodian had chosen for her that might mention the Ark: legal disputes, property matters, common gossip and reports of trials.

They were fortunate the custodian, Mrs. Dainfield, was immediately entranced by their search and enthusiastically joined them, providing a host of maps and documents. When Anna commented on this, the lady said, "In Canterbury we never throw anything away."

Anna, new to research, found herself diverted from the search for the Ark into a cattle market dispute that ended in a stampede and a herder falling under the stampede to survive without injury to his person and the robbery of a jeweller whose children were murdered before he had finally disclosed his treasure trove.

"What sort of father is that?"

Hazlitt raised his head to say, "Time flies. Don't let anything divert you from your search."

"Sorry!"

But the next document concerning the burning of heretics stole her attention. It was a faded paper relating to the burning

25

at the stake of Master Henry Radbrack & his wife Dora as accused & found guilty of heresy.

"Whereas at their house others conspired, only the Radbracks were taken by the Reeve and brought before the Ecclesiastical Court. Where they were found guilty & by command of her Majesty, Queen Mary, condemned to be burnt at the stake. The frantic behaviour of the heretics occasioned much merriment among the populace attending. The dwelling of the heretics, the tavern known as the Ark will be put up for sale by public auction, proceeds to the Cathedral Treasury."

The hair on the back of Anna's neck stood up and she struggled to breathe. She read the declaration through again and called, "Doctor? I think.."

Hazlitt looked up with one finger on the map before him and magnifying glass poised to strike.

"I hadn't realised it was so late. You must go. Your audience awaits."

Anna began to read the announcement aloud and Hazlitt interrupted.

"Queen Mary. Known as Bloody Mary. Probably more than three hundred burnings in her short reign. She was trying to restore the kingdom to the Roman Catholic Church. Sucks boo to her Daddy. She failed."

Anna waited until he had finished and returned his attention to the map. She continued to read aloud, "The frantic behaviour of the heretics occasioned much merriment among the populace attending. The dwelling of the heretics, the tavern known as the Ark will be put up for sale by public auction, proceeds to the Cathedral Treasury."

Hazlitt shot up as if he'd been shot.

"Good God!"

He galloped the length of the table faster than an excited schoolboy.

"Show me, please!"

Anna handed over the faded document to trembling hands. Hazlitt read the announcement. Anna watched his lips moving.

"Splendid! If there ever was any doubt about your veracity, which I never shared, here is the simple truth! The Ark existed!"

"But we don't know where."

"We'll find it. But we mustn't tell anyone of our good fortune."

Anna laughed.

"It's not a secret surely!"

"You'd be surprised how many would doubt you. So we stay mum. Okay?"

Anna nodded her agreement.

"My lips are sealed."

"Now, back to work!"

"Isn't that enough?"

"You search for notice of the auction. I will continue to search the streets for a pub called the Ark."

They worked steadily until six o'clock with no further success. Mrs. Dainfield came to remind them by her presence that it was beyond closing time.

"Have you had any success in your quest, doctor?"

Anna avoided Hazlitt's eye.

"Sadly no. May we come back another time?"

"Of course."

Anna and Hazlitt carefully folded or rolled the manuscripts & maps. They accepted the custodian's assurance she or a colleague would return the material to their showcases or storage. The doctor thanked Mrs. Dainfield for her invaluable assistance. The impressive door closed behind our heroes and they stood mildly triumphant in the late sunshine of Broad Street.

"Would you like to go for a drink?"

"Sorry! I must off to work. If I'm not in early, Gillian begins to worry."

"Perhaps I might buy a ticket and enjoy your performance?"

"Please don't. Your suggestion is death to any performance. The last thing any actor wants is someone out there who's come to enjoy their performance."

"But your audience?"

"Mostly Japanese. A wonderful audience. They come to enjoy themselves. If I tripped over a bucket they'd think it in the script and applaud my acrobatic recovery."

Had Anna and John Hazlitt remained in the hallway after the front door was closed, they would've been much confused. The apparition that was Mrs. Dainfield faded to nothing as the closing of the door echoed loudly in the hallway. The custodian, Mrs. Dainfield, appeared from a doorway on the left and regarded the empty hallway with some concern. She came to the front door and checked it was both locked and bolted. Mrs. Dainfield stood for a moment in puzzlement and called out twice, "Professor Parkinson?" Receiving no reply, she returned to her office.

At supper she amused her husband by relating the latest curious happening in the ancient building.

"I know you don't believe me, Arnold."

"I always believe you, my dear. But it is my earthy nature to baulk at any notion of the supernatural."

"Today someone or something went out the front door when I was the only person in the building."

The good man stopped eating to recite, "As I was going up the stair, I met a man who wasn't there. He wasn't there again today. I wish to God he'd go away."

"I wish you wouldn't, Arnold! You frighten me!"

"Apologies, my dear, but perhaps you should come home when the rest of the staff does?"

When the first flame flickered into life among the maps and documents on the boardroom table there was no human eye to raise the alarm. When the security system sprang into action and dowsed the fire, it was too late. The fate of Master Henry Radbrack & his wife Dora was idle ashes.

*

Gillian was delighted when her lead arrived at the theatre early and in the brightest of moods. They sat together in the office, drinking coffee and eating sandwiches made by Gillian's devoted slave, Eddie.

"How was Melanie?"

28

"She was fine, but she isn't my Peter. That wonderful, fantastical, sad, lost boy! So frightened of life! So eager to twist the world about him to the shape of his own cruel illusion. A boy who steals other people's children to populate his fantasy. A cruel monster, a child unloved, the boy who will never grow up."

"Wow! I never expected to be greeted with such a panegyric! I hope you've got that written down somewhere."

"I've lived a long time with Peter Pan. It isn't a children's story at all. Barrie has no idea how much of himself he reveals. You may not know Peter first appeared in Barrie's novel The Little White Bird?"

"I plead ignorance. I've no particular interest in Peter. It's just such a lovely part."

"A hundred and twenty years and the boy still hasn't grown up. I could list a dozen men who've never grown up either."

"How old are you, Anna?"

"Don't know. Twenty-four? Five? It comes of being abandoned on the convent doorstep."

"I envy you. You don't look more than sixteen, eighteen?"

"My curse."

"The girl who never grew up?"

That evening's performance was peerless. The audience was magnetised, unwilling to have coughing spasms or eat Chinese takeaways. Every mobile telephone fell silent. Every tongue was stilled. Anna became Peter Pan the boy who never grew up. When she declaimed, "I'll teach you how to jump on the wind's back and then away we go," the audience believed her. Anna displayed such swordsmanship as to bring men half-out of their seats and Malcolm McLeich to complain, "Steady on, old girl! It's not for real!"

She reached such heights of comic bravado and such depths of sorrow at the plight of this sad, loveless boy to bring her audience to both laughter & tears. When the final curtain closed every member of the cast knew they had engaged in a unique performance. Captain Hook demanded an ambulance to take him to hospital for the wound on his thigh to be treated under anaesthetic. Gillian scolded him, stuck a plaster on the scratch and threatened to do the same to his mouth.

Before she released them, Gillian talked to her cast.

"Tonight's performance was in a totally different class to so many run of the mill performances of Peter Pan. We've contributed our share. But tonight we gave an intensity of emotion that is often lacking. Peter is played as a children's story. The film, to its shame, was even more empty of meaning. Tonight we expressed clearly and heartbreakingly the true meaning of this play."

The director paused as if gathering the words.

"It is a play about heartbreak, loneliness, the unquenchable desire for home. The audience, many from a different culture were caught up in that longing the rest of the audience shared. That longing for home. Peter Pan is not a jolly romp. The Neverland is a desperate attempt to express the loneliness, the lovelessness, the longing for home that Barrie hid there. No one understood him. Tonight you unlocked the cage that imprisoned the play. Congratulations!"

As she walked home the director's words rang in Anna's head.

FOUR

From the handful of drinkers Annie knew it was almost closing time. The old man, Alwan, who lived most of his life on the bar stool knew it was closing time and presented Annie with his empty quart-sized wooden tankard. Annie smiled and refilled the tankard, took his coppers and dropped them into the red jug below the bar. She scanned the room, but the other drinkers were too far-gone to sink another drop.

Noah rang the bell and shouted, "Take theesels home afore I puts the dogs on thee!"

There were no dogs.

The barroom emptied as Noah's customers preferred not to be ejected nose down into the horse droppings that surfaced....

Anna suddenly realised she didn't know in which street, alley or court the Ark stood. She rinsed out the mugs & tankards on the bar and collected the strays. Alwan hadn't moved, but was steadily drinking his ale. Annie wiped down the bar and said to the old man, "Ye'll never finish that afore Noah comes back." Annie knew how to manipulate the customers. When Noah returned from seeing the last drinkers off the premises, Alwan was draining his wooden tankard.

"Yi can go now, Annie."

"Thank thee, Noah."

She slipped through the back for her cloak and returned to find Alwan gone.

"Got your wooden soldier?"

"Do I need to?"

"More than ever, lass. There's somebody taken a grudge against thee."

Anna went to collect the crossbow. Prepared by Noah. Armed and rewound. One tug and nothing could recall the bolt.

"Got it?"

"Yes."

"Show me."

31

Annie opened her cloak and Noah nodded.

"Go home safely, lass."

"God keep thee, Noah!"

He preceded her down the passage and opened the front door. To her surprise there were four gentlemen waiting. Noah was not surprised.

"Good evening, milord."

The taller man asked, "Is the room prepared?"

"All as thee wished, milord."

Annie stood aside as the men entered. They smelt quite differently from the Ark's usual clientele. Annie had never smelt such pleasant perfumes. One sword caught her leg.

"Beg pardon, milord," she piped obediently, looking at her feet.

The gentleman ignored her. They passed beyond to the stairs that could only mean they were here for a private supper.

"Don't thee need me, Noah?"

"I'll serve the gentlemen, lass. Get theeself home."

Annie felt he was uncertain, but stepped out and Noah closed the door. She heard him setting the bolts and turning the iron key. She felt shut out from the only security she knew.

As Anna struggled to see if there was a board above the door, she realised with a certain shock Alwan was standing in the shadows.

"Alwan! Yi fright me! Did thee wish so?"

"I wouldn't wish to scare thee, never ever, m'dear!"

"Then why're thee here? Nowheres better to be?"

Lights appeared in the upper floor.

Alwan ignored her questions to say, "Playing pokenose with gentlemen like these here present is dangerous, Annie."

"I'm not interested in their business. I were trying to see if there were a board saying like here is the Ark."

The old man laughed.

"Rotted away donkeys' years. Everybody that needs to know the Ark, knows the Ark."

"I don't know the lane neither."

Alwan was surprised, but answered readily.

"You is standing, my pretty, in the Frog."

"The frog?"

"Froggart's Lane. But all says the Frog"

The old man drew her away from the tavern to the corner of the building where a private carriage waited in the alley. The driver and the postillion were sheltering within.

"When the carriage come I wondered what such fine gentlemen would be doing here of the midnight hour."

"None of our business."

"The crest is cloaked. I would wager them fine gentlemen is conspiring."

Annie protested.

"Then we's safer not to know."

"And I'll tell thee someat else."

"Please, Alwan, don't tell me."

"The tall man is a lordship. One of the highest in the land. And he ain't most loyal to our good Queen Elizabeth,"

The postillion began to climb out of the carriage.

Annie said, "God be with thee Alwan!"

She began to walk away quickly, but the old man followed after her.

"Go away! Leave me be! If I tell Noah thou has fright me, ye'll regret it."

Alwan hesitated and turned away, calling, "Thou should listen to me, Annie. For thine own sake. But so be it."

Annie walked away, clutching the crossbow inside her cloak.

*

While Annie slept peacefully, Anna lay awake, trying to make sense of her situation. She became aware she had real memories of the Ark; much more engagement than she had thought. One evening the men had presented her with a stringed instrument and asked her to sing. She sang songs she didn't know she knew and realised she had sung them before: the men asked for their favourite songs. So she sang and sourfaced Marianne served the ale. The Ark was calm as the voice of the girl rose as the morning lark to fill the ancient rafters.

In the morning she was roused by Polly Parker's skivvy bustling in, saying, "Sorry ti disturb your Majesty, but if there's anythink solid in your chamber pot, yi'll clean it yoursel. Polly says what yi eat is disgusting."

The news bulletin was delivered with an engaging grin and a curtsey. She poured hot water from the kettle into the washbowl and left a jug of cold water.

"If yi want anything to eat, I'd suggest yi shift your carcass now, your Majesty!"

Annie threw a shoe at the skivvy who dodged with accustomed ease and vanished.

*

Carole was crouching in the lower passageway of Boxborough Manor examining the panelling. Daisy crouched beside her and Chris stood awaiting her decision."

"Sorry, Chris, but I have to agree with Daisy. Yes, the lower section is blemished, but on the whole it's in remarkably good condition, but it shouldn't be here."

Chris tried to interrupt, but Carole continued.

"They were fortunate servants who ran through panelled passageways to bring the master a lamb chop and a pint of porter. Give it a good dose of your secret jollop and fit it in one of the new bedrooms."

"Conniving witches," said Chris and Daisy punched his leg, "That's what you are."

"But you will do as I ask, won't you? Please? I need your brilliant work on display upstairs, not down here where only the mice appreciate it."

"Your wish is my command, madam."

Carole rose to kiss Chris on the cheek.

"There's Mamma's best boy!"

Carole and Daisy walked together the length of the subterranean passageway.

Daisy said, "There were literally two worlds. The moles ran these passageways unseen and unnoticed. While the gentry frolicked in spacious rooms above."

"Not only frolicked, but murdered too. The unfortunate men in the pit were murdered. The Earl must've known what was happening under his roof. The moles surely knew."

34

They paused at the foot of the staircase. There was a man on the landing above looking down at them. He was a stranger.

Daisy called, "Hello? Can we help you?"

It registered slowly on the women that the man was in Elizabethan costume. His breast bore a badge, a crest unreadable in the dim light.

Daisy said, "Stay there! We're coming up."

"I know the hotel people want to use costume, but that's months away."

They had almost topped the staircase when the actor vanished. Carole grabbed for the banister. Daisy gasped and seized Carole's arm. They were silent, regarding the empty landing on trembling legs.

Carole said, "I don't want to say this, but I think we saw a ghost."

It never occurred to her that Daisy might not have seen the apparition.

"I don't know what we saw, but it wasn't friendly. He saw us and looked at us with amusement. I didn't like him."

They climbed the last steps to the landing.

Daisy asked, "D'y'think our working here has awakened something? Something that doesn't like what we're doing?"

"I think we stop thinking, Daisy. Keep our mouths shut. Events like that happen in old buildings from time to time. But if it gets known we'll lose the students. Nobody will work late and every mishap'll be down to the ghost. So, keep mum! Okay?"

Daisy nodded agreement. Carole digested the thought that to abandon Boxborough Manor would bankrupt Truscott & Daughter.

*

"Let me see that again," said the youth in Walsingham's livery. Kit handed over the summons.

"You're late."

"I'm not going to excuse myself to you."

After tramping miles through the corridors of Westminster, Kit was becoming increasingly irritated. Only because he knew

35

Authority would miss this pimply young man sooner or later stopped him from strangling the idiot with his own ribbons and hiding him in the first cupboard behind a hundred doors.

"Your problem is that his Lordship does not carry out his duties in one office. He's liable to up and march off to see whoever he needs to see."

"So if I brought the news that the Spanish have landed in Kent they would be in London before you told his Lordship?"

"You're making mock of me, sir!"

"You've noticed?"

An elegantly dressed gentleman approached. The pimply youth stood aside, but Kit stepped forward.

"Forgive me delaying you, milord, but where should I find Lord Walsingham? I have been summoned."

Kit flourished the summons.

"How unfortunate! I've just left him," said the elegant young gentleman, "He's in a raging temper and looking for an arse to kick. Turn right and it's the second door to the right. Beware! He hides his moods well. Perhaps you may be fortunate and he's charged off to torment some other poor bastard. Anyway, good luck! You'll need it."

"Thank you, milord."

When Kit turned around his guide had vanished.

*

Sir Francis Walsingham settled himself into the chair, leaving Kit standing.

"Her Majesty is most impressed with your ability to encourage treacherous Catholics, nobility and plebeians, to betray themselves."

"Thank you, milord."

"I suppose it's to do with you being a scribbler and an actor. In short, an habitual liar and deceiver."

"I wouldn't put it quite like that, milord. A certain quickness of mind and action are essential in some circumstances to stay alive. These people are dangerous. I was present when a Christian gentleman was garrotted because he wouldn't tell a lie. Fortunately, I am, as you say, an habitual liar and so told enough lies to save my life"

"Yes, yes, quite unfortunate. But this is a war we're fighting. I suggest you recall some of her late Majesty, Bloody Mary's atrocities. However, that is all water under the bridge.."

"Bloody water, milord!"

"I have a delicate mission for you. Her Majesty has chosen you. Her most reliable, trustworthy agent."

"Before you go further, milord, may I respectfully beg off from this mission? And any further missions."

His Lordship did not reply until Kit was about to scream to break the tension.

"Have you not noticed the licence you are given to scribble and present the most outrageous, even heretical theatrical travesties, some very close to treason, without any question. Your friend, Thomas Kyd, does not share that freedom."

"He rightly complains of harassment in the pettiest manner."

"My dear Marlowe, I could have you arrested, found guilty and hanged, drawn and quartered for heresy on any day of the week and twice on Sunday."

"With due respect, milord, you cannot hang, draw and quarter any unfortunate twice."

Walsingham sighed deeply.

"You see? You believe you can play the fool even with me. How wrong you are."

Someone struck Kit from behind with appalling violence and his nose buried itself in the carpet at Lord Walsingham's feet.

"Does he know we have the girl?"

*

Sometime later Kit Marlowe was summoned from Death's door with ice water and constant slapping until he reached sufficient awareness as to recognise his tormenter.

The Queen's Spymaster said, "Her Majesty has a mission for you, Marlowe. Are you willing to serve your Queen?"

Someone moved his head up and down.

A different voice ordered, "Sign here, master."

37

A quill was held in his hand and miraculously began to scribe Christopher Marlowe. He lost interest by the time he reached the letter p. The quill was taken from his hand and someone else continued to write his name. Kit smelt the sealing wax and heard the crest being pressed into the hot wax. He heard someone say, "Let him sleep."

*

In the dream Anna found herself walking a long road flanked by very ordinary Council houses. She was carrying a heavy carrier bag in each hand. When she stopped at a garden wall to massage her numb hands and recover her breath, faces appeared at every window of the nearest house, hands pulling aside net curtains to stare at her, eyes expressing nothing. A woman came to the door and Anna smiled to call, "Hi! Hot, isn't it?" The woman stared and then turned to say something to a person inside the house.

Anna picked up her carrier bags to walk on when a young woman appeared at her elbow and took a carrier bag. The young woman spoke to her in a friendly manner. Anna couldn't hear what she said, but smiled and agreed. As they began to walk the young woman nodded back at the house where she had been stared at. She laughed, gestured and Anna understood that household was not popular in the road.

They walked together as the young woman talked. Anna realised she was supposed to know this friendly stranger and that she was not Anna or Annie, but someone else. The estate became more familiar as they walked the long road. She knew she lived here and had been happy. When they stopped outside a particular house she knew this was home.

Anna kicked the door. Somehow her foot knew what to do. She kicked the door three times. The door was opened by a young man who smiled upon her and took both carrier bags. Anna knew she loved him. He was a handsome young man with an unfashionable black beard & moustache with long midnight hair. He held a chewed biro between his teeth and Anna kissed him on the nose. The two young women went into the sitting room as the young man took the carrier bags into the kitchen.

When she stepped into that modest room Anna knew she was home and would love this bearded young man 'til life would end.

They sat down to talk and she turned to say something to the young man who carried in mugs of tea on a Coronation tray she knew so well, but Carole's voice and feet on the stairs awoke her.

She awoke from the dream angry and heartbroken, yet she knew she had to find that house and that young man. She knew without knowing where to look. The sense of loneliness, of loss was almost overwhelming. She hadn't come from nowhere. There was a life, love and home stolen from her.

FIVE

John Hazlitt completed his notes on the latest consultation with Mrs. Piper. He could smell her perfume lingering in the office. She was an intense woman and Hazlitt found her most demanding. She had made an attempt at suicide with nail scissors without breaking the skin of her wrist. Her relationships with both husband & children were fragile. He pressed the button and his secretary appeared with coffee. A ritual he always pretended surprised him.

"You must be telepathic, Sybil. Or is the office bugged? I'm dying for a cup of your admirable coffee. And here it is! Thank you!"

Sybil smiled to say, "You have twenty-five minutes, doctor, until your next appointment. Enjoy your coffee!"

Sybil disappeared. The good doctor sipped coffee and nibbled a biscuit. Then he came to a decision and dialled a number from his desk.

"George? John Hazlitt. Have I disturbed you? Let me steal two minutes. I have something that might interest you. A young woman serving as a barmaid in a pub called the Ark in sixteenth century Canterbury. She pops up for air every now and again as an actor performing in Peter Pan at the Queen's."

He stopped to listen, making appropriate grunts from time to time.

"But I believe her story may be true. That she is time walking."

He paused as his correspondent expressed dissent and continued; "We actually found mention of the Ark in a document in the city archives. George, if I thought it was self-delusion or fantasy, I wouldn't be wasting your time. In histories of this nature I've met recently, this is the only one that rings true to me. I thought perhaps I might interest you in meeting her. She's Anna Cato, a remarkable young woman."

40

He listened and continued, saying, "That's splendid, George! I'll send her notes over now. And we'll meet tomorrow at eleven? She has matinees in the afternoons."

His listener interrupted.

"She's plays Peter Pan."

Courtesies exchanged, Hazlitt returned to his coffee & biscuit.

*

When Kit Marlowe awoke he thought he was dreaming. He woke with alarm and throwing off the quilt, sprang from the bed. He found himself clothed in a fine linen nightshirt with a small crest at heart height. Kit thrust his nose into the shirt and smelled himself. He was shocked to find himself bathed and scented with lavender. His nails were neatly trimmed both hands & feet. In a panic he thrust himself towards the large mirror, scarcely according the pleasant bedchamber a glance. To his horror he found his beard, moustache and hair tidily trimmed.

He cried, "Great galloping Jesus! I'm bewitched!"

Kit took a second glance, peering closely at his face, flashing his teeth, turning about and inspecting his legs, thighs, genitalia and buttocks.

"God smite me, but I'm a handsome fellow!"

He galloped as a horse, watching himself in the mirror, admiring the dexterity of his limbs, the flair of his mane. Seizing an invisible sword, he fought a duel with himself in the mirror. Tiring of play, he examined the tall mirror in its gilt frame.

"Truly astonishing! I have never seen such a glass in all my life! Tis sure to make a fat toad like Walsingham appear a regular cavalier."

He turned to view the room in which he had slept. How long?

"If this is sorcery, Ned, then give up the stage! You would make a fortune in gold, preparing chambers such as this for our noble betters!"

41

There was a gilded couch, a dressing table in high style with a shining glass, upholstered stool and washstand with porcelain basin & jugs. But the high point of the chamber was the magnificent double bed with Romanesque pillars and brocaded curtains with gilded ties. Above the bed head there was a shield bearing a crest that made the playwright blink in horror. He searched the chamber in vain for his clothes.

"Holy Golgotha, I'm actually in Hell awaiting Beelzebub's pleasure or I'm . . ."

The short plump man bustled into the chamber, followed by a young maid. He carried clothes over his arm and waddled like a duck. The maid, graceful as a swan, carried a basket of shoes.

"Come, come, sir!" cried the duck, "Off with the nightshirt!"

"But!" cried Kit.

"Pure as she seems, Emily has seen everything of the human physique! There is no peculiarity of the human form she has not observed. Is that not so, m'dear?"

"If the gentleman is distressed, I shall turn me back," which she promptly did.

"I have a suspicion the pair of you are making mock of me!"

"Oh, dear me, no, sir!"

In less time than one might imagine Kit Marlowe found himself transformed to a gentleman in black satin. He gazed in wonder at his image in the mirror.

"Emily, you may turn about and give us your view of this fine gentleman."

Emily turned and curtseyed low, declaiming, "The very image of a Prince, sir!"

"I don't understand! What's this all about?"

"How else would one dress, sir, to meet her blessed Majesty?"

*

Sybil popped her head into Hazlitt's office to say, "It's George Bryce. He's almost half an hour early. What d'you want me to do with him?"

She wasn't to receive a reply as Bryce pushed her aside and barged into the office. His size & shape justified his nickname.

Bull Bryce. A colleague had once said to Hazlitt that he had never seen more frightening eyebrows. Yet his practice was very successful.

"There's no keeping an old friend parked on an uncomfortable chair."

Hazlitt would have contested the word friend, but at every conference Bryce would attach himself to Hazlitt.

"Good morning, John!"

Sybil retired from this display of bad manners with a glance to her employer that said more than any words.

"Good morning, George! I'm afraid we weren't expecting to see you for at least half an hour."

"I wouldn't let that little madam run your life, John. Now, which of these chairs did you not buy from a charity shop?"

Hazlitt knew from long acquaintance that this rude behaviour was intended to be eccentric & amusing.

"Sybil's more than a very good secretary, George. I wouldn't know what to do without her."

"Condemned out of your own mouth. Take warning. Never let her near any delicate matters. You'll regret it."

George Bryce found a chair to his liking, pulled it close to the desk and bounced it into submission.

Hazlitt sat down at his desk and sought to keep patience. Bryce seemed to be more unpleasantly ebullient than usual, but there was no aroma of alcohol. Bryce, without asking, produced a cigar, bit off the end, spat it nearly into the waste basket and lit the cigar.

"D'y'mind?"

"A custom loathsome to the eye, hateful to the nose, harmful to the brain, dangerous to the lungs..."

"Yes, yes! James, the party pooper! It calms me down."

"D'y'need calming?"

"What I have to say is completely confidential. Not a word to anyone, John."

He stared sternly at Hazlitt who felt compelled to respond.

"Completely confidential. I understand."

"Good chap."

He looked around the office, a subtly decorated room that evoked calm & security, an algorithm calculated to reduce tension.

Bryce asked, "Do you have any tincture that calms and celebrates?"

"You mean alcohol?"

"Indeed, I do!"

"Not in this office. The last thing I want is to suggest alcohol is beneficial to my patients."

"Good God, John, not for the patients! For you! For me!" George Bryce bounced in the chair alarmingly.

"Whoa, George! Calm down. There is something you wish to tell me. Can you imagine how frustrating it would be for me if you had a fatal heart attack?"

Bryce began to breathe a little easier.

"We have time before Miss Cato arrives to celebrate your good fortune that may change our lives."

"Not all change is welcome, George!"

*

Anna hung up the tea towel, returned the supper dishes to the cupboard, drank a glass of water, regarded the tidy kitchen with a certain satisfaction and found herself in a busy market tapping a tambourine on her knee. The young man was playing his guitar and singing. *My God*, thought Anna, *but he can sing.* There was a fair crowd listening and joining in the choruses. It was obvious the teenage girls adored him. Anna was surprised at her sudden urge to bang their pretty heads with her tambourine. She looked down to see a child dropping coins into the biscuit tin at her feet. She smiled and cried, "Thank you, sweetie!" as the child scurried back to her mother. Absently, she noticed how blue the sky was, how tantalising was the scent of sausages & burgers on the air and how happy she was, tambourine tapper to the market busker. Then it was gone and a bewildered Anna returned to Carole's kitchen. Rain was beating on the window pane.

*

44

"As you may know," George Bryce declared, " I spent the Spring lecturing in colleges on the East coast, ending in New York."

Hazlitt, not wishing to appear impolite, suggested, "I read your self-advertising eulogy in the Journal on your brave safari through the dorms of adolescent female university students."

"Now, now, John! That's absolutely untrue. I met with a television producer who had been following my humble footsteps. After the New York programme, which received wonderful, notices, we talked."

"And?"

"He has offered me the opportunity to present a television series on the lives of men and women who have experienced, shall we say, other worldly experiences. The money takes your breath away."

"Well, all I can do is offer congratulations, spiced with a touch of envy."

"No, no, there is room for you, John."

"I'm not sure I'm following you, George."

"John, let me investigate this story of the barmaid from the sixteenth century. It would make a blinding opening for the first series. And you'd name your own price."

"I can't do that."

"Why not?"

"I believe her."

George Bryce laughed.

"John! You old cuckoo! You know you don't. It's either an illusion, poor girl. Or it's a deception. I have some eighteen similar stories. It's perfect for the series! I will treat her with sympathy, gently teasing the story from her and with the utmost sympathy relieve her of this crippling fantasy"

Hazlitt was silent. The traffic in the street seemed to mount in volume to an unbearable level. He could hear Bryce's heart & breathing hammering at his consciousness.

Bryce said, "Well? Wha'd'y'say? Are we partners?"

He offered an enormous, moist hand which Hazlitt ignored.

"George, I should never have mentioned Anna to you. I promised her I wouldn't relay her story to anyone. I apologise, but I must ask you to leave before Miss Cato arrives."

At which point Sybil tapped and opened the office door to ask, "Miss Cato is here. D'you wish me to keep her in the waiting room or bring her into the office?"

"Take her into the Quiet Room and stay with her."

Conflicting emotions crossed Sybil's face; conflicting questions unspoken.

"As you say, doctor."

"Stay with her, Sybil. I want her isolated."

Bryce could hardly wait until the door closed before jumping up and blurting out, "Look here, John, you don't own that girl. She will have her own views. Let me speak to her."

"I'm sorry, but I don't think she should be exposed to public view on television. If she were older, perhaps. As a respected colleague, I'm asking you to leave now."

"You invited me here to interview her."

"My mistake. I apologise for wasting your time. Send me a bill."

For one moment Hazlitt believed Bryce was about to strike him. Then the big man drew a deep breath and spoke calmly.

"I have never had a subject refuse to be interviewed. On the East coast safari, as you call it, I interviewed thirty-four subjects. It could've been a hundred and fifty. They were fighting to take part. And they weren't being paid. Only the chosen subjects who appeared in the Fox show from New York were paid."

He paused to produce a cheque book and pen.

"I'm offering this girl a first payment of five thousand pounds just to talk with me. Do inform her of my offer."

"No can do."

"Wake up, John! In the plainest terms, she's probably an incorrigible liar who has thought up the weirdest fantasy. Annie Cato, barmaid at a shitty bothy, born in the sixteenth century. Keep your eye on the money, John. This is what the idiot box was invented for."

John Hazlitt took Bryce by the beefy arm.

46

"Time to go, George! Please don't disturb the other tenants. They often comment on how quiet we are up here under the tiles."

Bull Bryce shook off his colleague's restraining arm.

"You fancy your chances at putting me out?"

Hazlitt pressed the switch on the desk.

"No. I leave that sort of thing to Sybil. She'll dial nine, nine, nine and our boys in blue will come to escort you out. If you're rude to them, they'll spray you with pepper. Mind your footing on the stairs. The lighting is automatic."

The office door opened and Sybil appeared.

"Yes, doctor?"

"Mister Bryce is leaving. Please escort him to the front door."

*

"I knew of him as having a deal of experience with similar situations and thought perhaps he could guide us. I thought him to be a man of integrity. My mistake. He plans a freak circus on television. You are not a freak."

Hazlitt sat silent as Anna pondered upon his words. Her first anger had cooled, but the use of the word freak stung.

"I apologise wholeheartedly for my breach of trust. If you wish to end our association I wouldn't be surprised. I let you down."

He waited for her response, but Anna was silent.

"He is prepared to pay you a large sum of money for your co-operation."

"I don't want his money. I don't want to be on television. I just want to find out who I am and why I'm here."

Sybil tapped on the office door and entered.

"Mister Bryce has left the building."

"Thank you, Sybil."

"It's the first time I have ever been offered a bribe, sir."

Hazlitt laughed, but Anna asked, "Why would he do that?"

"A hundred pounds for your address or phone number. I refused either."

"Good grief! He's serious, isn't he?"

47

Hazlitt said, "Don't let him concern you, Anna. He'll cool down. Tomorrow he'll be ringing to apologise."

Sybil said, "I wouldn't count on it. He's sitting in his car across the road. He's not smiling."

Anna had never met George Bryce or even heard his voice, but the trickle of fear was so persistent she wished she had the bow Noah had given her.

Sybil and Anna went down the back stairs and out into the yard where Sybil's car was parked. As they drove to the theatre she remarked, "Forgive me saying so, Anna, but the first time we met I knew you were not who you appeared to be. Most disturbing."

"I don't know what you mean? That I was not who I appeared to be?"

"The best way to describe it? As if I had double vision. For the briefest moment I saw three people."

SIX

The bus dropped her at the end of the lane where a large board announced that the Luxury Boxborough Manor Elizabethan Hotel & Restaurant will be opening within its own grounds.

Carole was walking across the rear courtyard when Anna shouted.

"At last! Thank God! I thought I'd never find you!"

"What on earth's wrong, Anna? You look awful."

"I need you to drive me to Gilsford."

"Gilsford? Why?"

"It's crazy, but I just need you to do it. There's a house I have to find. I just have to go there."

"Have you the address?"

"I know what it looks like."

Carole regarded her distressed friend.

"Please, Carole! I wouldn't ask if it wasn't desperate."

"Alright, alright! If it's so important to you."

"Oh, thank you! Can we go now?"

"I must tell Harry I'm going somewhere."

"Thank you, Carole, I won't forget this!"

"I'm sure I won't either. Go to the car. It's not locked. I'll join you in a couple of ticks."

Anna sat in the car for ten minutes with no sight of Carole. Impatient, she climbed out and stood by the door, willing Carole to appear. When she did, Anna got back into the car, but Carole noted the impatience.

Starting the engine, she said, "Sorry for the delay, but I can't just walk off the job. They have to know what to do."

"I'm sorry. It's just I've never experienced anything like this. You'll think I've gone mad, but I haven't."

"It's an hour to Gilsford. Take your time and tell me why we're going."

Anna recited her dream experience and Carole drove the car into a layby and switched off the engine.

"We're going to Gilsford because you had a dream?"

"It's not like that, Carole."

"But it is like that, Anna. It's very, very, very much like that."

They sat in silence as the engine cooled and a large bluebottle settled on the windscreen.

"So, you won't drive me?"

Carole said nothing, but brushed the bluebottle away with a flick of the screen wipers.

"I swear to you on my heart and soul that dream is real. It was a clear message. Someone, something has wiped away my life for reasons I don't begin to understand."

"I'm struggling too, believe me."

"I know something I shouldn't. Or I will know something I shouldn't. And this man is the reason."

"Do you even know his name? He sounds like some actor out of a Thirties movie. He wasn't Rupert of Hentzau, was he?"

"He was in shirt and jeans. And bare feet. I beg you, please, please, take me to Gilsford."

A car drove into the layby and parked some distance behind. Carole locked the doors.

"You don't know who's on the road. Some madman."

Then she burst out laughing.

"Who is sitting next to me. And I'm worried about some nutter in the car behind?"

The rep unfolded his sandwiches and began to chew contentedly. On his expense sheet lunch would figure differently. He sipped his fizzy drink, watching the two women arguing in the car in front of his Honda.

"Okay, Anna, I'll take you to Gilsford."

Anna interrupted with effusive thanks.

"If you don't find the house and something, anything that makes sense to me, then tonight's the last night you sleep in my flat. We're finished. Do you understand?"

"I understand."

"You really need help, Anna."

The journey proceeded in silence until on the Western bypass of Gilsford, Anna cried, "There! There! That road!"

On the busy bypass Carole had difficulty returning to enter Springfield Park Avenue, which didn't improve her composure.

"I hope you know what you're doing."

As they drove slowly into the road, Anna said, "Here. Park here."

"Are you sure?"

"It's the longest road in the world. I've walked it a thousand times."

Carole surveyed the long road of modest Council houses.

"It's the entry to a Council estate. How the hell d'you expect to find a house when you don't know the address?"

"This is the right road. I walked twice a week to and from the shops. I could see the bypass the closer to home I walked. The house is near the end of this road. I need to get out."

Anna scrambled out of the car and Carole exited reluctantly. Anna started to walk along the pavement and Carole followed dutifully. Anna laid her hand on an iron gate.

"This is it. Number eighteen Springfield Park Avenue."

"Are you sure?"

"Absolutely. I recognise it. This is where we lived."

"You're beginning to remember. Or you're a very good liar. Of course, you're a professional actor!"

An older woman was leaning on her gate watching the strangers. On impulse Carole went to the woman, followed by Anna. Carole smiled and asked, "We're looking for old friends. A young couple. D'y'know who lives at eighteen?"

"That's the Palmers. But she's been taken into Care and Arthur goes to sit with her every day."

"Can you remember before the Palmers?"

"That would be a young couple and a little tot. A girl. But they didn't stay long."

"And before that?"

Carole smiled and the woman said, "There were the hippies. A young couple."

Anna said, "That sounds like them."

"The man was the wild one. With his motorbike. He used to sing on the Market."

"That sounds right."

51

"Then there was a big fight when the Council tried to evict them. All the men in the road joined in. He was at the top window firing his catapult."

Anna laughed for joy.

"I don't remember anything of that."

The neighbour regarded her oddly.

"Of course, they evicted them. Off they went on his motorbike. That's the last we saw of them. But you're not hippies?"

Carole responded, "Goodness me, no! Thank you! You've been a big help."

Satisfied that the visitors were not hippies the neighbour retired indoors. Carole and Anna returned to the gate of number eighteen.

Carole asked, "Can we go home now?"

Looking around, Anna said, "I've got to have a look."

She opened the gate.

"Anna!" cried Carole, but followed after her. Anna led the way to the rear of the house.

There was a neat vegetable garden, a small greenhouse and a shed. By the kitchen door there were two pairs of garden boots, one pair smaller than the other.

"You're not gona break in?"

"Ten to one it's not locked. Old people forget whether it's locked or not."

"It's still wrong!"

"The old gent's sitting with his wife in the Care home. He's probably just shared her lunch and they'll have a nap."

"I can't believe what you're doing."

"We're not gona take anything. I just want to see."

"If it's locked?"

"I'll think of something else."

Anna grasped the handle and opened the door.

"This is madness!"

"Then go and sit in the car."

Anna and a reluctant Carole stepped into a neat kitchen.

Anna cried, "It has doors!"

"Houses do have doors."

"I remember! He broke up all the doors."

"Why would he do that?"

"It was winter and we were freezing."

"Couldn't you buy coal then?"

"If you have money."

With some surprise, Carole said, "You're remembering stuff. Or making it up. I can't work out which."

Looking into the sitting room, Anna said, "The paraffin stove's gone. But you'd expect that. And their furniture matches."

She was halfway up the stairs before Carole joined her.

"We're going to get caught."

"The old man's dozing in the chair next to his wife."

On the landing were three doors to bedrooms and bathroom. Carole asked, "How did you manage without doors?"

"Very soon you don't notice. You're just more polite and we were warm. That was more important."

She stood at the entrance to the first tidy bedroom holding a single bed.

"I've dreamt about this bedroom. I slept here, but I had the bed against the other wall. This was my bedroom."

She gave it scarcely a glance and passed on to the main bedroom. Anna paused on the threshold, saying, "It seems odd going in here."

"Why?"

"We never went into each other's bedrooms."

"I find that hard to believe."

Anna regarded her friend.

"You misunderstand. I was. Am his adopted daughter. He rescued me from hell."

"This is either the most wonderful story. Or you're a complete fantasist. God's sake, show me something I can believe!"

They stood in a clean modest bedroom with a handsome quilt on the double bed. Anna lifted a chair away from below the window.

"If it's still there, I will."

"If it's still there?"

"Unless it's been discovered, behind this skirting board is one of his most precious possessions."

53

Carole felt the urge to laugh.

"What were the others?"

Anna thought for a moment.

"I don't know how I know, but I do."

She paused, and continued slowly, "His motorbike combo, paraffin stove, play scripts, Baked Beans, Hoola Hoops and."

Anna knelt down to pull & twist the skirting board, which came away in her hands. From the slim cavity she took out a package a metre or so long wrapped in a dark satin cloth. She laid it on the bed, astonished that it had survived.

Carole cried, "If it turns out to be a sixteenth century hair straightener I'll be so disappointed."

"It's not," Anna responded, recognising the article within.

She was struggling with the string bound tightly around the bundle. She couldn't break it and tried with her teeth.

"Give it here!"

Carole flourished a pair of nail scissors. She began to cut string at random until it fell from the bundle. Anna unfolded the satin folds with true showmanship pulling away the last fold with a flourish.

"A sword!" cried Carole, "A great big hunking sword!"

"What else would he have?"

Then they heard the front door hinges break and the door fall. Someone stumbled over the wreckage. Carole noted with puzzlement the bedroom door vanish.

"Oh, crumbs!" cried Peter Pan.

They stood frozen with terror. There was the sound of boots, but no voices. Someone walked through to the kitchen door. The bolts were pulled and the garden door was opened. Someone came into the house. Two men spoke together.

"This is definitely not the old man back from the Care Home," whispered Carole.

"What do we do?"

"Nothing. Just listen and pray."

They ventured to the bedroom door and tiptoed onto the landing. There were three men in the hallway; an older man in cloak, doublet, & hose. A silver badge shone on his breast and a feather in his hat. He wore a sword. His servants were in dirty tunic & kneebreeks: in appearance more simian than human.

"Why're they dressed up?" whispered Carole.

"They're not dressed up. The badge and the sword say guard your tongue. He has authority."

The older man spoke to his servants. His speech was inaudible as he moved about.

"Do not consider because he has not showed himself that he is not here. He is a sly dog. You must search every last crevice. His Lordship wished him in custody. You will destroy everything so he will know we have found his rat hole . . ."

His voice was lost as he moved into the sitting room followed by one servant. The second man came up the stairs slowly, cautiously.

"Oh, my God!" cried Anna. Carole stifled further speech with a warm hand. She pulled Anna into a corner of the bedroom and ordered her in whispers.

"When he comes, not a word."

She took the sword from Anna's hand, which alarmed her.

"What're you gona do with that?"

"Fight. I'm not gona stand here and be butchered."

"I have a pepper spray," Anna remembered.

"Then we'll surprise him."

Carole took the sword in two hands, prepared to strike.

The thug seemed to be in the bathroom forever, smashing bottles, breaking the mirror, pulling down a cabinet and turning on the taps. Anna thought she heard him use the word sorcery and found her anger growing and fears fading. She grasped the pepper spray and wished she was clutching Noah's bow instead.

He behaved in similar fashion in the first bedroom, destroying the bed, breaking up the wardrobe and destroying every object.

Carole murmured, "He's terrified of sorcery. Perhaps we can frighten him?"

"I don't think so. His response will be to destroy."

She was sure his master wasn't frightened of sorcery, but would willingly burn them as witches.

Then the thug loomed in the bedroom doorway and Anna almost cried out, but grasped the pepper spray more tightly. She felt Carole move beside her. They could smell his stink as he stepped cautiously into the bedroom. He stopped to stare at the two women. Carole raised the sword high to strike when he turned to destroy the bed, throwing over the bedding, mattress and bed frame. Astonished, Carole lowered the sword.

She whispered, "He cannot see us, thank God!"

The thug came close enough to share his stinking breath as he moved to destroy the wardrobe.

Carole whispered, "Let's get out of here. Slowly, very slowly, 'case he can sense movement."

The two friends crept from the bedroom and took refuge in the bathroom, sitting on the disordered bath to recover their breath. When the principal and the second man came upstairs to view the damage, Anna & Carole walked downstairs and out of the front door. They took time enough to restore the door to an upright position, leaning slightly into the door frame.

*

They sat in the car to recover composure.

"What was that all about?"

nna suggested, "Other people hunting for them too."

"How is it that monster didn't see us?"

"I don't know. But if they could, he would've killed us."

"Who are they?"

"From the sixteenth century. The gentleman had real authority. His badge has Elizabeth's crest. The orcs could be regulars at the Ark."

"And you're a barmaid at the Ark."

"They behave well to me. Noah doesn't need a Queen's crest."

Carole glanced in the wing mirror at 18, Springfield Park Avenue where all seemed serene.

"What'll happen at number eighteen now? Poor old chap!"

"The old man'll come home to find all in order. The rules changed when those three broke in. They created the past when we lived there. Kit's paraffin stove would've been in the sitting room. It was my bed he destroyed. But there would be very little else. That's why they couldn't see us."

"And the hunters?"

"Will continue to hunt. As I will."

Anna brought the sword up onto her knees.

"A rapier, slender, more sharply pointed than a sword. A gentleman's weapon, used for cutting and thrusting. Not like the plastic sword Peter waves about."

Carole said, "Even if I suspend disbelief, I don't see how it all fits together. First we have Peter Pan, twice daily except Monday, defeating Captain Hook and his ruffians. Then Annie in sixteenth century Canterbury serving ale in Noah's Ark. And now a Council house in Gilsford where you lived with a man who you believe is a playwright. A trip inspired by a dream. Did a dream bring you to Canterbury from London?"

"I wanted to be where Marlowe grew up."

The police car drew in behind them. A sharp tapping on the driver's window startled them. A police visage at each window caused blood pressure to soar.

Anna cried, "Oh, crumbs! The fuzz!"

"I'm surprised it took them so long," responded Carole, sourly.

They wound down both windows.

Carole recited, "Good morning, officer."

Anna smiled at the face inspecting her.

"Hi!"

"Step out of the car, please, ladies."

The ladies submitted.

"Names and addresses?"

They submitted names and address.

"You're not local. Where you from?"

In rough chorus they answered, "Canterbury."

The younger constable slammed shut the immaculate boot.

Carole & Anna jumped guiltily.

"It has been reported that you have been acting suspiciously."

Anna was indignant.

"We were sitting in the car. Is that illegal?"

The older constable reproved her.

"Don't waste my time."

The young constable began to rummage in the car.

Carole asked, "Can he just do that?"

Her complaint was ignored. Anna's heart slipped into her boots.

"You were reported asking about the tenants of number eighteen. Why would you do that?"

Anna hesitated and Carole answered, "We were asking about old friends."

"Names?"

Carole looked to Anna.

"Hannah. I don't know his name."

"Good friends were they?"

"Not that good."

"But you drove all the way from Canterbury to seek out good friends of whom you only know the name of one."

"It's been some time and they've moved on. We didn't know that."

The young constable called, "Take a dekko at this, Arthur," and waved the sword, almost removing Anna's left ear.

He came round the car to offer the sword to his colleague.

"Some sword you have here, ladies. You into sword fencing?"

Before Anna could blunder into speech, Carole explained, "It's mine. Well, actually it's for the redecoration of an Elizabethan manor in Canterbury. We're restoring it as a period hotel. The sword will hang on a wall with other props."

She fumbled with her wallet to produce a business card.

"Perhaps this will explain."

The officers studied the card. A disappointed constable returned the card to Carole. He nodded to his colleague who even more disappointedly returned the sword to Anna.

"A safe journey home to Canterbury, ladies."

As they reached the freedom of the bypass without hearing a police siren, Anna said, "Now you know I'm telling you the truth."

To which Carole replied, "Maybe, but I suspect I shall regret it."

Anna hugged the sword all the way home to the ancient city, but the darkness in her head persisted.

58

SEVEN

Kit Marlowe followed the silver-haired retainer dutifully. They halted at a crossroads of corridors to allow a flock of clergymen cross their path, chattering like jackdaws.

Kit asked, "If I'm allowed to know, sir, perhaps you'd tell me where we are. sir."

The old man turned his head slowly, ignoring the question, to reprove the young man.

"Lower your tone, sir. Where are you? You are here by privilege. That is all you need to know. Attend to your business and I shall attend to mine."

Kit thought it wiser to say nothing more and silently followed his guide to a particular door where a gentleman awaited.

"Master Christopher Marlowe, sir."

"Ah, Master Marlowe! There isn't a play of yours I haven't seen. A pleasure to meet you."

The guide vanished with a disdainful glance at Kit who dutifully bowed. The young gentleman was flaxen-haired, chin & head, blue-eyed, taller by a twelve-inch and well dressed. He smiled at Kit and announced ruefully, "I am about to recite."

Kit was at a loss to reply, but contrived, "I am prepared to be surprised or dismayed. Please enlighten me."

The emissary took a deep breath and declared, "I am Sir Ralph Boxborough of her Majesty's Court. You will shortly be meeting her Majesty who will present you with your Commission. When we are called, we will enter and bow to her Majesty. I will announce you to her Majesty. As I name you, you will bow again. We will be called forward and at a midway point we will stop and bow again."

"God's grief, but there's a pound or two of bowing in it!"

"Do not be concerned. An extra bow does no harm, but a bow missed is noted. Follow my lead always. Besides which, you're an actor, aren't you?"

"Not a very good one."

"You will be called forward and then you're on your own. Just answer her Majesty's questions and always agree whatever your private opinion. Receive the Commission, bow and say thank you. Wait lest there be more her Majesty wishes to impart to you. When she signals dismissal, retreat backwards until you come to me. We bow and leave her presence respectfully."

"Who wouldn't leave respectfully? Those halberds are exceedingly sharp."

"There have been occasions when the proceedings have been marred by nervous farting."

The double doors opened without warning. The light from the great window blinded Kit after the twilight of the corridor. Boxborough tugged his arm and they bowed together. Kit bowed so low as almost to topple over. His escort named his name. Kit lifted his head to see an Audience Room quite austere in decoration. The focus was on the gilded throne with the Great Seal of England above. In the centre of her attendants, counsellors and bodyguard sat Elizabeth, Queen of England, Scotland & Ireland.

A voice called, "You may approach the throne."

Step by step they approached to stop and bow again. Boxborough announced, "May it please your Majesty to receive your faithful servant, Master Christopher Marlowe, to receive your Commission."

A harsh female voice called, "Approach, Master Marlowe. I wish to take a good look at you, if not a smell of you."

There was the slightest ripple of amusement among the congregation. Boxborough whispered, "She is in a good mood. May fortune serve you!"

Kit tentatively approached the throne. A gentleman at the Queen's elbow raised a hand and he stopped. Kit Marlowe and the Queen of England gazed upon each other. Kit was shocked to see a face pasted white, only sharp eyes and active lips betrayed the woman within.

As she scrutinised her subject, Elizabeth said something to the tall gentleman at her elbow and he nodded.

"Master Marlowe, I have seen you before and you have performed good service for me. You are an admirable liar with a ready wit."

The sense of shock that rippled through the company amused Elizabeth who turned to proclaim to her audience, "He would most readily persuade a horse that he were a lion. And a nun to cast off her vows."

The company in the Audience Room laughed and the Queen enjoyed her success.

"He writes entertainments. He calls them plays. He believes he can offend anyone despite their rank and excuse it as all in play. There have been moments when I might have considered myself offended and have him pay the penalty, but . . ."

The company fell silent.

"But then, I need devious men like Master Marlowe who take great risks in the service of their Queen and Country. Master Marlowe, I have another mission for you to perform."

A courtier placed the vellum in Elizabeth's hands and she rose to present it to Kit. He was surprised to find he stood head & shoulders above her. The total lack of expression in the white mask was disturbing. There was something deathly about this Queen. Kit Marlowe accepted the vellum and listened to words he vaguely heard & comprehended. He bowed deeply.

"You are not free of me yet, Master Mischief."

"I will never be free of you, my sovereign Majesty. You have my given word."

Elizabeth turned to her Court to proclaim, "You see why, ladies, I warn you to be aware of this man. With a few words he will whisk away your petticoats and you will not notice what he has done until it is too late!"

The ladies & gentlemen of the Court laughed and her Majesty was pleased.

"I place upon this finger of your hand, my ring. And my Authority. Use it well."

Kit offered his hand and the queen placed upon the third finger of his right hand a gold ring bearing her crest.

"This will save you endlessly unrolling your Commission. This ring is my Authority. Do not abuse it. The price is too severe."

61

"Thank you, your Majesty. Whatever mission you give to me, I bear as an honour and will die before I fail you."

Kit felt Sir Ralph relax as he recited faultlessly the words his mentor had taught him.

At a nudge from Boxborough he bowed deeply and retreated backwards until Boxborough's hand sought his elbow. They bowed again and escaped through the double doors.

*

In the silence of the corridor his escort asked, "You did very well, Marlowe! You stood up to her bravely. No cringing and buckle licking. You'd be surprised how many shiver and shake. How was it for you, this first meeting with your Queen? A privilege not extended to many commoners."

"How was it? If I am honest. Disappointing. I had hoped to meet a real woman, not a plaster dummy with the voice of a crow."

"Ah, Elizabeth does not accept she is mortal and refuses to accept Time's judgement."

Kit smiled.

"I know now you have seen at least one of my plays, sir."

"It may sound theatrical, but I do suggest you turn the ring inward. It would be more discreet."

The playwright did as suggested and offered his hand to Boxborough.

"Splendid! A plain gold ring!"

As they walked Kit ventured to ask, "Do you do this often, sir?"

"Too often. Although my father the Earl is very proud that I have attained the position of footstool to her Majesty."

Kit failed to curb his laughter.

"Forgive me, sir!"

"My father broadcasts my son is at Court. I dare not tell him I am here like so many young men for Elizabeth's delectation."

They laughed together and Kit began to feel he had met a kindred spirit.

"Perhaps you might give up the high life and join Ned Alleyn's Company. And live off Dame Dorrie's mutton pies."

"What would I do?"

"Can you play a scurrilous monk or a timid shepherd?"

"I fear not."

"Can you sing?"

"Alas, no better than a rooster!"

"Then you must prance the boards for the delectation of the doxies in the pit."

They laughed together and walked with lighter hearts.

*

Gillian was right. That first evening when Anna had burst the bounds of convention and inspired her fellow thespians to create an insightful, soul-searching drama that brought the audience to laughter & tears was not a singular achievement. Cast and play grew in strength & insight as the days progressed. The tragedy that Barrie brought to the stage of life beginning in blood and tears of childhood and ending in solitary death without satisfying any of the great questions is a masterpiece of smoke & mirrors; a masterpiece as incisive as any of Marlowe's great tragedies. Any member of those audiences would understand the significance of the play; the crippling effect of this refusal to grow up, to shy away from the great challenges of life; in simplest terms the refusal of the tulip to flower, the foal to kick up its heels, the child to refuse to become the engineer, doctor, teacher, mother or father. For many of the cast their performances that season were the highpoint of their careers.

When Anna led the cast offstage, both exhausted & exhilarated by the extravagant applause, a surprise awaited her in the dressing room she shared with Wendy. On her dressing table there was an extravagant bouquet of red roses.

Anna was speechless, but Wendy cried out, "Oh, my! Oh, great grasshoppers, this has never happened to me!"

She sounded both wistful & envious.

"I don't suppose it ever will."

"I'm not sure I want them."

"If you don't, may I have them?"

63

Anna approached the bouquet and picked it up cautiously. It was surprisingly heavy.

Wendy said, "In the Naughty Nineties in London, there would be bouquets in all the dressing rooms and any number of carriages waiting in the street. And loads of dishy young men longing to take the actresses to supper and dance until the dawn dawns."

"How'd you know all that?"

"It was in a book."

"You must stop reading Barbara Cartland, Wendy."

"Never heard of her."

"How Time flies."

"There was a very naughty saying at the time. Don't judge a Johnnie by the size of his bouquet, feel for his wallet. They were called Stage Door Johnnies. Dashing young men with top hats, waxed moustaches and silver-topped canes."

"And wicked old men hunting foolish girls."

Wendy stood in a daydream as Anna laid down the roses and took the card from the ivory envelope.

"Who is it from? He must've been in the audience tonight. There was a very dishy young man in the first box. He never took his glasses from his face."

Anna read the card silently.

Wendy was downcast.

"Aren't you going to tell me? I promise I won't tell anyone. Please Anna?"

"I'm sorry but I did buy a ticket. It would seem the only way to get to know you. Perhaps you would like to have supper with me? It's the car across the road from the Theatre entrance. The ageing silver BMW."

Wendy was disappointed. Anna looked into blue-green eyes set in a milk chocolate skin framed by straw blonde hair and sighed for such innocence. Naiveté & beauty is a dangerous mix.

"That doesn't sound very romantic."

"I know him. He isn't a romantic person. I suppose you might call it business. I did tell him not to come to the theatre, but I suppose I haven't spoken to him since either."

"Will you go to supper with him?"

"Pizza? Perhaps."

"Well, that's a start."

"Wendy, when I cross the road to the silver BMW I don't want you at my hip, sighing and fluttering your delectable eye lashes at him. It's business."

"Are they really delectable?"

"Wendy, you are much too young to be fluttering anything."

"And how old are you?"

"Old enough to know better. But not wise enough to advise me."

*

Wendy came running back to the stage door faster than Eros's arrow. Anna couldn't help laughing.

"What it is to be so young!"

Struggling for an excited breath, Wendy cried, "He's there! The silver BMW!"

"You don't have to tell everyone."

There was no one in the alley.

"Where are you staying?"

"The Rosebank Boarding House. It's very nice. You should come to supper one night."

"Don't I see enough of you all every day? Now, please, go! Before Judith thinks one of her chicks is missing."

"I just want to.."

"Go!"

Wendy departed reluctantly.

Anna waited until the slim figure had departed before walking through the alley. The car stood across the street. As she waited for traffic to pass, Anna thought of how much she should tell Hazlitt of the Gilsford incident. The last taxi passed her and Anna sprinted across to the car. She was fastening her seat belt before she realised she wasn't sitting beside John Hazlitt. There was a big man, a stranger who reached to take her arm as she struggled to free the belt.

"Let go of me! This is the wrong car!"

The stranger let go of her arm.

65

"No, it's not! I'm George Bryce and I need to talk to you. I certainly won't hurt or harm you."

His voice was much more friendly than his face.

"I'm sorry to alarm you. I apologise for being large. My mater fed me too much plum pudden. But really I'm a regular softie."

His smile transformed his appearance.

Anna relaxed and smiled.

"My fault. I frightened myself. I should've looked in the car."

"You were expecting John Hazlitt?"

"Yes. He's the only person I know who would want to talk. Although I wasn't sure about the roses."

"Well, the door's not locked. You can leave if you wish, but not every word from John Hazlitt is gospel."

"What he said about you wasn't complimentary."

"Let me assure you I'm a respected psychotherapist. With all sorts of degrees and diplomas. But I've become more interested in people who say they have travelled in Time."

"John Hazlitt told me you didn't believe I was genuine and that you'd expose me on television as the Jeremy Kyle show used to do. Is that true?"

"Yes, of course it is!"

Anna put her seat belt aside.

"Wait! Let me explain. Exposing deception, fraud, trickery is what television excels at. I've done a number of people a service by exposing their mediums and spirit guides as dangerous. And much more."

He paused to give Anna time to think.

"If you are a trickster, of course, I'd expose you. Then prove to me you're the real thing. Then we can explore what's happening and perhaps discover why. Is that a fair offer?"

*

In the shadow of the theatre's portal columns Wendy was growing cold & tired. She thought of crossing the street at the traffic lights and walking down that pavement past the car to take a casual peep. She resisted the urge as the street was

66

deserted and she was easily recognised by Anna. Wendy was about to retire gracefully when the car engine started and pulled out to vanish down George Street bearing Anna Cato away. The girl skipped happily to the Boarding House, nursing a choice jewel of gossip, to delight the young cast.

*

Marlowe and Boxborough sat together in the dim reception chamber of Lord Francis Walsingham's private office. An old man lacking his left arm sat at a desk before the ornate door to the holy of holies. On their entry, he had said, "Sit there," pointing with his quill to the uncomfortable wooden bench on which they had been seated now for almost an hour. He returned to writing without ever looking up. Two halberdiers guarded the outer door, preventing any possibility of escape.

As they endured the bare bench, Boxborough said, "Master Marlowe, you must stop calling me sir."

"But you are a knight."

"But you have a commission."

"What has that to do with anything?"

"I would wager the moon it says one & all of whatever station and status are to render you whatever intelligence and action you seek and to serve you without question in whatever task or duty you deem necessary."

"Surely not! I cannot believe that."

"You have the Queen's Commission in this matter. There is no one can deny you. If you ordered the stout halberdier."

Hearing the word, but not the intention, both halberdiers glared at Boxborough who continued with, "To decapitate the old fool at the desk, he would do so."

The old fool at the desk gave no sign of hearing.

"You, good Master Marlowe, have power of life or death in your hands."

Kit broke the seal to read the Commission in an uneasy silence broken only by the harsh breathing of the halberdiers.

"Christ in torment!"

"It is as I say?"

"It is."

"What is your mission?"

"Will be imparted to me by Lord Walsingham. This is a matter of some importance to the Crown. It is imperative that the matter is concluded with speed & due secrecy."

"Oh, you lucky fellow! I only wish I were to accompany you. I am heartily sick of being a messenger boy in this place. I can assure you, my friend, I am most handy with a sword, pistols, fusil and horses."

"I too would wish you were to be with me. I believe you to be a true fellow. I would gladly take you to where we might both have our heads chopped off I could."

"But you may!" Boxborough claimed eagerly, "You have the Queen's Commission. You have only to say I will have Sir Ralph Boxborough accompany me and it is done. I know I can be of service to you. And I would escape the deadly doldrums of this palace. We are as much alike as brothers. If so, shall we dispense with titles and be just Ralph and Kit?"

EIGHT

They rode to the soothing tones of a Chopin nocturne until Bryce said, "Where would you like to go to eat?"

"Nothing extravagant."

"That's what restaurants are for. Worldwide, not just Canterbury."

"I wouldn't want you to spend money on me. I'm only here out of curiosity."

"Every word I say will be repeated to Hazlitt?"

"No. This isn't a competition. There!"

Anna pointed and Bryce exclaimed, "McDonald's? I've never been there. Are you sure?"

"Yes. You're going to miss the turn."

Bryce parked the car and they entered beneath the golden arches. He stood bewildered in the unexpected noise.

"I don't know what to do. Do we wait for the maitre d'?"

Anna laughed.

"What we do is, you go to find a table and I go to buy the burgers. So, money, please!"

Bryce produced a wallet and Anna took sufficient money for burgers & fries for two.

"Would you like a corn cob?"

"God, no! Is that what they sell?"

"Go and find a table. In a corner if you can."

Anna stood in line and in less than ten years, bought the biggest burgers, extra fries and buttered corn cobs. When she wriggled through the counter crowd she saw that Bryce had secured a corner table.

"That was very lucky. Getting a corner table."

"They'd finished scoffing whatever it was and were just talking. So I stood here until they decided to leave. I suggested they take their rubbish with them."

Anna laughed.

"You're not at all a nice man, Mister Bryce."

Anna laid out the food and began to eat. She noted that Bryce soon lost his cynicism and began to enjoy his burger.

In mock-journalistic tone, Anna asked, "How're you enjoying your first visit to McDonald's, Mister Bryce?"

He smiled his enticing smile to say, "Actually, it's enjoyable. I'd say it's a picnic indoors. Don't eat my corn cob. I may try it."

Anna laid the coins on the table, saying, "Sorry. Forgot. Your change."

Bryce picked up the coins and asked, "How much should we leave as a tip?"

Anna smiled.

"No tips. But I remember I did work somewhere where there were tips. But he said no tipping."

"No tipping? Who was he?"

"He said it was wrong. I was like a hound hanging about his Master's table, hoping some titbit would fall or be given to him. He said it was degrading."

"You listened to this man?"

"I gave my tips to the other girls. They thought I was gaga, but I knew he was right."

"And you always did what he said?"

Anna laughed, "You never knew him."

"I'd like to."

She saw his face and heard him sing. He smiled and spoke to her, but someone had tied her tongue & stuffed her ears. She struggled to remember his name and failed.

"He knew nothing of this world. Hated much of it."

"Was he into drugs?"

Anna laughed and there was a thin trickle of awareness.

"Never. I remember. He said he was born in Canterbury. On a cold February day in fifteen sixty-four. I remember him saying that."

Anna laughed again.

"His mother lost grip of him and he slipped to the floor on his cord. The first kindness he received was from the dog that licked him."

"You know that's impossible, don't you?"

"His mother was alone."

"That's not what I mean. He wasn't born in fifteen sixty four."

She could sense his disbelief. Stubbornly, Anna shook her head.

"Why would he tell me lies?."

"Did you love him?"

"I still love him."

She was amazed at the truth of these four words.

"You must've been very young. Sleeping with him. Surely that was wrong?"

"I never slept with him! You don't understand, do you? I am like his adopted daughter. He saved me from Hell!"

Anger flared within Anna.

"When did you come to Canterbury?"

"January. New Year's Day. I'd had enough of pantomime."

"Wasn't that an odd choice?"

"I had the chance to play Peter. The girl playing him had got pregnant. It was beginning to show. But I wanted to come to Canterbury anyway."

Anna tiring began to feel harassed.

"And that was when you began to be Annie, the barmaid at the Ark?"

"I want to go home now. Am I walking or will you take me?"

Anna shook off Bryce's guiding hand as they left the restaurant.

"I am capable of opening a door."

She was angry she had exposed so much to Bryce.

"I would very much enjoy working with you. I would also ensure you were well paid."

"You'll never understand."

"Hazlitt thinks you may be a Time Walker. That would look good as a book title, wouldn't it? Anna Cato, Time Walker. As the opening title of a TV documentary? As a feature film? Anna Cato played by? Anna Cato?"

*

71

Carole said, "A silver BMW? I say, you're stepping out, aren't you? And you're late home. If I were your Mother, I'd be phoning the fuzz. Where have you been, young lady?"

Anna flopped into the couch.

"Making more mistakes. I got a note with some flowers saying he was parked outside the theatre."

"He who?"

"I presumed it was Hazlitt, but it wasn't. I was in the car before I realised it was George Bryce."

"Who's George Bryce?"

"The psychologist Hazlitt told me to stay away from."

"But you didn't?"

"I was curious."

"So, he took you to Quadlino's and seduced you with gentle pats on the knee and soothing words? I've never been to Quadlino's. I could endure the pats and soothing words."

"Such cruelty!"

"We went to McDonalds and he got much more out of me than I should've given."

Carole lost her mockery.

"You definitely need a sherry."

"And a hug?"

"You shall have both."

Carole sought a half-full bottle of sherry and glasses from the cabinet.

"Stolen from dear Mama at Christmas. Good stuff. She may not be too quick on the uptake, but my Mama can spot a quality sherry at a hundred yards."

Carole returned to put down the sherry and glasses on the coffee table. She found the mobile and turned off the television.

To a slightly bewildered Anna she ordered, "Stand up!"

Anna obeyed.

"Prepare for the hug!"

They embraced and Anna began to feel calmer.

"Thank you, Carole! You're a good friend!"

They sat down and Carole poured two glasses of sherry. She gave one to Anna and sipped her own.

"Splendid! Just a hint of Christmas Past. We are going to sink Mama's sherry, but we must toast her first. Here's to my

72

Mama! God bless and keep her! And can we come for Christmas so I can borrow another bottle of delicious sherry?"

Anna laughed and life began again.

"Did you sign anything for this Bryce creature?"

"No."

"Never sign anything without consulting me. Agreed?"

Anna smiled to say, "Agreed."

"Did you tell him about our weird experience at Gilsford? Springfield Park Avenue?"

"No."

"Good! Now tell me what you told Mister Bryce."

*

Joseph Randolph, esteemed Truscott office manager, appeared before Carole's desk as the Angel of Doom. She looked up with the biro between her teeth from the notes she had taken of Anna's meeting with Bryce and sighed.

She removed the biro to say, "For someone as amiable and I may say, as competent as you, Joe, you offer the most gloomy appearance. Isn't there some way you could lighten your demeanour? A clown's nose? An illuminated whizz-around bow tie?"

Randolph laughed.

"There! You see that's much better!"

"Thank you. I'll take the propeller bow tie under advisement."

"Whose funeral have you to announce today?"

"Something rather jollier, I suspect. The Consulting Archaeologist, Mister Robin Camberley-Jarvis…"

Carole interrupted to ask, "Round Robin?"

"His weight is irrelevant. He would like to invite you.."

"I won't tell you about the last invitation I was foolish enough to accept to view his Egyptian phalluses."

"I'm not listening. The County Archaeologist is inviting you to a private viewing of the remains that were discovered in the pit at Boxborough Manor."

"When?"

"At your convenience."

73

"I haven't got a convenience. I share a loo."

"Before they go public."

Carole sprang up, surprising the older man.

"I go. I come back!"

Randolph asked, "Why do you make things so difficult, Carole?"

His question was unanswered. Carole had vanished, startling the pigeons as she sprinted for her car.

*

As the archaeologist and Carole walked the corridor together, Robin Camberley-Jarvis, pale, plump and pompous, said, "You do understand, don't you, my dear? This is a special privilege, this private viewing?"

"Oh, I do, Robin! I'm astonished to be here. A wonderful surprise. Much appreciated."

"We do owe a duty to the public, but I felt as the discoverers of this remarkable find, you should have first peep."

"You make it sound quite conspiratorial. Shouldn't we be talking in whispers?"

Carole laughed and punched his arm lightly to assure her benefactor that she was merely jesting. Robin laughed too, entering into the spirit of the moment.

"Then, perhaps, I should whisper if you can promise me the appropriate display, we may allow you to display the skeletons in this wonderful house you're restoring."

"Oh, my word! Really! That would be a great privilege!"

Delighted, Robin put a finger to his lips.

"As you say, only to be whispered to your father."

"Swelp me god, guvnor!"

She smiled sweetly at the Consulting Archaeologist as her inner being complained; *No way do they belong in a glass case in a museum. They belong at Boxborough House. They lived and died there.*

Camberley-Jarvis opened the door before them and stood aside for his guest to enter. With his eyes upon her posterior as Carole knew from previous experience. It was a disappointingly ordinary workroom with windows on one side with a dismal

74

view of a large yard. There was a large table in the centre of the room on which were laid out two skeletons. On a secondary table was a collection of clothing scraps, buckles, coins, buttons and the silver head of a cane.

"This is Miss Carole Truscott on whose property this remarkable discovery was made," trumpeted the Consulting Archaeologist, introducing Carole to a young woman who was working at a sink. She dried her hands and came forward to say, "I'm Lucy Foster, general dog's body."

"I'm sure that's not true."

Turning to the table, Carole said, knowing she was talking to the correct person, "Somebody's been working very hard, Lucy."

"We do our best," the Consulting Archaeologist agreed.

Lucy smiled, dismissing the compliment.

"Shall I put Miss Truscott..."

"Carole, please!"

"Carole in the picture, sir?"

"Carry on, Miss Foster!"

"This is the sixteenth, seventeenth century version of the shoot-out at the old corral."

Carole wasn't sure if she was supposed to laugh.

"Seriously?"

"All four men died by pistol fire. Times were changing. Gentlemen might carry swords, but not all killers were gentlemen. Let me introduce the cast."

She moved to stand behind the shorter of the two skeletons, allowing the windows to light the table.

"This is the Earl Boxborough, an English country gentleman. His title is ancient, originating in a lost Kentish village called Box. He was over sixty and took no interest in the politicking or skulduggery rampant in his day. His interests included gardening, fishing, cattle breeding, Latin texts and lepidoptera. There is actually a Boxborough moth. How less dangerous could an old gentleman be? He was attacked and murdered most probably in his own garden."

Carole interrupted to ask, "Why does it sound even worse to be murdered in your own garden?"

"The Earl, a completely inoffensive old man was murdered between fifteen eighty-four and ninety-five."

"How do you know this?"

Lucy gestured towards the smaller table.

"It's all there. Coins, clothing scraps, eye glasses, crest and buckles."

She returned her attention to the skeleton.

"The pistol was fired at close range and the Earl died almost instantly. The lead ball struck his right eye. To make sure of his silence someone pierced the chest cavity with a blade."

"Good God! What had the poor fellow done?"

"It was a very turbulent period of our history."

Lucy turned to the taller skeleton.

"Let me introduce you, Carole. This gallant young man is the Earl's eldest son, Ralph Boxborough."

"Oh, no! You'll have me in tears. This is total tragedy."

"We surmise Ralph surprised the murderers and tried to defend his father. But his sword was no defence against the pistol."

She turned to the two skeletons on the second table.

"Two heavyset men poorly dressed who we believe were members of the Earl's household staff who came to his aid and were shot down. The price of loyalty is sometimes severe."

Turning to the third table, Lucy added, "That you disturbed so little was a bonus for us. Everything is there. Every bone, button, coin, buckle and fragment of clothing. A sword and eye glasses, but no pistols. The sword in the pit belonged to Ralph."

She handed the weapon to Carole who was surprised by the weight.

"Oh, I see! It has the crest."

She returned the sword to the table.

"I suppose it's as good a way to die, defending your father."

"The murder of the Boxboroughs wasn't a spontaneous tragedy. It was carefully planned. The problem with murder is getting rid of the bodies. We believe the pit wasn't fortuitous. Members of this conspiracy arranged to dig a well where there was no prospect of finding water and if so, the dry pit would be filled in. There was connivance in the household. When the old

Earl watched the men digging he'd have no inkling it was to be his grave."

Carole found herself so moved by the fragments of lives destroyed as to be close to tears. Anger too began to grow.

"So they dumped the old man, his son and the servants in the pit, filled it in and went off to report to their master that the Boxboroughs had been silenced. And for four hundred years there was silence."

"Amen," said Lucy Foster.

NINE

Anna was pinning Peter's cap in place when Wendy burst into the dressing room. Anna lost control of the cap.

Wendy cried, "Oops!"

Anna bit back her exasperation. Wendy retrieved the cap, dusting off stray faerie dust before returning it to Anna.

"Sorry!"

"Let me guess."

"He's here. But not in the stalls. He's in the royal box tonight. Donny gave me this note he gave to Donny."

Under his jaunty cap, Peter sighed into the mirror. Wendy waggled the note under his nose and Anna took the note. She turned to pretend to tear up the paper into the waste basket.

Wendy struggled to stop her and cried, "Oh, no, please! Please do read it!"

Anna regarded the excited face.

"You are really very young, aren't you? Are you eleven? Twelve?"

Wendy laughed as a silver bell.

"Sixteen! And as my very best friend, you should know!"

"When did that happen?"

"January. When Gillian was going to dump me in with the kids and you said, 'Tammie can share with me.' Then you became my best friend ever."

"I would say Tinker Bell, the way she's always fluttering around my head."

The girl was hurt and the light drained from her. Anna felt uncomfortable and regretted her words.

"Silly joke! Didn't mean it! Look! I haven't torn up the wretched man's note."

"Then read it!"

Wendy jumped up and down. Anna read the note. It apologised for his behaviour, suggesting Anna have dinner with

78

him after the show to hear his good news of a research project Becket University were anxious to undertake.

"What's it say? Oh, Anna, do tell me. I won't tell anyone, I promise. Cross my heart!"

Anna kissed the child on the forehead.

"You really are a sweet kid, Tammie. Don't ever grow up, will you!"

"I promise!"

Anna prepared herself, cleared her throat and lied.

"My darling! My heart aches for you. Let me take you away from all this. Let us fly to Paris tonight. The seats are booked. The world is our oyster. Eternal love, my darling. Georgie."

Wendy sighed the longest sigh the world has ever heard.

"I knew it! I knew it was love. Let me see, please!"

Anna withheld the note, clutching it to Peter's manly chest.

"No! No one shall ever read it but me. I shall treasure it all my life! Will you make sure it's buried with me?"

Wendy nodded agreement, too near to tears to speak. She recovered enough to ask, "So, will you fly away tonight with Georgie to Paris and eat oysters?"

"I cannot. I am wedded to my art. I am a Thespian. I fear Georgie may find his love unrequited."

They sat together in a compassionate silence. Wendy stroked Anna's hand and Anna smiled on her best friend who constantly fluttered around her like Tinker Bell.

Wendy asked, "Anna?"

"Yes, best friend?"

"Is being a thespian the same as being a lesbian?"

*

When the clock chimed, Kit cried, "God's puddens, this is not endurable!"

Despite Boxborough's effort to detain him, Kit rose, waking the halberdiers and strode to the desk where the old man looked up in alarm. A dark moon of ink dropped from his quill on to the manuscript.

"Do you realise what you've done, you impudent . .?"

79

Kit interrupted the scribe as Ralph sought to drag him back to the bench. Hitching his backside onto the desk, he complained, "Do you realise the injury committed to my arse by an hour or more on that damned bench?"

The old man cowered back from the fierce face. The halberdiers elbowed Ralph aside and seized Kit by the arms, pulling him away from the desk. Kit resisted vigorously and Ralph joined the fray. The four men danced savagely. The dancing stopped when a voice said, "Compose yourselves, gentlemen."

The halberdiers sprang to attention. Kit and Ralph sought to recover breath. The old man behind the desk began to complain, but was silenced by a glance from his master. Elizabeth's spymaster and his clerk Thomas stood in the doorway to the inner sanctum. He was worthy of his nickname, the Dark Lord. He wore a full ivory beard, his eyes were dark & piercing and standing tall in black robes, Sir Francis Walsingham was a redoubtable personage.

The spymaster remarked, "There is only one man I know who would go to war over a piss splash. Christopher Marlowe."

"It would seem so. I apologise, milord."

"One day when you are of no further value to me, Thomas will make an account of your insolence and I shall punish you accordingly."

"Yes, milord. you will have right to do so."

"But that is not today's concern."

The dark satanic lord turned and retired to the inner office. Thomas at the threshold beckoned Kit forward. Ralph Boxborough moved with him.

The inner office was dark & shadowed; the windows heavily curtained. A visitor might not notice the men-at-arms standing in the corner shadows. His lordship returned to sit at his desk and Thomas to stand at his shoulder. The office was so steeped in twilight as to assure the hapless that there was no escape, no reprieve and no pity. Ralph Boxborough was unsure he would see the clear light of day again. Kit knew the purpose of the gloom and was not so easily subdued. Ralph came to stand beside Kit before the desk.

"Who is this bold spirit beside you, Marlowe?"

Ralph almost spoke, but a movement of Walsingham's hand silenced him.

"Ralph Boxborough, milord. He has agreed to join me in this endeavour."

"Why would he be so foolish?"

Ralph responded, "May I answer for myself, milord?"

The spymaster nodded.

"In the fewest words, sir."

"My work in running errands, sir, is a task that could be done by boys or carried by a dog. I came to Court to serve my Queen. Not to skivvy for her."

"Then you are best out of it. What qualities d'you believe he has that are valuable to you, Marlowe?"

"Loyalty. He came to Court to serve her Majesty. He is what I am not, a gentleman. Of gentle birth he has that extra quality."

"Common sense, I would wager. Of which you have not an iota. Good manners too?"

Kit tried not to smile and failed.

"So be it. You will also be accompanied by my choice. A gentleman. Loyal. An adventurous spirit. Sir Royan Armitage."

The stranger stepped from the shadows to bow with a theatrical flourish, declaiming, "Your servant, gentlemen!"

Ralph Boxborough bowed and Kit followed suit reluctantly. Armitage was of middle age, strongly built, balding but full bearded. Kit disliked him on sight.

"An honour to serve you, Master Marlowe! I trust I shall be of assistance in this matter. You may rely on me to offer more than good manners."

Kit sensed Armitage had been previously advised of the mission.; that he was Walsingham's creature. He formally introduced Boxborough. He and Ralph exchanged glances while welcoming the serpent to their company.

"The mission you will undertake is one of reconciliation. It will require both patience and diplomacy. Dealing with a most important personage may well require good humour. Amply served by Master Marlowe who is adept at entertaining an audience. Where diplomacy and political calculation may not prevail, my good friend Marlowe will captivate your prize."

Walsingham paused and was so long silent in his chair, Kit wondered whether he had fallen into sleep. As a child Kit had often awakened his Grandfather from dozing by whistling as a blackbird. The old man would wake, crying, "Confound that wretched bird! It haunts me, Kit. Is there not a boy in the house has a catapult?"

In the twilight room Kit awoke to the spymaster suddenly speaking.

"The matter is the Scots Queen, Mary Stuart. The lady is not only Scottish, but Catholic. A thorn in her Majesty's side. A camp of discontent. A rallying point for a flag. She is too subtle to be caught in any Jesuit plot although we know she is so involved. But we cannot charge King James's daughter and turn the Scots into the Spanish camp. So, what can we do in honour to resolve this problem, gentlemen?"

The gentlemen in question were silent, their brows racked suggesting thought, their heads bereft of inspiration..

"I know what Armitage would suggest. It is tempting. But who would kill a Queen? Who would reckon the consequences?

No, no, it will not do! It would be indeed foolish to teach the common people to cut off a sovereign's head."

Walsingham sat silent, regarding three men of which two wished fervently to be elsewhere.

"Tell me, Marlowe, is it particularly difficult to persuade a woman to do what you wish? I have little experience in this arena,"

"It depends on the woman. A combination of laughter, music, complimentary speech. Convince her she is a unique being and she will hasten to agree."

"Even a Queen?"

"A Queen is a woman. But surely, milord, you don't intend…!"

Walsingham interrupted. "Surely not indeed! A pregnant Queen is a double disaster."

The gentlemen sighed with relief.

"What I wish you to do, my dear Marlowe, is persuade this pestilential Queen of the Scots that she would be far happier in France from whence she came. We don't want her here and the Scots don't want her there. She is an unwelcome guest that we would dispatch with a heavy burden of English gold. Can you perform this service without stealing from the payment?"

"I will use my very best endeavour to remove this thorn that smarts our sovereign lady, milord. I will not fail you while I have breath."

"And you, Sir Ralph?"

"I am your devoted servant. I pledge my honour, milord."

Kit noted that no surety was requested from Sir Royan Armitage. Walsingham held out his hand and Thomas placed a sealed document on the palm.

"In the happenstance that the Stuart Queen is not amenable to a rich retirement in the French court, here are your final instructions. Only to be opened in the event of stalemate. Do you understand?"

"Yes, milord?"

"Then I wish you good fortune and a happy resolution."

"If I may ask? Where is the Scottish Queen, milord?"

"She is residing in Fotheringhay Castle, Northampton shire?"

"Will her majesty be informed of our coming, milord?"

"It is never wise to inform anyone of who is coming or going."

*

Kit & Ralph passed once more through endless anonymous corridors.

"Are you such a rake as you are described?"

Kit smiled.

"How easy it is to destroy a reputation. Do you know how many plays I have written?"

"A great many."

"Then how would I have time to chase the fair sex? We scribblers are more chaste than any monk in his lonely cell."

Ralph regarded Kit wondering how trustworthy were his words.

They walked on in silence until Ralph spoke.

"I have the odd feeling that this mission will not be as straightforward as his Lordship would have us believe."

"Ah, then I can reassure you there is no greater liar in the Kingdom than his Lordship."

*

In the privacy of his bed chamber Kit Marlowe examined the seal on the package given to him by Walsingham. It bore no crest, but a thumb print with which a miller might well have sealed his better wheat. Sufficient guarantee as all millers within his county would know the miller's thumb. The seal was not yet hard as the wax had been secured within the hour. Using his knife blade and a wary candle he began cautiously to peel the seal from the vellum. One might have supposed it was not the first time. His caution was repaid and the seal came away freely. Kit opened the folded document and reading, sat frozen in horror.

He rose to secure the latch & bolt the door. He returned to his chair and read the document again from first to last word. It was a royal warrant for the execution of the traitor Mary Stuart, Queen of Scots in the precincts of Fotheringhay Castle.

"Holy Mother of God! What treachery is worse than this!"

Kit's bladder was overflowing and his knees shaking. He had never felt such fear.

"I am doomed if I do or don't!"

The warrant was signed by Elizabeth R. There was no mistaking the crow's scratching. The execution was to be undertaken without delay in the presence of the Queen's Commissioner, Master Christopher Marlowe who would certify as to the death of the woman Mary Stuart.

"Dear Christ! What is this poor Commissioner to certify? A head rolling on the floor from a headless corpse?"

The warrant overruled any previous judgement or assignment regarding Mary Stuart, traitor to the Crown & criminally involved in the Papist plot to overturn the kingdom.

"This is sister to sister? Sharing a common blood? The great-granddaughter of Henry VII? What worse treason might there be? It outweighs Lear that might be taken for a comedy!"

Kit was overwhelmed by anger and sorrow. Unbidden tears flooded his eyes. Sorrow receded as anger grew.

84

"Is this to be? That a Queen may murder another noble being? Then nothing is in order. If a Queen may require murder then who may punish an ignorant labourer who follows her example?"

The traitor's corpse was to be transported to London in the coffin provided and buried according to the Queen's wishes. Kit refolded the execution order, used the candle to reseal the letter and hid it deep within his personal equipage. Kit found his way to the gardez l'eau.

He said aloud and the words echoed, "'Tis like unto a play. I hold the Fates bound fast in iron chains and with my hand turn Fortune's wheel about; and sooner shall the sun fall from his sphere than Tamburlaine be slain or overcome. Elizabeth shall be my Mycetes!"

*

When Anna had shed the guise of Peter Pan and barely closed the front door behind her she found Carole on the stairs.

"What's wrong?"

Carole came down the steps and Anna retreated. In the small hallway, Carole said, "That man Hazlitt is here."

"Oh, no!"

"About an hour. He said he wouldn't go away without seeing you."

"So, you let him in?"

"He looked so pathetic, poor man."

"Why didn't you tell him to buzz off?"

"He said he had something important to tell you."

"He's no different to Bryce. That man is in the audience every evening. It distracts the cast so much. To the children it has every thrill of the Great Romance. Of unrequited love. To Gillian it's exasperating. But he's wearing me down. If it goes on much longer, I swear I'll murder him with Peter's sword."

"Well, Mister Hazlitt's sitting upstairs in my Mama's chair."

"Then I'll jog around the block while you tell him to shift his sorry arse."

Anna turned to the door, but Carole forestalled her, placing her back to the door.

"Get yourself up there and talk to your visitor."

The door on the landing opened and a voice called, "It's a very pleasant room, but I'm beginning to feel rather silly. Wouldn't it be better if we talked upstairs?"

When they were comfortably seated with cups of tea and two custard cremes each, Anna said, "I'm sorry to sound unwelcoming, but I had an interrogation from your colleague that has left me feeling rather foolish."

"George Bryce in the strictest sense is not my colleague."

"For this relief much thanks."

"I've spent considerable hours searching for the Ark tavern. But I had an unpleasant surprise when I went back to Historic Documents. Missis Dainfield had no recollection of us ever having been there."

"But that's not true!"

Carole interrupted with, "She's covering her arse."

"But they did have a small fire on a table where documents had been left, carelessly exposed. The documents, of very little value, were destroyed."

"She's not going to admit she allowed you access and documents were damaged. She could lose her job."

Hazlitt admitted, "You could be right."

"So, the mention of the sale of the Ark was destroyed?"

John Hazlitt smiled.

"Fortunately, I made a copy."

"But someone, doesn't wish us to find the Ark."

"Then we must become even more determined to find it."

TEN

Kit had contrived to fall into an uneasy doze. He was aware of Armitage trotting past the carriage to chivvy the coachman to a faster pace. Kit and Ralph were shaken suddenly as the carriage gained speed and a satisfied horseman trotted past to return as escort to the following wagon.

"Fusspot, my father would say. This Armitage cannot abide but to control our every step," muttered Ralph Boxborough.

The carriage horses slackened pace.

"Every appearance of order, but order itself."

Kit sat up and opened his eyes.

"Have I disturbed you?"

"Morpheus had only whispered to me. Where are we?"

"Unless Armitage's bath tub falls off the wagon again we shall be in Buckingham within the hour where we shall pass the night."

Kit mused, "I wouldn't have marked Sir Royan as a man who bathed more than twice a year."

"I understand it is his mode of seduction. What maiden would refuse a hot scented bath?"

Kit laughed to say, "Then the chamber door opens and Sir Royan enters to dangle his fingers in the bath to test the heat of the water?"

*

Sir Royan on horseback passed the carriage window and the carriage came to a halt.

"Now what?"

As if in answer, Sir Royan appeared at the carriage door.

"The wagon has thrown a wheel. You will drive on to the Swan at Buckingham and secure our quarters. I will join you as soon as possible."

87

The empurpled face vanished and the carriage rolled forward.

"He's not such a bad fellow," Ralph commented, "He could've kept us out here in the wilderness until God knows when."

"And as he holds the purse strings, he'll find us sober."

As the carriage resumed its boring journey Ralph returned to the book he was reading and Kit trimmed his finger nails with his knife. Running out of fingers, Kit asked, "If I may ask, what are you reading?"

"All the great generals say to win a battle you must mark your enemy. You must learn of his strengths and weaknesses."

"I have a scholar for company as well as a swordsman. So?"

"So, I am reading about Mary Stuart, Catholic Queen of the Scots. More French than Scots or English."

"As I am more Shoreditch than Westminster."

"Mary is the great-granddaughter of Henry VII of England. She was next in line to the English throne because Henry VIII's children, are not recognised as legitimate. She has as valid a claim to the English throne as Elizabeth."

Kit sat up sharply.

"Boiled bunions, Ralph! Not so loud! I doubt Armitage would agree."

"No one can deny the truth, Kit. She has a valid claim to the English throne. Except she is Catholic and therefore a deadly enemy of Elizabeth. With Mary Stuart on the throne there would be civil war. And that's the truth of it."

"Sod the truth, Ralph! I don't want to find my head looking up at my arse from the floor. Does it not say anything useful about her?"

"She is lively, beautiful and clever."

"Now that encourages me."

"I sense sarcasm. Then there is more to come. Mary plays the lute and virginal. She is accomplished in prose and poetry, horsemanship, falconry and needlework. She speaks French, Italian, Latin, Spanish, Greek and native Gaelic. And, of course English."

The carriage chose to lumber over a series of bumps coinciding with Ralph's recitation of Mary's achievements; each collided bump registering on Kit's posterior.

"So, she is a regular paragon! A bride suitable for Zeus! Please tell me, dear friend, she is dwarfish, with blackened teeth, hunch-backed and a pockmarked face. With a body stench that kills stray dogs at a distance."

Ralph laughed; an openhearted honest laugh. Royan Armitage, in the saddle, appeared at the carriage window.

"Did ye call, sir?"

"I laughed, sir. Master Marlowe was telling me about a woman who offered him her bed if he would let her play Helen of Troy on stage."

"You lucky dog, Marlowe! I trust she played true! I am not a follower of theatre. But girls played by boys stirs the blood, eh! I shall leave you now and return to the wagon,"

He trotted away, every inch the gallant cavalier.

Kit shook his head in amazement.

"He believes that I would behave so!"

"And if Royan Armitage is feeling frisky, lock up your sons with your daughters."

The carriage vented its indignation with a wracking of limestone that bounced Kit in his seat as a pea on a drum.

"Is there any mention of her features?"

"The lady is described in her portrait as having a small, oval-shaped head, a long, graceful neck, bright auburn hair, hazel-brown eyes, smooth pale skin. ."

"Enough, enough! "

"She stands taller than most men. Nearly six feet tall."

"A formidable fortress."

"It becomes obvious why she is such a danger to our sovereign lady. Packing her off to France with a large dowry doesn't accord with the royal character I observe in these pages."

"So, I have in friendship a philosopher and a fusilier?"

"I do wonder to what lengths our Elizabeth might go to be rid of this thorn in her side."

Kit Marlowe was silent.

"And why are we lumbered with Armitage? Our Royan is no diplomat. He is not well regarded at court. He cheats at cards and borrows money. Requests for repayment are met with threats of violence. Ladies steer well clear of this man. The kindest word one might use is that he is a scoundrel."

"Why tell me this now, Ralph?"

"We are free of the politics of the court. Free for the moment from Walsingham. Forewarned is forearmed."

Kit tried to smile, but failed.

"Thank you, my friend. Though I shan't sleep tonight.

Yet he dozed peacefully until the carriage rumbled through the arch into the courtyard of the Swan at Buckingham. The horses expressed their tiredness, snorting & stamping. The ostlers rushed to free the horses, aware of the crest on the carriage doors. Ralph Boxborough shook Kit's shoulder. He awoke to proclaim, "God's arse, but I have a mouth as dry as Cuthbert's tomb."

Ralph sighed to say, "Even waking you spout blasphemy. How have you avoided decapitation for so long, Kit?"

"Have we pennies between us for a mug of beer?"

"Show them your Commission," suggested his friend.

*

The world changed when Kit Marlowe, feeling foolish, unrolled the Queen's Commission before the landlord of the Swan's surprised eyes. Kit & Ralph became honoured guests for whom even the best the Swan could offer may not be good enough for her Majesty's Commissioner.

They stumbled upstairs to fall onto goose feather beds with stomachs tight as kettledrums & breath fit to enflame a candle. They snored until the first false dawn when Kit was aroused by commotion in the yard below. He dragged himself bleary-eyed to the window to stare into the yard. Ralph followed him. The wagon had arrived with Sir Royan on a tired horse. Ralph moved to return to bed, but Kit stopped him. A sleepy ostler grumbled across the yard to the horses. Another took Armitage's mount.

"Look, Ralph!"

Three men dismounted from the wagon. Ralph yawned.

Kit stared and stated, "They are not the men who started this journey with us."

Ralph woke up, looking at the men who were listening to Armitage, stamping feet in the chilly morning as horses do.

"I suspect those poor fellows are dead."

The three men were brawny, shaven-headed, with tunics and breeks below the knee.

Ralph said slowly, "They look like ruffians."

"Armitage is better dressed, but he's of the same breed."

"What do we do?"

"We pretend all is well, but we mark our enemies."

"I have two pistols, Kit. I would be happy to show you how to use one."

*

In that same dawn a labourer trimming the hedge of the Buckingham road beyond the hamlet of Kilwert found blood on the road stones. He stooped to find three coins, but no more. He pocketed the coins and wiped his hands on the grass.

Moving on, he found a dead man blocking the ditch. He had the neatly cropped grey head of a household servant. The labourer stole his shoes and the crucifix on a chain about his neck. He found two more dead men in the ditch. All three had been bludgeoned to death, but the third man, taller & stronger, had resisted. For which he was rewarded with his face beaten beyond recognition. Their discoverer stole all three pairs of shoes and the ring from the big man's hand. He had little understanding so the crest on the ring was meaningless to him. Rejoicing at this windfall the labourer made his way along the hedge. He was disappointed to find the farther ditch lacking dead men & shoes.

*

"That there was never an Ark in the city isn't true," Anna asserted angrily.

Hazlitt assured her, soothing her ruffled feelings..

"The Ark existed because you, Annie Cato, work there. I am inclined to believe you."

"Thank you. Sometimes I feel."

Hazlitt produced a notebook and thumbing to a certain page, began to read, "*Master Henry Radbrack & his wife Dora were accused & found guilty of heresy and burnt at the stake. And the tavern known as the Ark was put up for sale by public auction, proceeds to the Cathedral Treasury.* Someone burnt the original note and the custodian chickened out on us, but I have my copy. Someone wanted the Ark forgotten. You Annie Cato, barmaid by profession, has let the fox into the chicken coop. The Ark is much more than a dingy beer swamp. The lost scrap of vellum mentions that there were other conspirators who escaped."

Carole said, "I'm struggling somewhat to catch up."

Hazlitt quoted from his notebook again.

"*Whereas at their house others conspired, only the Radbracks were taken by the Reeve and brought before the Ecclesiastical Court.* And the conspiracy? At this date in our history the ongoing conspiracy.."

Carole interrupted to say, "Is this conspiracy an attempt to return England to the Holy Roman Church and overthrow Elizabeth?"

To which Hazlitt added, "And the threat of Spain invading England. The Armada and Frankie Drake in the Channel, Medina in the Spanish Netherlands and Henry Garnet the Jesuit plotting bloody revolution."

Anna and Carole looked in some surprise at Hazlitt who smiled to say, "I've been doing some reading. And more. Anna and her lost life are tied up in this tangle of treacheries. When we find the Ark we'll begin to unravel Anna & Annie's story. Do we deserve coffee now?"

"Better. We have three inches of port in a bottle purloined from Mama that I was keeping for the End of the World. Sucks boo to the end of the world! We'll have a tiny tipple now."

Struggling with the neglected bottle Carole suddenly felt dizzy.

For the briefest moment it seemed to her that the familiar sitting room dissolved and she stood in a dark street of impressive houses. The stink of horse dung was sharp to her nostrils. Torches burned outside some doors. Beneath these torches stood footmen. As she watched, a girl, cloak flying, hurried along the street. The sitting room returned. No one seemed to have noticed her disappearance.

*

After Hazlitt had departed the girls settled into the couch and Carole commented, "He's a better man than Bryce. He favours the chase, less the slaughter of the hind. Someone said that was the measure of a man."

"Where do you get all this stuff from?"

"Boarding school. They fill your head with quotes to avoid any unfortunate silences at dinner."

"What did they offer for breakfast?"

"Mostly cold beans, fat bacon and stale bread."

"No fried eggs?"

"Not unless you were down first."

"Wasn't there anything good about boarding school?"

"Absence of parents and brothers? Learning girls are cleverer than boys but you mustn't show it? Hanging perilously out of the dorm window smoking your first cigarette and being sick? Whacking Jane Margaret Turnstone's fat ankles with a hockey stick? Shall I go on?"

Anna laughed.

"Those are your happy memories of boarding school? Wasn't there anything really good?"

Carole rose to say, "Something good happened at work today. Chris found a brassbound box hidden in the wall of Bedroom Five. He has a knack of finding things in walls. Remember the priest hole under the stairs? The Communion set?"

"I thought the Boxboroughs were Loyalist?"

"The old Earl would've found it difficult to abandon the Faith he was brought up in. But the House was solidly Protestant."

"Just a little Catholicky on the side?"

Seeing Carole's expression Anna wisely changed course.

93

"What was in the box? I don't suppose it was gold doubloons?" "Love letters. Heartbreaking. Written to a young man in the household. Whichever of the Earl's sons. Begging him to elope with her as their fathers were opposed to their marriage."

"But he didn't?"

Carole shook her head.

"Oh, how stupid of him! I would've eloped."

"Time's living stream flows on. What happened today was Robin Camberley-Jarvis, the Consulting Archaeologist to the Council, phoned me to say the City are considering allowing us to display the Boxborough remains in the new hotel."

"Is that good?"

"It's the best news ever. The hotel makes or breaks us. I don't like Camberley-Jarvis, but this opens up a totally new clientele. Archaeologists, historians.."

"Ghouls?" interrupted Anna.

"Where did you say you went to school? Bash Street?"

"Should've been so lucky."

"I wonder whether you deserve to share the bottle of champagne I bought myself on the way home to celebrate?"

She took a quizzical look at Anna and decided, "I suspect you need a glass of champers more than I do."

"I do, I do, I really do!"

From the kitchen Carole brought the champagne on ice broken from the freezer in a plastic bucket and Anna found two flutes in the cabinet. The cork ricocheted about the sitting room like an angry wasp. Carole raised her glass.

"Here's to the Earl Boxborough and his gallant son! May they enjoy returning to Boxborough House!"

They toasted the Earl and his oldest son separately,

"What about the lovelorn girl?" asked Anna, "Have you tracked her down?"

"Chris played Sherlock Holmes. He believes she was Catherine de Meurnier. Her father was a French silk merchant in Canterbury. There are two mentions of her in the Christchurch Chronicle, but nothing more. She vanishes. It's possible her father sent her to a convent, but unlikely. I propose she is our next toast."

94

They raised refilled flutes to lost Love.

"To Catherine! May she find her true love yet!"

Which sounded odd to Anna, but worthy of a second toast.

"May her lover find his Catherine!"

It was the best evening Anna could ever remember.

"Are we going to have lots of toasts?"

"Until the bottle runs dry."

"And then what?"

"One of us will have to crawl round to Asquith's for fresh supplies."

ELEVEN

Kit and Ralph brought their bundles out to the carriage where their driver was standing. As Ralph loaded the bundles the driver, an older man, enquired of Kit, "May I speak with you, sir?"

"Of course, Jonard. Speak freely."

They moved together to the patient horses where Jonard pretended to test the harness. Ralph Boxborough called, "I'll sign for our reckoning, Kit."

He vanished into the Swan.

The old man hesitated before he spoke.

"Sir, I beg you to release me from my duty."

Kit recognised his fear. His hands shook on the harness.

"That would leave us in great difficulty. Tell me why."

"Sir, we are in the hands of murderers. Sadly, I have to include Sir Royan Armitage. He must know."

"As we do, Jonard."

The man seemed as much relieved as surprised.

"Sadly, we assume your friends from the Household have been murdered."

"They say they deserted and they were recruited from a nearby village. Richard, he was the Queen's man. He'd been a soldier. A good man. He wouldn't desert. He'd've made a fight of it. I didn't believe a word they said, butt I thought it best to accept their story."

He looked hopefully to Kit who clasped his shoulder and grinned. He could sense the tension slackening.

"Good man! Now there are three of us looking out for each other. Boxborough and I have swords and pistols. Do you have a knife?"

"And a crossbow on the carriage, sir."

"Good. I have a mission to complete for her Majesty and I intend to do so. Forewarned and forearmed, we'll not be plucked like chickens. This night we shall reach Fotheringhay

Castle where help will be at hand. Whatever mischief they intend we will overcome it. Are you with me, Jonard, on her Majesty's business?"

"Yes, sir. Much relieved, sir. I won't fail you, sir."

They shook hands. The driver's hand was strong & dry.

Over Jonard's shoulder Kit watched the rogues help the ostlers bring out the wagon horses from the stabling.. From the front door Sir Royan Armitage appeared to savour the early morning sunlight. To Jonard, Kit said, "Not a word. Trust me. Now play at checking the wheels and axles."

The old man vanished and Armitage wandered across to hail Kit.

"Good day, Marlowe! The sun shines upon us. By God's grace, we'll reach the castle before dark."

Kit regarded an uncertain sky.

"In such hope I'm checking the harness. The old man is, shall we say, likely to drop the chestnuts into the fire. Perhaps her Majesty cannot afford to pension him off? But then I don't wish him to fall from the box today either."

They shared a laugh. As ringing as a competent actor could devise. Kit rapped the carriage to offer, "This tyrant has hammered my arse too long. One more day is all I can endure!"

"Tonight we shall sleep in the Castle," Sir Royan Armitage promised.

*

Storm clouds darkened the day and by noon it had began to rain as if it were Saint Swithin's Day. When lightning flashed and thunder rolled the carriage horses became skittish. The driver climbed down to comfort his horses, standing between the pair with a hand on each neck. Kit, jumping down from the carriage, called to Ralph behind him, "You can always judge a man by the way he treats his horses."

The driver was already drenched. When he turned his head he grinned at the friends. Beyond the trees smoke curled upwards from a solitary chimney. A lane wandered through the trees towards the farm. Armitage rode up alongside to berate the driver.

"Turn into the lane, man! We will seek some shelter. The wagon goods will be ruined."

Kit & Ralph protested.

"We need to press on."

Armitage declared, "I see a barn. We'll make shelter for the horses."

When Kit protested Armitage said, "You are the diplomat. I am master on the road."

"Very well. Then take the wagon first."

"Agreed."

The carriage driver took his horses forward to clear the lane and the wagon turned, led by Armitage on horseback and the surly trio on the wagon. The wagon trundled into the lane.

Ralph warned, "This is not right, Kit."

Patiently the carriage driver backed his alarmed horses to turn onto the unpaved lane. They gathered together under an oiled tarpaulin over the horses' heads & shoulders to confer; in a warm, wet breath of horses and rain hammering on the canvas.

Kit said, "We must not be separated. If we sleep in a chamber, we sleep together. In a barn, like three rams. Bring the bow and bolts. We may surprise them yet."

"Yes, sir."

"First concern, shelter for the horses."

They sat in the carriage to prepare. Reloading pistols and wrapping them dry, hidden in the groin. Swords free in the sheath. The crossbow was the small weapon, deadly at short range, favoured by assassins. Johan wore it in his shirt and spare bolts belted into his breeches. They secreted knives in their boots.

"Who was it said," asked Ralph, "Keep your powder dry and your bladder empty?"

They lined up along the lane entry and did just that. It was a cheering moment. Then they climbed aboard the carriage and plunged into the lane.

Kit said, "D'y'know what?"

"D'y'know what a source of constant irritation it is for you to constantly ask me, do I know what? Of course, I don't know. Just tell me what it is I don't know."

"I shall scribe a wonderful play of this adventure, Ralph."

"If you live, Kit. That's something you don't know what."

They had been struggling along the lane for perhaps fifteen minutes when the carriage stopped.

"God skin a Persian! What now?"

The wagon was firmly embedded in the mud. Jonad shook his head as Kit and Ralph joined him.

"Those ruffians are not wagoners. They've run it back and forwards and the wheels have dug deep."

Kit commented, "At least they've taken the horses."

Ralph was poking his nose into the wagon's goods; household needs, garrison supplies, fourteen gunpowder tubs, eight bags of lead shot for the fusils, food, smoked meat, wines, fabric bundles and Sir Royan Armitage's bath tub. He stopped at one particular item.

"Kit?"

Kit and Jonad joined him.

"Why would the castle want a coffin? They must have their own carpenters."

"Somewhat more expensive than the one I was buried in," said Kit, "This is a ride to the Pearly Gates for someone of substantial means."

When Ralph gathered speech his friend advised, "Keep your thoughts to yourself. Shall we follow Armitage's example?"

As they led the horses along the lane the rain began to slacken as the storm passed away to frighten chickens & children elsewhere. The farmhouse became clear; the smoking chimney a cheering sight. To the right of the house stood a large barn. Beyond that an open-fronted blacksmith's shop. The furnace was cold. As they approached, Armitage's three companions came out of the barn and walked towards the house. The open door of the barn showed lantern light within. As they entered the yard a collie came to meet them. He didn't bark, but cringed.

Jonad said, "That dog's been sore beaten. He's learned not to bark at strangers."

When they walked into the barn, a man stopped spreading hay for the wagon horses. The dog went to join him. The man, thin, wiry, accustomed to labour at little profit, clutched the hay

99

fork and regarded the newcomers, trying to suppress both anger & fear.

Ralph asked, "You are the farmer?"

"Farmer. Blacksmith. Soldier. Whatever it takes. Sir."

Kit remarked, "Your dog's been beaten. And so have you."

He saw the man's hand grip the fork tighter.

"Ye won't surprise me a second time."

"Is your wife in the house?"

"Do not put your hand on my wife."

"Any one else?"

"No."

"I am the Queen's Commissioner on our way to Fotheringhay Castle. The men in your house are planning to kill us. But they don't know we're aware. We are not your enemy."

The farmer inspected the trio with suspicion. Jonad insisted, "The Commissioner is telling ye the truth. They have already murdered my friends."

Kit repeated his question.

"Is your wife in the house?"

"She's giving supper to those bastards."

"I want you out of here alive. I will try to get their leader to let your wife bring you some supper. Then you will flee from here and return tomorrow."

"Thank you, sir."

When they walked into the farmhouse the hallway was comfortingly warm. In the big room Armitage and his men were sitting at the table gobbling stew.

"There you are, Marlowe! Horses safely in the barn?"

"The man is rubbing them down. He's agreed to feed them."

"Agreed?"

Armitage laughed.

"You're the Queen's Commissioner. He cannot refuse you."

"A little courtesy costs nothing."

"Sit yourselves down. The woman will serve you the best stew you'll ever taste."

Kit hadn't noticed the woman crouched on a stool by the fire. She was clearly terrified.

"Yes, sir! I will, sir."

Her teeth chattered as she spoke.

100

"What is this meat, woman?" Armitage asked.

"Rabbit, sir."

"Rabbit? You live very well here."

Armitage and his crew laughed.

"Thank ye, sir."

From the cauldron over the fire the woman filled three wood bowls with stew and found three wooden spoons. She delivered the bowls to the newcomers, shivering with fear.

"Be careful now! I whip those who spill stew on my friends."

His companions laughed. One man lunged at the woman who shied away, but Ralph took the bowl without spilling a drop. The woman fled to the stool.

Armitage turned a smiling face upon the newcomers.

"Talking of horses, there was some barbarian chief who was rebuked that he favoured horses rather than his men. D'ye know how he answered, Master Marlowe?"

"I can make men, but I can't make horses. I was tempted to give the line to Tamburlaine, but it wasn't mine to give."

The three ruffians, lacking understanding, laughed and Armitage turned on them a devil's glare. The room was suddenly chill.

Kit took advantage to ask, "The fellow seeing to the horses. A good man. Could the woman not take out a bowl of her admirable stew for him?"

"Why not, why not. After all you're the Commissioner. Who am I to refuse?"

The voice clearly displayed contempt, but Kit chose to ignore it.

The woman looked to Kit who nodded. She departed speedily with the bowl of stew.

Ralph asked, "I know of your high reputation as a horseman, Sir Royan. What style of horse would you favour? Ignoring expense."

Sir Royan was slow to recognise flattery. He was applauding the quality of the Arabian stock before he realised the woman had not returned.

"Tub, go and see where the woman has got to!"

Ralph rose, saying, "Then I shall excuse myself a moment to clear my bladder against these venerable bricks."

With a laugh and a bow to the company he vanished.

*

As Ralph ran to the barn, Kit realised Jonard and he were without Ralph's sword. Armitage and his two ruffians rose, kicking away the benches. The younger rogue turned upon Jonard as he struggled to free the crossbow from his shirt.

Armitage cried to the thug at his side, "Earn your money, man! Put him down! Or I'll do for ye!"

Sir Royan drew sword and pistol, but didn't challenge Kit who backed away, struggling to free an unfamiliar sword, until his back found the wall. It all happened in the briefest moment of time.

The younger rogue laughed at Jonard struggling to free his weapon until the bolt fired and buried itself in his right eye. Kit gave up on the sword to pull out Ralph's pistol and aimed at his murderous assailant. In desperation he pulled the trigger and in a great flash the pistol misfired, throwing a cloud of burning powder into the man's grinning face. He turned away, screaming, clawing at his eyes. Armitage moved in to kill Kit.

In the single moment that encompassed the entire fight, they found themselves seemingly on a theatre stage where children screamed & fled and actors stood frozen, open-mouthed. The pirate captain dropped his sword and jumped off the stage to vanish up the centre aisle. From above a slight figure in scarlet dropped between the combatants and drove a shining blade through Sir Royan Armitage.

The audience exploded into applause and the theatre vanished, leaving the survivors of the battle in the farmhouse bewildered & breathless. Armitage lay pulsing blood & groaning on the floor. He lay across the corpse with the bolt in its head. The dying cavalier struggled for breath & cried for a priest from a bloody mouth. The last ruffian stumbled blinded from the room.

Jonard was the first to speak.

"What in God's name was that, sir? A Devil or an Angel?"

"Angel or Devil, he was very timely."

*

Ralph Boxborough stood at the barn door, sword in his right hand and pistol in his left. Then he heard weeping and entered. The farmer was embracing his sobbing wife. He had buried his pitchfork in the chest of their would-be murderer. He lay sprawled on the strewn hay. Ralph lowered the pistol and sheathed his sword.

"Well done, sir! Well done! Let me shake you by the hand."

"I told ye, didn't I? I told ye I wouldn't be surprised a second time."

On the way back to the house, Ralph found himself seized by a ruffian and a knife blade pressed to his neck.

"Cause I'm blind don't mistake iss. I want a horse and I want it saddled. And you'll do it, sir, I promise ye!"

"No, sir, I won't."

He pulled away and asked, "You killed the men on the wagon?"

"The young un squealed like a lass!"

He laughed and Sir Ralph Boxborough, at the risk of his soul, ran the despicable creature through twice. Then he sprinted for the house.

*

"Armitage, tell me who ordered you to do this?"

The dying man struggled to breathe. The words were lost in a flood of bloody bubbles from his mouth.

"Tell me. You have nothing to lose now."

Armitage struggled to raise his head in a final effort to speak and fell back defeated. He beckoned feebly with his left hand to draw Kit closer. He was holding the hand when Sir Royan Armitage died as calmly as a babe falls asleep. He was about to arrange both hands on the dead man's chest when Ralph stopped him.

"Hold hard! Let me see."

Ralph took the hand to display the ring on the third finger. The face of the ring lay in the palm. When he turned the ring, Ralph gasped, "He was a Papist!"

Kit took the hand to see the stone set in the gold ring. "Garnet. Of course! Father Henry Garnet. A most unworthy priest. Involved in murder and torture. Who would see our beloved Elizabeth burnt at the stake. This man is a traitor!"

"No more, dear Ralph. See, he is gone! Dead & unshriven. Denied Heaven, may he rot in Hell. If Hell exists which I doubt. Life on Earth is hell enough. But the accursed ring explains a lot."

Ralph tore the ring from the dead finger and made to throw it into the fire.

"Whoa, whoa! That might be useful some day. If I wish to identify myself in the wrong company."

Kit took the ring and slipped it on to the third finger of his left hand. He turned the garnet inwards. Holding up his hand, he declared, "A simple gold ring. Which binds me to a dear lady who worships me though I have forgot her name. I wonder how many Marlowes I have sired?"

Ralph and Jonard laughed while the farmer and his wife struggled with perplexity.

"A quieter signal than a flag. A venomous snake among good men. Yet if I turn the ring I have access to Papish conspiracy."

Ralph said, "Or wriggling on a rope."

The company was quieted.

"No, no, on the other hand, I have her Majesty's authority."

He held up his right hand displaying the Royal crest and the farmer's wife curtsied. Kit helped her rise.

"Thank you, madam, you have shown such courage and your husband is a very brave man."

TWELVE

When the applause died away and the audience regained its seats, the performance continued, jubilant, well paced, ending on a high emotional note whereafter Gillian had to plead for the audience to disperse and allow the cast to go home to bed. It was by sheer chance that Julian Middleton, the doyen of theatre critics, had been persuaded by his wife to join her sister & family for a weekend in Canterbury. It is sufficient to quote a few words from his subsequent review. *In my entire career I have never seen Captain Hook and the Pirates vanquished in such a wonderful maelstrom of action, magic, blood & terror. A truly memorable, terrifying performance. Watch out for Peter herself, Ms Anna Cato, swordsman supreme.*

As the cast left by the stage door, Wendy asked the question they almost all longed to ask, "How did you do that, Gillian?"

"Trade secret, darling."

"You mean you don't want to tell us."

"I'm sworn to secrecy."

"Well, I can tell you," pronounced Wendy, "it was the most scary thing I've ever seen in all my life."

The children agreed wholeheartedly. On cue the taxi arrived to whisk the director away.

Anna found herself alone on the pavement with Wendy who as usual was reluctant to part company.

"Your Prince is waiting. The royal coach awaits."

"I see a second-hand car."

"Aren't you going to join him?"

Anna ignored the question, but began to walk away. Wendy was disappointed and lagged behind.

"I would! I've never ridden in a Beamer."

Anna stopped walking to allow Tammie to join her.

"Didn't your Mother ever tell you not to get into cars with strange men?"

Wendy laughed. A child's honest laugh.

"He's not a strange man, Anna."

"He is a very strange man. I wouldn't trust him with a Barbie doll."

Wendy found this statement very funny.

"I still have my Barbie."

Wendy laughed. Anna stopped walking.

"'How're you gona get to Rosebank?"

"Walk."

"It was arranged for you all to live at Rosebank Boarding House. Why did Gillian do that, Wendy?"

"I know they didn't arrange it, but Missis Seaberg's son Laurie is absolutely gorgeous. So, I'm grateful for that."

Anna laughed despite herself.

"Wendy, you have to start growing up."

"That's not what Peter Pan says."

Anna was surprised.

"Golly gumdrops! Behind that sweet face there's a brain? I am surprised. You win."

She linked arms with the girl who responded happily.

"Best friends?"

Anna ignored the invitation, but said, "You are with Missis Seaberg to keep you safe. We're very late tonight and you shouldn't be walking home alone. I'll walk you to Rosebank. And I'll tell you some of the things your Mother should've told you."

Both noticed the BMW was following them, but only Anna was angry.

*

Anna waited until Wendy stepped inside the boarding house and waved to Mrs. Seaberg as she closed the door. The BMW was idling at the kerb. Anna made to pass by, but from the open window George Bryce said, "Let me give you a lift home. You know very well I'm not going to jump on you."

Anna hesitated. It was late and she was tired. Anna sank gratefully into the comfort of the BMW. The car pulled away.

"That was a remarkable performance this evening."

"Every evening is remarkable that we stagger through without knocking the scenery over."

"I know what I saw. As do you."

"Gillian is a very enterprising director."

Bryce turned his head to smile at Anna.

"You're not a good liar."

"A change of heart? Your previous opinion was that I was an accomplished liar."

The car stopped obediently at the traffic lights. Driver & passenger were silent. The lights changed and the car pulled away smoothly.

"I saw you interrupt the performance of the play to fly back to the sixteenth century and intervene in a bloody brawl, saving a young man's life. Then you hightailed it back to the twenty-first century and continued your performance without missing a beat. The audience was too bewildered to do more than applaud. An astonishing performance!"

Anna despite herself couldn't help laughing.

"Ah, we are friends again!"

"Never!"

"Participants in a unique venture?"

Anna did not respond.

"It must've been the most extreme impulse that pulled you through Time to save that young man. What's his name?"

"I don't know and I wouldn't tell you if I did."

Bryce turned his head to regard Anna.

"I wasn't thinking to torture you."

"Whatever it is you want, you can't buy it from me."

"Where others wish to travel to the Moon, I want to travel in Time. Is that unreasonable? You are a true Time Walker. I want you to help me."

"Do you understand how beastly you have been to me?"

"I'm sorry. I do most sincerely apologise. I have in my pocket five thousand pounds. A gift for you in apology for my behaviour."

"I don't want your money. Put it away!"

They travelled in silence.

Anna was relieved to see the familiar street.

"You even know where I live!"

"What do you want, Anna?"

"My life has been stolen. I want my real life back."

Exiting the car she remembered her manners.

"Thank you for bringing me home. That was kindly."

"I'd bring you safely home every evening."

"But at what price?"

Anna found her key and opened the door. She stood in the safety of the tiny hallway and heard the car draw away. Tackling the stairs, she heard music and called out, "It's only me."

Anna was midstair when she realised she was Annie carrying a tray of glasses & bottle upstairs at the Ark. She stopped bewildered on the landing and the nearest door opened to Noah's familiar face.

"Annie! Whata ye doing here?"

The room was enlivened by candles and a brisk fire. Four gentlemen sat at the table. The eldest was black-bearded and dressed in black.

"Marianne said take up the gentlemen's drinks. Has I done wrong, master?"

On the landing there was a chill in the air that frightened Annie. The gentlemen at the table sat very still. Noah took the tray from her.

"I only done what Marianne said."

"Go now! I'll speak to Marianne."

Annie turned away, but the bearded man at the table commanded, "Stay! I wish to speak to the girl."

Noah gestured the girl into the room and closed the door, which frightened Annie even more.

"I never meant."

The man rose slowly to silence Annie with a raised hand.

"There is nothing to be frightened of, child. If you tell the truth."

Annie nodded. He was tall and thin and somehow frightening.

"Do you always tell the truth?"

"I hopes so."

The cold dark eyes menaced her soul.

"Do you know who I am?"

108

She tried to look to Noah, but her questioner said, "Don't look elsewhere. Look at me."

He repeated his question.

"No, sir. Never seen ye afore."

"I am the Inquisitor. I do God's work. I seek out the faithless."

"I swear I am a good girl, sir."

"Do you know these gentlemen?"

"No, sir. Never, sir."

Annie made a clumsy attempt to curtsey to the table.

"What is your name?"

"Annie Cato."

"Do you work at the Ark?"

Annie nodded.

"Speak!"

"Yes, milord."

"What do you do?"

"I serve the bar and keep it clean. And I clean the barroom."

"Do you serve upstairs?"

"No, milord. Never. But Marianne told me."

"Noah will speak with this Marianne. Do you like working here?"

Annie came to life.

"Oh, yes! Noah is very kind to me."

"How long have you been here?"

"Long as I remember. Noah found me when a man was hurting me."

The Inquisitor regarded the girl for what seemed an eternity.

"So, are you walking out with a young man?"

"No, milord."

"Do you attend church?"

"No, milord. Does I has to?"

The man stood looking at Annie until she thought her bladder would burst.

"You may go."

"Oh, thank ye! Thank ye, milord!"

Noah closed the door on her gratitude.

"Harmless. But beware of with whom she talks. Deal with this Marianne, Noah. She was careless. Do you understand me?"

"Yes, father."

"You may go."

Noah left the upper room, scarcely less frightened than Annie.

When the tavern keeper departed, the man who wore the Queen's medallion on his breast reassured his companions at the table.

"We are secure. This girl has no more intellect than a Bayswater hog. Otherwise I might find it difficult to explain to my sovereign lady why her minister seeks company in a bothy such as this dung heap."

His companions smiled.

The Inquisitor inquired, "Have we further word of Armitage and his companions?"

"Not since Buckingham, father. All is progressing satisfactorily."

"We offer prayers for the safe conclusion of their enterprise. We are committed now, gentlemen. There will be no turning back. There is one queen too many for this small island."

Annie sat sobbing on the cold wooden seat of the privy. Anna shared the same wooden seat trying to understand the scene she had shared while fearful of some monster pulling her down through the hole into the stinking cesspit.

*

It was with more than the usual sense of relief to find herself on the familiar landing. Anna entered the sitting room to find Carole comfortably ensconced in the couch cushions sipping a glass of sherry while watching television.

"How long have you been lounging there in the lap of luxury?"

"Forever. Worrying and waiting for my dear friend to come home. Hoping you haven't been abducted by aliens. Where've you been anyway?"

"Plonked on a sixteenth century privy hole above an ocean of shit while Annie sobs her heart out. But that's only for starters. My tale of woe I'll relate after I gobble whatever delicacy you've lined up in the microwave and two sherries to catch up."

"Top chef's fish pie with ambrosial Cheddar cheese."

Heading for the kitchen Anna called, "Thank you! Pollard trimmings and mould scraped off the factory wall."

"Ungrateful pig!"

The fish pie was surprisingly tasty. The sherry was as soothing to the spirit as it was numbing to the brain. Anna recalled the exciting events of the evening.

"But did no one question what they saw?"

"It all happened too fast. I jumped down from the mast to confront Captain Hook and landed in the middle of a real fight. There was blood everywhere. The children were screaming. I landed astride a young man on his back on the floor and I'm facing this brute who's about to kill him with a sword."

Anna stopped, seeing again the grisly scene; a man on the floor, his face flooded with blood, a man screaming and clutching his face and the triumphant grin of the man about to drive his blade through the young man.

"This beast was about to kill him. So, what could I do?"

"You could've tried to interpose yourself between the two of them."

"Well, I didn't. I ran him through and he died. That's what I was sent to do. Save that man. But that murderous beast was most astonished."

"I'll bet he was. But, hang on, you don't have a real sword. Peter's sword's plastic, isn't it? It would just bend."

Anna hesitated.

"You remember the sword we found in Gilsford? The Council house?"

"You mean you're waving around a real sword while playing Peter Pan?"

"The weight of it makes all the difference. You try waving a plastic stick. It lacks reality."

"Reality? Remind me never to sit in the front row. Anything else before I ring the police?"

111

"I took Wendy home to the boarding house and Bryce followed us. Then he brought me home."

"What!"

"He understood what he saw on stage. Nobody else seemed to. He wants to be a Time Walker."

"Time Creep surely?"

"And he offered me five thousand pounds in apology. Which I refused."

"Well, I'm not sure I'd've refused the money. Did he actually have the money?"

"Yes."

"A man who follows through. That's rare. In apology? Not for a jaunt through Time? Which you can't deliver. You have no control over when or where you go."

*

Carole awoke from a bewildering dream. The street outside was silent. Inside her head something buzzed as a wasp.

She said aloud, "I know Anna is Annie Cato. Fact. Therefore."

She pushed off the bedding and sat with her feet on the sheepskin rug. Carole had lived with this rug since childhood. In teenage it was her Determinator. With her toes in the fleece she would determine whether she had to rise to her books now and find the answer or leave it for the morrow and slide back into bed.

"I saw Anna in the street. I didn't imagine it."

She rose and went to seek the answer in her bookcase in the sitting room. Bell Harry chimed four as Carole whispered an exultant, "Yes!"

No one questioned her whisper. Carrying the heavy volume of *A HISTORY OF CANTERBURY*, Carole went to disturb Anna. She didn't wait to knock, but entered abruptly, planted herself and the book heavily on the bed and switched on the bedside lamp.

Anna awoke in alarm, struggling to sit up as book & Carole were imprisoning her under the duvet.

She cried, "Someone breaking in? Have you phoned the police?"

"Calm it! Nothing's wrong. I have something to tell you."

Anna, free of the duvet, complained, "At four in the morning?"

"It couldn't wait."

"My father's dead?"

"God, what a gruesome girl you are! Hazlitt's wrong."

"Wha'd'y'mean?"

"There is no Ark. But there is the Archangel Inn, Northgate."

"So?" enquired a sleepy Anna.

"If I was to invite you out for a pint, I wouldn't say Archangel. I'd say d'y'fancy a pint at the Ark?"

"No, thanks. Just let me sleep."

*

Parking in North Gate was impossible. Carole had driven up and down twice seeking whatever might remain of the Archangel Tavern without success. North Gate had become a centre of luxury shopping drawing shoppers & visitors by the magnificence of its seventeenth century architecture. The ground floors had been transformed into major-brand stores with their frontage a seventeenth- twentieth century pastiche. Carole judged that the upper floors were genuine. A renowned architectural historian had once advised her; *Ignore the ground floor. The jewels are above.*

Anna complained, "We're wasting our time."

Carole stopped the car to be hooted impatiently. She ignored the protests.

Hazlitt said, "If we find any indication.."

Cars began to edge past.

"Don't you understand how heartily sick of it all I am? I wish to God I'd kept my mouth shut."

"What sparked this off anyway?"

"Last night. I couldn't sleep after you woke me. I want to be Anna Cato, sometimes unemployed actor."

Carole responded, "Shall we do that then? Get out of here and pretend it was all a sour joke?"

Carole put the car into gear and when Anna spoke returned it to neutral.

"You have no idea how I feel."

"I think I do."

"I doubt it."

Carole moved the car forward another two car lengths ever hopeful of a parked car moving off.

"Anna, you're never going to have any peace 'til this is sorted."

Anna was silent.

"If we were in Soviet Russia," John Hazlitt suggested.

"We're not in Soviet Russia."

"Please, Anna, it's the only way I can explain what I believe is happening to you."

"Okay, tovarisch, we're in Soviet Russia,"

"A young woman called Anna Cato is arrested on the street without charge. Despite protests she is whisked away to live an alien life in a gulag. Why she is there she doesn't know. Every now and again she suffers the cruelty of being freed, but re-arrested again. Do you follow me?"

"I suppose so."

"You say there was a man you love. Your memory has been suppressed, but there are moments of clarity because love is the strongest bond. He may not know what has been done to you. His memory of you may have been suppressed. The State holds him to its tasks. It has a hostage. Pressure can be applied at any time. If he refuses or fails, he will be killed or join you in the gulag."

Anna hesitated before answering him.

"To be with him anywhere would be heaven!"

"Then we must find him. We have a lead. The Archangel."

THIRTEEN

They were all startled when the police officer tapped on the window. Carole wound down the glass to say, "I was hoping somebody would've spent enough and go home."

The officer smiled and responded, "Hell'll freeze over first, miss. Take the first left and you might find somewhere."

"Thank you, officer."

To the relief of the drivers behind her, Carole took the first left.

Halfway down the lane a red car pulled out. As gracefully as a seal, Carole slipped into the space and turned off the engine.

"Made it! Not too far to walk back."

She unbuckled her seat belt. Anna sat silent & unmoving.

"Lost in admiration at my parking skill, Peter? One of the advantages of growing up."

"The alley. The name. Didn't you see it?"

"I was more concerned with avoiding that Sherman tank. What about it?"

"Froggart's Side. The men at the Ark called it the Frog. This is where the Ark was. At the end of the lane."

As they walked along the lane the buildings became less interesting. It would be a resolute tourist who wouldn't close the camera and turn away. Carole pointed out to Anna the seedy Gentleman's Club with its bouncer dressed as no Elizabethan gentleman would, complete with bowler hat & codpiece.

"Abandon hope and your holiday money whoever enters there," Carole suggested.

But Anna had stopped, frozen.

"It's still here! The Ark! Still here!"

Closing the cul de sac was a building whose structure attested to the passing of the centuries from early casements & pillared doorway to Victorian chimneys.

"You're sure?"

115

"Absolutely. One of the ruins that Cromwell knocked about a bit. But unforgettable."

They examined the building before them. There was now a third storey of attics. Contradicting the sage advice given to Carole to look for the gems in upper storeys it was the humble lower storeys that bore the genuine traces of a sixteenth-seventeenth century heritage. Above the front door hung a shabby board that bore the image of a saucy angel and the words, *Archangel Tavern*. A second board carried more information. *The oldest surviving Tavern in the City, Birthplace of our National Playwright, wherein Christopher Marlowe would carouse with his friends.*

"Absolute nonsense!" Anna cried, "He was never born here."

Hazlitt suggested, "If you read it carefully, it refers to the city as the birthplace of your hero."

Anna laughed.

"That's very clever! It must annoy the Council heaps. I'm beginning to like the old Ark."

"You might call it a tarted-up old whore who still makes a living at a familiar trade."

"You might call it a trusty old survivor."

"You might call it Annie's prison."

"That was a long, long time ago. And it wasn't a prison. It was the only place I felt safe."

"The Stockholm syndrome?"

"No!"

They were silent as a couple came chattering happily out of the doorway.

"It's really astonishing to see it's still standing," Carole admitted.

"As is the old manor that's going to become an expensive hotel?"

"Bullseye!"

Hazlitt suggested, "It's a pub. Shall we pop in and have a glass of wine?"

Anna laughed to exclaim, "You're right. It's a pub. I was going crazy. But now I know it's real. Let's go in and have a drink. The liquor won't be any worse than it was four hundred years ago."

Being a gentleman, John Hazlitt said, "The treat's on me."

He held open the door and followed the girls into the Ark. The barroom was decorated in the mock Elizabethan style favoured in the city by most pubs to attract tourists. The walls displayed extracts & woodcuts from Marlowe's plays while busts stood at each end of the bar. Henry the Eighth's composition *Green Sleeves* flavoured the air. The pub was busy, but Anna & Carole found a table while Hazlitt went to the bar.

"Is it like coming home?"

Anna laughed.

"The bar itself is in the same place. Beyond that door there should be a hallway and stairs. The door behind the bar opens into the back room and kitchen. Of course, it could all be different, but our customers would think they'd died and gone to Heaven."

Hazlitt came to sit down empty-handed.

"Table service," he explained.

"We stayed behind the bar. Marianne and I didn't mingle with the customers. Too risky."

A serving girl made her way across the room and smiled at the trio.

"Greetings, master and mistresses, what be your pleasure this day?"

The Elizabethan speech parody seemed less awful in the context of this modern Ark.

"We has all manner of ales, wines and spirits for your delectation. We has seven ales of rare quality and the finest wines and spirits from as far afield as France and Spain. Finally, we offers a special rare draught. Home brewed cider from our Kentish orchards. A rare treat for our visitors from foreign climes."

The girl finished her recitation and smiling, awaited their pleasure, biro at the alert to take the order. It was all so ridiculous Anna burst out laughing, struggling to apologise for her ill manners.

117

John Hazlitt explained, "She means no harm. The recital was excellent. It must take some learning."

"What d'y'want?"

"I think we'd all like to try the cider from the Kentish orchards."

"In a dirty glass."

The girl didn't smile and no one laughed.

"It's a Bob Hope movie. Bob orders lemonade and Bing adds *in a dirty glass*. To show he's not a cissy," apologised Anna.

"Did we need to know that?""

The question remained unanswered. As swiftly as the magician strips away the tablecloth while not disturbing the crockery, the trio found themselves alone in the barroom. "Green Sleeves" was silenced. Everyone was gone. The room was stripped of all pretension. The ugly bones of the earlier Ark showed through. They arose in alarm. Time stopped.

Carole said, "Well, we've found the Ark."

"How long is it likely to last? This enchantment," Hazlitt asked.

He was opening up his mobile to snatch pictures of the barroom.

Anna said, "That won't work. I've no idea. Ten minutes? A week?"

Carole was at the bar.

"It's exactly as you said it was."

She picked up the red jug below the bar counter and rattled the coins.

"Don't let Noah catch you doing that."

Carole hastily replaced the jug.

Hazlitt asked, "Shouldn't he be here?"

He was busily scribbling in a notebook as he moved about the room.

"This isn't normal. We wanted to find the Ark and here we are."

Anna moved to the farther door and after some hesitation opened it onto the familiar hallway and stairs. Carole and Hazlitt joined her. Anna stepped into the hallway and stood listening to the silence.

Hazlitt suggested, "I doubt we'll get another chance. Shall we explore?"

Anna called out, "Noah! Just me. Annie. With me friends."

There was no response.

"You wouldn't want to surprise Noah."

Anna led the way up the stairs, which creaked most ominously.

"Triple crumbs!" breathed Carole, "What a location for a Gothic thriller!"

On the landing they paused facing three doors. Anna gestured to the door on the left.

"I took drinks to that door and feared for my life. There were four gentlemen at the table. The man with the black beard. The Inquisitor questioned me. I was absolutely terrified. I knew if he so wished I would be killed. I wasn't supposed to come upstairs. Marianne sent me when she shouldn't."

Anna opened the door. Carole stepped behind Hazlitt. The room was empty. Four chairs and a table. The fireplace was cold. The candles were puddle wax. Anna stepped into the room. Hazlitt joined her and surveyed the room.

"This is the sort of room where great conspiracies begin. Four gentlemen? Well-dressed? And Noah?"

"Just as a gofer."

"Did the conspiracy succeed? Or have the echoes not reached us yet?"

Carole joined them, saying, "I think I heard voices in the farther room."

They stood together outside the room reluctant to enter.

Hazlitt surmised, "We've made enough noise for an angry man to come at us with an axe. But he hasn't. Therefore, he's not here."

He took the latch and opened the door.

Anna recognised it immediately. It was the sitting room of the Council house in Gilsford. The paraffin stove was in the fireplace. The furniture was ill-matching pieces from half a dozen alien rooms, but polished, clean and obviously loved. Two odd armchairs faced one another across the fireplace. The couch was of wickerwork with animal cushions. The bureau may have been rescued from the office of a retiring solicitor or

119

a deposed crime lord. On the bureau stood the laptop. It was open. The chair once had been a swivel chair. There was no television set. It was the home of a young couple that were starting out with nothing and would end up with nothing. Despite the flood of adrenalin Anna wanted to weep.

Carole pushed past her into the room. She went to the window to pull the net curtains aside.

"Gilsford! It's Gilsford! Springfield Park Whatever! That motorbike contraption's out here."

Hazlitt was making notes of everything and scribbling sketches of the room.

"How on earth have we landed here, Anna?"

"We got off the train at the wrong station."

At the edge of her vision she noticed the image of the room was trembling.

"Good Heavens, Evans! I have never seen a Standard Vauxhall in donkeys' years. Should be in a motoring museum."

"Vernon Gresty had a Standard Vauxhall,," said Anna without thought. She came to join Carole at the window.

"Yes, that's Vernon's car."

She surveyed the room, noting the guitar on an armchair by one chair and the saddle bags tucked in beside the bureau. She repressed the impulse to straighten the cushions on their couch still holding Kit's shape. She knew someone had pulled him off the couch to go to.

Reality flickered and Anna said, "It's time to go. Before the roundabout waltzes on."

They were seated at the table in the Ark. The girl was leaving with their order.

Carole commented, "She's a regular smiler, that one."

When she had gone, Anna said, "In all the time I've worked at the Ark I've never seen anything like that."

"But you weren't allowed upstairs, were you? The only time you were, you were lucky to escape alive."

Carole asked, "What has that Council house to do with the Ark?" Hazlitt said, "I'm beginning to understand."

The girl arrived with the drinks. They fell silent.

After a precautionary sip Hazlitt announced, "You're right about the cider."

He read her name card.

"Excellent, Marianne!"

"Sorry, but the manager wouldn't let me serve you drinks in dirty glasses. I had t'wash them."

When she had gone Carole suggested, "She wouldn't wash them in the toilet bowl, would she?"

"Well, it is the Ark," said Anna.

*

It was noon before the carriage and wagon were prepared to continue their progress to Fotheringhay Castle. Kit agreed to help the farmer dig the hole into which to bury the murderous quartet. Surveying the farmyard and the orchard beyond, Kit asked, "Where would you plant this scum, master?"

"Where would you put them, sir?"

"I suppose the bee paddock? The orchard?"

"When they come to find what happened with their friends, where'd they look, sir?"

"Wha'd'y'mean? When they come."

"They're coming sure as x is x. Wouldn't you, sir?"

Kit felt the rain begin to whisper.

"Yes, I would. I would have to know."

"And they'll find where the ground is dug. In the paddock. In the orchard. Wherever."

"I fear we have put you in great peril, my friend. Come with us! We're safer together."

The man shook his head.

"This is our ground, sir."

"I admire your spirit. But you know these are very dangerous men. Their leader is a Papist. Can you claim to be Catholic?"

"We've never had much use for either. Whoever they are they still demand the tithe."

"I suspect you know where we're going to bury these creatures."

They had cleared the centre of the dung heap before Kit realised that he couldn't smell anything. The rain had drizzled as they dug into the wet soil to shoulder depth before they

121

stopped to climb out and take large gulps of ale from the farmer's wife who was pretending she couldn't smell anything. Kit and the woman passed the rogues, one by one, to the farmer who dragged & pulled the corpses to the burial hole. Ralph & Jonard arrived as Kit and his companion lifted up the corpse of Sir Royan Armitage.

Ralph cried, "Whoa! You cannot bury a gentleman in a dung heap, Kit!"

"Why not!"

"Because he was a gentleman!"

Kit and the farmer looked to one another.

"He was never a gentleman, Ralph. He was a treacherous rogue."

"He has an ancient lineage. His ancestor came over with William the Conqueror."

"His ancestor didn't 'come' here. He was with an invading army. A pack of Norman rogues."

"Kit, you cannot bury a gentleman in a dung heap."

"But you would so bury this honourable man beside me? And Jonard? And Gilbert here? And me? But not you?"

Ralph was silent.

Kit offered, "We must beg to differ. We're wasting time and I will have no quarrel with you, Ralph. You can have your precious gentleman. Hide him securely so the Papists don't find him."

Ralph and Jonard carried away the corpse. Kit and Gilbert the farmer & his wife began to fill in the pit, first with the diggings and then with decomposing dung. With a certain degree of pride they regarded the recomposed dung heap.

"I don't see any sign of digging."

"No, sir. Neat as ninepence."

"Would you wish to say a prayer for the dead?"

"May they rot in hell!"

The three workers shook hands.

"Where's the pump? Nothing refreshes a man more than to surrender his head to the pump."

*

Anna was drying herself from the shower when she found herself sitting under a tree with a book in her lap. The motorcycle combo stood on the verge and the young man was on his knees working at the engine. She tried not to laugh, but looked down to her book. She was surprised to find it was entitled MOTORCYCLE MECHANICS, but not surprised she didn't understand anything on the pages before her. The young man turned to her, enquiring, "Anything?"

"Sorry."

"You're the clever one."

"I don't remember getting a Distinction in mechanics."

Her companion rose with a volley of strange oaths some of which Anna had never heard before, marching around the combo kicking & cursing it ferociously. Pausing for breath he threatened to set fire to the machine and drew a knife to frighten the blameless tyres. Anna didn't respond as she presumed she had witnessed such performances before.

Finally the young man, so handsome thought Anna, threw up his arms in despair and demanded of the sky & any passing deities an explanation as to why he was being so mercilessly persecuted. Receiving no reply, he turned upon Anna, gesturing, "Well, what do you suggest, oh, Mistress of my Fate?"

"Checked the cables?"

His face suggested she was an idiot.

"Changed the plugs?"

He shook his head sadly at his favourite idiot.

"Could it be we have no juice?"

He sought around for a twig. Anna threw the nearest at him. She watched him dip the tank. She heard his muffled curses. From a pannier he took the petrol can and without a word marched away. Anna called after him.

"Bring me back a tin of something fizzy, sweet idiot boy!"

He gave no sign of hearing. Anna laughed, brushed away the attentions of a bumblebee and lay back to doze until he returned.

Anna awoke in the bathroom with the towel in her hand and wept.

FOURTEEN

When they returned to the farmhouse the horses were harnessed to the carriage and the wagon.

Ralph spoke as if they had never disagreed.

"I have given the good wife a subsidy from the Castle supplies. I trust you agree?"

"No. Take it back. Every last crumb. Every last drop."

Ralph & Jonard were shocked.

"How can you say that, Kit? When they have endured so much?"

"When Father Garnet comes with his murderous brutes, as they surely will, anything that doesn't belong here will cost these people their lives."

Ralph looked to Gilbert who nodded.

"Let it be done as quickly as possible. Or we may be caught flat footed."

As they turned to obey, Kit asked, "Ralph, if I may ask, where have you hidden the gentleman, the deceased Sir Rotten Apple?"

"On the wagon. In his bath tub."

Kit was astonished.

"Tell me I misheard you, sir."

"There stood the bath tub. Filled with robes and towels and bottles of scented water. Smelling more like a lady's boudoir than a gentleman's dressing box."

"So you decided to hide him in the bath tub?"

"You said securely and I had a cadaver to hide. He is well hidden in the bath tub. No one need disturb it."

"I hope your God agrees. How long do you propose dragging this increasingly malodorous box with us? Have you considered the possibility that Fotheringhay has a need for a coffin?"

Ralph hesitated.

"First come, first served?"

124

Kit didn't smile.

"My friend, you are totally unfitted for this work."

"How so?"

"I am ready to do anything, say anything to save my skin. You, Saint Ralph, are too honest. Brought up in gentility, you are unable to accept that Armitage was a vile, corrupt traitor and sodomite. Certainly no gentleman. I assure you he would've warmed his toes happily at your bonfire."

"De mortuis nihil nisi bonum."

"You must leave the schoolroom behind. I will suffice for your Mentor and endeavour to save both our skins. Although if this were an entertainment of mine, I cannot foresee how I would contrive a happy resolution. So, then we must all play our parts manfully and pretend to valour."

"I suspect, Kit, a speech used afore? Indulge me and confess."

"To inspire the troops when Dame Dorrie refuses any more of her admirable mutton pies until she is paid and the Company is penniless and the actors are hungry and mutinous."

They laughed together and all was mended, but for the shadow of the coffin.

*

Carole was working at her desk, absorbed in the drawing before her when a sombre shadow fell across the desk. She looked up simply to say, "The bow tie actually does work, Joe."

"Thank you. But I didn't come solely for your approval of my apparel."

Carole surrendered her attention to the drawing to say, "I had a most unusual day yesterday. Please bring me good news."

"I shall recite what your father said, omitting the blasphemy. Thank you, my dearest daughter, for dropping in to work occasionally. I had Robin Camberley-Jarvis the archaeologist on about some display we've promised to erect and maintain. What have you got us into, dear daughter?"

"Oh, crunchy toast, I was meaning to tell him!"

"Message ends. Robin Camberley-Jarvis will be with you at twelve. Sort it out."

Carole looked at her watch and groaned.

"You have ten minutes."

"Have you been sitting on this?"

"No! Mister Truscott stopped to tell me as he left for the Cranebrook site."

Carole wasn't listening, digging into her desk for the Boxborough file. On the run, she cried, "Thank you, Joe!"

She found her least favourite archaeologist, Robin Camberley-Jarvis, standing in the centre of the rejuvenated Great Hall that would be the principal dining room of the new hotel. He closed his notebook & pocketed his pencil to call to Carole, hurrying in by the far double doors.

"I have to admit I was dreading something expensively awful. It's very good. Authentic almost. Your father must be proud of what he's achieved."

Carole joined him to say, "Thank you! But why the *almost*? Every item is authentic. I made sure of that."

"The candles are electric."

Carole laughed.

"And there are no rushes on the floor."

"That can be remedied. Have you the address of a good reed cutter?"

"Show me where you'll put the Boxborough display."

Carole's heart stopped beating.

"That sounds as if you've decided it should be here?"

"The Council has so decided."

Frightening yesterday was swept away by a brilliant today.

"Oh, that's wonderful, Robin! No ifs and buts? No mebbes?"

"All subject to my approval. It must, of course, be viewed by the public."

"Absolutely! Our thoughts are in synch. I have the perfect space. The coffee lounge. Open to the public. Let me show you!"

The coffee lounge had been enlarged by turning two sitting rooms into one large room. Carole thought, as she entered with Camberley-Jarvis, she wouldn't have been surprised to find Elizabethan gentlemen conversing with friends, older gentlemen dozing in the chairs by the great fireplace and daring young gentlemen smoking long-stemmed pipes.

"You should be working with me, Carole."

She laughed to say, "No, thank you! The money's rubbish. Here I get to bring the past to life. As close to reality as money and craftsmen can buy. To be able to walk into an Elizabethan room and share coffee with friends is a rare privilege."

They were sitting on a couch with the blueprint of the Boxborough presentation open before them when they were interrupted.

Camberley-Jarvis was at first amused when what appeared to be a bearded actor in black Elizabethan dress poked him with his cane and demanded of Carole, "Who is this fellow?"

The actor was accompanied by two sullen rogues in shirt & breeches. Carole found herself speechless in a state of deadly dread. She rose, struggling to overcome her fear.

Camberley-Jarvis laughed & responded, "This *fellow* is actually the Consulting Archaeologist to the County of Kent. Robin Camberley-Jarvis, at your service. Be careful with that stick. Please don't overact."

He smiled at Carole, but seeing the distress in her face, offered, "Very authentic, chaps! Remarkable! But this is a private meeting, so if you will excuse us. Thank you for the audition! I look forward to the full performance."

He smiled to Carole, saying, "Perhaps it would be simpler if we excused ourselves?"

Before she could speak the gentleman raised his cane to Camberley-Jarvis's face as if to poke him in the eye, saying, "Stay! I do not excuse you."

The archaeologist made to rise, but with the stick on his cheek, sat back.

"Look at me!"

Camberley-Jarvis looked into the burning eyes and struggled to control his bladder.

"Please take your stick from my face."

The archaeologist feared for his eye, but the stick didn't move.

"We have an interest here, fellow. There be no Boxborough shrine. There is an excommunication upon that

127

faithless family. Take this warning, Master Robin Camberley-Jarvis. There will not be another."

The three visitors vanished. Camberley-Jarvis fell back into the couch, gasping for breath. Carole sat down slowly, her intellect numbed. Without conscious thought she folded up the blueprints and gathered the documents together. In a fearful silence she returned everything to her briefcase.

Robin Camberley-Jarvis was pale and sweating.

"That wasn't a performance, was it?"

Carole said slowly, "It's a very old house, Robin. We've had the odd incident. Men appearing where no one was working. Two occasions where panelling and a door were damaged. I've played it down for the sake of our workers, but we seem to have awakened something we don't understand. It appears to be completely harmless, if mischievous."

"Harmless? He threatened me personally, Carole. He didn't threaten you."

"It was an apparition, Robin. It has no reality. What could it possibly do?"

"The stick was hard on my face. No illusion. I feared I was going to lose my eye. That's not mischievous."

Carole slowly became aware that the architect had soiled himself.

"Would you like me to escort you to the gents, Robin?"

*

The carriage and the wagon made good progress with Ralph and Jonard at the reins and Kit riding Armitage's gelding. They stopped in a ford to rest and refresh the horses. Kit rode on ahead to see how close Fotheringhay Castle stood as they had passed an almost indecipherable signpost to Fotheringhay. The wagon brushed the rotten post as it passed into the lane and the post fell down, losing its fingers. Kit tried to prop up the fallen without success.

Jonard said, "They'll bear it no mind, sir. They knows where they is."

The track followed the reedy bank of the broad River Nene without sight of castle or village. Kit began to wonder if they were going in the right direction; that the signpost may have misdirected them. He was relieved to find a man laying fishing nets from a small reed & willow craft. Carriage and wagon stopped. Kit went to speak to the fisherman who ignored his calls. When the man finally turned to him he saw a goblin of a man, hunchbacked with a forest of a beard and an unfriendly face.

"The fishing good, is it?"

"Are ye blind? I's jest putting out me nets. Ye has to pull the nets afore ye can say whether the fishing's good."

Ralph and Jonard came to join Kit.

"Yee's not from round here. Wha'd'ye want?"

"Fotheringhay Castle?"

"Wha'd'ye want that for?"

"We have our reasons."

"Ye won't like it there."

"How d'ye know?"

"Me daughter worked there 'til she got wed and then there was the babby, Eric they called him. But at the Castle they said they don't want her no more and turned her away with not a penny for the babby. And she was pregnant again."

Struggling to halt the flow of the fisherman's family chronicle,

Kit asked, "Why won't we like it?"

"They don't want nobody there, that's why. Yee go there and they'll kick your arse half a mile or more."

Ralph decided to try a question.

"They has someone there they don't want us to see? That's why they kick arses?"

"Adam went just to ask why they had turned his good wife away and that's what they done. Kicked his arse from Castle to village if you can call it a village. He were standing up to sleep seven nights and that's no lie."

The ferocious little man in the fragile craft was silent and Kit was about to ride on when the fisherman spoke.

"I heard they has a foreign lady there. She's been there nigh on a year, poor woman. Mary Sanscliffe says she's a queen. Mary's keeping company with one of the guards. He's foreign,

129

but no fancy airs. Sarah, me wife, she fancies there's a wedding in the air."

"This foreign Queen.."

"They won't let ye see her though."

Kit decided to end the conversation before being invited to contribute to the wedding costs.

"How far to the castle?"

"Follow the river. May be three mile. Mebbes four. Five?"

"How is it ye don't know how far?"

"We uses the river. Ye'll see the castle. On the tussock. T'other side of the river."

"Is there a ford?"

"No. This is the River Nene. Not a piddle pond. When they built the castle they brought the stone up the river."

"There's a bridge?"

"Yes. How otherways would the cattle cross the water?""

To Ralph, Kit said, "Godspite, but this is pulling teeth!"

Ralph called to the fisherman, "Thank you, sir! May your fishing be fruitful!"

"Does ye not has a drop of ale on your fine wagon?"

Kit nodded to Jonard who went to the wagon and returned with a bottle of wine. Kit winced.

"Is there nowt else?"

"No, sir. They'll brew their own ale at the castle."

"You might enjoy this," Kit suggested and threw the bottle.

The hairy goblin caught it nimbly and rejoiced, despite his willow & reed craft dancing erratically.

"Thank ye, master!" he cried as the carriage & wagon trundled away, "May fortune favour ye!".

"I hope your God notices my good deed," sighed Kit.

"It was worth it to rid ourselves of his endless chatter. I feared we were going to be invited to Mary Sanscliffe's wedding."

*

Anna was peacefully sipping coffee, staring mindlessly at the television and waiting for the frenzied dance of the washing machine in the kitchen to stop when she heard Carole open the front door, but not close it. When she didn't immediately bounce up the stairs, grab some forgotten file and bounce out again, Anna, provoked by curiosity, went onto the landing to find her friend sorting through the accumulated bumph.

Carole looked up to ask, "Why don't you ever pick up this crud?"

"I'm bumph blind."

Anna thought that a pretty nifty response.

"Bumph blind is patented Anna Cato. But I'll except you."

"Too kind!"

Carole's front door bore a neat notice stating Do Not Put Bumph In This Door. Beside the doorstep stood a green bin in which fresh bumph was deposited. Recently, Anna had noted, by most of the street.

"Well, here's a surprise! A letter for Mizz Anna Cato! From Lloyd's."

"I haven't an account at Lloyd's. In fact, I haven't an account anywhere."

"Well, they're on to you now. Shall I open it for you?"

"Don't you dare!"

Anna flew down the stairs, grabbed the offered envelope and flew up again.

Sitting on the couch clutching the ominous envelope and trying to overcome a sense of foreboding, she wondered why her life should have become so overwhelming. Carole arrived to slump into the couch beside her.

"Go on! Open it! It won't be half as bad as you fear. It'll be twice as bad."

"Oh, gee! Thanks!"

"Open it for grief's sake! Your Uncle Wally in Oz has conked out and you own his diamond mine. Only they built the Sydney Opera House on top ot it. Pity, but there yo go, cobber!"

Anna hit Carole with the envelope and opened it. She read the enclosed letter as Carole tried to read over her shoulder, even going so far as to run round the couch to get a better squint.. Anna folded up the letter and stuffed it back into the envelope. She threw it at Carole's nearest bumph bin and

131

Carole was after it like a terrier after a fallen chip. She didn't attempt to read it.

"What does it say?"

Carole couldn't read Anna's face.

"No Uncle Wally? There's a new Time Walker's Tax?"

"I have a new bank account."

"But no money? Can they do that?"

"I have five thousand pounds."

"Then it's a mistake."

"No."

"Then I can put up the rent."

"I haven't paid rent."

"Then you can start."

"It's from my Uncle."

"Not Uncle Wally?"

No. Bastard Uncle George Bryce."

"Why didn't he do that to me? I'd let him pat my knee."

"I hate you, Carole. This is not funny."

"Sorry, old duck."

"My debit card will be forwarded separately. The overdraft level will be three thousand pounds. And I may wish to apply for a Credit Card."

They sat in silence.

Carole said, "If it had been Uncle Wally we'd both be dancing on the furniture."

"The bastard. The totally evil bastard."

"If you're gona return the money, I'd keep the Credit card."

"No."

"No?"

"Canterbury races."

"Next month! How opportune! I'm applauding your thinking, Einstein. We have a word with a jockey. Get a hot tip."

"Not a hot tip. The lamest horse in the Glenville Challenge and back it with five thousand paper representations of the Queen."

"But it doesn't go as planned, Donkey Kong wins the race at mountainous odds and we're off on a life of luxury. First stop Disneyland! But we leave the winnings in the taxi and a deserving immigrant family finds the money and the sun sets on our vie libre! Alas, twas ever thus!"

They laughed together. Carole said, "I'm sorry, kiddo. What're you gona do?"

"I choose a charity. Close the account. And teach the pig the lesson of a lifetime."

"How?"

"Take him Time Walking."

"And maybe keep the credit card?"

"Stop saying that!"

FIFTEEN

The day was dying when the castle appeared on a large mound across the river.

Kit said, "Like a painted picture with the sun setting behind it. If I was a religious man I would take it as an omen."

"It's a very old castle.."

"Aren't they all?"

"This is ancient. A Norman castle. Motte and bailey. The tower is the donjon. Built first in wood. Then in stone."

"Thank thee, dominie!"

"We can look to no comfort there. They'll still be pissing from the walls."

"Tell me, do all earls' sons speak so crudely?"

"Only if they have the misfortunate to fall into company with Christopher Marlowe."

Kit spurred forward to the cottages to find the bridge.

He returned to say, "The miserable hamlet has a pump and thus strives to appear a village. The bridge is old. Built with wood salvaged from the Ark. Otherwise Fotheringhay is deserted."

Johan offered, "They'll have hidden themselves. If I saw a horseman approaching in these troubled times I would hide. You spell trouble, sir."

Kit smiled.

"Me. Kindly Kit?"

"You has a horse and a sword. And justice does not reach out to the poor, sir"

Impatiently, Ralph asked, "But the bridge? Can we cross?"

"Sound enough. The toll keeper ran away when I rode towards him."

"I don't blame him. I should've done when first I saw you, Kit."

"Shall we cross the river before the toll keeper returns with the Sheriff?"

The short cavalcade crossed the river without incident with Jonard leading both teams of skittish horses & wheels over the bridge. The mound loomed larger and the Castle appeared impregnable.

"Fotheringhay Castle!" Ralph sighed. He was astride Armitage's horse, an honour won by the spinning of a coin. The loser, Kit, held the reins of the carriage, "A hot meal. Clean linen. A warm bed. All our troubles locked outside the castle walls. Bliss in simplicity, thou ever wert!"

"Wouldn't your earlship wish to partake of a hot bath, sir?"

Ralph was dismayed.

""Do you think this is the proper time.."

Kit completed the question.

"To remind you there is a scented cadaver in the bath on the wagon? Yes. Tread warily and let no one onto the wagon."

*

Anna awoke to the motorcycle combo bumping in the gateway and coughing its way around the house. A voice she knew called from the kitchen.

"I'm preparing you breakfast. A surprise."

"That's certainly a surprise."

Anna lay back in half-waking contentment, listening to him sing an Elizabethan love song, innocent, but so seductive. Happiness is so simple. She drifted into a doze only to be summoned.

"Breakfast's on the table! The cat's on your chair."

Anna grabbed her robe and flew down the stairs.

"Hang on! We don't have a cat."

The scent of fried fish made her mouth water. She sat down saying, "Where'd you get the fish?"

"Like the solitary heron the dawn fisher comes and goes but no one sees him."

It was a good sized fish, temptingly parting to her fork.

"It isn't roach, is it? That was truly dreadful."

"Bream. The choice of kings. Barges used to bring sweet bream into London daily. For our richer and betters. Dig in!"

Anna raised a forkful of prime bream to her lips and found herself in the green room of the Queen's Theatre. Wendy was regarding her curiously.

"Are you alright, Anna?"

*

Carole raised a hand in salute as the Consulting Archaeologist's

car sprayed her shoes with gravel as it sped from the courtyard of the Manor that had once belonged to the Boxboroughs.

"Triple shit!"

As she stamped across the yard to the Manor stroke Hotel Under Renovation, she cried, "Triple triple shit!"

The jackdaws called out in angry echo. In the corridor she was confronted by Joe Randolph.

"Has he gone?"

"If you mean pigface, yes. I was tempted, but I'm still here. What is it, Joe?"

"The figures on the Boxborough presentation."

He gestured with a fat file.

"I wanted to catch you and Camberley-Jarvis. So he'd have the costs of this exercise. He should know what it's going to cost us. Lighting and sound alone…"

"Forget it, Joe. It ain't gona happen."

"Why not?"

"The Consulting Archaeologist got shitscared, Joe. As simple as that."

"I don't understand what you mean. The Council's getting a free ride."

"Blame the Boxboroughs."

Randolph almost laughed.

"What have they done?"

"They were a Catholic family. Or they renounced the Faith. Whatever. They annoyed some very nasty people."

"But what does that matter today?"

"Until twenty fifteen Royalty couldn't marry a Catholic. That's how much it matters."

Randolph was silent.

"What do you want me to do with this?"

He indicated the file.

"What do I care?"

*

Anna said, "It sounds pretty horrific."

Carole agreed.

"It was. Utterly terrifying. What Camberley-Jarvis said is true. The apparition didn't threaten me. It threatened him. Camberley-Jarvis said he felt the cane on his face. He was afraid he'd have his eye put out."

"But what has it to do with me?"

"Everything. You may be the barmaid at the Ark who glimpses a conspiracy. We find the Ark and an old woman. Maybe you are a Time Walker, living a life that isn't yours. There is a man you say you love. A man whose name you don't know. This man is involved in a Catholic-Protestant conflict that rages through Time. If half of that is true, I'd say you're a dangerous person to know. Camberley-Jarvis would certainly agree. He was so terrified meeting this man he shit himself."

"I'm not a danger to you, Carole. I promise you."

Carole smiled.

"Walking the same path with you is dangerous."

"Then don't!"

"Aren't you performing this evening?"

"Oh, God yes! I'm going to be late. First time ever."

"No, you won't. I'll drive you. But you'll have to crouch down on the floor so nobody sees you're with me."

"Really?"

*

Tameeyah was already Wendy when Anna arrived in the dressing room. She jumped off her stool to relate the latest news and Anna laughed which stopped the girl in her tracks.

"Why're you laughing, Anna?"

137

"I'm not laughing at you. A simple laugh of pleasure. Whenever I get here you're always here before me. That's dedication. Can't you find anything to do in this magic city?"

Wendy grimaced.

"Mebbe it's because you're older, but it's not magic. It's boring, full of old buildings ready to fall down. And creepy old men."

"I suppose you're right about the city. It's looking back, not forward. Augustine 604. Christopher Marlowe 1600."

"I was in Ferguson's *Women*, at the Doner in Liverpool last year. Liverpool is brilliant. I had a great time and I was mentioned in the reviews. This place is a dump. Liverpool is alive. I'd jump at the chance to go back there."

"Okay, kidder, you win! But as we're in employment in this 'dump', let's not shout too loud. How stands the hour?"

"He's not booked in stalls or box today.."

"Thank God for small mercies!"

"But he left you a package. Mebbes a CD?"

Wendy cautiously offered a slim cardboard envelope.

"It's not a bomb, is it?"

"No! He's saving that for Christmas."

It was a silver photo frame featuring a smiling Bryce & Anna. The photograph had been taken by a camera in his car.

Wendy ventured, "It's a very nice photograph. You're both smiling."

"How dare he take a photograph of me without my knowing!"

She felt anger mounting, but also fear lurking in the background.

"It doesn't do any harm."

"Wendy, it may do any harm he may contrive. He can manipulate that photo in any way he chooses. If he wishes I can be nude. Do you understand me, Wendy?"

Wendy shook her head solemnly.

"He wouldn't do that!"

"Believe me, Wendy, men'll do anything to get what they want."

"What does Mister Bryce want?"

Anna slammed the photo frame into the waste bin.

"You really are angry, aren't you, Anna?"

*

Once there may have been a moat. An antique drawbridge lay before them, but the gate was closed.

"Come, let us march against the powers of heaven, And set black streamers in the firmament, To signify the slaughter of the gods."

"Tamburlaine," Ralph affirmed.

"Then I am not forgotten," the playwright declared, "If we survive this mission, I will transmogrify our antics justly."

"Will I play the lead?"

"That's down to Ned Alleyn. Or an arrow from these forbidding walls."

Horseman and conveyances crept across the doubtful timbers above the shadow of a moat. No arrows flew from the wall. A soldier in plain tunic appeared above the gate. Without preamble, he shouted, "Wha'd'y'want?"

The voice rattled on the walls and the horse jerked at his bit. Horses are wiser than men.

"Open the gate! I am Master Christopher Marlowe and I hold the Queen's Commission. So, it is best you mind me. My companion is Sir Ralph Boxborough. I will not discuss my business with you, fellow. Fetch me the Castellan. I will have speech with him."

The soldier scowled and almost responded, but thought better of it and vanished.

Ralph admitted, "That was well done, Kit. Most impressive. As to the manner born."

Kit smiled to say, "'Tis as another part to play."

The soldier reappeared with an officer who addressed himself to Kit.

"You can identify yourself as the Queen's Commissioner?"

"You do yourself no good delaying me here."

*

139

Wendy reported as soon as Anna set foot in the dressing room.

"He's in the box tonight."

"I saw the car."

Anna hung up her coat & beret watched by Wendy.

"Why are you looking at me?"

"You're my best friend, aren't you?"

"As you insist, yes, you are. You certainly persist."

"I admire you. You're really brave. You stand up for yourself."

"But do you have to watch me hang up my coat?"

"You don't look right."

"What does that mean? I haven't put on a pound. Fact is I'm losing weight."

"You looked so sad when you came in."

"Maybe I've played Peter too long?"

"No, no! When you're out there, you're alive and alight. You make it wonderful. As if it was all new."

Anna couldn't find anything better to say than, "Okay, I'll buy you a burger and chips after the show."

Which Wendy ignored, offering, "You just look so sad. I don't mean just sad, but sad sad. Like someone has died."

She paused, but Anna didn't respond.

"What's wrong, Anna? If you can tell me, maybe it will help?"

They heard the children arriving and Gillian put her head in the door to say, "All serene?"

Anna and Tameeyah answered in rough chorus as they uttered every evening, "Serene as serene can been!"

Gillian smiled and vanished, saying, "Best of luck tonight! The Mayoress and grandchildren are in. Could be a grant in the wind."

When the door closed, Wendy suggested, "But it's not serene, is it?"

Anna shook her head.

"What d'you think of Mister Bryce?"

The girl hesitated and declared, "At first I liked him. You would wish to have a Dad like that. Y'know, a big car. And

140

money. But I've changed my mind. I don't like the way he harasses you. If it's not too rude, what does he want of you?"

"He wants to make me rich and famous. Or perhaps better choice of words, notorious."

"D'y'not want that?"

"Not from him?"

"Have you told him?"

"Yes. Near as shouting. But he won't listen."

"The police?"

"And tell them he wants to make me famous?"

The children's dressing room door opened to a burst of chatter and closed. They both smiled at odd memories.

"If I gave you five thousand pounds. . ."

"You haven't got five hundred."

"What would you do with it? Would you waste it? No, no, I'm serious. Take your time. But answer me truthfully."

"It's what I've always wanted to do."

"Then tell me!"

"If I had five thousand pounds, I'd find the best drama school in London I could afford."

"Should I believe you?"

"That's the truth. A drama school."

Anna studied the girl's honest face. The smile was replaced by puzzlement.

"Why're you looking at me now?"

"To see if you're worth five thousand pounds."

Wendy laughed and asked, "Am I?"

"I think so."

"And I'm your best friend? For real?"

"Really real. Five thousand pounds worth my best friend."

Anna reached into her handbag to find a brand new chequebook.

"What're you doing?"

"I'm writing you a cheque for five thousand pounds."

"You're not!"

"I am. On the back I am writing. To finance Tammy Wells' fees at Drama School and for no other purpose."

"But you haven't got five thousand pounds."

"Not now I haven't."

141

Anna handed the cheque to Wendy.

"I almost wrote it out to Wendy."

"I am Wendy."

She studied the cheque.

"I don't understand."

"Bryce gave me a bribe. I'm spending it on a good cause. No one will argue with that."

Anna began to tear up the chequebook into the waste bin.

"That is the first and last cheque ever written from this book. Cash it. Bank the money. Don't spend a penny or I won't ever be your best friend again. When you stop being Wendy Darling and you are Tameeyah Wells, go to drama school. Is that a deal?"

"Better than a deal! A miracle! I don't know what to say. Except thank you. I'll never forget this. Thank you, Anna. Can I hug you?"

"If you must."

Anna struggled in her passionate embrace.

"Are you still sad sad?"

"Once I shake you off I'll begin to worry whether I've done the right thing."

"You have, you have! Absolutely the right thing!"

The performance was high-level energy from first word to last bows. Then Wendy watched anxiously as her best friend went to talk to the gentleman in the secondhand Beamer.

*

The gate to Fotheringhay Castle began to open, revealing a broad bailey with stabling, workshops, barracks and high on the motte, the donjon, the keep. Kit led the carriage and wagon into the bailey. He noted there were four cannons & two carronades mounted on the walls. The gate was closed behind them. Men appeared who came to stare at the arrivals. Grooms issued from the stable and began to unharness the horses. Kit rode round the carriage & wagon pushing away the over-curious.

He paused to say, "Jonard, do not let anyone on the wagon. Cause a hullabaloo and I'll attend you."

The officer who had spoken from the wall arrived with a sergeant at arms. Ralph joined Kit. There was no sense of good fellowship. Kit withdrew his glove and turning the ring, raised his hand.

"I am here on the authority of her Majesty."

"Welcome, Commissioner to Fotheringhay Castle!"

The words were uttered without any pretence of welcome.

"I am Captain Louis de Saint des Vosges."

Kit introduced himself and Ralph.

"You are French?"

"I have that honour, monsieur."

"Vous parlez anglais mieux comme moi, Monsieur."

Saint des Vosges smiled and bowed.

"An English nursemaid. At eight I was interpreting for my father. Saving him from being cheated by the English."

"And the garrison?"

"A company of twenty halberdiers. Four fusiliers. Twelve gunners."

"And your commission, sir?"

"To safeguard the Castle."

"Excellent! Security is vital to my mission."

Kit turned to the bearded Sergeant-at-Arms.

"Sergeant!"

"Yes, sir."

"Close the pigeon loft now. No bird flies. Put reliable sentries on guard. If any bird flies without my authority the punishment will be most severe. No bird flies without my script. Do you understand?"

"Yes, sir. No bird flies unless from your hand."

"Look to it!"

Ralph looked to Kit who responded, "We will decide what we tell her Majesty's spymaster. And when. Not the Castellan. Not the Queen's Chamberlain."

He turned to Captain Des Vosges.

"Were you expecting us?"

"No. May I ask why there are only three of you, Commissioner?"

143

"There were those who did not wish us to reach Fotheringhay. We endured a skirmish. Eight men died to bring us here. I did not have your halberdiers."

Des Vosges nodded as if this was to be expected. The atmosphere began to warm a little.

"I regret the Castellan, Sir John Nottingsley, is in poor health and has retired early. I am loath to disturb him."

"Where is Mary Stuart lodged?"

Des Vosges was startled at the bluntness of the question. It seemed he was about to lie, but changed his mind.

"We are not here to do her harm, sir. I presume you are loyal to the Scottish Queen?"

"There are those who would prefer Mary Stuart dead. Elizabeth has her throne. Therefore, she is in peril."

"My companion and I wish only for her safety. Where is she lodged?"

"In the donjon. The tower you call the keep. She has the prime apartment."

Kit nodded and turned to Boxborough.

"Have you a question, Ralph?"

"How many of the garrison are French, sir?"

"Four. The fusiliers. The gunners are Flemings."

Kit declared, "We shall attend upon your Queen in the morrow to discuss private matters. If you would arrange an audience?"

"I shall inform her Chamberlain."

SIXTEEN

The minibus arrived and the children scrambled aboard.

Anna sighed, "I wish I was as carefree."

The last aboard was Tameeyah, reluctant to leave Anna.

"Good luck and be careful!"

"I have my lucky hat pin."

Mr. & Mrs. Darling said goodnight and wandered off together, hand in hand. The lighting on the theatre portico died. Anna was left standing on the dark pavement. Across the road the passenger door on the car opened. Anna crossed the road avoiding a late night taxi and slid into the seat, closing the door.

"I'm so glad you've joined me, Anna. Where would you like to go? McDonalds?"

He started the car before Anna could say, "I'm not going anywhere with you."

Bryce switched off the engine.

"But surely we can talk? You have some independence now thanks to your Uncle."

"I wouldn't touch a penny of it. Your money's gone to a good cause."

"The money's of no account. But I can help you become very successful. Of all those who claim to have travelled in Time, none have ever made repeat trips. Only you."

"I'm not listening, Mister Bryce. I want you to leave me alone. Don't ever contact me again. If you do, I'll phone Equity's legal department. Perhaps they'll be able to persuade you to leave me alone."

She sat silent, but Bryce did not respond.

"Do not try to stop me getting out of the car."

"The door's not locked."

Anna exited the car and closed the door. The BMW drove away. She felt both nauseous and exhilerated. To the sympathetic stars she proclaimed, "I did it! I didn't think I

145

could. That's more like Peter Pan. I wish I'd brought my sword. I could've slashed up the seats."

Then she walked home. There were no flaring torches, no footmen to walk with her, but no following footsteps.

Carole was watching a horror movie so it was to funereal music & cackling that Anna climbed the stairs. Carole was clutching a cushion when Anna entered and switched off the television.

"Thank Gawd! I didn't dare move. I need a pee so badly!"

Carole vanished and Anna collapsed into the couch. Carole returned and fell into the couch.

"I don't know why I put the damn movie on. Went the day well?"

"The show went very well. I love Peter. If Barrie had gone to a psychiatrist we'd have lost a great piece. And I told Bryce to bugger off."

Carole awoke with a start of surprise.

"You actually told the bastard to get lost?"

"I warned him if he didn't leave me alone, I'd get on to Equity."

"Wow! Then he wouldn't let you out of the car?"

"No. He said the door wasn't locked."

"Oh!"

"You sound disappointed? D'y'want me in a life and death struggle with a sixteen stone rugby player? You'd be trying to fit all the bits back together."

"The door's not locked. Didn't he want his money back?"

"Too late. It's paying for Wendy's Drama school."

"So that's it?"

"That's it."

Carole rose to rummage in the cabinet.

"It's all we've got. It's called Eggnog. But it has alcohol in it."

Anna leapt up to hunt out two clean glasses in the kitchen. She returned with two half-pints.

"Best I could find."

They settled down happily sucking Eggnog from the glasses and finally using fingers to collect the last of egg & nog.

"I just hope he does leave you alone," Carole commented.

"I must remember to renew my Equity membership."

*

Later at ease in their private chamber, Ralph said, "You have my greatest respect, Kit."

"How so?"

"You act the part of Commissioner as if suckled right royally. How do you do it? You did not blaspheme once."

"You said it yourself. *Act the part.* To me it is all a play. I am questioning an actor for a part he wants. They're all liars. It's their occupation. I have learned to interrogate them and winkle out what I need to know."

"Such as?"

"I would hire Monsieur Captain Louis de Saint des Vosges as my leading man. He is a good soldier. His sergeant at arms is glad of a good officer. He will play second lead. The cast are the four French fusiliers."

Ralph couldn't resist laughing.

"Then I will play the clown as Dickie Tarleton!"

"We can count on two pistols and four fusils. I cannot count on the garrison or the gunners. The pit is too fickle. They may join us on the stage as they have often done. Or they may pull down the scenery."

"Surely they will follow their officer?"

"They will follow their sergeant at arms who may hold loyal to his captain. Louis des Vosges loves his Queen and would die for her. But the Castle smells wrong and we haven't met the principal players yet."

"All this you learned?"

"Easier than any actor. And I would wager the Castellan, Sir John Nottingsley is drunk in his bed."

*

Freed of the matinee, Anna had spent the afternoon in Canterbury's oldest cinema, the Bijou. Late afternoon sunshine welcomed her to reality, encouraged by the improbabilities of the silver screen to become once again the imperturbable Peter

147

Pan, free of Bryce's malign influence. Approaching the Queen's Theatre she became aware of men and women at the front door.

"Either I'm late. Or they're dead keen for returns."

She walked past the façade of the theatre, stopped at the lane entry to look back at the group waiting at the theatre doors. It was then Anna became aware there were five people, three women and two men at the stage door.

"What's going on?"

She walked around the block to the back lane entry. The door was locked, but she could hear Tom Parker's voice in the yard, talking to his assistant caretaker.

"Tom! Tom?"

The voices stopped.

"It's me. Anna. Let me in, please."

When the door was opened she smiled at Tom.

"Thanks. Something's going on out front."

Tom didn't speak or smile which was unusual. His assistant, known only as The Lad, ignored her.

"Gillian in yet?"

"She's in her office."

Anna tapped on the office door and walked in. Gillian was sitting at her desk.

"Anna! I'm glad you're in early."

"I hope that's my fan club laying siege to us."

"That's what I want to talk to you about. Take a seat."

With growing unease Anna sat down slowly.

"I don't understand. Is something wrong?"

"Have you been telling people you travel in time?"

"Not from a soapbox. But that's my business, isn't it?"

"Not when the papers get hold of it, it isn't."

Gillian flourished a newspaper.

"Time walking is not something I chose to do. It just happened."

"So, you do believe you can travel back in time?"

Anna was silent, struggling to gather her wits.

"Do you want me to say, no, I don't? I can do that if it helps. But I will still, without my consent, from time to time, find myself back in a scruffy Canterbury tavern in fifteen eighty something serving at the bar. I have no control over this."

"So you speak with dead people?"

Anna tried to laugh, but failed.

"Do you speak with dead people?"

Anna surrendered.

"I suppose I do. But they're alive when I'm talking to them."

Gillian passed the early edition of the Canterbury Chronicle to a reluctant Anna. The headline read ACTRESS SPEAKS TO THE DEAD. There was her photograph and a full story of which she recognised the origin. There was a full paragraph describing her mental state.

"Bryce! You bastard!"

"So this isn't all lies?"

The telephone rang. Gillian lifted the receiver and replaced it.

"Not lies then?"

"My *fragile mental state* is a lie."

The telephone rang again and Gillian lifted and dropped the receiver.

"That has been ringing since I got in. The Trustees were not the first I answered. The first and third cancelled school bookings. An hysterical actress who travels in time and talks to dead people is not what parents want for their children. And neither do I. I want actors with their focus on the performance. And not an audience watching for what the mad woman will do next."

"I'm not mad!"

"And that stunt when the stage was invaded and you apparently killed a man with a sword?"

Anna sat silent, defeated.

"I do have a contract."

"I'm not firing you. The Trustees would've done so toot sweet. You're suspended. You'll be paid for the remainder of your contract. But you won't play Peter at the Queen's again."

Anna wanted to weep, but she contrived to say, "Melanie's a good kid. She deserves a break."

"I'd rather you went now and didn't disturb the cast."

149

"I have a few things in the dressing room."

Gillian looked at her watch.

"That should be okay."

"Best of luck with the show. I've really enjoyed working here."

"Don't think I wouldn't pen a good word for you, Anna."

"Thanks, Gillian."

"Go out the back way. I'll deal with the press."

There wasn't much to pack beyond the sword that Anna rolled in a plastic sack. She was about to leave, turning off the lights when Wendy exploded into the dressing room.

"Is it true?"

"Why the sea is boiling hot, and whether pigs have wings?"

Wendy slapped at Anna.

"No! Have you got the bum's rush?"

There were tears in the child's eyes.

"As you so elegantly phrase it, I answer, No, I have not had the bum's rush. I have been suspended."

The relief in the girl's face was as the rising of the sun on a fine May morning.

"Suspended? How long for?"

"Forever as far as the Queen's is concerned. Now don't start blubbing. We're still best friends."

"Then I'll suspend myself. I'l go on strike!"

"No, you won't! I would never be best friends with a striker?"

"You wouldn't?"

"Never! What are the words we Thespians live by?"

"I didn't know we had any."

"The show must go on! That's what we live by. You are a true Thespian, aren't you?"

"Yes. Now you've explained what a Thespian is."

"Then you cannot disappoint your public by going on strike. Besides which you'd never get another gig."

"But what about you?"

"I'll be fine. Knowing my best friend is on the job. One day soon we'll be strutting the boards together in another show."

"Best friends ever!"

Anna finally extracted herself from the octopus embrace and departed the theatre by the back yard door. In the lane she wept in the shadow of a telegraph pole. When she felt better she bought a six-pack of lagers from Cheapskate and went home to the empty flat. Carole was at work. Anna put three cans at Carole's end of the couch and sat down to drink herself silly. She fell asleep with the first can unopened.

*

Anna awoke startled as someone beat a tattoo on the front door. Hope springs eternal and immediately she hoped, prayed it was Gillian who had rushed to tell her she was defying the Trustees' order to give Peter Pan the bum's rush. Tumbling down the stairs she could almost see Gillian bravely facing the stony faces of the Trustees, the spitting image of the Easter Island images.

Anna fumbled with the door, but succeeded in opening it to John Hazlitt. Not Gillian. The disappointment must have been evident in her face.

"I've come at the wrong time. I'm sorry. I'll go."

"No. No, I've been napping."

The connection between a nap and disappointment wasn't immediately obvious to Hazlitt.

"I see. You're expecting someone? I was told at the theatre you weren't performing today. I thought you might be free. Perhaps we can arrange a time at the office?"

"Come on in, Mister Hazlitt."

He stepped into the hallway.

"I'm not being a nuisance?"

Anna gestured for him to precede her up the stairs, being aware that her derriere wasn't her best feature.

At her invitation he sat down on the couch and discovered the lager cans.

"Carole is an alcoholic. I need to have alcohol waiting for her when she comes home."

"Of course," said John Hazlitt.

Anna knew he wasn't listening.

"What was so important that . . .?"

151

"I understand how it works now."

"What does?"

"Time walking."

"Explain?"

"The past is still there. We've always been aware of crumbs of the past. We've begun now to record it in sound and picture, but retrieving the past is more difficult than travelling to the moon.

"They make it look easy."

"It's a process even Einstein would approve. Time walking is not accidental. The simplest way to describe it is transmitter and receiver."

Anna interrupted to say, "You are seriously saying...?"

"The Ark is a way station in the chain. That room in the Council house in Gilsford we saw at the Ark is part of your story."

"And tomorrow it's the New Theatre and I'm watching Ned Alleyn play Christopher Marlowe's Tamburlaine."

"Someone you know is the twenty-first century transmitter and receiver. That someone need not be close, but he or she has awoken your ability to cross Time. That person has no notion of the power they wield."

"How curious?"

"One last thing. I know who you are."

"Then tell me, please."

"You must find your own way. But I will tell you what bars your path. One question. What happens to Anna Cato when you find your true self?

*

Kit slept soundly in the guardroom. Jonard slept with the horses. He had reported the horses were treated in kindly fashion and well-fed. The stablemen were friendly and eager for news of London. Ralph supervised the unloading of the household goods and gained the goodwill of the guardroom with a bottle of brandy. Thereafter, Ralph checked the guard on the wagon hourly and met enquiries about the bathtub & the coffin, saying, "One never knows when one may require either or both."

Which won the sentries' respect.

With the sun rising over the castle wall, Kit and Ralph in company with the Captain presented themselves at the armoured door on the keep and requested admission. Kit and Ralph were admitted and they stood in the echoing hall until the doorkeeper returned with a spindly old man with the longest white beard Kit had ever seen. He was formally dressed in black and carried a staff. A rapping of such on the flagstones punctuated his words.

"I am Sir Geoffrey Hamilton. I am the Queen's Chamberlain. You say you have her Majesty, Queen Elizabeth's authority to invade our domain?"

He barely glanced at Kit, but spoke to Ralph. Kit overcame the temptation to yank hard on the old man's beard.. With an apologetic glance to Kit, Ralph answered the Chamberlain's question in his most courtly manner.

With a bow that almost swept the unswept floor with his journey-stained hat, he responded, "I am Sir Ralph Boxborough. My father is the Earl Boxborough. I am aide de camp to my companion the honourable Master Christopher Marlowe, her Majesty's Commissioner."

The Chamberlain visibly paled and fluttered his hands. Kit sought to ease his discomfort.

"Fear not! I am not your executioner. We have satisfied our Queen's appetite for slaughter this season, have we not, Sir Ralph?"

"Indeed, we have, Master. Indeed, we have. I have the figures here, sir, if you. . ."

Kit sighed. In his head he wondered why no actor ever stays with the script.

"Enough! You will alarm Sir Geoffrey."

Turning to the humbled old man, Kit offered, "You are too cowardly to ask to see my Commission."

Brushing aside the few bumbled words, Kit declared, "Then I insist you read it, sir."

He flourished the travel-worn document and the Chamberlain accepted it with a shaking hand. Kit took Ralph aside.

"Never over-egg the cake. The less said, the less likely are you to be caught out."

Ralph looked sheepish. Kit was not impressed.

The Chamberlain returned the Commission and bowed.

"I am at your command, sir. But I cannot command the presence of the Queen, Mary Stuart, at this hour of day."

"I understand. Please arrange a meeting with her Majesty at two hours past noon?"

"I will, sir."

"Now I will rouse the Castellan from his bed."

"But, sir, he is ill-disposed."

"So am I! Ill disposed towards him. Last night he should've carried his bed down to the bailey to greet her Majesty's Commissioner. But he did not! Take me to him!"

SEVENTEEN

Anna was watching Hazlitt's car move away when within the blinking of an eye she was Annie, standing at the bar in the Ark. Without a clock she knew it was mid-afternoon. There were only two customers in the bar, an old man who was dozing in the corner and a drunken man who was explaining to Annie that all women were bitches and should be chained up to stop them wandering. He didn't seem to be aware he was talking to a woman. He continued to relate what atrocities should be inflicted on all women to teach them to behave. He cursed women to Hell & damnation and explained exactly what he'd done or would do to his wife when he caught up with her. Anna was inflicted with nausea & fought not to vomit. Annie poured his next pint and wondered where Noah was. Anna was astonished how the girl controlled her fear. She was immensely relieved when Noah appeared and grasped the situation. With the skill born of experience he steered the drunkard to a table in a corner.

"Bring him another pint of Best, Annie! There ye are, sir. Take thee ease."

Anna carried the pint of Best to the table.

"Say thank thee to Annie, Rob. Good lass, she is. She's me favourite, Rob. Of all the lasses, she's me true love. So, don't upset her, treat her right, sir, treat her right! Or uzz'll fall out! Dost understand me?"

Anna whispered thank you and returned to the bar. Noah watched the drunk beginning to doze and joined Annie.

"I has an errand t'do. If ye has any bother. Which ye won't. Threaten him with the dogs. But ye'll clean up afterwards."

There were no dogs. They smiled and Noah vanished. Presently there were two snoring men in the barroom. Anna went to slip the latch on the door and then took the door to the passageway and the stairs. The old house was silent. She hesitated and then cautiously, silently climbed the stairs.

155

*

Hearing Sir Geoffrey's voice the Castellan opened his chamber door, but on glimpsing Kit & Ralph cried out and fled to his bed.

"I don't deserve this!"

To the Chamberlain, Kit said, "You are dismissed!"

Kit & Ralph entered the chamber and closed the door.

Sir John Nottingsley clutched the bedclothes and whimpered, "Please don't kill me. I'll do whatever you want. I'll swear to anything."

Ralph was astonished and said, "But, Sir John, we. ."

"What did I say about eggs, Ralph?" Kit interrupted.

He turned to the shivering man.

"You are correct. We have come to kill you. Slowly or speedily as you deserve."

Sir John began to weep. Kit with a warning glance to a discomforted Ralph, asked, "Do you know why my friend is going to fillet your ribs so we may view your beating heart?"

Kit waited for the outburst of terrified sobbing to slacken and repeated his question.

"Because you're going to kill the Scottish Queen."

"How'd you know that is our intention?"

"You've brought the coffin, haven't you?"

"Yes."

"And you are our sovereign Queen's Commissioner."

The Castellan turned to Ralph.

"And I know who you are."

"Who am I?"

"Sir Royan Armitage."

Ralph laughed which frightened Nottingsley even more so.

"Does Mary know of her danger?"

"No."

"Surely she does?"

"She has been a prisoner so long she believes she would've been executed earlier. Elizabeth is her sister. Sisters do not harm sisters."

"Who is closest to her?"

156

"The Frenchman."

"His name?"

"I know not. He does not speak to me, but gives orders. A gentleman, but surly and ill-favoured."

"But Mary favours him?"

"It is difficult to tell. He gives instruction and she obeys."

"Surely she has a lady in attendance?"

"She has one attendant and her bodyguard. An enormous man. He frightens me, but I believe he is loyal to Mary Stuart. When I have seen her, he is always with her."

"And you?"

"I wish to God I were out of it. Kill me cleanly, I beg of you. I am loyal to Elizabeth, but we are in the hands of Papists."

"We will be in attendance on the Scottish Queen past noon. You will be present."

"Yes, your honour. Are you not going to kill me?""

"Not yet. Tell me, is there anyone in the castle you trust?"

The Castellan pondered.

"No one."

EIGHTEEN

Anna found herself on the landing struggling to control Annie's terror.

"Ye shouldn'ts be here, Annie. Yee's going to be in such trouble." Anna's own fear overwhelmed her and she turned back to the staircase only to stop when an old voice cried out for a pot. Anna opened the third door & was shocked to find not the sitting room of the Gilsford Council house, but a well-furnished room of sixteenth century style. Annie was surprised to see an old woman propped upright by cushions in a comfortable bed.

"Who are ye? What's ye doing here? Ye's not Noah's mammy that I do know."

The old woman was equally indignant.

"I's Betty Trumble and I has every right to be here. And you'd best watch your tongue, my girl. I only has to say a word to his Lordship and ye'll be back in the gutter ye came from."

Annie was deflated and Anna took over, taking out the chamber pot from its closet.

"Now ye wouldn't do that to me, would ye, Betty? Not when your bladder's busting, would ye?"

The old woman laughed and Annie settled her onto the chamber pot. The steady purr of urine into the pot was accompanied by a loud fart. Annie kneeling on the floor with one arm about Betty chuckled & chided her.

"Naughty girl, Betty! Imagine if your Lordship were in the room."

"Don't ye mistake him. He's a Goliath. Not a prancing Percy. It's like a volley of cannon when he fires off!"

They both laughed and Anna asked, "Does ye has many visitorst?"

"Oh, that I can't be saying. It's all coming and going. I ne'er know as much as Nick's name, but they is very kind. They calls me Grandmother and I has had strawberries. Strawberries!

Imagine that! Nor will they have iss thirsting. I likes a drop of stout, but I has had French brandy. A whole bottle. Can yi believe that? French brandy. All the way from France. They's lovely gen'lemen."

Anna lifted the old woman back into bed, asking, "And wha does thee have t'do for that brandy, Betty?"

The old woman tittered, "I knows what you saying, but no one lays a finger on me. All I has to do is lie here and be civil."

"And the gentlemen?"

"They comes and may be brings a gift. May be sit on the bed. Or ask after me cough. And then they's gone."

"How'd'y'mean, gone."

"I may be looking at the pretty flowers and when I looks up to say thank ye, milord. He's gone."

"Goodness gracious! I'm glad to see you so well, Betty. Give iss a shout when you want the pot."

Anna made her way to the door.

"I has t'go. Work calls."

"God bless ye, lass. May yi be so fortunate as meself."

Until it doesn't work any more and they throw you out on the street for burning as a witch, Betty.

*

Anna was halfway down the stairs when she realised Noah was standing at the foot. She stopped, suddenly weak at the knees.

"Come down, Annie!"

Anna descended slowly, desperately trying to think of any excuse for being upstairs. She stood before Noah and awaited justice.

"What lie has ye ready, lass?"

"None. The old woman needed her chamber pot."

"None of thee business."

"I am so sorry, Noah."

"Sorry don't skim no milk."

They stood in silence.

"I fear ye has killed us both, Annie."

With a sudden shock Anna realised the man was terrified.

159

"I don't know what ye mean, master. I saw an old woman who was to soil the bed if I hadn't put her on the pot. I swear to God that's all!"

"And when she has her next visitor? Her gentlemen callers?"

"I'll go now and never come back. I promise. You'll never see me again, Noah."

"Too late. Betty cannot hold her tongue."

"I'll tell them the truth. Ye never knew what I done."

Noah smiled and shook his head.

"When ye come here, Annie, my life was foresworn too."

"I don't understand."

"We is prisoners both, lass. Chained to the same wall."

"Yous fritting me, Noah. I don't understand what ye saying."

"Marianne is dead. I killed her. I was so ordered. Do ye understand that?"

Annie began to tremble on the verge of hysteria.

"Oh, dear God! Ye've been so kind t'me, Noah. Please, please don't hurt me."

Anna began to struggle as Noah seized her arm and dragged her along the passage. Annie began to scream when Noah opened the door at the passage end. He threw her into the darkness. Annie fell down the cellar steps and Anna was caught up in the nightmare, striking her head on the stone floor. Noah struck flint to steel and lit a torch. He followed Annie into the cellar.

"Be quiet, lass. Ye is still alive. Be grateful."

The darkness fell away, but farther into the cellar rats' feet panicked from the torchlight.

"Get up!"

Annie rose, taking Anna with her.

"To the wall!"

Noah gestured and Annie retreated, brushing against the chains hanging on the cellar wall. When she realised his intention she began to scream. Noah punched Annie in the face. To her horror, Anna found herself chained, neck, hands and ankles to the wall.

Her face was afire and blood trickled down to her tongue. She heard Noah climb the cellar steps. He dowsed the torch and closed the door, drowning the cellar in darkness. Anna heard the key turn in the lock and Annie began to wail.

*

Kit sighed mightily and the sigh echoed around the stone walls. Ralph kept his head buried in *The English Succession*. The Castellan Sir John Nottingsley apologised yet again.

"I regret, Commissioner, that I cannot order the Queen's presence. If she delays I cannot summon her."

Kit growled, "We have been sat here over two hours. Cannot is your answer? What do you do here at Fotheringhay?"

"I maintain the castle and keep all in order."

"Mary Stuart is detained here by our Sovereign's order. Who has authority over her."

The Castellan hesitated to speak.

"Speak up, sir!"

"No one. She is a law unto herself."

"Then carry this message to her. Her enemies are not far behind me. If she will not speak with me I shall withdraw and leave her to her enemies. Do you wish me to repeat the message?"

Sir John Nottingsley opened his mouth and then changed his mind. He rose, bowed and left the antechamber.

Ralph was uneasy.

"Do you understand what you've done?"

"Spoken directly."

"You've threatened the Queen Mary Stuart."

"This castle is in faerieland. I know London awaits an answer. They've waited too long already. Her life depends upon her word."

"Then she will not speak with you."

Ralph tapped the volume on his lap.

"Mary Stuart is the true claimant to the English throne denied because of her religious persuasion. She will not compromise."

161

"On a mission to the Duke of Alba for her Majesty seven men died because they would not compromise. They wouldn't have died if the Duke had listened to me. We are told Mary is an intelligent woman. This is her examination."

*

John Hazlitt walked in Victoria Park with his dog Mush to shed his patients' problems before dinner. His evening walk was predictable; once around the lake, fifteen minutes of sheer pleasure for Mush to retrieve his favourite stick and then to share the bench where he might best watch the swans returning to the lake.

The two gentlemen who were passing the bench stopped to regard the dog. John Hazlitt offered, "You're wondering what breed of dog this is?"

He smiled at the strangers who remained solemnly serious.

The red bearded man replied, "Indeed, I was, sir. It is a breed I have never encountered before."

The younger man appeared wary of dogs.

"Mush is an Alaskan husky. His ancestors pulled sledges through the wilds of Alaska for both the native people and the fur trappers."

"Indeed! Remarkable! But weren't the sledges very heavy?"

"Ah, I have misled you. There were eight, ten, twelve dogs in a team. Depending upon, as you say, how heavy the sledges were."

"I understand. Will he bite me if I lay a hand on him? May I stroke him?"

John Hazlitt laughed at the notion.

"No! Mush is an old softy. He runs from next door's cat. Please stroke him if you wish."

The red bearded man began to stroke Mush and the dog responded favourably wagging his tail.

"A fine, fine dog! Black, brown and white! A kaleidoscope indeed. I envy you."

Before Hazlitt had time to blink the blade cut the dog's throat deeply.

"What're you doing?"

162

Mush became a red dog and died struggling & bewildered. Hazlitt made to rise, but was pushed back onto the bench and seized from behind. Then the man who slaughtered his dog passed the razor to the thug behind Hazlitt. He hadn't heard his murderer approach to pull back his head and open his throat from ear to ear. The thug returned the razor to his master who pressed the bloodied weapon into Hazlitt's dying & bloody hand.

To the pale young man the master declared, "You see? He has killed himself and his faithful dog. How sad! He will not interfere in what is not his business again."

He looked to his companion, saying, "You have no stomach for this work, have you? Go into the greenery if you are about to discharge your dinner."

The young man stumbled into the trees. The older man and his cutthroat shared a smile to hear the sounds of vomiting. When the shocked young man, returned, wiping his mouth, the assassins walked away quickly.

The swans circled the lake & landed on the green water, surfing almost the length of the manmade lake. The evening starlings flocked to smother the Victorian Yacht House roofs in chattering birds. John Hazlitt and his dog were silent.

*

They had not waited more than a quarter of an hour before Sir John Nottingsley returned to announce, "Her Majesty Mary Stuart will see you, now, gentlemen."

As they climbed the stairs Ralph whispered, "Well done, Kit! Elizabeth has sent the right man."

"Let's see where we are when we retire."

Sir Geoffrey Hamilton, the Queen's Chamberlain, met them at the door to the apartment. The Castellan made the introductions, but as he turned to enter at the Chamberlain's invitation, Kit declared, "Your usefulness ends here, Sir John. Go count the pigeons."

In the apartment, the best & most elevated of the donjon, Mary Stuart sat in a plain wooden armchair. Behind her stood a pennant bearing the words *In My End is my Beginning*. To

163

either side of her chair stood a dark young man in military garb and her giant bodyguard. At the Queen's elbow stood a grimfaced older woman. Kit & Ralph approached. They bowed and Kit presented his Commission, which the Queen began to read.

Mary sat tall in her chair and Kit could well believe she stood taller than many men. He saw a long graceful neck bent over the Commission vellum and arched brows, bright auburn hair and hazel-brown eyes whenever she raised her head to seek answers from her Chamberlain. When she had finished reading she looked to Kit who was instantly struck as to how attractive she was. In his experience the exalted were most often exceedingly plain or disfigured. The Chamberlain rapped with his staff on the flagstones to signify the importance of his own presence.

"I have now read of your Authority, Master Marlowe and I am assured my sister did not send me un tete de noeud. What do you wish to persuade me to do against my best interest?"

"I would like to clear the room except for your Majesty and your advisor.."

Kit bowed to the dark Frenchman at the Queen's side and continued, " My aide de camp and myself."

There was a rattle of protest, but Mary raised her hand.

"Allez sors!"

Kit and Ralph were alone with Mary Stuart and her advisor.

"Why do you wish Monsieur Boxborough to stay?"

"I need a witness to my words. No one will question a Queen."

Mary smiled and Kit learned why men were prepared to die for her.

"I wish to speak clearly, your Majesty."

"It will be a welcome change."

"Elizabeth wishes you to return to the French Court with a large amount of silver and trouble her no more. But there are those who think it cheaper to have your life extinguished. Father Henry Garnet would like to use you as the figurehead of a Catholic rebellion. There is talk of a Spanish invasion. Garnet would be content for you to be the martyr of a failed revolution."

"Where do you stand?"

"I wish to see you safely across the Channel into France."

"And you believe there are men coming to kill me?"

"Yes."

"Mon Dieu! But I am the Queen!"

"We set out from London seven strong. We discovered we were among murderers. There was a fight and we killed four of them. . If we had not, the murderers would be in the castle now. With no news of their success another party will follow. We must have you out of here before they arrive."

Kit & Ralph stood in silence as Mary Stuart pondered upon her choices. She whispered to her young advisor. He nodded his agreement. The Queen declared, "We shall speak again," and gestured their dismissal.

*

As our heroes found their way to the guardroom Kit enquired, "How many of the garrison d'you think we can depend upon if it comes to a brawl?"

"Perhaps the fusiliers under the Frenchman's command. But if they come against us in the name of Elizabeth. . ."

"And the cannons?"

"The crews are Flemings. They bear no loyalty, but they are Protestants."

"Have they been paid recently?"

At the guardroom door, Kit said, "Tomorrow, dear Ralph, I will have need of your muscles."

"How may I assist you?"

"We must take her coffin to her Majesty."

*

The announcement in the Chronicle stated simply that Ms Sybil Crowther had died of smoke inhalation in a fire caused by faulty wiring in the offices of Dr. John Hazlitt in the Royal Albert building which is now closed for investigation.

165

NINETEEN

"How do you secure the loyalty of the common soldier, Ralph?"

The morning sun had barely cleared the castle walls, but Kit & Ralph had eaten breakfast and were as smart in appearance as Ralph's limited wardrobe could provide. They were waiting as ever for an answer from Mary Stuart that they may attend upon her. At whatever hour of the day she might choose. They waited, Kit in thought and Ralph with his head deep in *The English Succession*. He trapped a stray feather in the volume to mark his place and gave his reluctant attention to his friend.

"Your question again, if yu please?"

"How do you secure the loyalty of the common soldier?"

Ralph gathered his thoughts.

"I suppose by pride in his Company. Having good officers. Honest sergeants. Hopes of reward. I have an award presented to me after the siege of.."

Kit laughed in interruption.

"You are a dear fellow to suggest you would endanger your life for a pretty riband. Have you yet begun to shave that handsome chin? Do you still believe in true love?"

"One day, dear scribbler, you will test me too far. Yes, I would die for honour. Upon my soul, I believe in true love!"

"When so many pretty girls hang on the arms of pox-faced rich old men? Does that not fox your argument?"

Ralph is silent.

"Actors have much in common with soldiers. Ask me how I secure the loyalty of my cast for a play."

"This is all nonsense, Kit. But I will humour you. How do you secure an actor's loyalty?"

"You feed him Dame Dorrie's mutton pies. And secure his credit at the nearest alehouse. He cares naught for Ned Alleyn or Christopher Marlowe and never reads a script beyond the page on which he is poisoned, stabbed, throttled or dismissed."

166

"You judge your fellow peacocks too harshly, Kit."

"Which is why I retreated from the limelight. Mutton pies and Best Ale secure the actor. And the soldier too. But how does one secure the pies and ale?"

Ralph laughs.

"Money, of course! The only enduring loyalty. But what of it?"

A solemn Kit pressed Ralph into a chair.

"We are in a very dangerous situation, my friend. We must take this stubborn Queen to safety. We need loyalty to succeed. Within days a fresh reinforcement of her enemies will arrive and if we are still here, we will all most likely die. You will never finish reading the English Succession and I will never have scribbled my play of the Queen's Escape. We must buy loyalty."

"But how?"

"We will pay the garrison with Elizabeth's silver."

Ralph was driven aghast from the chair to stride the chamber.

"You cannot do that! It would be a shameful breach of trust. That money is to ensure the Queen's future!"

"So?"

"I cannot permit you to do so."

"It will buy us time to spirit Mary Stuart from Fotheringhay."

"I cannot stop you, but I will have no part in this."

*

Sunshine filled the bailey of the castle. Captain Louis de Saint des Vosges was surprised to be summoned by the Commissioner and informed to present the garrison for a Pay Parade within thirty minutes. Opening the moneybox was easy once Ralph could be persuaded to surrender the key.

"You will have to take the key from me."

Jonard apologised as he seized Sir Ralph Boxborough's arms to bind them behind his back. The key was easily discovered sewn into his doublet.

167

"Believe me," said Kit as he turned the key in the locks, "I will testify to the insufferable torture you suffered before yielding up the key."

Ralph was silent.

"If you wish I will not mention that your genitalia were torn from your body before you regurgitated the key hanging by a silk thread from a back tooth in your stomach. It may damage your marital prospects."

Ralph could not keep himself from laughing.

"You are no gentleman, sir!"

To which Kit replied, "When did I claim so?"

The garrison was drawn up beyond the large table. All eyes were upon the cash bags on the table until Kit approached and the garrison stood to attention. Led by des Vosges, the Commissioner inspected the ranks, having a word of praise for every man.

As they turned away, Kit said, "This is splendid theatre! I must find a place for it in my next play."

"What would that be, sir?" asked the polite Captain.

"Either a Queen Betrayed. Or a Queen Restored."

"I prefer the second title, sir."

"As I do also."

The Castellan and his clerk rose as the Commissioner took centre chair. Captain Louis de Saint des Vosges stood in attendance. The Pay Parade began. The first Halberdier was called forward. His name was recorded. Five silver coins were counted into his hand by the Commissioner. The man affirmed his loyalty to the Queen's Commissioner in a loud voice. Silent surprise rippled through the ranks as man after man returned jubilant with five silver coins. The pay parade ended with rousing cheers for the Commissioner led by the sergeants who had received ten coins. Kit rose, smiling, to accept their gratitude.

In their private quarters Kit asked Ralph, "Find Jonard. Enlist extra help and bring the coffin here."

"With my hands bound?"

Kit cut his hands free.

"You should've been out there, Ralph. A splendid parade. All we lacked was fife and drums. Such happy faces. Nay, nay, loyal faces. We have bought the Castle, my friend."
"I have bought naught, but sold my integrity."
"Then you got a fine price for it."

*

In the darkness the rat bit Annie's foot. Annie shrieked and the rat fled. Annie began to weep & wail and woke Anna. The neck shackle was very painful, made more so by Annie's vigorous lamentation.

Anna cried, "Shut up, Annie!"

To her surprise the wailing dwindled to sniffles & ceased. In the blind darkness Anna checked her arms were locked to the walls. Similarly her shackled legs gave her little freedom. Then she felt Annie was about to empty her bladder and didn't protest. The release was oddly calming; the urine striking the cobbled floor of the cellar very ordinary. It was the first normal happening in recent memory.

Then everything changed and though Anna knew she was shackled to a wall of the Ark cellar she found herself in a school hall and saw herself sitting on a stool to one side of the school stage. The hall was filled with young people in school uniform. The young man was standing in the middle of the stage, waiting until absolute silence prevailed. Then as if a rocket blossomed in midnight darkness she knew his name was Kit and she loved him.

Into the stillness, this man proclaimed, "There isn't a worse play than Romeo and Juliet for young people because of senile professors and idle teachers who believe their duty is to bore their charges. And thwart any interest young people might develop in a play written especially for them."

There was a ripple of interest across the hall.

"There are exceptions among pedagogues. Mostly they are too old to understand the play. I have been to Grammar school. Boring, I know it to be so. Yet language, the gift of language can transform a dull soul, illuminate the darkest life, raise up the child of poverty to the highest heights of the spirit."

169

About Kit as he spoke, shade by shade, grew the New Theatre until all were encompassed within its walls, the young people in the pit and Ned Alleyn & his Company on stage. Actors in full flow of dialogue appeared & conflicted in high style around the teenagers until all were caught up in the magic world of theatre.

"This play of mine, this Romeo and Juliet, was written for you. And has been stolen from you. It is your testament. It tells you all you need to know of young love. Of its joys, its anguish, its dangers. The blindness of parents is as true today as it was when the play was written. It is your play. It is all about you."

From where she sat Anna saw the children transformed, both boys and girls. Kit conjured for his audience a theatre set within Gilsford Grammar and the play began. The students lived, loved, swore eternal love, betrayed one another, parted and in anguish turned to new love. All the pain, exultation and despair of youth were played out. When he had finished speaking and the images dissolved, his audience understood the meaning of the play. When he recited the silence was as a calm sea after a storm.

"A glooming peace this morning with it brings. The sun, for sorrow, will not show his head. Go hence, to have more talk of these sad things. Some shall be pardoned, and some punishèd. For never was a story of more woe than this of Juliet and her Romeo."

The young people began to applaud. Anna knew who the girl was who sat on the stool at the side of the stage.

Then the cellar returned and in the midnight darkness Annie cried out, "We's all done now," and wept.

Anna responded with those same lips.

"No, no! It's just beginning. I know who I am. I know who he is."

Her voice echoed in the cavernous cellar.

"Cheer up, Annie! We's still alive. Long as we's breathing there's always hope."

It didn't sound at all like her own voice, but it was oddly comforting. Annie gave a tremulous sigh and Anna took that as agreement.

170

*

The simple lunch had been eaten in silence. Kit, Ralph and Captain Louis de Saint des Vosges had waited all morning to be called to the presence of Mary Stuart, Queen of Scots. There had been no word. Kit was becoming increasingly irritated. When des Vosges attempted to apologise, Kit had refused, saying, "The reason I am happy enough to have boys take the women's parts on stage is women's insatiable desire to argue. In the theatre no words would be good enough but that they would change them. And if they refused, off they would go to sulk. I will give her Majesty, Mary Stuart a quarter hour longer. Then, Ralph, we are free to depart."

Captain Louis de Saint des Vosges rose, excused himself and quitted the chamber.

"Now we will see!" Kit announced.

Ten minutes later the chamber door opened and the Captain declared, "Her Majesty will see you now, Master Marlowe."

"Our surprise is prepared, Captain?"

"It awaits your word, sir."

At the Queen's apartment they were parted from des Vosges and entered into the Royal presence. Kit noticed that her company was as before, but that the dark Frenchman stood before her. The bodyguard and the sour older maid stood at some distance.

After polite exchanges, Kit declared, "I am hopeful that since our last audience her Majesty will understand her present danger. Hopefully, we may now arrange your safe return to France. Your enemies know their venture has failed and must be within two, three days riding. We must be gone tomorrow or Friday at the latest."

There was a long silence in the chamber while the jackdaws of the Tower continued with their unending squabbles. The Frenchman spoke into the Queen's ear, which Kit wished had been his privilege. There was a flurry of jackdaws at the Tower window. To lighten the atmosphere Kit suggested, "Let us hope we can find agreement sooner than the crows."

No one smiled.

171

The Frenchman stepped forward to say, "You are free to go whenever you wish. Her Majesty thanks you for your consideration."

Kit stood dumbfounded, unsure of the meaning of what he had just heard. He looked to Ralph whose face demonstrated similar confusion. He spoke in French to the Queen's spokesman who answered & nodded. Ralph turned to interpret, but Kit held up a hand stilling his tongue.

To the Frenchman Kit enquired, "Who am I speaking with?"

"I am the Chevalier de Orleanais Duvios. I speak for her Majesty."

"Is she not allowed to speak for herself, Chevalier?"

"Her Majesty has decided to remain at Fotheringhay Castle. She does not believe her sister Elizabeth would harm her. She can understand the need for Elizabeth to keep her in restraint, but that is a matter of politics. She is not uncomfortable at Fotheringhay."

Kit stood silent.

"Her Majesty is anxious to conclude this audience."

"Is this her last word?"

"It is."

"There is nothing I can say that will alter her mind. I am sure you have tried strenuously to move her."

The insult was received & ignored.

"Nothing. The matter is ended."

Kit spoke directly to the Queen.

"Your 'sister' Elizabeth has sent you a parting gift, your Majesty. I trust it pleases."

Before anyone could intervene Ralph went to the chamber door and spoke to someone outside. The Captain entered to bow to Mary Stuart and four halberdiers carried in the coffin and placed it before the throne. Mary Stuart's complexion paled and she rose in alarm. Her bodyguard moved to shield her. The Chevalier put hand to sword hilt, but shrank away from the foreboding gift. Ralph Boxborough put hands to sheath and sword hilt.

The Chevalier de Orleanais Duvios cried, "How dare you present such an insult to her Majesty! You will pay for this, English!"

Kit ignored the Chevalier and spoke directly.

"Your Majesty, your loving 'sister' has also been kind enough to send you a farewell letter."

Kit took out the execution warrant and pulled away the seal.

"Sir Ralph, if you would be so kind as to present this death warrant to the Queen herself?"

The young man was most obviously shocked.

"Not to the poltroon who would keep her here as a sitting duck before the sportsman."

Her bodyguard refused to allow Ralph to hand the warrant directly to Mary Stuart. He surrendered the paper to the bodyguard who offered it to his mistress with courtesy. Mary Stuart read her own death warrant in icy calm.

Kit whispered to a stunned Ralph, "It is extraordinarily alike to theatre, is it not? All the world's a stage, and all the men and women merely players: they have their exits and their entrances; and one man in his time plays many parts. This is one of my better parts, don't you agree?"

Ralph didn't speak, but nodded which alarmed the Scottish Queen further.

"Are you planning to murder me, Monsieur Commissioner?"

"No, your Majesty, we are going to take you to safety in France, But you must do what I say if we are to succeed."

The Chevalier protested, "You cannot," but decided it was safer to keep his mouth closed at the lisp of Ralph's scabbard.

"Very well. What do you wish me to do?"

TWENTY

With curses & bruises abounding, Kit, Ralph, Des Vosges and Jonard manhandled the coffin from the Queen's apartment, down the winding stairs with yelps of pain and across the bailey finally to hoist it onto the wagon. They struggled to gain breath and lick their wounds.

"Could not the halberdiers have borne this burden?" complained Ralph, nursing skinned knuckles.

The Captain might have spoken, but Kit replied, "This is a private matter. And it is not yet undertaken. You are not going to enjoy what we have to do, but I assure you it is essential to the Queen's safety."

He handed his companions a morsel of soft white bread.

"Chew it well, but don't swallow."

Taken from his bathtub the corpse of Sir Royan Armitage was surprisingly short on stink as being dressed with all the perfumes of Arabia fit for a Scottish queen. Yet every man worked with chewed bread in each nostril. No one volunteered to decapitate the corpse so Kit performed the task so badly all four of them vomited onto the bailey. Kit also burnt off the beard and dressed the head in the horsehair wig. No one was prepared to undress the headless corpse. Even Kit couldn't stomach the task.

Des Vosges solved the problem.

"It is sacrilege, but we cut the Queen's robe at the back from collar to hem and lay it on the body as one would dress a bed."

Despite doubts they agreed it looked well, but although Jonard removed the boots there was no disguising the feet.

"They are not a Queen's feet," Ralph observed.

Kit said, "I will return. Do nothing further until I return."

The shaken undertakers sat down gratefully in the shadow of the wagon.

Ralph declared, "I cannot believe we are doing this."

174

"But we are," commented the Captain, "A foul business. But we need a dead queen to save a living queen."

When Kit returned he covered the feet with the dead Skye terrier and the face with the wig.

Ralph was outraged.

"You killed her dog?"

"She understood she couldn't take the dog with her."

They regarded the confection in the coffin with some satisfaction before they sealed it.

"If anyone has the authority to open the coffin they may do so. They will meet with stink, rot and horror. They will take no more than a glance. A queen's decapitated corpse and her pet dog. They will hasten to fasten down the lid. And the traitor Armitage will redeem himself in this last service to the Scottish Queen."

In comment Sir Ralph Boxborough added, "Although you have turned my stomach, Kit, I see Elizabeth has sent the right man on this mission. Although it may not turn out as she would have wished. We whisk the Queen away to France, but surrender the dead Queen to Elizabeth."

Kit smiled to say, "Think of it all as a play, my friend. I have seen worse at the Globe, but none of my making. Now we must dress the wagon in funeral green."

*

It was early evening when Kit and Ralph left the Queen's apartment, seeing her prepared for her journey. Walking down the endless spiral staircase, Ralph said, "Do you think they are committed?"

"The Queen is prepared. It's a simple dress. With her hair braided she may pass unnoticed. But we cannot hide her height."

"It's those around her who trouble me. That brute of a bodyguard. Her attendant lady was as impolite as she dared. The Chevalier de Orleanais Duvios was barely civil."

"I wouldn't expect them to rejoice. The open road is not comfortable. But you're right. We can't afford any delay."

175

The four best horses were being harnessed to the wagon that was now suitably dressed in funereal greenery. The carriage stood ready, the horses stamping with impatience. Jonard sat up on the box surely as impatient. Kit complimented Captain Louis de Saint des Vosges.

"Well done! The next time I am buried I will insist you are Master of Ceremonies. The last time the priest was drunk so we hung him upside down from a tree to shake the liquor out of him."

The Captain smiled politely and looked to Ralph who shook his head sadly.

"As per your orders, Commissioner, I have confined the Castellan and the Queen's Chamberlain to their quarters."

"I'm sure Sir John Nottingsley has his head in a bottle already. The carriage is prepared?"

"Horses chafing at the bit to go. They hate to be idle. The halberdiers too."

"And the escort is trustworthy?"

"Yes, sir."

Ralph added, "They have all sworn loyalty with gold coins. But I'm sure they're all good men, loyal to the Captain."

To Kit he said, "One day I shall have to face a court to answer to misusing her Majesty's money."

"Not for saving a Queen you won't. We will release the carriage with the Queen first. Good luck, Captain. Ralph, I'll see you in France. I may need a hidey hole."

"Let me come with you to escort the Queen to her carriage."

*

On the staircase below the Queen's apartment the friends were met by the Chevalier and the bodyguard.

"Well met by moonlight, gentlemen! I presume the Queen and her attendant are behind you?"

"Her Majesty is not leaving the Castle."

The silence lasted too long.

Kit said, "I understand now."

Turning to Ralph, he explained, "There are cockroaches in the house."

Ralph laid hands to sheath and sword hilt. The Chevalier laughed.

"This staircase has a right hand spiral. You will find difficulty drawing and fighting."

Kit drew his pistol and shot the bodyguard in the chest. The man mountain looked surprised, began to say something and fell on Kit. They tumbled together down the steps. When Kit disencumbered himself from the dead man he climbed upward to find the Chevalier similarly deceased farther up the staircase. He realised Ralph had forsaken chivalry and shot the Frenchman in the back of the head.

Kit found Ralph comforting the Queen who was quietly sobbing.

Ralph cried, "Are you hurt?"

Kit looked down at his bloody doublet.

"Not my blood."

There was a further corpse lying on the chamber floor.

"She had a knife and threatened to cut the Queen's throat."

Kit dragged the woman's body out of her Majesty's eye.

"Your Majesty, your people intended to hand you over to whoever came to take the Castle."

The Queen was silent.

"We must go now. Before we are trapped within these walls."

The Queen nodded and with Ralph at her elbow rose obediently. There was a clatter of boots on the staircase and the Sergeant-at-arms stumbled into the chamber.

"There's a man arrived at the gate, sir. Says he has to talk with the Lordship that give him the wine, sir. Life or death, he says."

*

Wendy was in the foyer posting newly taken photographs of Melanie and taking down the images of Anna when Carole arrived to demand, "Is Anna here?"

"No."

"She hasn't been home three days now."

"Oh, golly jeepers! She was suspended Monday."

177

"Suspended?"

"Don't you read the papers?"

"Haven't got time."

"There was a fuss about time travel and talking to dead people. But she didn't get the bum's rush. She's only suspended."

"Who's playing Peter?"

"Melanie. She's okay, but not like Anna."

"And you haven't seen her since Monday?"

Wendy shook her head and asked, "Has she done a bunk?"

"Wha'd'y'mean?"

"Has she taken her stuff?"

"Nothing at all."

Wide-eyed Wendy asked, "Could that man Bryce have kidnapped her?"

Carole almost smiled.

"No. He's not that stupid."

"Sometimes they have cellars. With lots of photographs and slinky music."

Wendy became aware she had an armful of photographs.

"George Bryce is a nasty greedy man. But he's also has a highly paid solicitor. Please don't say nasty greedy to anyone."

Clutching the photographs Wendy was suddenly aware something precious was in danger.

"Do you know where Anna is?"

"I think I know where she is."

Wendy looked to her expectantly.

"Somewhere in the past."

The girl smiled hesitantly.

"You don't believe she can travel in time, do you?"

Carole was surprised how wide Wendy's eyes opened.

She said briskly, "I don't want to stop you working. If she turns up ask her.."

Wendy interrupted to say, "I'm only doing this because I've got nothing to do. There's no matinee. P'rhaps I could help you look for Anna? I'm her best friend."

The child's innocent face signalled *choose me, I could help.*

"Have you got a time machine?"

Wendy shook her head. The auditorium door opened and Gillian came into the foyer. Carole vanished. It's possible Gillian never saw her, but Wendy was astonished.

"Did you see that?"

"See what?"

"Anna's friend Carole just vanished."

"She must need to be somewhere."

Gillian helped Wendy pick up the photographs she had dropped. She hesitated, looking into the child's worried face and said, "Tammie, if you'd like to keep Anna's photos, please do."

"Oh, thank you, thank you, Gillian! You're very kind really!"

As she passed from the theatre onto Broad Street, Gillian said to herself, "At least I've made someone happy today," and then, "What did she mean by you're very kind, really? Why really?"

*

When Carole opened her eyes she knew exactly where she was and was disappointed. She was standing in the garden of Boxborough Manor. She was disappointed that she wasn't elsewhere. To be snatched away by Time and..

Slowly, she began to realise that the garden seemed more mature. The knee-high box hedges about the flowerbeds seemed sturdier; the carefully sited trees & bushes stronger. The little summerhouse was overgrown with vines: a sweet haven for young lovers.

A gardener was working with a hoe some distance from Carole. She walked the path towards him and realised how cleverly the walks were laid out to distract the visitor: every path was the longest way to anywhere. The creator of the garden was holding his guests to hostage for as long as possible.

"How clever!"

Within the walled garden her voice carried. The gardener looked up from his hoe. He was a stranger. A younger man than Sean. As she approached he removed his shapeless cap and

179

stood to attention with a hoe rather than a rifle. The thought made her smile, but the gardener looked to his boots. All in character.

"I think. . . No, I'm sure this is the finest garden I've ever seen."

"Very kind, milady."

"We haven't met before, have we?"

"No, milady."

"I'm Carole Truscott."

The young man didn't respond and it finally dawned on Carole that she was talking with a sixteenth century gardener.

"Thank you for your hard work," Carole complimented the young man. He mumbled something and either nodded or bowed. Carole walked away, overflowing with embarrassment. *How awful of me. I sounded just like the Queen. Thank you for your hard work. How patronising! At least, I didn't ask have you come far?*

"What a ninny I am!" she chided herself, but she spent another hour in the garden sketching the gardener & garden features that would enhance the twenty-first century version.

"Of course, every garden architect has their own ideas. We assume they all used the same layout. Well, the man or woman here was an original thinker."

As she walked contentedly amid birdsong and the buzzing of bees she pondered whether he had read the Gardener's Labyrinth, published by Didymus Mountain. Published fifteen seventy one? Five hundred years away? Or recently published?

Carole went into the Manor and time vanished. The house was silent; a profound silence not to be found in the twenty-first century. She could most clearly hear the imperious blackbirds from the garden and stood still in a corridor to listen. The doves would calm any troubled spirit. She inspected the dining room and a sitting room. It was disappointing that her camera didn't function, but she had a good visual memory. She was pleased to find she had reworked the principal features correctly. She met no one. No one enquired as to whether she had any right to be examining dining chairs or sitting in the Earl's armchair. It was a most wonderful afternoon.

Passing from the dining room, opening doors to peep inside, Carole realised she'd passed a small door almost without noticing. She went back to look again. To describe the hooped door she might've used the word commonplace. There was no shining brass handle, but a simple latch. The dark surface matched the wall panelling in appearance. It was as if someone had wished to hide a door in full sight.

*

Ralph and Kit recognised the goblin fisherman, Ganda, before they reached the gate. More surprising was to welcome into the bailey the farmer Gilbert and his wife Marion.

Ralph cried, "Good to see you, Ganda! But the wine is all drunk."

Kit shook hands with Gilbert.

"It's good to see you alive and well."

When they were settled in privacy, Kit declared, "Ganda hasn't brought you for wine. Something has happened. I would wager not good news."

Gilbert began, "When you left us, I knew there'd be others to come. We laid a patch of the lane with caltrops. Like we did in the Low Country."

To Kit, Ralph said, "D'y'know what they are? Caltrops."

Kit shook his head.

"Iron hedgehogs. However you drop them there's always a spike pointing up. Easy for a blacksmith to make. Deadly to horses." "Marion didn't like me doing it. Crippling the horses. We prepared to leave on any warning. Then sure enough there was trouble at Stephen's Cross on market day."

The goblin fisherman took up the story.

"A mob of maybes three score hoodlums led by a red bearded man come on us. And a flock of women and childer. They dragged out and burnt the priest at the foot of the Cross, God forgive iss. He wudn't recant. Screamed like a pig. They has Papist banners. The red-bearded man declared this the beginning of the revolution. England would return to the true faith and Stephen's Cross would be viscerated."

Ganda paused, proud of his acquisition of this astonishing word although mangled & misspoken.

"Viscerated as the birthplace of the revolution. He said a Spanish Armada was setting sail even now to invade with an army from across the Channel. He axed the villagers to join the revolution. Said they'd have a true priest of the Faith restored to 'em. A handful joined, but others was killed 'cause they refused."

Ganda wiped his nose on his raggy sleeve and Gilbert the farmer continued the story.

"We knew it were our turn next. Needed our corn and stock. Revolutions has to be fed. They stole five horses. Father Garnet, that's his name and his cronies took to horseback. They charged up our lane with the mob behind them. The horses hit the caltrops and down they went, throwing the riders, arse over thumbs. We was gone afore the first horse screamed. Without horses we've slowed them down summat."

Gilbert looked to Ganda who continued, "They come on to us at Throstle's boatyard. To take the boats. So, we come on to ye. Tell ye they'll take the Scottish woman from the Castle and march on London. They plans to raise an army as they marches and overthrow our own dear Queen. They'll have your cannons."

Kit interrupted. "Have they taken your boats?"

Ganda laughed as the cackling of geese, displaying blackened teeth at rare intervals in a generous mouth. He stopped laughing long enough to cry, "Has theys taken them? How daft dost thee think us is?"

He continued to laugh until Kit couldn't bear it any longer and took the goblin by the shoulders and shook him like a child's doll.

Ralph cried, "What on earth are you doing?"

"I'm going to shake an answer out of this sweet fellow even if his head flies off. Has Garnet got your boats?"

Ralph rescued the fisherman from Kit with apologies.

"Please, dear man, tell my friend. Has Father Garnet taken your boats?"

Ganda dusted himself down.

"There weren't nowt at Throstle's boatyard t'take."

182

"Then, where are they?"

"Take yasel a promenady down t'the river. We'd never let any take our craft."

Kit turned to Ralph.

"Please tell Jonard his services are not needed. Release the horses. Her Majesty is not going to London today."

TWENTY-ONE

Carole lifted the latch and gasped when she descended five, six stairs into the twilight of the family chapel. It was no bigger than a small sitting room. She was embarrassed when she realised she had marked it on her reconstruction as a storeroom. The walls were hung with ancestral banners. The small altar was dressed in virgin white linen and the cross bearing the image of Christ shone as a beacon in the candlelight. The statue of the Virgin Mary & Child and the paintings of the Saints behind the altar declared it a Catholic chapel. There was a handful of chairs. Carole sat down on the nearest both awed & exhilarated. Her pagan ego was overwhelmed by the knowledge that the punishment for its use was paid in betrayal, torture & death. She was a clumsy intruder upon the family secret. The Boxboroughs paid homage to the Protestant church, but were worshippers of the old faith. Carole vowed the anonymous storeroom would be restored to its true function.

Slowly she became aware a plain coffin lay before the altar. Carole rose, drawn to the coffin. Her footsteps sounded as thunder on the plain flagstones. The coffin was open. Carole's legs faltered. She dreaded what she would see and prayed earnestly for the first time since childhood.

"Please, please, God, don't let it be Anna!"

*

When out of the silence of the dark cellar Annie asked, "D'ye think Noah will murder uzz?"

With surprise Anna realised her fellow-self accepted her presence. Or believed she had gone mad.

"Why would he murder uzz?"

"Noah does what his Lordship says. He strangled Marianne cos she sent me upstairs. I never asked where he buried her."

Anna struggled not to let fear overcome her.

184

"That don't answer why."

"The old King, bless his memory."

She paused so Anna recited, "Blessed be his memory."

"They said his queen was trying to bear him a son. But that don't excuse her sleeping in other beds to make one, do it?"

"No, indeed not!"

Anna wondered if she was losing her mind.

"The churches had to change so's the king could get shot of his wife. I never been since I were baptised so it made no matter to me. That's what it was all about as I heard. The king kicked the Pope out. Took over his job."

Anna realised she'd never heard a more succinct explanation of the Reformation.

"Then he kicked out the monks. That was for the money."

Anna felt a warm regard for her sister-self. Her explanation of the Dissolution of the Monasteries couldn't have been more accurate.

The silence lasted forever. Annie shivered.

"I don't believe Noah would ever do you harm, Annie."

"Holy God, I prays not!"

Annie began to weep, wailing loudly, struggling with the chains. In sheer desperation Anna began to sing, "When you walk through a storm. Hold your head up high. And don't be afraid of the dark. At the end of the storm. There's a golden sky. And the sweet silver song of the lark."

Even as she sang it seemed ridiculous, insane, but it silenced Annie. The cellar walls echoed the absurd words as Anna faltered to silence. The cellar door opened, but there was no golden sky; no sweet silver song of the lark. A stone-faced Noah, bearing a flaming torch, stood in the doorway.

"God quit ya row, Annie!"

"It just come on me."

He came down to stand before Annie who raised a tearstained face.

"Oh, Noah, I's so glad t'see thee."

He began to release her bonds.

"I'll go to Timbuktu, Noah. Anywhere! Ye'll never see me again, I promise!"

185

The chains fell free and Annie flung her arms around the man.

"They wants ye upstairs."

Annie gave a shrill cry of terror and clung to Noah. He freed himself as gently as he could.

"Hush thee! There's nowt I can do, but if it shud come to the worst, I will die with thee, Annie. Just play the dafty!"

Anna followed Noah on Annie's shaky legs up the cellar steps.

*

Carole gripped the rim of the coffin and looked down into the pale dead face of Christopher Marlowe. She gasped with relief that it wasn't Anna. She knew who the man was. This was the man Anna was seeking; a man without a name with whom she'd lived a previous life. On his grubby shirt lay a fresh quill & an inkhorn. He lay sleeping peacefully, innocence regained. He looked as if he might awaken at any moment and Carole almost reached to shake the sleeper ino wakefulness.

"Poor Anna! Life is so cruel."

*

"What manner of banners do they carry?"

"Bed sheets hung from two poles. I never learnt reading so what they say.."

Marion the farmer's wife interrupted Ganda, "I can read. One say, Rejoice the True Faith Arises. Another says England will be free. The largest uses our Lord's words. I am the Truth, the Way and the Life. A banner with Christian crosses. A banner with martyrs' names. Banners with pictures. One ye don't want t'see. The Lord burns heretics."

Kit said, "You have a good memory."

"Who'd forget?"

Ralph asked of Kit, "Why're you so interested?"

"If you has no cannon, banners are a powerful weapon. They threaten and frighten people."

Ralph was not convinced.

186

"But we have cannon."

"Then are you prepared to fire upn a banner declaring In Christ's Name, carried by women! Will you fire on children? Would you not hesitate?"

Ralph had no answer. Kit could read the Captain's face.

"I wish Ned were here. He is a master at handling crowd scenes. Ned can make a baker's dozen appear to be five hundred."

Des Vosges asked, "Who is this Ned? He is a general, yes?"

Ralph laughed and answered, "He's an actor and the director of a Theatre Company. A master of make-believe. Kit is his disciple. He sees everything in terms of theatre."

Kit defended himself.

"Believe me, Captain, only a fool takes life seriously. Regard it as a play upon a larger stage. With good fortune before we reach the final Act you'll be written out."

"I'm so pleased I am not English," was the gallant Captain's reply.

The Sergeant-at-arms arrived to report.

"There's an armada on the river, sir. Eight good vessels with sail. Fifteen smaller craft. On the pasture a considerable herd of cattle and goats that have followed the fleet. And a large flock of geese. And the dog that is the master of the geese. The birds follow the dog. So I understand, Commissioner."

Ganda offered, "Wherever Hannibal goes the geese follows him."

Ralph offered, "As a good sergeant with sound soldiers."

The Sergeant smiled in his beard.

"A movable town. The Israelites out of Egypt. Better than the fall of Troy! I could keep Ned in business for a lifetime on this one adventure alone."

Ganda said, "Theys maybe two days ahind us, master. But theys won't take us. We're off to the Wash."

"You can reach the Wash?"

"I telt thee the Nene is no piddle pot. Us'll be drinking in Boston afore the Papists take the castle from yous."

Gilbert commented sombrely, "They want the castle, sir. There's the armoury and the walls. A strong base for revolution."

Kit said, "Women and childer? Kine and goats? Geese? That won't be a comfortable cargo, Ganda. Have you room enough?"

Ganda hesitated to suggest, "Ye has good pasture here."

Kit paced the chamber and whistled through his teeth. Ganda wiped his nose on his sleeve. Ralph regarded his feet and the Captain examined the ceiling for water stains. Kit slammed his hand on the table, which startled one & all.

"Ganda, my dear friend, if I give you two bottles of wine. Play stockman to your cattle and goats. Enlist Hannibal and his geese. Give you a heavy bag of silver coin and buss you on both cheeks. Would you swear to take the Scottish lady and her escort safely to the Wash where they can buy passage for France?"

The little man didn't hesitate.

"Forget the bussing, but give me four bottles of wine and I'm your man to the death!"

He offered a grubby calloused hand.

"I'd rather have you drunk in some pigsty in Boston. Never dead."

Kit suffered the crushing of his hand.

*

Carole became aware an old man sat in the nearby chair. He wore a fine robe with a gold chain about his neck that bore a gold crest. His hair was snowy white, which indicated it was washed regularly in the reign of a Queen who bathed twice a year whether she needed to or not. It was a well-fed face with a flush that betrayed his indulgence in foreign wines while his serfs drank ditch water. Carole recognised the Earl Boxborough. He stank of alcohol. There were two wine bottles and a glass by his chair.

She smiled and enquired, "How goes the day, milord?"

Startled out of his nap, the tipsy Earl belched & cried, "Heaven 'fend me! Are you devil or angel?"

Carole smiled at the question. The old man blinked anxiously.

"My name is Carole. I'm not a devil. Perhaps one day I may graduate as an angel third class."

188

She watched the earl gather himself to ask, "Sweet spirit, do you bring me sad news of my son?"

"No, milord. Is he in danger?"

The Earl tried to reach for the glass by the chair leg & failed. He looked to Carole who didn't move to assist him. He indicated the coffin.

"Alas, here lies my son's unworthy friend. But he was much dear to my son. Who, God be thanked, is grievously wounded, but alive!"

"God be thanked, indeed! How did such a tragedy unfold?"

The old man took a moment to control his feelings.

"If you would not wish to.."

The Earl interrupted to say, "No, no! My son, Ralph, is in service to her Majesty. There was an attempt at Tilbury to assassinate our dear Queen. My son, Ralph, was taken by surprise and took three sword thrusts. More tragically, Master Marlowe stood before her and received the pistol ball. It is a barbaric age in which we live, sweet spirit."

"And the Queen?"

"Unhurt. Praise be to God!"

"And your son?"

"The doctors have him. They have bound his wounds with fresh placenta which they assure me will restore his vitality and hasten his recovery."

Carole shuddered.

"Would it not be better to pepper the wounds with sulphur, fire the sulphur and bandage his wounds?"

"The doctors know best."

"I doubt they do. But may I sit with you and hear the story?"

Carole took a chair and sat with the Earl.

"Then you have not come to punish me for my mortal sins?"

Carole took the old man's hand.

"No, no, milord! You have behaved most properly. Despite your anxiety over your son's wounding, you have taken Master Marlowe's body into your home. Treated him with respect when you acknowledge your mistrust of him."

"For Ralph's sake."

Carole looked about the chapel.

189

"Into the utmost privacy of your home. At considerable risk to you and your family."

The visitor surprised the Earl Boxborough by kissing his brow.

"You are a brave man, milord."

The old man essayed to laugh & failed.

"What courage I display, sweet spirit, comes out of the neck of a bottle."

Carole knelt to pour the last of the wine into the glass and presented it to the old man.

"Take a little wine for thy stomach's sake. And tell me the story. From the beginning."

The Earl Boxborough sipped the wine.

"A remarkable wine. French. Sadly flawed by bubbles. But if you have patience the bubbles are soon subdued."

"The story, milord."

*

After the midnight cellar the passageway and the stairs were blindingly bright. Anna's eyes had begun to adjust when she was pushed into the now familiar room where the gentlemen had met to conspire. Noah followed and closed the door. Annie began to whimper until someone declared, "Please stop wailing! It is a most distressing sound."

Annie fell silent. Anna regarded the speaker. He was a young man dressed in sombre style. Anna realised she was looking at a priest of the Inquisition yet he had the sweet face of an angel, which was both bewildering & frightening. Behind him stood a man of brutal appearance, but it was the coldness of this young man that filled Anna with dread.

As Annie fought to contain her bladder Anna struggled with the growing certainty that this man's pleasure was to create pain. Anna fought to calm Annie; not to allow this man see or sense their weakness.

Annie, this man takes joy from hurting women. She felt the girl stir with surprise. *We must spoil his game and hide our fear. See! He's not so brave. He has a bully with him. If he were*

190

alone Noah would tear him into pieces and dispatch the pieces to his mother.

Anna felt Annie trying to hide a smile. The inquisitor caught the moment and stepped forward to take Annie's left hand. He smiled upon her, stroked her hand and counted the fingers.

"Please do not be afraid, child."

"I try not to be,"

He took her hand in his two hands and smiled into her face.

"Such a pretty sweet hand!"

"Thank you, sir."

He pulled back the little finger and broke it. The pain was excruciating to Anna who locked Annie's jaw shut. The girl stood shaking but silent before her tormentor. The broken finger stood up from her hand The tormentor stepped back, his smile fading.

Well done, Annie! That hurt and will hurt long. But he's disappointed. We hid our pain.

"My dear girl, I am the Inquisitor. I am bound to seek out the enemies of our Lord Jesus Christ. When the apostate Elizabeth is overthrown I will reap the Great Harvest of those who resist and I will restore justice. Therefore. I am not as concerned for your body as I am for your soul. When you stand before me to answer my questions, you stand before Our Lord as you are answerable to Him."

Anna interrupted to say, "Lord Jesus wouldn't break me finger."

Noah cried, "Oh, Annie lass! Don't speak so to the Father."

"How else should I speak? He hurt me. While you watched."

Noah punched Annie in the face. Anna reeled back to find his hands upon her shoulders a strange comfort. Blood ran from her nose and her head rang with pain. Annie was weeping.

"Annie's just a silly bit lass, Father. A dafty. I took her in from the street 'cause she's willing. She don't understand nowt. She does what I say. Simple tasks even a dimwit can do."

"If she does what you say, how did she disobey you not once, but twice?"

"The first time the lass Marianne sent her up. That has been dealt with. The second time she heard Betty calling for her chamber pot. Being a kindly lass she set her on the pot. I found her coming down and she told me so. Then I told the Father as I has to."

"When Marianne sent you upstairs do you remember the gentlemen who were gathered here?"

Before Anna could stop her, Annie blurted out, "Yes, sir, I do! The red-bearded gentleman told me I done wrong, but he was kindly to me."

"How so?"

"He didn't have Noah strangle me."

*

It seemed to Carole that the Earl Boxborough was dozing.

"The story, milord!"

The old man recognised her presence.

"Ah, yes! The story. It was all because the Queen wished to hold tight a man who has no fear of spirits or demons or respect for Almighty God. She needed him to perform a fearful task."

"Christopher Marlowe?"

"The scribbler Kit Marlowe. A known blasphemer."

"You hold a poor opinion of Master Marlowe?"

"He has turned my son's head."

"We all have faults, milord."

"Forgive me. De mortuis nil nisi bonum."

For some moments the old man was silent.

"To that end it was decided to take & hold his daughter from him, but the witch swept away her life as a maid clears a table. Marlowe lost all memory of his beloved daughter, Hannah. That was not so intended. Worse was, the witch could not restore their lives despite torture and finally the fire."

"Brain washing fifteen-eighty-eight style."

"If so, I pray it scoured out the blasphemy that endangered his soul."

"I'm sure he's a nicer person dead. But who will pray for Hannah?"

TWENTY-TWO

The Inquisitor was silent. Annie tried to move away before her bladder rattled the floorboards, but failed. The Inquisitor stood in the growing flood of urine.

"The lass is frightened to death, Father. She has no more wit than a goat."

"You understand, do you not, Noah, that we are engaged in a most dangerous enterprise?"

"I do, Father, I surely do!"

"Within days an army of the True Faith will march upon London, growing at every step to surprise the usurper and cast her from the throne. The Duke of Parma and fifteen thousand Spanish troops will land to secure that victory."

"May that day be soon, Father!"

"All depends upon secrecy. I could force the truth from her. What she heard and who she tattled to, but I haven't the hours."

He nodded to his bully who came forward grinning. Anna felt Noah release her shoulders. Annie turned to Noah.

"Ye promised, Noah! Ye promised!"

*

The last image Carole retained was of the Earl Boxborough's anxious face before she was suddenly cast into the crowded foyer of the Queen's Theatre. Around her swirled a whirlpool of excited children & adults, local theatre-goers & tourists. The clamour rose as the doors to the auditorium opened and faded as the audience surged into the auditorium. The doors closed and silence prevailed. To Carole it seemed the tide ran out and left her stranded on the shore.

Carole tapped on the hatch marked BOOKINGS & RETURNS. After somewhat of a pause the hatch opened. An older lady asked, "How can I help?"

193

"I know I'm late, but I wondered if there was a spare seat for this evening, please?"

The lady vanished, closing the hatch. When Carole had begun to accept that the lady wasn't returning or had dropped dead, the hatch reopened. The old lady smiled to say, "You're lucky. Returns. You have a choice. Stalls or Circle?"

Five minutes later an embarrassed Carole apologised encore as she shuffled along the row to her seat in the comfortable dusk of the Circle. She quickly identified Wendy and during the interval sought to remember what John Hazlitt had said of time travel.

"I've come full circle. Back where I started. The girl was changing the photographs. Someone came in as I was swept away. I was looking for Anna, but instead."

Carole was captured by the performance. She wished to be loyal, but could find no fault with Melanie's performance as Peter. When the final bows had been taken and the audience dispersed, Carole went to the stage door and presented herself to the keeper.

Smiling her charm-the-archaeologist-smile, she asked breathlessly, "Could I please see Tameeyah? She's my niece. She plays Wendy. I just have to tell her how wonderful she was tonight. Please?"

The doorkeeper whose main concern was to keep doubtful men away from the children saw no fault in this excited Aunt.

"Please? I'd love to surprise her."

The keeper stood aside.

"Dressing room four."

"Oh, thank you! How kind!"

Carole tapped on the door and a voice cried, "If you've come for the rent, we're not in."

She took this an invitation to enter. Both girls were out of costume and looked somehow smaller. Melanie looked puzzled, but Tammie cried, "Have you found Anna?"

"Sorry. Not yet at least."

Wendy turned to Melanie, saying, "This is Anna's friend. Carole. She's been looking for Anna."

Melanie offered, "Believe me I feel guilty about this. That it was about me playing Peter. I just hope she's alright."

194

"Believe me, Melanie," Carole consoled, "You had nothing to do with Anna being suspended. I know she recommended you to the director."

"See! I keep telling you."

"I saw the show tonight and I thoroughly enjoyed your performance. Bright and sparky! Clear as a bell! Any girl will be inspired to take on the world."

"Thank you. That's very kind."

"I hope I don't sound impolite, but I came to talk to Tameeyah about something else."

"No, no! You've really made my day."

"I thought I'd take Tammie or Wendy for a burger so we can talk."

"I must tell Gillian."

On their way to the stage door Carole said, "Almost forgot. I'm your Auntie Carole. That's how I got in."

"He's a sweetie. He keeps the creeps out."

At the door Wendy smiled at the keeper.

"Thanks for letting Auntie Carole in. It was a lovely surprise. She's taking me out to a posh restaurant because I'm a star."

"No, I'm not! For a burger and fries. I'm not gona spoil you."

The trio laughed together.

"I'll deliver her safely to the boarding house."

"I've told Gillian."

*

Carole watched the girl devour the largest burger and both packets of fries without pause. She then drank her Cola and rattled the ice cubes. Carole sipped her coffee.

"We don't know much about each other, do we? I'm Anna's friend Carole. Carole Truscott. My dad's a builder and together we restore very old buildings. We're working on a building over four hundred years old. Originally called Boxborough Manor."

"Wow! That's really fabulous. I'm not so interesting. My name is Tameeyah Wells. Tammie for short."

195

"An unusual name."

"Family. My Dad's a DJ. He's really good and my Mum's my Mum. You can call me Wendy. I'm so used to it now. Can I get another drink?"

The girl fled without waiting for an answer. When she returned she said, "I told her you're the boss's girlfriend."

"I wondered why they were all looking at me. I'll pay for the drink before we leave."

Tammie settled to imbibe the drink.

"Anna told me one night there was something really odd happened when she was fighting with Captain Hook?"

"Oh, yeah! Really scary. One moment it was going really well. And then it was a real fight. There were these men fighting on stage and it looked like this man was gona get hurt and Anna jumped down and poked this other man with her sword. Then it all vanished. The audience went mad and we got on with the performance."

"Wow! That was quite something."

"Captain Hook ran away. Yellow belly!"

"And you?"

"I was too scared to move."

"Maybe I would've run away. But somebody must've arranged a stunt like that?"

"When I asked Gillian, she said it was secret, but she wasn't there until late on."

"How'd'y'mean?"

"Just in time to see the fight."

Tammie gurgled the last drops and rattled the ice. Carole asked, "D'y'know if they do ice cream?"

The girl nodded enthusiastically. Carole opened her handbag.

"Have yourself an ice cream, fresh coffee for me. And be sure to pay for that drink."

When Tammie returned Carole was relieved to see the ice cream was not enormous.

"How'd you not blow up like a balloon, sweetheart?"

"You won't be buying me supper tomorrow."

"Makes sense."

196

"And I don't take meals from just anybody. Anna says I'm knave, but time will cure that."

"Knave?"

Carole let it go. The girl spooned ice cream.

"Something odd happened to me. Shall I tell you about it?"

Tammie nodded.

"I was in the foyer when you were taking down Anna's photos and putting up the new photos of Melanie."

The ice cream had vanished. The girl sucked the empty spoon.

"Gillian told me to.."

Carole silenced her with a gesture.

"You're not going to believe me, but what I tell you is the absolute truth."

"Sounds dead serious."

"I was talking with you about Anna. Then I found myself in the garden of Boxborough Manor."

"The house you're doing up?"

"But not the Manor 2021. The Manor 1588."

The girl broke the silence, saying, "Fifteen eighty-eight? In the past? Are you telling me the truth?"

"I swear. I was transported through time. I met Earl Boxborough and what I learnt was very disturbing. There's something very important I must do for Anna."

"You're frightening me. Talking to dead people."

"I need you to help me, please."

Tammie laughed.

"There's nothing I can do. I don't even believe in time travel."

"The past is still there and there are travellers who journey in both directions."

"I don't see what it has to do with me."

"You're the key that unlocks the door."

Wendy laughed to say, "No, I'm not!"

Carole took out her notebook, thumbed the pages and began to read aloud.

"To travel in time two stations are required, one transmitting and one receiving. Travellers are dispatched between stations. Men and women who have this unique ability often don't know they are active. A person who comes within the orbit of a time station may be dispatched where there is need for an intervention. The Russian philosopher, Nicholas Kolubin wrote that. Disappeared October, nineteen thirty-six."

"So?"

"Anna has vanished into Time. You are very close to Anna. I was with you when I was dispatched to the Manor. I returned to the foyer this evening. I need you to dispatch me again to where I'm needed. You have the gift."

Tammie laughed.

"I don't think so. I'm just a kid. Even if it were true, I don't know what to do."

"Everything will go wrong for Anna unless you help me. Please?"

Tammie surrendered.

"I'd do anything for Anna. What d'y'want me to do?"

"Where do you live?"

"Rosebank Boarding House. Missis Seaberg's very nice."

"I'll take you home. Keep Anna in your thoughts. Have you a photo?"

"Lots. D'y'want one?"

"Thank you, but no. Just keep Anna in your thoughts."

*

As Annie struggled Noah took her arm to lead the terrified girl from the room, but the bully elbowed him aside. He dragged Annie onto the landing and on to the stairhead. Noah followed behind. Anna, sick with the pain from the broken finger, bit the man's arm. He swore and released her. Noah kicked the bully boy in the back and he flew downstairs to land on his head. He lay still and blood began to create a dark halo about his broken skull. Annie sat down on the stair to say, "We's doomed now."

When Noah turned back to the room Anna forced Annie to her feet and followed. The pale inquisitor stood behind the table holding his Bible as if it were a shield.

He pronounced, "I am a priest chosen by God Almighty to forward the restoration of His Church in this sorry land. You may not harm me. Stand aside and do not impede my progress. It would be advisable that you surrender yourself to the Justices."

Noah surprised the priest by vaulting over the table, driving him into a corner. When Noah advanced on him the inquisitor began to whimper and then scream when Noah took him in a chokehold.

Annie cried, "Don't kill him, Noah! It'll only make it worser!"

As Anna watched hypnotised, Noah cut off the priest's nose, grinding through the gristle with his unyielding blade. The girls screamed with one voice. The pig screamed too. Blood flooded from the destroyed face.

Noah came to Annie and took her unhurt hand.

"Time to go, lass. As far away as we can go."

Anna agreed wholeheartedly.

As they proceeded to the front door Noah dropped every burning torch to the floor. As they hurried from Froggart's Side the Archangel tavern behind them was burning fiercely.

Annie asked anxiously, "Will he die in there?"

"Do you care?"

"I never wanted nobody to die."

*

Contentment reigned at 18, Springfield Park Avenue. The paraffin stove glowed cheerily and filled the room with Kit's second favourite parfum domestique: paraffin oil. His latest passion was for kippers. Kit was reciting the new scene from his project, THE FALL OF THE TYRANT, the ink scarcely dry on the page. Hannah at her laptop listened and applauded. When Kit had amended the scene with as many scratchings out as to create an untidy nest of ink ants, Hannah would have the task of transcribing the scene to the laptop. It was the happiest of domestic scenes.

Hannah applauded the last words as Carole appeared on the goatskin rug; their newest acquisition from a charity sale. Carole had wit enough to say, "Apologies for this intrusion."

She looked again at a confused Hannah.

"Of course! You're Hannah. You don't know me, but I'm Carole.

Anna's gone. I have no idea where she is. I must find her."

Her image rippled. Carole said, "I'm so pleased to see you both together."

Carole vanished. The ripples of Time swayed the net curtains.

Hannah said, "You would never leave me, would you, Kit?"

The national playwright, time displaced, considered his answer.

"I would consider life without you, tiresome person as you are, as unbearable as a boil on the arse."

"But you would never leave me, would you?"

"As you would never leave me, my sweet peasecod. We are so sworn."

"I can never tell whether you're serious or not."

"Then don't ask serious questions."

"There are no other questions I want to ask."

"I'll recite the scene again, shall I?"

Because she loved him and because he did have a fine voice, she said, "It deserves a second hearing."

An actor's voice, thought Hannah, but no one ever says, a house painter's voice or a butcher's voice or. . .

Peace returned to the house in Springfield Park Avenue.

*

"Come away!" Kit ordered, "They've forgotten us already."

The sails and smaller craft were already distant upon the broad breast of the Nene.

Ralph said, "I had never heard of this river before."

"Being rowed back and forth across the Thames narrows your vision of life."

They had parted with Ganda & his people, Captain Louis de Saint des Vosges, six halberdiers, four fusiliers, a Scottish Queen and a considerable sum of money. As they rode back across the pasture to the castle Ralph commented, "You've given her Majesty enough money to fly to the moon."

"If it will ensure her silence, it is money well-spent."

"And gold pieces to the escort here and to be paid again in France?"

"I wish a live Queen to arrive in France."

"And Louis refused a bribe?"

"He is a chevalier serving his Queen. He will have a secret to share with his grandchildren on his deathbed."

"I would've preferred to have his sword here."

"I have your sword here. That is surely well enough, my chevalier?"

"Kit, there are reports that Garnet's army is growing. Perhaps a hundred? Perhaps more?"

"It's not an army, Ralph, it's a mob."

They dismounted on the bailey amid the complaining voices of cattle, goats and geese.

"Why are they not out at pasture, Kit?"

"As the new Castellan of Fotheringhay my first restraint is to restrict the number of questions you ask. Do you wish to have your question answered?"

"I'd like it to be."

"The kine, goats and Hannibal and his geese being now part of my garrison are confined to camp."

"Speak sense, please! The mob as you call it will be upon us any day now."

"Out to pasture they will be stolen and eaten. I am not going to feed Garnet's mob. They are members of the garrison. Therefore, you as my adjutant will add them to the payroll."

"You are jesting with me, surely!"

"How otherwise will we begin to explain the money we have spent of Elizabeth's money?"

"We? I don't recall any *we* in our discussions."

"The garrison consists of me, you, the Sergeant-at-arms, Jonard, Gilbert, sixteen halberdiers, twelve gunners, Corporal Hannibal, kine, goats and geese. As named."

"Such do not have names, Kit."

"Give them names. Write them into the payroll."

"This is sheer madness, Kit! One day there will be a reckoning."

"And what would you do, Sir Ralph?"

"I would have kept the fusiliers. In the armoury we have too many tubs of lead shot."

"And you would wish them fired upon this mob? Men, women and children?"

"At the first volley the charge would wither and die."

Kit sighed & shook his head.

"Ralph, I thought you had finally grown up. Now you're reverting to childhood. Try to think as I do. Trumpets! The Siege of Fotheringhay! This is a play in which we are taking part. Don't interrupt! I have always wished to play Tamburlaine. Defending the castle I mean to kill no one. Or as few as possible. Do you agree?"

"Yes."

"Then you must behave as if you do. Kine and goats must stay on the bailey. Gilbert and Jonard will help you. Hannibal will keep his flock calm. Our first line of defence is our walls. Walls don't kill anyone. Unless some idiot falls off. Talk to our Sergeant-at-Arms. I want as many halberdiers on the walls as possible. Give every gunner a halberd. The sergeant will arrange a routine so that we appear twice as strong as we are. And torches on the walls at night to let the spectators see the sentries. A splendid scene with moonlight. Later we'll check the Armoury."

"What about the Chamberlain and the Castellan?"

"Keep them locked up and feed them gruel."

Ralph laughed and walked away. Kit shouted after him.

"That was not a jest. Keep them on short rations. They speak to no one. Is that understood?"

"When it comes to the trial I shall plead madness and be sent to Bedlam."

TWENTY-THREE

Kit surveyed his kingdom: busy soldiers, singing from the laundry, thirsty cattle and bad tempered goats, faithful geese following Hannibal in search of any scrap of green. He recited aloud, "I hold the Fates bound fast in iron chains and with my hand turn Fortune's wheel about. Sooner shall the sun fall from his sphere than Tamburlaine be slain or overcome."

Gilbert appeared at his side.

"How many questions am I allowed, sir?"

He grinned at Kit.

"Sir Ralph warned me."

"How many questions do you have?"

"We can stretch the feed for horses and kine to a week. The geese too. The soldiers already love Hannibal. But we must water all at the river."

"Water the horses when Sir Ralph sends out patrols."

"And the kine?"

"The kine, goats and the geese stay on the bailey. They must not go to water. That is an absolute order."

Gilbert looked anxious.

"Do you trust me?"

"Yes, sir."

"Then you must accept my word. Kine, goats and Hannibal's company must go without water. I will not feed Garnet's mob."

*

It's like travelling on the Tube with your eyes closed, thought Carole, a confusion of noise, voices and unexpected bumps from inconsiderate shoulders. Yet why am I travelling standing up? I will be very disappointed if I am on the Tube. Though I don't want to be in a tumbril rubbing shoulders with aristos on our way to the guillotine.

Carole opened one eye and then the other without surprise. She knew exactly where she was. She was standing in the pit of the New Theatre. She had only ever seen a print of the theatre, but she knew she was watching Ned Alleyn bring Faustus to its dramatic close. The groundlings about her were mesmerised by the great actor, all disbelief suspended.

When the performance came to its end the audience was slow to disperse, immersed in the magic of theatre, reluctant to break the spell and return to a drab existence. Carole saw that Ned Alleyn was still on stage talking to friends, smiling, occasionally breaking into laughter. She made her way slowly through the parting crowd to the foot of the stage.

*

John Hazlitt and his secretary Sybil Crowther were buried together in New Christchurch graveyard. As usual in such circumstances it rained steadily throughout the service at the graveside. The funeral was attended by three former colleagues including George Bryce and two older ladies who might have been sisters of either deceased.. Wendy and Detective Sergeant Stanley Robertson attended.

It was a cheerless occasion as the Vicar had never met Hazlitt or Sybil Crowther and had nothing to offer but platitudes. His patients did not attend. Bryce attended so he couldn't be accused of not attending. The two women psychologists were from London where they had both worked with Hazlitt.

Throughout the graveside charade Wendy stared stolidly across the flooding grave at Bryce, which annoyed him as he had never met this girl. The grey-haired Sergeant attended the burial because he was puzzled by Hazlitt's suicide. But the killing of his dog was in character with what he had learnt of the man. The death of the secretary seemed an unrelated incident.

The burial party did not linger. Skating through the last words the Vicar left the graveside followed by the burial party. Only Wendy and the Sergeant stayed to drop a handful of mud on the coffin.

"How well did you know Mister Hazlitt?"

"I never knew him. My friend did."

"Then what're you doing here in the rain?"

"I hate Mister Bryce."

"The big bloke?"

"That's him. He's a psychologist. He wants to go time travelling. That's why he was pestering my friend Anna. To take him time travelling."

The sergeant considered the child's face, the straggling wet hair, the slight form in the plastic mack.

"Let's start again. I'm Detective Sergeant Stanley Robertson."

"Show me your I.D."

"Do I have to? It's raining."

He started to unbutton his mackintosh.

"Never mind. I'll see it another time. I'm Tameeyah Wells. I'm an actor. I play Wendy in Peter Pan at the Queen's Theatre. Call me Wendy. Everybody does."

"Really? My grandson's your biggest fan."

"Gosh! Brilliant!"

"Not when I'm paying again and again for tickets."

"I could give you my autograph for him."

The sergeant sighed.

"I suppose so."

He pulled out his notebook and offered a clean page and a biro. Wendy added her signature and then hesitated.

"What's his name?"

"Who?"

"Your son."

"His mates call him Bobby."

Wendy amended the inscription.

"How old is he?"

"Twelve."

Wendy hid her disappointment. A fan is a fan.

"Is the interrogation over, miss?"

Wendy smiled. The rain began to fall ever faster.

"D'y'fancy a burger and chips, Tammie?"

"If you're paying."

"I suppose I am. Let's find the car."

Robertson watched respectfully as Wendy demolished the biggest burger on sale and large fries.

"I wouldn't want to keep you for a week."

"I'm only eating with you cos you're a copper. Anna says, don't take a free meal. He thinks he's buying you."

"Anna sounds a sensible woman."

"She is. I'm her best friend."

"Tell me what I don't know."

"Have you seen in the papers about the actress who time travels and talks to dead people?"

"Yes. Sounds dodgy."

"That's Anna. She's not dodgy. They're alive when she talks to them, she says. She may travel in time, but I've never seen it. She played Peter and she was wonderful."

"You say played?"

"Bryce got her sacked. Suspended. Whatever. He was pestering her. Every performance. And odd things started happening."

"Like?"

"There was suddenly a real fight on stage. Anna killed this man and there was blood everywhere. It was terrifying. Then just as suddenly it all vanished and the audience applauded like mad. We went on performing as if nothing had happened. Carole disappeared when I was taking down the photographs and Anna hasn't been seen for days now."

"D'y'think that is connected with this 'time travelling'?"

"Anna said Mister Hazlitt told her it was all connected."

"Do you think Bryce killed this other psychologist?"

"He got Anna suspended from performing. But I don't think he'd have the guts to kill anybody."

"I'd like to find out more about time travel. Where'll I find Anna?"

"She's been missing for days now."

"What's her full name?"

She recited Carole's name & address.

The sergeant made a note to pay another visit to the park and the fatal bench.

*

206

The Armoury was below the guardroom with gutter windows at ground level as it is risky to take torches near gunpowder. Kit, Ralph and the Sergeant-at-arms were carrying out an inspection of the Armoury. Kit noted there were more than ample gunpowder casks to supply four cannon & two carronades. There were also enough casks of lead shot to supply a regiment of fusiliers on a long campaign. The Sergeant opened box upon box of coils of German 'Blitzschnell' fuses in long & short lengths.

"Which castle was Fotheringhay planning to undermine?"

"I cannot answer your question, sir."

"It had no serious intent."

There was also a rack of antique fusils & boxes of flints. In the twilight behind these outdated weapons was a rack of chained modern muskets.

"Explain this to me, Sergeant."

"Where should I start, sir?"

"Gunpowder and fuses to blow up the White Tower ten times over. Enough lead shot and weapons to win a war."

"I've only been here just over a year, Commissioner. There is no Master Armourer here and supplies arrive every quarter and more often. All are duly marked in the Register. You, sir, brought the muskets. I locked them away."

"I suppose my answer would be that I didn't load the wagon. Didn't you think to question this?"

"I told the Castellan, but he said let it be. So, I let it be."

Kit nodded acceptance. There were also racks of halberds and cutlasses that Kit questioned.

"What're we doing with cutlasses? Boarding ships on the Nene?"

"I would suppose discarded by Lord Howard, sir," commented the Sergeant-at-arms, "He prefers cannon,"

"When this Papist mob arrives I am not going to turn the cannon on them. Nor the carronades. Let Frankie Drake clear the decks of this Armada we hear about. Two hundred and fifty Spaniards at one blow. Well done! Two hundred and fifty men, women and children waving banners?"

"No, Commissioner! I would be shamed as a soldier to commit such murder!"

"A man after my own heart. So, what do we have to frighten the Papists into surrender?"

"I'm hoping you will laugh, sir and not curse me."

The Sergeant led Kit & Ralph to the farther wall where in the dim light he pointed to the wall racks.

"We have, sir, two hundred and fourteen long bows. And two hundred sheaves of arrows."

The good Sergeant awaited laughter from his betters. Sir Ralph laughed, but the Queen's Commissioner was unmoved.

"Splendid!" cried the Commissioner, "I want them cleaned, oiled and strings checked. The garrison will begin archery practice today."

"But, sir, the fletching of the arrows may be!"

"Whatever is amiss, we have geese and geese have feathers. I'm sure Corporal Hannibal cannot count."

"Yes, sir!"

Ralph said, "As you have an interest in antiquities, Commissioner,

Perhaps I may show you a rare object?"

Wary of jests, the Commissioner followed Sir Ralph Boxborough and the Sergeant to a dark corner where a jumble of timbers & ropes lay ignored.

"You think to throw this at the mob?"

"It's a ballista, Kit. You throw stones with it. Or they did in olden times."

Ralph and the Sergeant laughed, but the Commissioner bent down to examine the clutter.

"Is it all here?"

"Just as the Romans left it."

Kit straightened up to say, "Capital! You and the sergeant will rebuild this machine today. It's always good for the actors to see the gaffer at work too."

Ralph was too astonished to complain, but the Sergeant complied.

"Yes, sir. Today, sir."

Kit stood deep in thought for a moment.

"You, Sergeant and Sir Ralph are two of the few people I trust at Fotheringhay. Am I right to do so?"

The answers of both men were immediate & sincere.

"This is not a matter of bad housekeeping. This is a long laid conspiracy. Someone of authority has provisioned this castle in anticipation of this Papist rebellion. If they take the castle they will have more than pitchforks and hoes. It will be a different matter when they have muskets, cannon, black powder and fuses."

The Sergeant hid his surprise. Ralph proclaimed, "I keep saying you're the right man for this mission, Kit. But I must admit in the beginning that I thought otherwise. I believed that I should have played the diplomat. My apologies!"

"No, no! No place for apologies. I would've thought the worse of you if you hadn't wished to be the Commissioner. Am I right, Sergeant?"

"Yes, sir. But this is no place for a gentleman, begging your pardon, sir."

Ralph laughed wholeheartedly and clapped the good soldier on the shoulder.

"One last thing. Have Armitage's bathtub moved to beside the barracks. Daily Orders. All shit to be deposited here."

Ralph opened & closed his mouth. The Sergeant agreed.

"Yes, sir. Daily Orders. All shit to be deposited in the bath tub."

Kit marched away leaving Ralph and the Sergeant in silence until the Sergeant ventured to ask, "Do you think, sir, the Commissioner is in his right mind?"

"Without a doubt, Sergeant. You may rely on him. A very clever man. He has my total loyalty."

"Thank you, sir. Then I will follow your example."

He saluted Ralph and exited saying, "I will set men to the bows and I'll find a cart to move our bits and pieces onto the bailey. We can start when you're ready, sir."

Left to himself Ralph informed the Armoury walls, "No, I do not lie. Master Marlowe knows what he is doing. But he is not preparing the defence of this castle, but a dramatic production that would bring the groundlings storming onto the stage to tear the unhappy actor playing Father Henry Garnet limb from limb. Then all duty done we would retire to Mistress Brown's House at Cheapside to fill our bellies with pork bones and too much beer. Here at Fotheringhay the outcome may be quite different."

Kit found the Quartermaster at the tubs where the women were boiling the castle's dirty washing, uniforms, bedding et cetera. He explained to the doughty old soldier what he needed done and why it must be done today. The Quartermaster agreed because he was accustomed to being told what to do, but he also realised that this was the rare occasion in a lifetime of service that someone took the trouble to explain why it was needed.

"Wha'do his lordship want of us, Billie?" a woman asked.

"He wants us to make some banners."

"Why'd he want that?"

"The holies has banners. So shud us."

"He's a queer one."

"No, Maisie, he's a right one. There'll be sparks, ye'll see."

"Will they take the castle?"

"Sir John Piss-his-britches Nottingsley would open the gate for them and kiss their arse. This one won't. He'll snuff out their piddling rebellion, so don't you be feared, woman."

With his ears burning with unheard compliments, Kit Marlowe went off to find the Ensign of Gunners and talk about bombs.

That day an industrious peace settled upon Fotheringhay Castle.

Idle soldiers are a dangerous fodder for mutiny. They're happier working together at tasks they understand.

*

Carole waited at the foot of the stage until the men talking with Ned Alleyn departed. When the actor turned to go, Carole called, "May I speak with you, sir?"

The famous actor appraised her and said, "Why would I not speak with you, m'lady? If not your appearance, your dress intrigues me."

Carole realised that a woman in jeans, Buffalo teeshirt and a leather jacket might seem unusual in 1588.

"I dress as I need."

"But not for propriety?"

"I know of you, sir and I have the highest regard for your reputation."

Intrigued, Ned Alleyn, manager-actor, came to sit on the edge of the stage; Dionysus approaching Artemis, the lover of alcohol and the huntress.

"What do you seek?"

"He seems invisible. The playwright Christopher Marlowe."

Ned laughed and Carole rewarded him with the smile that charmed the owners of venerable properties Truscott & Daughter wanted to save from falling down.

"Ah, Kit! The master of distraction. Now he is here and now he is not. But always my lifelong friend and a scribbler of some merit."

A well-phrased warning, thought Carole.

"So I have heard."

"When did women play the bailiff? I doubt you have come to begger him. He has nothing."

"I don't come to bear him harm. But I would wish to talk with him."

"You come too late. He has vanished to fulfil a mission for her Majesty, good Queen Bess."

"And you won't tell me where he has gone?"

"I know not. From time to time he does some service for her Majesty. I have not seen Hannah since…."

An unconscious slip of the tongue. Carole's heart beat loudly. *Surely he could hear it?*

The actor-manager paused to regard Carole sharply.

"I have not seen you before, m'lady."

"I am concerned for Hannah."

Ned Alleyn jumped down from the stage to regard her from top-knot to toe. A voice in her head warned Carole she was skating on thin ice.

"Are you a daughter of Lesbos?"

Carole was indignant.

"Indeed, no! You mistake me, sir! I seek my sister."

"Your sister?"

"Hannah. Sometimes Hannah Cato. Sometimes Hannah Marlon. Whatever takes her fancy. She is always with Kit."

Ned Alleyn seemed to relax.

211

"When last Kit was with me, Hannah was not. He never mentioned her and when I did, refused an answer, saying I know her not. Then the summons to attend Court came and I have not seen hide nor hair of either of them since."

"Then they have had a falling out."

Ned Alleyn was silent until reluctantly he offered, "You come at a very bad time. Complaints have been made to the Justices that playing Faustus is proselytising for the Devil. This was our last performance. We are leaving until the dust settles."

"Where are you going?"

"To Canterbury. Kit's birthplace. I will expect him to attend. Perhaps Hannah too?"

Carole refused beer at the Black Horse and to Ned's surprise shook his hand in farewell.

"By krise, but ye has a fierce grip for a woman."

Carole overcame the temptation to take him in a headlock and force him to cry quits.

"But, sir, you have a sure tongue to please the weaker sex."

*

From outside the Black Horse on a crowded sunlit street stinking of horses and horse dung, Carole suddenly found herself alone on a rainy country lane where before she had time to draw breath she was almost struck down by a motorcycle combination that clattered on without stopping. She shouted after the solitary rider, but he gave no indication that he had heard or seen Carole although almost swatting her like a fly.

The rain began to flood Carole's world so that when she smelt a particularly disgusting stink a Roman legion marching towards her came as no surprise. Roman legions on the march were always smelt before being heard & seen. She hid in the trees beyond the road and cursed the rain, listening to the stolid thump of iron-nailed boots, creaking wagons, chattering women & the bleating of goats as it seemed the entire Roman Army in Britain marched in review past her soaking wet self. Surprisingly, Carole fell asleep and woke up in her own bed.

TWENTY-FOUR

Tammie adopted a defiant, appealing stance before the receptionist's desk.

"I just have to see Mister Bryce. I just do! Please!"

She added a little sob of sadness, appealing blue eyes holding back a flood of tears.

"I really need to see him. I really do. My father."

She bit her lip and ceased to speak. Mrs. Fleurpart, a sympathetic middle-aged woman, almost came around the desk to wrap a chubby arm about the child's thin shoulders. Wendy turned her head away from the receptionist. Her breath smelt of peppermint. She was well into her stride as Jenny the abused child she played in *Bad People* at the Liverpool Barn.

"Mister Bryce only sees patients by appointment, sweetheart. His time is very valuable. He's talking with a lady at the moment. I can't interrupt him, but if you're prepared to wait perhaps he'll see you. It's his last appointment of the day."

Wendy gave a little sob, nodded and took a seat under the wall littered with photographs of Mr. George Bryce engaged in many therapeutic activities.

"What's your full name, dear?"

"Wendy Darling."

"Can I get you anything, Wendy?"

Tammie suppressed her natural reaction to ask, "What you got?"

"Just to see Mister Bryce."

She smiled sadly and Mrs. Fleurpart smiled fondly.

It was perhaps thirty minutes later the door to the inner office opened. Mr. Bryce and his patient emerged. Tammie came to life and Mrs. Fleurpart raised a warning finger to her. The child subsided. The psychologist escorted his patient to the outer door murmuring reassuring platitudes that were gratefully received.

213

The door closed and George Bryce said, "There's one in every basket, is there not, Missis Fleurpart?"

He hadn't noticed Tammie and appeared startled as if she had suddenly materialised.

"Who have we here?"

The receptionist pleaded for the child.

"Wendy Darling. I wonder if you would have time, sir, to listen to this distressed child. She really needs help."

Mr. Bryce sparkled upon the forlorn figure that rose to stand before him.

"I won't keep you long, sir. But I've heard about you and I really need."

With a warm smile George Bryce put an arm about her shoulders and drew Wendy towards the inner sanctum.

"I won't be taking notes, Missis Fleurpart. So, I'll see you in the morning?"

At the threshold of the study, Tammie stopped to say, "Thank you, Missis Fleurpart. You've been ever so kind."

To the closing door, the good lady answered, "Bless you, darling!"

*

Bryce invited Wendy, "Please sit down, my dear."

Wendy remained standing.

He smiled upon her, teeth glittering with virtue to say, "There is no need to be anxious. This is the place where people share their troubles and I try to solve.."

He took two steps towards Wendy and suddenly stopped, switching off the smile.

"You're the brat at that damned funeral that kept staring at me! Out you go!"

He waved his hands at her, advancing another step, Goliath looming over dwarfed David.

"And you're the slimy bugger that lost Anna her job, you bastard!"

He waved his hands again at her, protesting innocence and Wendy lunged at him. With the Stanley knife she slashed at the back of his right hand. As he stared at his hand, Wendy moved

214

in again to slash wildly at his left hand. Bryce shrieked with pain.

He cried, "Missis Fleurpart, ring the police! I'm being attacked!"

There was no answer as the good lady was opening the door of her Honda Classic, casting a smile upwards to the shining light where the saintly gentleman whom she adored was surely easing that poor girl's pain. In truth, she had him pinned against the desk desperately trying to fend off the vicious blade. The child was very quick and slashed at his expensive suit again & again. He tried desperately to save his suit, exposing his hands to repeated cuts.

"For krise sake!" he whimpered, "Stop it! Stop it!"

Wendy stared at him in amazement.

"You're not only a nasty bastard, but you're fucking gutless coward!"

When Wendy cut his face he began to weep. When he covered his face with bleeding hands she cut at his sleeves leaving them hanging in tatters. He made one last desperate attempt to break free and fell striking his head on the edge of his desk. He didn't move again. Wendy enjoyed a last fury slashing at his expensive waistcoat.

She regarded the silent figure on the floor for a moment to say politely, "Thank you, Mister Bryce for giving me this chance to explain my position. I love Anna and I hate you."

She turned off the lights in the sanctum and the outer office. She pulled the outer door to and heard it lock. She walked quietly down the stairs, met no one and walked through the rain to the theatre to play Wendy Darling in the evening performance.

*

It had been a long & tiresome journey and although the bedroom was an attic storeroom Anna was grateful for the clean bed & the oil lamp. Annie was worried that something with teeth would drop from the dark rafters above. Anna had stood on the bed with the oil lamp to prove her wrong. Before Annie voiced her fear, Anna got down on hands and knees to

215

investigate under the bed. She found three ornamental hairpins that Annie was pleased to receive. Anna could hear below the familiar racket of evening in a busy pub. She found it reassuring, but Annie was restless. She spoke to her firmly.

"Annie, goodness sake, if the bed falls through you'll be to blame. I know you're tired. There is nothing to fuss ye. Noah is working in the bar for friendship's sake. We have a full belly. There's a bolt on the door and a pot under the bed. Tomorrow we'll be in London. Give us a bit of peace, girl!"

"It's a strange bed!"

"It's fit for a Queen."

"Do ye think so?"

"I do dearly! Fit for a queen, your Majesty!"

This silenced Annie. Dear, simple Annie! Anna was surprised to find she was becoming fond of her sister. Annie seemed to accept the voice in her head. Anna wondered what she sounded like to the girl and would she feel abandoned or relieved when the voice stopped giving advice. Annie began to snore and Anna relaxed from sentry duty. She pretended she was riding on a steam train. As she fell asleep Anna found herself hoping she wouldn't wake in Canterbury.

*

The sunlit park was cool and calming to the spirit. Contrary to the sagging police tape about the area of the deadly bench. The solitary constable i/c park bench recognised the veteran Sergeant Robertson, but not his thin bespectacled companion.

"You must be short of someat to do, Stan?"

"You've not been mobbed then?"

"The odd dog walker no more."

"Just taking a last look. Don't think we've missed nothing."

As they stepped over the tape the constable said, "I give it to him that he didn't leave his dog."

"True. A man and his dog."

The sergeant and his companion, Alan Thurston, approached the bench. It was clean, washed by the rain or a fire hose. Backed by a spinney of trees it offered a fine view of the lake.

"Tell me what you think," Stan Robertson urged his friend.

216

"I have no idea if I'll be able to tell you anything. I've little experience of working outdoors."

"Alan, we're here because you are the real thing. You've helped me before when you've seen and heard what I cannot."

"Your fellow officers would dispute that."

"Some of my fellow officers wouldn't accept the truth if it crept up and bit their arse. You do have that extra sense. When I first met you I thought you were as phoney as the rest, but.."

He stopped because the medium was standing very still.

"A man who must be Hazlitt is sitting on the bench with his dog. They approach. There are three of them."

Alan Thurston pulled the Sergeant aside as if to let the killers pass.

"They're talking about the dog. The leader sits to fondle the dog."

He pauses, becoming disturbed and appeals to the sergeant.

"Krise sake, he's cutting the dog's throat and smiling at Hazlitt! He holds the dog as it dies. Hazlitt is frozen. It's unbelievable! He passes the razor to the brute behind the bench who cuts Hazlitt's throat. Oh, my God! The third man is terrified. I can smell his fear. He runs off to vomit in the trees."

Thurston is badly shaken.

"Show me!"

"I'd rather not."

The Sergeant took his friend by the arm and pulled him towards the trees. The site of vomiting was still visible. The medium returned quickly to the bench and Robertson followed him.

The Sergeant queried, "They're not spirits, are they, Alan? They're real! Something to do with Time?"

The medium began to shiver.

"We really shouldn't be here, Stan. This is very dangerous!"

"What can you see?"

"They're close. Very close. If we don't go they will kill us too! Oh, my God!"

Three figures appeared among the trees, vague shapes becoming clearly precise. In what Sergeant Robertson recognised as historical dress. The medium fled to the car. The Sergeant was sorely tempted to join him.

The constable called, "What's up with your mate?"

The assassins stood behind the bench. Stan saw the eternal brute, the young man who vomited and the Jesuit. When the lordling opened his mouth to speak, Sergeant Stanley Robertson cut him short, saying, "I don't know why you did this, but if ever we meet again, I'll bring such force against you as you'll never have seen and I will destroy you."

He took out his service torch and switched it to flutter, which disorientated the toughest burglars in Canterbury. The assassins raised hands to protect their eyes and Stan set the horn to squeal and advanced under cover of flutter & squeal. He had scarcely taken three steps before the vision flickered and was extinguished.

He found himself shaking and knew he had never been so terrified in all his life. His ears were ringing with the high intensity sound that befuddled many a criminal brain.

He called to the constable.

"You can shut it down, Mick. Clear the tape. Don't leave a mess. I'll get them to move the bench."

Then he went farther into the spinney to empty his bladder and throw up his breakfast. As he returned to the car, he advised himself, "Let's not do that again, Stan. We're too old for the historical."

Alan Thurston asked, "What did you say to them?"

"Stay off my patch."

"God, I never knew you were so brave, Stan."

The sergeant looked at him wryly.

"Brave? I've been shot once and stabbed twice, but I tell you, Alan, I was shitting meself. I don't blame you scooting. I nearly did."

"You're right. They were from the Past, Stan. I know the past is still there, but I never knew it to react so violently before. What did Hazlitt do to provoke them?"

The sergeant didn't respond.

"What're you going to do about it?"

"Nothing. Mister Hazlitt for personal reasons killed his dog and then killed himself."

When Alan Thurston looked at him, Sergeant Stanley Robertson replied, "Nobody would believe me and I am not going to end up in the loony bin."

*

"Everything in order?"

Everything in the grim chamber had been stripped away leaving only the small table and the two chairs occupied by Kit and Ralph Boxborough. There were velli enough on the table to start a small library and two inkhorns & quills.

"Yes, sir," replied the Sergeant-at-arms.

"Then bring in the prisoner."

The Sergeant exited the chamber and returned with Sir John Nottingsley between two halberdiers.

"You are Sir John Nottingsley? Formerly Castellan of Fotheringhay Castle?"

Kit could smell the stink of sour wine even from where he sat. He regarded the pitiful old man with contempt.

Ralph proclaimed, "Do you wish to address the Commissioner?"

"I protest my treatment and the usurpation of my authority."

It was a pitiful quaver which Kit admired as it would bring tears to the eyes of older women in the boxes.

"I am the Queen's Commissioner. Both are denied. You are charged with failing in your duty. I find you guilty."

The old man required support from his escort.

"What is the penalty, Sir Ralph?"

Kit turned to a solemn Ralph who sought an answer among the velli on the table.

"Execution by hanging, Commissioner."

Kit took and signed an old laundry list. Ralph added a wax seal.

"So be it. Unless he prefers the axe."

The former Castellan cried out, "You cannot do this to me! This is beyond your remit! I appeal to her Majesty."

Kit rose in his chair and a future audience at the New Theatre held its breath.

219

"Cannot? Cannot? I can and I will. I have executed Mary Stuart, Queen of Scots! Her coffin stands in the yard ready to be transported to London. A man who executes a queen may execute anyone. You won't see such courtesy. We will drown you in the dung pit and drag you out seven times before we hang you. If I am in a merciful mood, I will permit the executioner to open your belly and you may regard your own guts before he opens the trap door to eternity."

Sir John Nottingsley fell to the floor whimpering.

"Prepare your soul. You will be executed forthwith."

The poor man was dragged from the chamber to be locked away in Fotheringhay's drear dungeon. When the door closed, Ralph accused Kit.

"That was a most unworthy act of bullying. You should be ashamed, Kit. But then you are not a gentleman."

"No, I'm what is mockingly called a scribbler. If I could reach I would pat myself on the back. We must find a clerk to record such splendid performances. It would be a sin to lose such wizardry."

"Such cruelty is a sin."

"Did I sneer enough? Was my contempt for the creature evident? At the end was there just the slightest suggestion of sympathy for the traitor from my generous heart?"

"What was the purpose of that disgusting charade, Kit?"

"The word is out. Mary Stuart is dead. Executed by the Queen's Commissioner. I shall write a description of the occasion. God's balls, but there is a masterpiece to be devised from this adventure."

Ralph struggled to hold his tongue and failed.

"Why this foolery? Who would Sir John tell?"

"He's not important. The garrison now know I am a man to be feared. I must remember to scowl more. I have too friendly a face."

"And the Queen's Chamberlain? Sir Geoffrey Hamilton?"

"Ah, yes! The old clown with the longest beard in England! We shall have a glass of wine before we proceed to roast the bastard. Or perhaps two?"

"These are serious matters, Kit. I do protest your levity."

220

"Without levity how could we bear to proceed? Perchance I might add jollity to the proceedings by setting that ridiculous beard afire? Or should I leap upon the table and strike at him with my sword in righteous anger? Setting fire to his beard? That would be a lark to remember! Wha'd'y'say, milord? Jolly sport?"

"Promise me you aren't going to execute those poor old fools."

"Those bastards have conspired to surrender a Queen and this Castle to the Papists. They deserve to die."

With a complete change of intention, Kit proclaimed upon his longsuffering friend, "Perhaps I should command the seamstress to create for me a regal Commissioner's costume? To be worn at executions and occasions of State. Stronger shoulders. Gold to set off the midnight black. A cloak to swirl when having given judgement I sweep out, ignoring the plaintive pleading of the condemned."

He paused to laugh at Ralph's solemn face.

"I tell you, Ralph, it is all theatre, this politicking and prancing. It's all acting! Never mind truth or justice, it is the roar of the crowd they seek. And so do I in my humble striving after fame. Or do you think I am of a more pastoral disposition, too tender in my feelings, that perhaps I should seek a shepherd's tenure in some gentle shade?"

Ralph's granite face was unmoved.

"If you harm those foolish old men I will quit you, Kit. I promise!"

"And miss the entertainment? I doubt you, Ralph."

TWENTY-FIVE

Sir Geoffrey Hamilton, Mary Stuart's Chamberlain, suffered Kit's taunts with more grace than the former Castellan.

"Whatever the cost I maintain my devotion to Queen Mary Stuart. A lady grievously misjudged. The longer I served her the more my respect for her grew."

He drew strength from Ralph's face, which could not conceal his agreement. Kit hardened his tone.

"I have already executed her advisor, the Chevalier de Orleanais Duvios and her attendants. They were discovered as traitors willing to give over their charge to the leaders of the Papist rebellion now bearing down upon us."

"I had suspected their inclination."

"And you did nothing?"

Hamilton didn't respond.

"Couldn't you have disposed of their service?"

"I was alone."

"You had only to call upon Captain Louis de Saint des Vosges."

"But he is French!"

"He is a man of honour. Whereas you are not. You failed in your duty. Hereby, I sentence you to death by execution."

The Chamberlain began to speak but fell silent.

"Would you wish to see the Queen's body. I can open the coffin."

Kit felt Ralph stiffen by his side.

"I would prefer to remember her Majesty as she was."

"As previously the Queen's Chamberlain, you will visit the coffin to confirm her death."

On the staircase Ralph hissed in Kit's ear, "Are you mad?"

"You will open the coffin and as swiftly close it. To have his signature on a document certifying her death is invaluable. I'll hold him back as you prepare."

Kit and Sir Geoffrey approached the funeral wagon. The Sergeant-at-arms offered a muscular arm to assist the old man up onto the wagon floor. Ralph stood at the head of the coffin and the Sergeant at the foot.

"This won't be a pleasant experience, sir. I couldn't ask anyone else to execute a Queen. I regret I am a sorry axe man."

Kit put a sheltering arm about the old man and nodded to Ralph. The coffin lid was lifted.

"Oh, dear Christ!"

The stink was not as overwhelming under the canvas hood as might have been expected. But the corpse was alarming. The head had separated from the body, staring into the side of the coffin, darkly unrecognisable. The coffin lid descended at the Chamberlain's distressed cry.

"And her dog too! She doted on ma Cherie! How could you? You are indeed a capital villain."

The old man began to weep. Kit turned him away from the coffin and the Sergeant leapt down to lift the Chamberlain to the ground. Kit followed.

"When you are calmer, sir, I'll have you sign the release. But I won't press you now."

The Sergeant returned Sir Geoffrey to his apartment. Kit and Ralph watched as the ill-matched pair crossed the bailey.

"You were right about the dog, Kit. That made the case."

"A wonderful scene at the coffin! We must have Ned as the Commissioner."

"But when will we take our final bow on this drama?"

"When we're comfortably sated with Dame Dorrie's mutton pies and wallowing in good Cheapside ale. Safe home in London."

"I'm not so sure we'll be safe in the city. If we were so lucky as to find ourselves there. I'd rather be in Northumberland."

"Why Northumberland?"

"They speak a different tongue and the law walks in dread. A fearsome people."

"A tempting offer, Ralph. But to business. We must have the pigeons away to London with the sad news of Mary Stuart's death. Pigeons too aboard Ganda's craft. It would be cheering to know they had arrived safely at the Wash. Place the bombs with the gunners and spend our day rehearsing the next Act."

"And what is the next Act, oh, scribbler supreme?"

"The Defence of Fotheringhay Castle! Devised by Master Christopher Marlowe. A Noble Conflict Enacted by a Noble Company led by Sir Ralph Boxborough."

"You do me too much honour, sir. Let's hope I survive."

*

Sergeant Stanley Robertson was seated comfortably on the toilet reviewing the racing page, biro in hand when he was interrupted. A familiar voice called, "Stan?"

"What now, Margie?"

"There's a girl at the desk wanting to see you."

Stan groaned, recognising his visitor.

"Five feet two. Chocolate complexion. Eyes of blue-green. Sort of blonde brown hair? Wistful smile? Persistent?"

"That's the one. Wendy Darling."

"Tell her to go away."

"She won't. She's sitting there so sad, Stan."

"Why did you let her sit down?"

The unseen constable made no reply.

"Have you no mercy? I've not been to bed. I've been clobbered in the face with a bottle, but I brought in Willie Bishop. The county's been after him for months. The woman wasn't hurt, but terrified for her life. He's a vicious bastard! Isn't that enough for today from little Stanley?"

The constable coughed politely.

"Couldn't I have ten minutes to pick the nag I'm gona lose me dosh on?"

"She says she's very sorry, but she needs to confess and she won't talk to nobody else. She says she has a poison pill in her mouth and she'll bite on it if you won't.."

"Alright, alright! But forget the poison pill. There's no poison pill."

"Yeah, but if she had?"

"She's an actress! Actually very good. A born liar. More dangerous than a dozen Willie Bishops."

224

Sergeant Robertson emerged from sanctuary to wash his hands and scowl at himself in the mirror, surveying his battered face.

"That's the wrong face for a copper, Geordie. Should be brutal, but it's not. Lead on McDuff!"

Tammie leapt up from the chair when Sergeant Robertson entered the interview room.

"Oh, am I glad you see you! I couldn't sleep! I know you'll understand. Oh my! You've been in a fight! Did you beat him up?"

"I restrained him."

She sank back in the chair and the woman police constable released her shoulder and stood back.

"Don't go too far. This one's a wild beast."

The constable nodded, but doubtfully.

"Girl, you have disturbed me on a very important case. If you are wasting my time, I'll drive you to Margate and you can walk back. Understand?"

A subdued Wendy nodded.

"State your name and your age."

"Tameeyah Wells and I'm sixteen."

The sergeant was disappointed.

"Sure about the sixteen?"

"Seventeen next month. You can come to my party if you like."

"God forbid! Tell me what you've done. The truth, mind!"

Wendy looked around at the policewoman.

"Margaret wants to hear as well, don't you?"

"Can hardly wait."

"Well, I was very upset and I went to Mister Bryce's office and I killed him. With this knife."

Wendy brought out the Stanley knife and laid it on the table.

"Then I was sorry for what I done. So, I came this morning to tell you. I'm really sorry."

The sergeant picked up and studied the knife.

"It's difficult to kill anyone with this knife. You have to know where to cut. The blade's only an inch long."

"I cut him again and again and again."

The sergeant exchanged glances with the constable who stepped forward to inform Wendy that she was under arrest on suspicion of murder and recited her rights. Wendy was excited to be handcuffed.

"This is real, isn't it? You're not just joshing me?"

She was reassured of reality.

"There was that Scottish detective on telly used to say murrrder with a mouthful of rs. Really chilled the blood! Could you say it like that for me?"

Wendy glowed with excitement. Robertson shared bewilderment with the policewoman.

"It's the first time ever I've been arrested for murrrder."

A puzzled Sergeant Robertson asked why she was so delighted.

"Experience is the making of an actor. If I go to an audition and they ask me, has you ever been arrested, I can say, yes, for murrrder. And I was handcuffed. I'll get the parrrt."

The woman constable raised her eyes to the ceiling in amazement.

"Well, I'm glad you're pleased. I thought I was the only person round here who was certifiably insane."

*

When the elevator spoke to Sergeant Robertson he was startled. He had chosen the elevator rather than the stairs when he read the board of tenants. George Bryce & his numerous qualifications inhabited the fifth floor.

"Who are you, please?" asked the recorded voice.

Wendy responded more quickly than the sergeant.

"Wendy Darling and friend. I've been in handcuffs but not now."

"Detective Sergeant Robertson."

"Have you an appointment?"

"No."

"Wait a moment, please."

"What's the point if we can walk up the stairs?"

"There are cameras on the stairs."

226

Without warning the doors closed and the elevator began to rise.

"I am definitely obsolete," said the guardian of the law.

"They have lifts in shops. You musta been in a lift before."

"Don't patronise me."

The elevator stopped and the doors opened. There was only one door on the pleasantly decorated landing.

"A lot of money must travel in that lift."

"Not going down," suggested Wendy shrewdly.

Wendy opened the door into the large reception area. Mrs. Fleurpart was already on her feet, coming forward to crush Wendy in her feverish embrace.

"Oh, Wendy! I haven't slept a wink. I've been so worried for you."

"I'm alright, Missis Fleurpart, really I am. This is Sergeant Robertson.."

"Good morning, madam, I need.."

A glowing Wendy interrupted to say, "I've been arrested. For murrrder. I even had handcuffs, but they took them away. It's the first time I've ever been arrested. It was wonderful."

An astonished Mrs. Fleurpart looked to the sergeant.

"I don't believe it! Not for a moment. Who is she supposed to have murdered?"

"Your employer. Doctor Bryce."

Mrs. Fleurpart laughed and shook a reproving finger at Wendy.

"Oh, Wendy, how could you tell such a story!"

"But I did. In his office. With my knife."

Sergeant Robertson asked, "Could we speak with the doctor, please?"

"The doctor hasn't been in attendance this morning. But that's not unusual. If needed he often goes directly to the patient."

"Could we see his office, please?"

"Of course."

The receptionist led the way into the inner sanctum. Wendy was surprised. The room was immaculate. There was no deceased psychologist sprawled at the foot of the desk. The

227

sergeant went into the bathroom and returned to look stony-faced upon Wendy.

"But it's true! He was lying there. His face was all blood."

"You're not troubled by his absence?"

"No, sergeant. He goes where he's needed. He is a remarkable man."

An irritated Sergeant Robertson offered Mrs. Fleurpart a business card.

"If you would ask him to ring me, please?"

"I can't dictate to him, but I will certainly ask him to ring you."

As the elevator descended, the sergeant said, "I hope you've nothing arranged for today."

"No. Why?"

"I'm driving you to Margate. You can walk back."

"Oh, no, please don't! That's such a long way."

"Fair enough! When we get out onto the street, run away. I won't run after you."

"Oh, thank you!"

"Don't murder anyone else today."

Wendy laughed happily. The sergeant shook his had sadly.

"Seriously, I must hand you over to a responsible person."

"Why?"

"You're a juvenile. I don't suppose your mother's in Canterbury?"

"Carole's my best friend. She's like a mother to me."

"Have you got her number?"

*

"I have scraped this vellum until my fingers bleed. But you can still see it's a supply order from Nottingsley. Dear Zeus! He must bathe in wine."

"Which reminds me, Ralph. They can stop shitting in the bath tub. With the kine and goat dung we have more than enough. And set a guard on the ballista. Warn the kitchen and laundry women. Their children think it a plaything to climb on. One of the brats goes whizzing over the wall you're explaining to his mother."

"You never listen to a word I say, do you, Kit? Yet you belabour me with orders."

"I heard you. You were complaining about scraping a piece of vellum. Let me see it."

Ralph passed the well-scraped vellum and stretched his aching shoulders. They were sitting at a table in their private chamber. Kit was preparing the message for Walsingham & Cecil, the Queen's spymaster and advisor reporting Mary Stuart's death.

"Well scraped! You forget we need only a petty piece to attach to a pigeon's leg. Too weighty and the poor beast will fly in circles until exhausted. Let me read you what I have written. *Scots Queen dispatched. Coffin prepared for London. Marlowe Commissioner.*"

He paused and looked to his longsuffering friend.

"Or should I sign it Sir Geoffrey Hamilton? What think you?"

"What they need to know is that Mary Stuart is dead. Dispatched is as near as dammit to the truth. I don't think Elizabeth will want her rival's mortal remains in London. Would you in her place? Signed by Hamilton is as good as saying that he has supervised the execution."

"So be it. *Scots Queen dispatched. Sir Geoffrey Hamilton.* Anything else to report?"

"The garrison has taken to the sport of archery. They would play all day if the Sergeant and his corporals allowed them. Some are excellent marksmen. They've even started a competition among themselves. English versus the Flemings."

"Splendid! Then we'll offer a prize and award a rank."

"And give away even more of the Queen's money?"

"Certainly! Money is for spending."

"I pray she never learns you said that."

"Anything else I should know?"

"A Papist priest and escort visited the village last evening. As we've sealed off the village they learnt nothing. But he threatened the village with eternal damnation."

"Did he see the barricades on the bridge?"

"He took particular note. How will we know when to set it afire?"

229

"We don't fire the bridge. We stand to arms when they start the tedious task of taking down the barricade. We need warning not angry villagers marching with them because we burnt their bridge."

*

Wendy had almost completed the jigsaw of the Teddy Bears Picnic when Detective Sergeant Robertson opened the door to say, "She's all yours. Have a chat. Then I'll sign you out."

At Wendy's gesture of protest he added, "We are not serving, lunch."

Then as an afterthought added, "You might like to know Mister Bryce has vanished. Before a now distraught patient in her own home. Says he just vanished in front of her. How reliable
she is I don't know. Just don't vanish. I need a signature."

When the door closed Carole said, "What did you do to Bryce?"

"I killed him, but they say I didn't. They're not charging me with murder."

Carole could see the girl was disappointed.

"I can't believe I was ever so young as you."

"I don't know what you mean."

"You left him lying on the floor, but when you and the sergeant returned, he wasn't there."

"Somebody stole his body."

"Well, I'm just glad you didn't kill him."

"He deserved it."

Carole kept patience.

"You care for Anna, don't you?"

"I love her. Mister Bryce was.."

Carole interrupted sharply.

"Anna is our concern. Anna is Anna Cato, an actor and our friend. By some twist of Time, in the sixteenth century she is the barmaid Annie at the Archangel Tavern. Anna in what I believe is her real life is Kit Marlowe's adopted daughter, Hannah Cato."

"Golly!"

"So you understand?"

"I think I do. Anna is Annie and Hannah. And Hannah is Anna. And.."

"Near enough. What happens to Anna and Hannah if Annie dies?"

The girl took time to think before answering.

"We have to make sure nothing happens to Annie."

"Gold star!"

Carole looked upon the honest face and wanted to hug her, but desisted.

"Then that's what we will do!"

"Can I play the matinee first?"

TWENTY-SIX

George Bryce, gentleman & psychologist, landed outside the old city wall in the most odoriferous swamp of refuse known to sixteenth century mankind. He had merely asked where he might find a cab to be assaulted by the savages who had swiftly surrounded him. He had parted with his spectacles, wallet, cigar case, lighter, mobile phone and his shoes with the minimum of protest, but had struggled when the creatures began to free him from his bespoke suit, tie, shirt, vest, underwear and socks. He made a run for it, falling into slimy pools, disturbing crows and harassed by hungry dogs. Having stripped him of everything the undeserving poor gave the weird creature a good kicking before losing interest in George Bryce. They were not cannibals, but his porkly person provided much amusement.

*

"How much longer, Noah?"

The cold wind swept the river and Annie shivered despite Noah's cloak wrapped about her. They were sitting at Broadnail landing waiting for the promised waterman to take them out of London. The city had not provided the refuge they sought, but buzzed with rumours of invasion and a Papist rebellion. Those that Noah had assumed would offer shelter were reluctant to help. The Inquisitor that Noah had mutilated was apparently an important personage.

"Patience, lass! He'll come to us."

"We've been waiting since dawn."

"He has work to do. He'll come when he can."

Anna knew the waterman wasn't coming. That he had been warned or bought off. Yet she didn't want to tell Annie. Her spirits were at their lowest after the previous night in a dismal cellar and no more of a breakfast than stale crusts and sour milk. Last night was the lowest of a descending order of refuges. Anna knew because Noah had cut off the Jesuit's nose they were being hunted and when caught Noah & Annie would be tortured and murdered.

When St. Anne's clock began to toll the noon bell a boat with a hooped canvas cover began to approach the landing. The waterman in the stern sculled vigorously.

"Thank God!" cried Noah, "He's here!"

He fastened his cloak about Annie's shoulders as she stood up unsteadily.

"I had given up hope."

Noah didn't answer, but knelt to seize the prow of the boat to bring it to the landing. The waterman used his oar to bring the stern to shore.

Noah called, "Quickly aboard, Annie!" as she hesitated to jump.

He moved to help her when two bully boys burst out from under the canvas surprising him. As he fell backwards the bully was upon him.

"Run, Annie! Run for thee life!"

Fuelled by terror, Anna ran up the landing, planks echoing beneath her feet. Annie screamed as the second bully tackled her and was carried back to where Noah was pinned to the ground with a blade at his throat.

"So, ye has me! Let the lass go! She's no harm to nobody. Let her go!"

A man stepped out from under the canvas. Noah groaned and Annie whimpered. Anna struggled for calm, clinging to the thought; *Can I die here before I am born?*

"So you recognise me?"

Noah and Annie were mute.

"Then you remember what you have done to me."

He pulled away the mask. Anna saw eyes that blazed with anger.

The face shorn of the nose was alien; the visage of a pig with bare nostrils dribbling snot & blood.

"I cannot preach from a pulpit without a mask. How can I officiate at a wedding or a funeral? Do you see what you have done to me?"

233

Anna never understood why she spoke; unless it was the certainty of agony & death to come.

"Exposed your true nature. You're not a priest, but a pig!"

The world stood still. Anna felt her captor shift his stance behind her. She stifled Annie's whimper. The Jesuit raised a hand and the bully relaxed.

"You will pay for those words. Your last hours will be a passage of pain lasting as long as I can contrive before I send you to Hell and the Devil."

The Inquisitor replaced his mask.

"That does not hide what you are," countered Anna.

"Let us embark."

Noah picked up Annie when a bully boy reached to drag her into the boat. He jumped in and the fragile craft rocked.

"Steady!" called the waterman.

Noah began to step from side to side and the boat picked up his rhythm.

"Steady on!"

The first bully to jump onboard struck at Noah's shoulders with his club. Annie & Noah sat down together. The bully laughed at their discomfort. The other man assisted the Inquisitor to step down into the boat.

The boat was midstream when a black creature with a tortured face appeared before the Inquisitor. Noah & Annie jumped up.

Noah cried, "God save us all! It's the Devil hisself!"

In the confine of the hood panic & confusion reigned. The bully boys struggled to escape the Devil, crying out in fear.

The boat turned turtle. The shock was immediate. Anna was sure she was to die under the flooded craft gasping for air and swallowing green water. Anna was kicked by the flailing legs of the Inquisitor and heard the bullies screaming. They couldn't swim. Her arm was seized roughly and Noah pulled her out from under the capsized boat, gasping for breath. Then she lost consciousness.

When Anna came to herself she was floating downriver clinging to the turtle with Noah and George Bryce. There was no sign of the bully boys or the Inquisitor. But George Bryce?

He was naked, dirty, disoriented and constantly whimpering. He didn't recognise Anna.

*

Standing on the smaller table carried out from the barrack room, Kit addressed the assembled population of Fotheringhay Castle against the protesting voice of kine, goats & geese penned against the gates who had been deprived of water for two days. Kit had been forced to water the horses once because the Papists had failed to attack.

Using the brass trumpet created by the blacksmith, Kit addressed his audience, two & four-legged alike.

"Last evening, there were Papist scouts at the bridge again. They have called a total curfew on the village with burning of any who disobey."

"Why burning?" interrupted Ralph.

"To save their souls.

The brass trumpet seared the ears of the assembly.

"Three brave villagers defied that curfew, but didn't return to be toasted."

The laughter encouraged kine, goats and geese to raise a tumultuous racket.

"So we know tomorrow they will attempt to take the castle."

"We too have scouts who have paid visits to the camp at Bairlie Edge. There are perhaps a hundred & score Papists. Men, women and children. Very few firearms. Abundent old swords, pitchforks and sickles. Enough sharp knives even among the children. They want the Scotch Queen's coffin as the figurehead of their rebellion against our Queen Elizabeth. They want the Armoury. We will refuse them both."

He looked out on their attentive faces, soldier, farrier, blacksmith, gunner, horse master, young men, old men, old women and mothers, children and babes in arms. Bawling kine & bleating goats. Hannibal and the geese. The garrison of Fotheringhay Castle.

"But it will be an odd battle. They will kill us if they can. We will try not to kill them. Everything you've been working at these past days will make sense if you stand fast. Why not kill them? Because they are misled. They follow the wrong banner. They believe they can take their women and children into battle and God will protect them. Wrong. Meanwhile the Papist priests, the Jesuits, the Inquisitors, the Pope himself are safely out of harm's way."

He looked out on the solemn faces.

"If you wish to leave. To join the Papists. Because you wish to take no part. The postern will be opened for you."

Kit was silent and held his breath. No one moved.

"Thank you for your loyalty. The Spanish Armada under a seasick Duke Medina Sidonia is reported in the Channel with Frankie Drake and Lord Howard chasing them. The Duke of Parma and fifteen thousand Spanish troops are waiting to cross the Channel. Who will remember the battle of Fotheringhay Castle where no one died?"

Someone laughed and then the laughter grew until the defenders of Fotheringhay laughed loud enough for their enemies to hear them.

That evening at the castle there was a great feast with four bullocks roasted and everyone from scullery boy to the Commissioner retiring to bed with a full stomach. Surprisingly, there was no drunkenness. Wine & beer were restricted, as all would need a clear head in the dawn to follow.

Ralph quizzed his leader.

"I have some slight experience of battle. Surely, Kit, celebrations of victory take place after victory is achieved? Not before."

"In all my reading of the matter you are correct. Have you never considered how unfair this is on the fallen? Do they not deserve to die with a full stomach and an aching head?"

Sir Ralph shook his head in amazement.

"I am heartedly relieved, Kit, that you are a scribbler rather than a general."

*

It seemed simpler to Carole that she should stay to watch the matinee. The foyer was buzzing with excitement; a noisier elation than the theatregoers of the evening performance. The tide that swirled about her was composed principally of children and parents. Wendy was pleased she had decided to stay.

"Clap hard for me," she declared, "When we're taking our bows."

"I shall clap until it hurts."

Once again Carole tapped on BOOKINGS and RETURNS. Before she had decided the old lady had died or forgotten to turn up to work, the trap opened.

Gillian said, "How can I help?"

"Oh, hi! I wondered if there was a vacant seat anywhere?"

"Give me a minute!"

Gillian vanished and Carole stood wondering whether she should introduce herself. Gillian returned to say, "Front circle? A little more expensive. Mums with three children would rather not."

"Front circle will be fine."

While Carole sought to pay, Gillian said, "I think I know you? You're restoring some Manor House?"

"Someone's been talking. Anna is my friend.."

"Oh, dear! A difficult decision."

"No, no! I'm not involved. I'm here today at the 'invitation' of Wendy. I'm posing as her Auntie Carole. I'm to clap my very best."

Gillian laughed.

"That's Wendy! After the show we offer coffee in the green room to special visitors. I'd like to invite you to join us."

"How kind! I'll accept if you let Wendy join us. As her Auntie Carole."

"I can't keep her out. I'll send Wendy to bring you backstage. I'd like to hear more of the restoration of the Manor."

*

At eight o'clock the following morning a group of three adults, an old man, two young women, a boy & girl child leading a dog approached the Great Gate of Fotheringhay Castle to be addressed by the Corporal of the Guard.

237

"What is your business here?"

When the dog had stopped barking the old man replied to the Corporal who was chewing on his breakfast.

"We are here to request you to surrender the castle to the venerable Cardinal Henry Garnet, acting with the righteous authority of his Holiness Pope Sixtus the Fifth. No one will be hurt or admonished."

"I didn't catch it all. Say it again."

The old man struggled through the request to surrender once more and the Corporal swallowed a mouthful of breakfast.

"What Pope was that you said? Was it Fiftus the Sixth? Or Sixtus the Fifth?"

The old man had a coughing fit and the exasperated children shouted, "Sixtus the Fifth!"

"I will report what you said to me Sergeant."

The Corporal vanished never to be seen again.

"Cleverly done!"

"How so?"

"The first rule of drama. Appeal to the right audience. The old man to grandparents. The young women to young men. The children to parents. The dog? Everyone of kindly nature. The audience says, They're just like us! Open the gates and welcome them in."

Ralph admitted, "I did think they were reasonable. The old man didn't threaten us. No one was hurt or admonished. He has a nasty cough."

"And the fox may bark as loudly as the house dog. Regardez!"

After a considerable period of time two children, boy & girl appeared above the gate and threw down meaty bones to the dog who could not be restrained from seizing the nearest morsel.

"What's your name?" the girl cried from above.

"Judith."

"I'm Rebecca. You should've been here last night."

"Why? What happened?"

"We had a party. The biggest party in all my life. Loads to eat. We had four bullocks on the spit. If you want to chew on one of them bones. They are fresh from last night. Very tasty."

Rebecca produced a meaty bone and began to chew. Judith hesitated and then followed her example.

The Sergeant-at-Arms appeared, spick & span, black beard glistening in the sunlight.

"Wha'd'y'want?"

The old man repeated his request for surrender and the two young women opened their banner to display the words I AM THE WAY, THE TRUTH AND THE LIFE.

The Sergeant studied the banner.

"You've spelt TRUTH wrong. You've missed out the E."

The Sergeant was prevaricating, but the party examined the banner. The two young women started to quarrel as to who was to blame.

The Sergeant said, "Don't go away. I must speak to me officer."

He vanished never to be seen again.

On the walls women began to attach rolled banners that might be displayed by pulling the laces.

No officer appeared to talk to the Papist party. After an hour or so they walked away. The two young women were still arguing who was to blame for the mispelt banner. Judith and the little boy carried as many meaty bones as they could manage. The dog had his stomach and jaws full. The old man was very tired. Kit & Ralph were satisfied with this first encounter. The battle royal began at noon. The garrison went to arms. Everyone became a soldier.

TWENTY-SEVEN

The green room was larger than Carole expected; a pleasant sitting room. Cast members were talking to family and fans. Wendy was buzzing with excitement. Carole and Gillian let her talk herself out and steal their biscuits. When she was called away by an eager fan for photographs with the Darling boys, Michael & John, Gillian smiled to say, "She's very young, but determined to learn. I'd wager on her making a name."

"I understand the show closes soon?"

"Another couple of weeks. Which I must confess is why I really did want to talk to you."

"Speak the speech I pray you. Sorry. Living with Anna."

"The restoration of Boxborough Manor. I wonder if an Elizabethan Masque might find a place? Excerpts from the plays? We are Marlowe's home town. If I'm being too pushy.."

"Not at all. I'll talk to my father. We're putting everything into this venture. It's not just going to be a posh hotel."

Gillian's smiling face vanished even as she spoke. Carole found herself standing in a crowd watching men dissembling a barricade on a bridge. She looked across the broad meadow as cannon thundered from the castle walls beyond. There was noise & commotion all about her. Someone put a hand to her shoulder. The image vanished. The green room returned.

Wendy was standing beside her with a hand on Carole's shoulder. She was smiling, saying to Gillian, "Thank you, boss! I owe you. Fiona won't let you down. She's a real Wendy."

To Carole she said, "We can do what we were hoping to do. You know. For Anna."

*

The rebels began to take apart the carefully complicated barricades on the bridge. To encourage progress Kit ordered the four heavy cannon to fire. The noise of the cannons was excessively loud and the collected rubbish of the Castle darkened the sky. The rebels fled from the bridge. The charge of kitchen rubbish, odd detritus, broken china & discarded metal almost reached the bridge.

Cautiously, the bravest of the rebels, men & children,, returned to their task. The cannons boomed again expelling nothing more dangerous than smoke, but the workers fled to safety. The soldiers on the walls roared with delight. The gunners loaded broken bricks and looked to Kit who shook his head. The gunners were disappointed.

"When we fire again, we will break heads. If matters turn against us, we may be forced to fire again. But only if.."

He turned to call down to the crew about the ballista.

"Can you better that? Send them running as from a nest of wasps?"

Everyone on the bailey assured him they would.

"I see the strategy, Kit. If they will not be otherwise persuaded, we will throw stones at them."

"I would wish they would leave the children out of this. It's hard to believe that every decent Catholic mother wishes her son to be a martyr for the obnoxious Henry Garnet."

There was cheering from across the pasture.

"They've cleared the bridge. Now they will come. The Prologue is out of the way. Act One of our drama begins," Kit decided and called out through his brass trumpet, "Be all a scourge and terror to the world, or else you are not sons of Tamburlaine."

The castle shook with the roar of defiance of its defenders as the rebels poured out onto the pasture and began to march towards the castle.

"When they break. For by God's balls, we shall break them! There is one man only who deserves to die. The Jesuit, Cardinal Henry Garnet. Red-bearded in priestly black. Musket, arrow, whatever! If there is a clear shot the marksman takes ten gold coins. But no one other may be hurt."

The crowd flourishing few weapons came to a stop facing the castle. The banners with threats and promises were planted broadwise to be read from the walls, bed sheets between stout poles. The threats were terrifying. The promises of salvation false. Behind all lurked the shadow of the Inquisition.

"Now!" called Kit.

Stout halberdiers began to raise the drawbridge. It rose slowly, reluctantly over the missing moat.

"Drop!"

The old drawbridge faltered and fell in a host of dust & damaged struts. The followers of a distant Pope roared with laughter. The red-bearded priest stepped before the banners to cry, "Is that all you can do? A rotten bridge for a rotten castle! Open the gates and let the army of our Lord Jesus Christ enter this sad Jerusalem!"

The rebels cheered and surged only to stop when the fire arrows struck the bed sheets and the banners began to burn briskly. Men, women and children struggled to halt the flames, pulling down and trampling on their own banners. There were cries of protest & disappointment ending in a sullen silence.

At that moment the laces were cut and the banners unfolded on the walls of Fotheringhay. Suffice to say they displayed every heretical word, every blasphemy, every slur on the Pope's character & physique true or false. The effect was stunning.

"Begin!" cried Kit.

The fuses were lit and the shit bombs began to explode among the Papist crowd, drenching the Chosen People in a mixture of human & animal shit.

Kit said, "You cannot beat a good German fuse, Ralph,. Worth every penny! Blitzschnell!"

Ralph agreed and laughed when the ballista began to heave further human & animal waste on the bewildered enemy. The company outside the gates was beginning to break up, mothers pulling away their children, men turning away, losing faith in the leaders.

"And now," declared the Queen's Commissioner, "The Cavalry!"

The Sergeant-at-Arms swung the axe that opened the gates. The thirst-maddened herd of kine, goats and geese on the wing stampeded for the river through the ranks of the rebellion. Behind followed the rank of halberdiers offering the steel that

242

thrusts and strikes, spear & axe; a fearsome weapon beyond the reach of swords. There was no opposition.

When silence fell there was no attacking force, but such few wretches who had borne the brunt of the stampede and struggled with broken limbs to escape the field of battle. Kit and Ralph accompanied by the astonished garrison came out from the walls to view the empty pasture.

"Savour the moment! This is the field of battle where no one died and few bones were broken. Who can claim to be a hero at the battle of Fotheringhay! What statue should we erect? A goat? A bullock? I favour Hannibal who led the charge!"

The soldiers began to laugh and the laughter to spread throughout the castle.

"The vile papist Garnet's rebellion is broken. He flees from laughter, not the cannon. Tomorrow the tragic Queen, Mary Stuart will begin her honoured Progress to London. It will be our privilege to escort her."

The garrison cheered and the audience of the Globe echoed their applause. Such was the noise that the walls of the wooden castle on stage wobbled. The acclaimed scribbler accepted the plaudits of the audience from the stage, arm in arm with Sir Ralph Boxborough played by Ned Alleyn. In such fashion did his new tragi-comedy play out in the scribbler's head.

*

Ensconced in the cushions of the couch Wendy called, "This is a lovely flat. I'll have a flat like this one day."

Carole returned from the kitchen with two mugs of coffee and gave one to the girl.

"You did say three spoons of sugar?"

"You get energy from sugar."

"You get fat from sugar."

Carole sat down cautiously so as not to jar any elbows and sipped her coffee.

"Is that true?"

"If you eat too much sugar. And it rots your teeth."

There was silence as Wendy checked her teeth.

"What's too much?"

"Three spoonfuls in a cup of coffee."

"It's still a lovely flat anyway."

"Thank you."

"Do you have any biscuits?"

Carole rose as cautiously as she had sat down to find the biscuit tin.

"Same rules apply."

"I haven't eaten one yet."

"Nibble to your heart's content. You'll need all your energy if you're to send me to help Anna."

"What do I do?"

"Nothing. We were in the foyer. You were changing photographs. I vanished."

"I wish I'd gone with you."

"Doesn't work like that. Apparently. If poor Mister Hazlitt is right. The transmitter doesn't time travel."

"So I just sit here."

"In the green room I vanished. Probably just for seconds. Nobody noticed, but you were in the room. And I returned. If I vanish, please, lock the door when you leave."

"Shouldn't I wait for you to come back."

They sat for half an hour and nothing happened. The telephone rang and rang. Carole finally picked up the receiver.

"Wardley Chinese Laundry."

"Oops! Sorry! Wrong number."

Carole recognised the voice.

"Gillian?"

"Yes, it's me."

"I'm sorry. Just a silly.."

Carole & Wendy vanished because Wendy wasn't the transmitter.

*

Kit declared to Ralph, "What a play this will make! I have found the title. It came to me as I emptied my bowel into her Majesty's gardez l'eau at dawn this morning. Do you know she has a sponge on a silver stick to wipe her arse?"

244

Sir Ralph Boxborough waited for an answer until he could wait no longer.

"Is this title a secret, Kit?"

"Indeed it is. The title of this grand drama is THE GREAT SECRET."

"And this is the Grand Secret? Mary Stuart has a sponge on a silver stick to wipe her arse?"

"Our performance is not yet played out. We have yet to persuade her gracious Majesty, Elizabeth, to believe her dear sister is deceased. Who knows what is to come?"

"How will we explain why her money has dwindled so rapidly?"

"Fotheringhay Castle was overrun with mice. How does that appeal?"

When the gallant birds and beasts had been gathered from the river & pasture, the garrison of Fotheringhay Castle enjoyed food & drink enough and retired to bed contented. In the early light of morning Kit & Ralph were supervising the harnessing of the best horses to the funeral wagon and the Halberdiers were falling in for the long march to deliver the coffin to her grieving sister Elizabeth in London when the cry arose of pigeons in flight.

The garrison watched three pigeons circling the castle and descending to land on the entry of the cote. Three boys came running in full excitement to offer the pigeons to Kit and Ralph who demurred to his friend. Kit soothed the bird and cut free the vellum scrap attached to its leg. He released the bird and unrolled the message.

"Do you know why the pigeon flies so speedily to its destination, Ralph?"

"I cannot guess."

"He flies to his true love. As with all mortal beings love is the answer. He flies to ride his hen. As men do to their mistress."

"Please read the message, Kit!"

"Your success will be rewarded Return to London all speed Cecil."

The growing crowd applauded. Kit accepted the second bird and relieved the bird of its charge.

"Wash in sight. The Queen in good spirits Saint des Vosges."

The crowd cheered surprising Kit.

"She has more support that I believed."

"Which is why our gracious queen wished her dead."

Accepting the third bird, Kit commented, "Still, she is off our hands and I feel much relief."

He opened the third message and cried. "Great steaming puddens! Someone has been speaking with Elizabeth."

He read the instruction aloud.

"Coffin to Peterborough Cathedral. Immediate. Walsingham."

"What does that mean?"

"Walsingham has overruled Cecil. And explained to Elizabeth the danger of Mary Stuart's coffin in London."

"And why are you delighted?"

An astonished Kit Marlowe stared at his friend.

"No one is going to travel to Peterborough to check the coffin before burial. And it's many fewer miles for us to march. Sometimes I question your mental agility, Sir Ralph."

*

Wendy cried out. Carole opened her eyes. They were standing in the empty marketplace in Gilsford.

The girl asked, "Where are we?"

"This is wrong. This cannot be right. We're here because I've been in Gilsford with Anna. But it's wrong."

Carole called to a passing woman. "No market today?"

"Wednesday."

She stopped as if expecting another question. Carole obliged. "What day would I find the busker here?"

"Mebbes Thursday. But definite Saturday."

"Thank you."

Carole went to sit on a bench and Wendy followed her.

"I don't get it."

"This is where they were together. And happy."

"What do we do now?"

"We wait."

246

TWENTY-EIGHT

The turtle snagged on a submerged broken quay and came to rest within five yards of a muddy strand. Abandoned warehouses sagged beyond. Noah surveyed the unwelcoming shore. Nothing disturbed the silence.

"Seems, lass, we's arrived."

"Where's that?"

"Nowhere. But we's alive."

"I has me feet on rocks and such."

"Then no need for me t'carry ye ashore like a bride o'er the threshold."

Annie laughed, but Anna caught the wistful echo. She too took stock of their situation; the distressed shore, no sight nor sound of human activity, standing shoulder-deep in cold Thames water that surged to invade the mouth. She took in sight a bewildered Bryce holding to the wreckage and staring about him in bewilderment. Annie had edged along the turtle as far from Bryce as possible. It was the presence of an undaunted Noah that kept Anna's spirits from drowning.

"I know ye're enjoying bathing yoursel, Annie, but it might be safer to be out. Afore the crabs start on your toes."

Annie gave a startled shriek and released the wreckage to seek shelter within Noah's sheltering arm. They started to trudge carefully towards the shore. Bryce gave a pitiful cry and Noah stopped.

"Shallis cut its throat and be done with the imp?"

He released Annie, but Anna cried, "He's a poor creature. Not likely an angel turned out of Heaven. Most probable a demon that wasn't devilish enough. But his arrival was like a miracle. We's be floating with us throats cut."

Anna felt quite pleased with her defence of a man she detested. But to watch him being murdered was a throat slit too far. Annie added her twopennorth.

"Poor thing don't mean no harm."

247

Anna was amazed at how both Noah & Annie accepted the notion that they had a possible demon in tow. *When I write my book on Elizabethan beliefs & customs...*

Noah gestured and called, "Come with us if ye must."

Bryce gave a pathetic cry and struggled against the river to join Noah & Annie. Bryce began to explain himself, but having lost his upper denture his speech was indistinct and barely comprehensible to Anna.

"I am George Bryce, a renowned, respected psychologist and able to pay any ransom. I know I was attacked in my office by the girl Wendy Darling and since then everything has been distinctly odd. I believe I was drugged. I will pay you any amount. Name your price and let me go home."

"Can ye make anything of that, lass?"

Anna adlibbed freely.

"He's a very rich man. He has won awards in farting competitions. He were out looking for adventure. Ye can imagine what like, the dirty bugger, when this girl attacked him and serves him right."

Noah turned to give Bryce a most threatening glance and Bryce began to cry, whimpering how sorry he was. In her battered inner mind, Anna wondered: *Wendy? Why on earth would she attack Bryce? And then he goes time wandering?*

Annie wondered why she could hear soothing music, but she was too happy to question, wading through muddy water and thick mud with Noah's arm about her shoulder.

*

Carole grabbed Wendy's hand and pulled her from the path of the lorry that hurtled past them. It was dusk and they were standing on the scrubby verge of an unknown road. Behind and before them were fields. They could hear the evening gossiping of sheep.

"I don't like this," said Wendy.

"You wanted to go Time wandering."

Looking at the girl, she added, "I'm sorry. That was a silly thing to say. We're worried about Anna and we're trying to find her. You're being very brave. I know Anna was in the market. So, she must've been here."

"But there's nothing here."

A car passed them and as they watched some two hundred yards farther on it turned off and stopped; rear lights still glowing.

"That's it! Come on!"

The illuminated burger van stood in the layby. A man was carrying a package & plastic coffee cups to the car. He passed his burden in through the passenger window and entered by the driver's door.

"They were here," Carole affirmed, "That's why we're here."

Wendy suggested, "Smells great."

"I'm sure they thought the same."

There were a man and a woman working the van.

"Could we not have a burger?"

"I'm not sure you're taking this seriously."

"Burgers are serious too."

"I'm not sure we're meant to have them. But you're right. It smells delicious."

They approached the burger van. They were almost at the counter when Time's jigsaw fell apart.

*

It was what Sir Ralph Boxborough termed the finest or worst moment of Kit's tenure as Queen's Commissioner. The Bishop had resisted the entry to Peterborough Cathedral of the coffin of Mary Stuart, Queen of the Scots. Kit took the miserable little man and threw him to the limestone of his nave and placed a boot on his fat neck.

"I am the Queen's Commissioner and you may not be aware that the Head of the Church of England is our sovereign lady, Queen Elizabeth. In opposing her Majesty you are guilty of treason and thereby stripped of your office."

To make his meaning to the rapidly arriving clergy of all degrees, Kit bent to rip the robe from the whimpering creature at his feet.

249

"Sergeant!"

"Yes, Commissioner?"

"Take this traitor out of God's house and prepare to hang him from the nearest tree."

The former bishop screamed and struggled futilely in the grasp of two muscular halberdiers, escorted by the Sergeant as escort. His screams died away as the party left the Cathedral. A dread silence fell upon the nave and the clergy.

Ralph whispered to Kit. "God's blood, Kit! Are you serious! This isn't play-acting!"

"Of course, it is! He is merely a simple player. I can have him burnt at the stake if I wish."

"But you won't, will you?"

Kit didn't respond. Ralph whispered, "I excuse myself, Commissioner, to see no harm comes to the bishop."

"Do what you will."

Kit listened to his angry footsteps retreat and commanded his petrified audience, "All but the canons lie down on the floor."

There was a moment of hesitation. Suddenly the floor of the nave was littered with black beetles. Five men were standing. Kit beckoned them forward. They approached cautious of the halberdiers. Kit held up a hand and they stopped. He walked about them and saw the oldest and the youngest were trembling.

Kit asked, "Who would like to be bishop here?"

Two men put up their hands immediately; a plump balding man who smiled at Kit and an older thin man with a scar to his face.

"Lie down," Kit said and three men lay down.

*

They were standing in darkness watching a building burn fiercely. Flames reached for the dark Heaven obliterating the stars. Carole smelt rather than saw the growing crowd about her. Wendy was at her side. No one was making any effort to tackle the blaze. As at a firework display the spectators cried out their pleasure as roof timbers fell into the furnace and a galaxy of sparks ascended.

Carole addressed the shape beside her. "Excuse me ignorance, mistress. I am a stranger hereabouts. It seems a worthy structure."

The woman looked at her oddly.

"It was a pothouse . They called it the Ark. I am not sorry to see it burn. An unholy place. Not an ark at all."

Carole nodded agreement.

"Amen to that, mistress."

She nudged Wendy into movement before the woman became too friendly. The girl was unwilling to leave the spectacle, but Carole urged her through the crowd. Beyond the crowd they stopped to watch the building fall in on itself to appreciative applause from the crowd.

"Why don't the fire brigade turn up?"

"Because it's August fifteen eighty-eight and there is no fire brigade. If any volunteer company had got here with their hand pump it would always be too late. Most of the Ark is made of wood."

"And we're here because Anna has been here."

"Anna as Annie is. Was the barmaid at the Ark."

Tameeyah was quiet too long. The applause of the crowd mounted as the brick chimneys fell into the flames.

Carole said, "I don't believe Anna was in the Ark when the fire started. If that's what's worrying you."

"It just seems to me the past is a horrible place. I wouldn't want to be stuck here working in a scummy bar. Just the idea frightens me."

"Anna and you are both brave girls. Like a cork in water she'll bob up!"

Carole put an arm about Wendy for reassurance.

"And we'll get home."

*

The muddy trio, Noah, Annie & whimpering Bryce, flopped exhausted onto the scurvy shore; feeble grass struggling to hold a place between thistles, stones and wooden flotsam. Noah aroused himself.

"Stay thee there, lass. Lets iss get me bearings,"

251

Annie protested, but was ignored. Noah poked the muddy bulk that was Bryce and threatened, "Any harm come to this lass I will cut thee into a thousand pieces."

The black imp whimpered a protest. Noah responded with a kick to the head.

"Keep thee self away from it, Annie," he ordered and made off towards the derelict warehouses.

Anna waited until Noah vanished until she walked over to Bryce and said, "I know who you are."

"I doubt you do, madam."

"You are George Bryce, a respected psychologist. Although God knows why. You are a repulsive snot of human garbage who feeds on others' distress."

"This is a nightmare. You're not real. My god, why don't I wake up?"

"Because it's not a dream. You wanted to travel in time. Well, your wish has been granted. How I know not, but Georgie boy, you're on Thameside, August, fifteen eighty-eight. Good Queen Bess is on the throne and Frankie Drake is chasing the Spanish Armada. Either Noah or the Inquisitor will cut your throat. How're you enjoying your trip?"

"You're wrong! I'm suffering a nervous breakdown. It's all in my mind."

"It's real. Perhaps you'll begin to understand the misery of patients you exploit."

"If you are a nurse. Please call the doctor who is attending me."

Wherever the Inquisitor and his bullies appeared from Anna was taken by surprise. Annie screamed and ran. The bullyboys were on to her as wolves upon a lamb and dragged her back to face the pig face.

"We meet again, witch! And here you consort with demons!"

He bent to examine Bryce who began to scream until a blow from the smaller thug silenced him. He crouched on the stones and whimpered like a beaten dog.

"As I said, you consort with creatures out of Hell. I cast aside care for your body. I am intent tto save your soul. You

252

and your familiar are condemned to die by fire that will cleanse your soul and carry your imp back to Hell."

The bullyboys released Anna at a gesture from the Inquisitor. To her horror she saw they began to build a pyre of flotsam from the shore. The Inquisitor anticipated Annie's clumsy attempt to run and struck her a savage blow to the head with his staff. Shocked by pain, Anna fell stunned and struggled to stay conscious. Annie was bleeding from nose & mouth. Anna glimpsed the muddy fat man set to work to build his own pyre.

From time to time he cried, "This is not real! I demand to see a doctor!" The bullyboys laughed and joined in chanting the words. Out of the corner of her eye Anna saw Noah emerge from a broken doorway. Anna tried to close Annie's mouth, but was too slow.

Annie cried, "Oh, Noah! I knew you'd come. They's gona burn me!"

*

Ralph's angry feet returned and demanded without pretence of a whisper, "Are these also under sentence of death?"

"Is the late bishop still breathing?"

"He is being mocked by the scum of the streets. He is very distressed. The soldiers do little to protect him."

"He denied the Queen's authority."

"And these two gentlemen?"

"One will become the next lawful bishop of Peterborough. I may execute the other. Help me choose."

"I will take no hand in the matter."

"Let us examine the fat one first. He has enjoyed a good life here. Whatever is proposed he agrees. I would not wish to be a novice in his care. I suspect he is a cruel man. I doubt his dedication."

"Dedication? You're not choosing an actor. This is not a play."

"Unless an actor is dedicated to his task the play fails. I need a man who trusts me."

"And this other gentleman?"

253

"Let me have men about me that are fat, sleek-headed men and such as sleep a-nights. Yond Cassius has a lean and hungry look,

He thinks too much; such men are dangerous."

Ralph laughed despite himself.

"You counsel against yourself? Then the die is cast."

"I'll take the thin man. His dress is simple. His face records he has seen life. I would wager he is not well-regarded here. Passed over for privileges. This is his opportunity too often denied. What is your name?"

"Canon Finan Heathwred, Commissioner."

"Would you wish to be the fat bishop of Peterborough?"

"If such a title means a dishonest bishop, I would rather be canon."

"Why not free of it all?"

"As canon I may alleviate some of the Bishop's failings."

Kit turned to the second man to say, "Lie down and pray I do not recall your face."

To his Corporal, he ordered, "Carry the coffin most reverently and lay it before the altar. This is her Majesty's last journey. Treasure the occasion."

The coffin escorted by halberdiers proceeded to the altar. Bishop Finan Heathwred followed. The sound of his voice in prayer echoed through the nave. The halberdiers knelt to one knee and bowed their heads.

"Won't this make a wonderful scene, Ralph. The Queen's last progress. Simple soldiers bowed in reverence."

Clergy in the Cathedral stood with heads bowed, regarding their shoes, praying not to be noticed.

Ralph sniped, "A traitor's last progress."

"A mere detail. D'y'know, Ralph, we need a man who can sketch. Paper and charcoal."

"Not so! We need a magician to explain where the Queen's money has gone."

*

Kit and Ralph were occupied in the Cathedral Treasury exploring the accounts; assisted by a timid clerk who protested his innocence in a mouse's squeak. He was sweating and stank.

"Do we have all the account books or are there more hidden in some privy place?"

The clerk didn't respond. Kit placed a kindly hand upon the thin shoulder. A tremor ran through the man.

"Would you give me an answer if I threatened to take an axe to your legs?"

"Oh, sir, please! I have only done as ordered by Bishop Giland. How could I refuse?"

"There is no Bishop Giland. I am the Queen's Commissioner. Do you stand against her Majesty? If so, I will take off your legs. Possibly your arms."

The clerk began to weep.

"Go! And return with the true accounts."

The clerk rose as someone knocked upon the door. Ralph opened the door to Bishop Heathwred whom he noted wore the same simple black robe. The Bishop stood aside to allow the weeping clerk to pass.

"Good morning, my Lord Bishop!"

"God be with you, Commissioner! If I am not intruding there are matters I need to discuss."

Ralph sought a chair and Heathwred sat down.

TWENTY-NINE

With a roar Noah launched himself across the strand at the thugs. The Inquisitor stepped back in alarm. Muddy Bryce began to scream hysterically. Anna bit the nearest arm as savagely as she could. The thug released her and struck her in the face as Noah collided with him. As she fell Anna saw the flash of Noah's blade as he stabbed repeatedly at the bigger man who shuddered and collapsed dying.

At the shattered warehouse door a bewildered Carole and Wendy

appeared. As Anna fell Carole cried out in despair.

"Too late! Too late!"

Wendy ran to drop to her knees by Anna.

"Don't die, Anna! Don't die! Please don't die!"

As Noah came at him the shorter thug backed away and slashed at Noah's parrying arm to cut deeply. Noah stumbled, the blood spurting from his arm, struggling to close the wound. He sat down heavily, grasping his arm. A frozen Carole came to life & ran to help, pulling his belt away to serve as a tourniquet. Her snarling face warned off the thug who decided discretion was the better part of valour.

The Inquisitor cried out in triumph.

"So shall die the witch! So do we deal with Satan's imps!"

He towered over Wendy and Anna, fumbling in his cloak to bring out a pistol. He cocked the weapon and aimed directly at Anna.

"Get thee to Hell, Spawn of Satan!"

Ignoring the pistol, Wendy rose screaming to launch herself at the Inquisitor, clawed hands seeking his eyes. The frightened man struck her with the pistol butt. Wendy clung desperately to the pistol arm.

"No, you won't, you bastard! I won't let you!"

She spat in his face and her tormentor swung her around, a dog refusing to release a stick, her legs flying off the ground. Bryce began to scream and scream.

A pistol fired and the Inquisitor cried out. He clutched his leg and released Wendy who flew feet away. Carole crouched by Noah holding her Grandfather's Webley Mark 4 Revolver. The gun with which he had demanded the surrender of a vital blockhouse and forty-seven soldiers. At that moment the pistol was empty. The German captain had meekly surrendered.

"Sorry! I didn't know it was loaded."

Carole began to laugh as Time rattled the dice again.

*

Detective Sergeant Stanley Robertson was parked where he could see who came and went from the small shop in Lombard Alley. He knew Dickie Thomas of old. He always waited until the twenty-seventh of the month, his lucky day, before dropping off his ill-gotten gains at Morris's pawnshop. Despite previous experience of being nicked.

The sergeant was enjoying a lettuce & tomato sandwich prepared by his good lady for his lunch when the call came through.

"What you doing, Stan?"

"Margie, don't you ever think to use standard procedure?"

"Well, this isn't standard."

Sergeant Robertson groaned.

"I haven't anybody else."

"I know, they're all busy. Well, I'm busy."

"No, you're not. I can hear you eating."

The sergeant surrendered.

"What d'y'want?"

"There's a lunatic in St. Oswin's graveyard. There's a funeral going on and he's scaring the pants off the vicar and the mourners. He's lying down in the grave. On the coffin."

Stan put the sandwich back in his Snoopy lunchbox.

"On my way."

"One more thing. He's bollock naked and very big."

257

"Oh, good! I enjoy wrestling with lunatics. I hope you've booked an ambulance."

"Will he need one?"

"No, I will!"

Detective Sergeant Stanley Robertson started the engine of the car.

"Your lucky day, Dickie, you thieving little bugger. But I'll get you next month."

THIRTY

"Firstly, I must say that I am unworthy of the office of bishop."
Kit interrupted to say, "We shall find out your quality by
action not words. The matter is discussed."

It seemed to Ralph the man's face flushed.

"I have to report that the arrival of the late Mary Stuart's
coffin has been well-received in the city. As I speak the nave
holds a host of citizens who have come to pay their respects and
the line flows past the coffin. I also sense from reports that the
citizens are hoping for…"

Kit interrupted again to say, "An honest bishop. An honest
church."

"I would've hesitated to say it, but you speak truly."

"Sir Ralph and I are beginning to discover just how greedy
the late Bishop Giland was."

A timid hand tapped the door. Ralph took from the tearful
clerk an enormous armful of account books.

"Until you are dealt with, you will remain within the
Cathedral grounds," ordered Kit.

The man whimpered and Ralph closed the door. He placed
the mountain on the table.

"There is the truth. If you have honest clergy you will go
through every page and come up with a true accounting."

"I will. For your entertainment you may have noticed that
the Cathedral has only three towers. This is not what was
planned. The money to complete that tower vanished. There is a
tradition of mismanagement in this Cathedral."

"I am only concerned with one matter. Settling the deceased
Queen to eternal rest in this Cathedral. Once done, we will
leave you to cleanse the Temple as I believe Our Lord did."

"Then I can help you, Commissioner. The late King Henry
wished his late wife Catherine of Arragon to rest here. So she
does in a simple grave. The necessary royal style has not been
applied to the grave site although fashioned by the craftsmen

because in the same mysterious fashion the money vanished. Their work lies abandoned in a corner of the crypt."

"I am sure there is room enough for two coffins. We have the money. We need a craftsman to renew the inscriptions. Perhaps the image of Catherine could become the image of Mary? Who has seen either? Dust off whatever railings, decoration, heraldry is necessary. No longer will you be the invisible Cathedral. Scots and English will flock to Peterborough to mourn the tragic Queen. And at long last the craftsmen will be paid for their work. Is that agreeable, Lord Bishop?"

When Bishop Heathwred had departed smiling, Ralph accused his friend. "You are a most dangerous man, Kit. I shudder to think what disasters you would engineer if you had real authority. The lies fly without conscience from your lips. And the man believes you! Even I trembled on the verge of belief when you spouted about cleansing the Temple as Our Lord did. The voice! The face! The tremor of emotion!"

"Don't you understand, dear Ralph? It's all a play. The scene we have just played is a key scene. In a day or so we will be free from our task and may rush to London to receive our due reward. We have rid Elizabeth of her dreaded rival. We have suppressed the Papist rebellion!"

"And spent the Queen's money!"

"And well spent the Queen's money! Look forward to being embraced by our sovereign lady and laden with honours and purses of gold. Rejoice! On to London!"

"I wish I shared your present joy."

"Is your father as flaming miserable as you are?"

*

"I believe we can safely assume Anna escaped when we did."

"Then where is she?"

"Where are we?"

They were sitting in the empty bar of the Queen's Theatre eating crisps and sipping fizzy drinks. They were the only people in the building. The clock above the bar signified ten

260

past eleven signalling all should be home watching television and not eating stolen crisps & sipping sugary drinks.

"You know where we are."

"Time has restored us to a familiar location."

"Then where is Anna?"

"Somewhere familiar."

Wendy took another packet of crisps from the box.

"Shouldn't you ask?"

"Who?"

"Me. I'll be paying for them."

"You don't have to."

"You were very brave. Fighting for Anna. You were quite remarkable."

"You nearly killed me."

"I was aiming for his foot."

"Where did you get the gun?"

"My Grandad. He used to be a bank robber."

"Crumbs! Was he any good?"

"Wendy, I don't want you to go time walking again."

The girl's face displayed emotions alpha to omega and settled on disappointment.

"You'll get yourself killed."

Carole left Wendy safely at Rosebank Boarding House with profuse apologies to Mrs. Seaberg for keeping the girl out late. Wendy left Carole promising not to speak a word to anyone on pain of being cast down to Hell. Carole left hoping for the best. She drank no alcohol and retired to bed. She slept well and woke without memory of any dreams. She woke in her own bed and the calendar clock assured her the year was 2021. Anna's bed was empty.

*

The early evening was a triumph. Kit had arranged for Ned Alleyn and his Company to present an entertainment for her Majesty and select guests. Ned had accomplished miracles in bringing his actors from London to Canterbury, Kent when those who could afford to were scurrying North & West for fear of the Spanish invasion. News was scanty, but the fearsome

261

Armada was in the Channel and fifteen thousand Spanish soldiers awaited ferrying from the Spanish Netherlands to the English shore. To divert the Queen the Great Hall of Boxborough Manor had been transformed into a playhouse.

When the royal party were seated comfortably and |Lord Walsingham's gouty foot had been elevated to the most comfortable position, Kit announced, "This is an entertainment devised by me alone. If it offends only I am to blame. Do not lay the fault upon the actors who are here most willingly to entertain your Majesty, but not to offend you. And beg forgiveness before they perform.."

Elizabeth interrupted to cry, "Enough making amends when no amends are needed. If I am offended you will know it, Master Scribbler. The actors are mere puppets. I will take the puppet master to task."

The Queen's party laughed & applauded.

"Begin!" cried the crow's voice and the entertainment began.

The servants scurried about moving & changing furniture. Flowers were set to delight the royal visitor. Trumpets sounded. The courtiers stood in line and the Queen made her entrance.

The gasp from the audience was most audible. The Elizabeth on stage was Elizabeth Regina beyond simple recognition. The appearance, the white doll face, the voice, the movement, the gestures were astonishingly true. It was a most remarkable performance. In those first moments all eyes turned upon Elizabeth Regina and all hearts began to beat again to find the Sovereign shaking with laughter.

The Queen's laughter released the cast who so encouraged gave a splendid performance. The Elizabeth on stage became ever more outrageous as she rode the Spanish Ambassador around the Hall belabouring him with a riding crop. The peak of *her* performance was when she made a rousing speech to the army before she drove the Spanish army over Dover cliffs, piddled on Admiral Medina Sidonia and punished his backside all the way to the Tower. Elizabeth in her chair jeered, hoorayed and in her passion kicked her legs about in a most unladylike fashion.

The play ended in tumultuous applause as Elizabeth & her party threw boots and shoes at the unfortunate actor portraying Admiral Medina Sidonia who was by custom forced to stand under bombardment bowing to the applause. Kit was brought before Elizabeth and to his horror was firmly bussed on both cheeks by his Sovereign lady. Elizabeth was notorious for issuing death warrants by embrace.

Then the royal party led by the Queen and Master Marlowe adjourned to the Great Chamber for dinner. As they walked together, Elizabeth declared, "I have need to give such a speech to my Army to rouse their blood, Master Scribbler."

"Indeed so, your Majesty! It will be an honour to shape your words!"

Inwardly, Kit sighed such a sigh as might have been heard at the sack of Carthage.

*

Carole skipped breakfast, but found herself nibbling stale biscuits and drinking coffee loaded with sugar at her desk. She was pleased to see Daisy.

"You haven't come to tell me something's gone wrong."

Daisy was startled.

"No! At least, I don't know. Is there something I should know?"

"Dear Daisy, you're not of this world, are you? Your heart and soul are with Tudor panelling. Come on, confess! If it's not wooden, you don't want to know."

Daisy laughed. "You have a visitor."

"Anna!"

"Robin Camberley-Jarvis."

The day darkened. "Consulting Shitbag to the County."

"The very man."

"Where is he?"

"He won't come into the house."

"Where is he?"

"In the courtyard."

"Tell him I'll be down in two minutes."

Carole waited fifteen minutes before she left her desk.

"My father," Ralph Boxborough pronounced, " has never been happier in all his modest life than now. Just look at him, Kit! He sits at supper with his Sovereign. A little more under the spell of Bacchus he might reach out to squeeze Elizabeth's thigh in a mad moment of adoration!"

"Then congratulations, Ralph! You will accede to the Earldom!"

Earl Boxborough, face shining with happiness, nose glowing with excess Burgundy and plump personage almost shaking with excitement, sat at his own table entertaining the Queen of England. She ate very little and only sipped the very expensive wine for which purchase the Earl had pledged the hamlet of Hanwren Parva.

"How will he feel tomorrow when he views the cost of Belshazzar's feast?"

"He will ignore the writing on the wall and bumble on towards bankruptcy."

Our Heroes, Kit & Ralph, were not in London, but at Boxborough Manor, Canterbury. Elizabeth was in Kent because of the threat of the Spanish Army in the Netherlands preparing to invade her realm. She had quarrelled with her closest adviser, Lord Walsingham.

"Where should a Sovereign be when her kingdom is threatened, milord? No arse licking, sir. I must have the cleanest buttocks in Christendom. Speak freely!"

The noble lord weighed his words.

"A Queen should be secure in the Tower. Not risking her sacred neck, your Majesty. We have hundreds, thousands willing, nay, eager to risk their dirty necks."

"A leader must lead. I must be where my army is. And my army will be at the enemy."

"Then I suggest you don't unpack your trunks and portmanteaus, your Majesty. The Armada are in the Channel looking for an open door."

His lordship sulked and his gout punished him in return.

The parting from Fotheringhay had been most amiable. Gilbert and his wife returned to their farm with a reward of Elizabeth's gold. Jonard resolved to stay as Sir Ralph's man. The Flemings remained to garrison the Castle. Their Captain was appointed Castellan a l'heure. The previous office holder having fled Fotheringhay in company with the Queen's Chamberlain. Both had tongues & fingers removed to avoid tale-telling. Kit thought to brand them both as thieves, but Ralph thought that excessive.

On leaving Peterborough Cathedral Canon Finan Heathwred was ordained Bishop by Kit, giving him the opportunity to wear the elaborate robes, heavy with jewels purloined by the previous Bishop. To his honour Bishop Finan Heathwred did not, but wore his simple robe throughout his tenure. The Sergeant-at-Arms and the Halberdiers received due gratuities in gold and resolved to return to garrison duty at Fotheringhay. As Kit said, "No soldier refuses a warm billet with a dry roof and three meals a day.

*

In the courtyard Robin Camberley-Jarvis stood by his car kicking at the gravel that Jacob had calmed with the mechanical rake the day before. The old man was a perfectionist; an ally of Carole's father who aimed to create Paradise. When Carole started across the gravel the archaeologist composed himself, but Carole sensed his pomposity was not fully inflated. There was less of the Consulting Archaeologist to the County greeting a modest trowel toiler on her knees before his Magnificence. *Maybe it's just that I hate his piggy little eyes.*

"Carole! How good of you to spare me five minutes! I know you must be awfully busy."

He shook her warmly by the hand; *Stanley greeting Livingstone? Or Livingstone warily shaking hands with a journalist?*

"Good to see you, Robin! I understand why you don't wish to enter the building. I have been concerned for you."

"How kind! I've put it aside, but it was very real."

"Fortunately, we've had no further incidents. How can I help you?"

"I think you'll be pleased to learn I have succeeded in persuading the Council to accept your offer of housing the Boxborough burials in the new hotel." He beamed upon Carole.

Big liar! You advised the Council to withdraw, but they're not entirely stupid.

"They decided it would raise the image of the city. Probably a different calibre of tourist?"

"We've discovered the hidden chapel used by the family. Secret Catholics. It will be restored to its original state."

"Oh, my word! How exciting!"

"Which will be offered to guests as a working chapel and a wedding venue. With a suitable grant we'll consider opening a Visitors Centre in the grounds as a separate project from the hotel. There's a wonderful story here yet to be told."

"I must arrange for you to meet the sub-committee. Do not be concerned. They sit or beg as I command."

He's your boy, Adolf!

"I'd be happy to talk with them."

Robin Camberley-Jarvis hesitated to say, "Then I'll leave you to your work. I'll go and start the ball rolling. I'm sure we'll be able to work well together."

"Fortunately, there's only one snag, Robin."

"Oh?"

"You not being able to enter the House. But I'll make sure you have photos. And perhaps a video."

*

From what he perceived, Kit learnt that except for her Majesty and Lord Walsingham their dinner companions were military officers of rank. Elizabeth was in rare good humour and most complimentary to Kit & Ralph.

"I am sure, gentlemen, you are unaware you are seated with two gentlemen who have done me great service. Have you heard of the battle of Fotheringhay? The Papists defeated? The

266

enemy crushed and driven from the field? Garnet running like a rabbit!"

It appeared no general at her table had an inkling of the bravery displayed at Fotheringhay.

"Shall I tell them, my dear Kit, or would you wish to inflame their passions with a description of your own gallantry and that of your comrade in arms, Sir Ralph Boxborough?"

Every eye was turned upon the embarrassed gentlemen, seated modestly at the foot of the table.

"Pissed Purgatory! Your gracious Majesty, please, please, do not embarrass us further. We did what we needed to do. We would not wish to boast. I would rather you executed me than spin such a story."

Ralph looked alarmed at this generous offer.

"And so I will do one day, Master Marlowe. I shall have your head on a pike. But not tonight. I will accept your insolence so long as you please me. You please me greatly tonight. I will tell the story of the great battle of Fotheringhay."

"May we be excused, your Majesty?"Kit half-rose from his chair.

"To leave the hunter without his prize stag? Certainly not! You two villains will come and stand by me, one gallant gentleman on my left and my favoured lying, cheating, but successful scribbler on my right."

Elizabeth began to tell the story and her military gentlemen vastly enjoyed the entertainment.

"He choked the bridge because he didn't want to set it afire. The Papists spent time unravelling the barricade. They approached the Castle and flourished their banners. The scribbler set fire to the banners with flaming arrows. The rebels had to stamp on their own banners. The walls of the castle were hung with banners displaying the most outrageous calumnies about the Pope. In such manner was their spear blunted. Bombs loaded with dung and shite began to explode among the throng. An ancient ballista.."

Elizabeth paused until the laughter died down.

"A ballista began to shower the Papists with a good mixture of the same unpleasant mixture. Finally the cavalry!"

The audience roared again.

"The gates were opened and a thirsty herd of kine, goats and geese stampeded through the Papist horde to the river."

The military men stood up to cheer and applaud. When order was restored Elizabeth, Sovereign Queen, finished the story.

"The battle was won. No one died. No child or woman were hurt, but most stank to high Heaven. The rebellion was broken. Why have I taken time to tell you the story?"

No one suggested a reason.

"Because it was an English victory. The style of victory that gallant captain Frankie Drake has achieved according to recent reports. He sent fire ships into the Armada and scattered the fleet just as Master Marlowe and Sir Ralph did with the stampede of the kine. There is a way with the English. We do not do what is expected of us. We do what surprises the enemy."

The generals stamped their feet and mumbled their agreement.

"We don't marry off our country to foreign princes. We don't knuckle under to Italian Popes. We don't quake under threats of invasion. Come the world against us we will surprise them."

In the uproar Ralph knew exactly what Kit was thinking; itching for quill, ink and paper. *What a wonderful scene this will make! The final scene that brings the pit onto the stage and endangers the actors' lives by fierce embrace! Someone should be sketching this!*

When the applause finally subsided and the servants were able to refill all the glasses, Elizabeth broke the news to the gathering.

"Admiral Medina Sidonia might have taken the Isle of Wight, but he has missed his opportunity. The Armada has passed Folkestone. It seems their prize is London. Admiral Medina Sidonia is to force a landing in the Thames Estuary. If he can secure a foothold on Thameside, then two thousand Spanish troops will become near twenty thousand as Parma's troops join them from the Netherlands. It is all or nothing for the Spanish now. Our Army is gathering at Tilbury. We move at first light to join the Army."

THIRTY-ONE

Ned Alleyn swore that despite any threat of the rack, blinding, castration, multiple mutilation, hanging, drawing and quartering, he and the Company would never work with Kit Marlowe again if they survived the journey. It was undoubtedly the worst journey in the world. Men who had been nibbled by sharks, pin-cushioned by sixteen swords, stumbled headlong into the flaming abyss, men who had been stuffing the cannon ball down the muzzle when the wretched machine exploded, all who had so suffered agreed that the journey undertaken by the Company and Kit from London to Tilbury as guests of her Royal Majesty was the ultimate Hell on wheels.

The Queen's principal caravanserai consisted of six great wagons containing the few simple items her Majesty would need to survive two or three days in Tilbury. The Queen's personal carriage was bigger than a barn on eight wheels. Twelve Shire horses pulled the carriage with a second team in attendance. It was the height of luxury with a royal gardez l'eau that cleared itself onto the road. An Indian tracker would have easily followed it by the droppings.

The only slight inconvenience was that every shock of the primitive road surface was transmitted to the travellers. The Queen's chair was immovable, being built into the floor. On a really bad road everyone else in the royal carriage performed Saint Vitus's dance. Older ministers would have resigned before accompanying her Majesty on such royal jaunt if they had dared.

Throughout the journey Ned Alleyn & Company performed every scrap of Kit's work they remembered to entertain the gracious Elizabeth; the longest theatre festival in human history. Tragedy is difficult to sustain when actors & audience are bouncing about like peas on a drum. Elizabeth found King Lear most amusing and threw Lord Walsingham's slippers at the unfortunate king.

"Serves him right!" cried England's Queen, "If the fool had kept it in his codpiece," and dissolved into raucous laughter at his plight. Kit was reminded of stories of her royal father who would roar with laughter at a friend's jest and sign his death warrant within moments; a cruel mirth as frightening as the crying of ravens.

Our hero enjoyed the privilege of holding the back of the throne to stay upright. Sir Ralph was spared humiliation as he was on horseback with the advance guard. Performances didn't stop while her Majesty used the gardez l'eau. But every so often Elizabeth would stop the performance. The unfortunate actors would hold onto one another swaying backwards & forwards like drunkards before the magistrate.

"I wish to see the play where I am whipping the Spanish gentleman and piddling on the Admiral. I believe it is my finest performance."

Those who did not wish to have head separated from body did not groan aloud. After the first request to repeat the performance' caused a delay that created a storm of bad temper, the veteran mimic Matthew Querrilon stayed in costume. It was a wise decision. The skit was performed three more times before the Queen relented and permitted the Company to sleep.

When the curtain was withdrawn about the royal bed for the doctor to present the Queen with a sleep potion, Kit seized the opportunity & the glass from the old man to approach his sovereign mistress.

"If I may take but a moment of your time, your Majesty?"

"Do you know how much I desire to sleep? But speak up, Master Impudence. You have much pleased me today."

"I wondered, your Majesty, if you would consider being the Patron of Master Alleyn's Company? They would be honoured to call themselves The Queen's Company. Master Alleyn does not know I am asking you. So, if I offend, he is blameless."

Elizabeth drank the potion and Kit's confidence began to drain away. The Queen returned the glass to Kit.

"Master Marlowe, you have done me as always, great service. The Scottish woman is no longer a threat and you have made a mockery of Henry Garnet. I owe you much for both.

The actors have filled the day for me most gladly and taken my mind from other matters."

"Service given most willingly, your Majesty!"

"When Lord Howard has swept this Armada into the cruel embrace of the North Sea, I will have a document drawn up that gifts Master Alleyn's Company with the title of The Queen's Company. I will be their Patron. The New Theatre will become the Queen's Theatre. Will that satisfy you, Master Scribbler?"

Kit's joy was apparent. He subdued the impulse to embrace the royal personage. Her breath would've cast down the walls of Jericho.

"Thank you, your Majesty! Thank you! I can assure you Master Alleyn and the Company will be even more grateful than I am. A wonderful gift! The Queen's Company will always be at your service as I am, your Majesty!"

"Enough! Enough! I don't want your spit all over me! Close the curtain and let me rest in peace. Cast your spittle on my Company!"

"I will, your Majesty, I surely will!"

So passed the journey to Tilbury.

*

Kit was astonished at the great panoply of tents and the vast numbers of soldiers of all branches busy about their tasks. The artillery park was most impressive, row upon row of gleaming brass dragons of death: and their sombre iron brothers with their attendant artillerymen. The scent of hundreds of horses drew attention to busy farriers and attentive stablemen burnishing already-shining coats in the cavalry lines. There Kit saw Ralph in his true element engaged in boisterous conversation with the gentlemen of the Queen's Horse. There was total bustle in the encampment to prepare for the Royal Visit in two days time.

Upon a central mount stood a fair pavilion emblazoned with pennants & banners where her Majesty would dine in company and from which she would sally forth to address her Army. For security her Majesty & household were settled into Tilbury Fort less than an hour distant. Kit had already skirmished with

Elizabeth over the speech he had written for his Sovereign; the first warrior Queen since Boudicca of the Iceni. He had also secreted a copy that would figure in his soon-to-be-written drama, ELIZABETH REGINA.

Kit, Ned and the Queen's Company were billeted in a clean tavern in the town of Tilbury. They were expected to perform for a select audience. Kit was at the Queen's beck & call with constant changes to her speech. Yet all was set fair for a remarkable Great Parade that Spanish spies were welcome to report to their master.

*

The hospital was silent in a mid-night calm. Every synchronised clock clicked to display three a.m. On Mary Seacole ward a soul slipped away quietly and the night nurse obediently recorded the time of death. Elsewhere only the nursing staff were unsleeping except for Hannah. She was sitting by Anna's bedside holding her hand.

"I know so little about you, Anna. I was me, Hannah and then I wasn't. My life was stolen. Forgotten. We were unwitting lodgers, you, me and Annie."

She sat silent regarding Anna's face.

"You look somewhat like me. But these hands aren't yours. They're Annie's hands. Rough and calloused. I hope she stays with Noah. Will you stay to help Wendy grow up? I hope you stay together. You were always so brave."

Hannah laughed quietly.

"I wish I had time to tell you about life with Kit. But maybe one day I will write a book. Kit is always scribbling. What would he say if I showed him a book I'd written? First he'd sulk and scribble and then he'd find where I hid my book and read it. Then he'd sulk again and pretend I wasn't there."

She stroked the hard hand and smiled in the electric twilight.

"Such a child. I want to say thank you. For all the care you and Annie took of me. Now I am awakened."

Hannah kissed Anna's sleeping brow and rose, reluctant to release her hand.

"I have to go. Where am I going? I'll follow the trail as a good hound should. I'll find him. As we Thespians say, break a leg! Maybe we'll meet again. So, I won't say farewell."

A nurse entered the cubicle as Hannah left, but she didn't see her. She checked pulse & drip and continued on her solitary way.

*

A distracted Carole left work early and drove home to an empty flat. She lingered at the foot of the stairs, hoping to hear a cheery voice. She announced her presence, but there was no reply.

As she sipped from a bottle of Cathedral Brewery Light Ale, Carole reasoned with herself that being so tense was interfering with any time transfer. She agreed and drank a second bottle of Light Ale while she ran a bath wilfully adding whatever scents & oils were at hand.

"Sorry, Anna! Tahiti Heaven is too good to ignore."

The deep foam & heavenly scents waited no longer than for Carole to strip and plunge into Paradise with a fresh bottle in her hand. She had barely taken a sip when she found herself stark naked on a pleasant woodland path. She glimpsed a large country house beyond the trees. Carole was suddenly aware of her situation. Light Ale in hand, she stood horrified & naked.

"Not again! Please, not again!"

Her confusion was redoubled when Elizabeth, Sovereign Queen of England, Scotland and Ireland appeared on the path, accompanied by two gentlemen in Elizabethan dress; the elder accompanied by his clerk. Kit and Ralph completed the close company. Four members of her Majesty's bodyguard followed at a discreet five paces.

The Queen was enjoying a gentle morning stroll to rehearse the speech, which she was to deliver tomorrow to the Army. The Royal party was aghast & open-mouthed at the appearance of a naked female woodland spirit in their path. Kit and Ralph stepped forward to shield Her Majesty from any evil intent of this uninvited intruder.

To complicate matters further a creature with the face of a pig, in black costume & cloak, stepped out of the undergrowth to point a pistol at Kit. At either flank of the creature stood an ogre. Kit & Ralph drew their swords.

Kit stepped out to cry, "You shall not pass!"

The pig laughed and gestured with the pistol for Kit to step aside. Kit stood fast and Ralph joined him. The Inquisitor aimed the pistol and shouted, "Death and damnation to all spawn of Satan!"

Carole threw the beer bottle at the creature. The pistol exploded and Elizabeth Regina fell to the ground. Kit and Ralph leapt forward.

The Inquisitor turned and ran into the woodland. Ralph's blade ran through the scowling ogre twice who barred his way and the man fell cursing, dying. Kit tackled the other man who was brave enough to face a blade with a club & a knife. Most surprising was Thomas, Lord Walsingham's clerk, who displayed a pistol and killed Kit's man. The woodland spirit vanished.

Ralph commented, "Braver than their master."

The whole affair had taken little more than a minute. The two gentlemen, Walsingham and Cecil knelt by the Queen. Thomas was loading his pistol against a return of the Papists.

"I fear the worst," his Lordship declared.

Ralph picked up the Queen. The body had already lost all muscle tone. He looked to Kit who agreed.

"The future lies with the pistol."

When they reached Hambleton House with Ralph carrying the Queen's corpse, Lord Walsingham ordered the household to assemble in the Great Hall & be so recorded by the Housekeeper. The Queen's Body Guard closed & locked all entrances & exits. No one was to enter or leave the house on pain of death.

Carole hammered on the locked door, but no one was listening. She pressed her lips to the Ogre's mouth that served as a keyhole.

"I'm sorry! I'm really so sorry! It's all my fault. I don't know why I threw the bottle. I'm sorry. I wasn't thinking."

The rooks mocked her anguish. She sat down on the steps and found herself sinking into a foaming hot bath perfumed with all the scents of Araby that Anna could afford.

*

The image of the lead ball striking the Queen's left eye in the white painted face replayed itself. The mouth opened in pain & anger again & again. She felt about in the bath for the beer bottle, but it lay among last year's leaves in the woodland by the fatal path. Cathedral Brewery Light Ale. She had thrown the bottle. Kit was not dead. The Earl's son was without a scratch. But she had interfered from the distant future to kill a Queen.

Carole remained in the bath until the water was lukewarm and the scented foam was cold. Anna's footsteps did not sound on the stairs. No cheery voice shouted it's just me. Someone pushed unwanted bumph through the letterbox.

*

"Come in!" called Superintendent Musgrave.

The door opened to Detective Sergeant Stanley Robertson.

"You sent for me, sir?"

"That sounds so severe, Stan. Called to the Headmaster's office."

"You knew you were in trouble then, sir."

"Never you, Stan. Last of the bulldog breed. I just wanted to say how sorry I am that you've put in your papers."

"I've done my thirty years, sir. Shot and stabbed. My lady thought we should have time for us. I've never been there when she needed me."

"She's right, of course. D'y'think you'll miss the job?"

"I think not. I just don't understand crime any more."

The Superintendent laughed. "Why's that?"

"There's a young woman in Saint Clement's. Badly beaten. Won't give any information. Says she lost her memory. Finally get her to talk to me. She says she was going to be burned as a witch. Only she was whizzed through time and landed in the old railway workshop. And listen to this. She says she must've landed there because her father was a railwayman and she's always loved railway engines."

"Sounds very reasonable."

The Sergeant gave his superior a sharp look.

"Then I find she's the actress at the Queen's who claims to travel in time and talk to dead people. The theatre suspended her."

"You're too conscientious, Stan. Dump this stuff on young Lambert."

The Sergeant took a moment to ponder this advice.

"He'd make it worse. He has no feeling for people."

"But he's a good policeman."

"Any pub, any night, yes."

The Superintendent gestured.

"D'y'want to hear the rest of this?"

"Carry on."

"Her best mate confessed to killing a psychologist, which she didn't. To complicate matters said psychologist ends up lying on a coffin in a fresh grave begging to be buried. Now confined under the Mental Health Act 1983. A danger to himself and others. Do you understand what's going on, sir? Because I don't. Is there a crime here? Stuff like that takes up acres of my time."

"So what've you written it up as?"

"N.F.A."

"No further action required."

The Superintendent nodded agreement.

"Any ideas for the future."

"Little village in Northumberland I know well.."

"What would you do there?"

"Forget this and start living."

Stan smiled at his superior officer.

"I will arise and go now, for always ever more, I hear the North Sea tides in conflict with that rocky shore while I stand on the roadway, or on the pavements grey, I hear it in the deep heart's core. Nearly W. B. Yeats."

"Get out of here, Stan! You'll have me putting in me papers next."

276

What the Sergeant forbore from mentioning was the odd suicide of the psychologist John Hazlitt & his dog. N.F.A.

*

In the privacy of the Queen's chamber, Lord Walsingham declared, "I cannot recall a more difficult situation."

William Cecil shook his head sadly.

Ralph Boxborough cried out before Kit could stop him.

"A more difficult situation? Milord, our Sovereign has been murdered! Have you no thought of her? Of this brave woman, King Henry's daughter?"

Kit viewed the slight body lying on the bed. The voice of the crow silenced forever.

God's teeth, but this will be a scene to wring the women's tears to flood the pit!

"How does your milk & water philosophy assist us, sir? Leave the wailing and gnashing of teeth to the women."

Before Ralph's temper boiled over Kit put a hand to his friend's shoulder and turned him away from Walsingham.

"His lordship is an old man, Sir Ralph and has no understanding of our desperate situation. But he is right in that there is a time and place for everything. This is not the time for grieving."

William Cecil who had been silent throughout agreed, "I understand your sorrow, sir. Tomorrow the Queen was to speak to the Army. No one doubts the seriousness of England's peril. Without the Queen's rallying cry.."

He gestured, leaving the thought unspoken.

Walsingham took his gouty foot to a chair. Kit regarded the damaged face of the figure lying asleep forever.

"Then the Queen must ride among her Army tomorrow…"

Kit ignored the protesting voices and continued. "She must be viewed by Papist spies who will carry the tale. Her soldiers must see Boadicea astride her charger. She must give her speech and inspire every man to do or die for England. There has to be a Queen of England at Tilbury tomorrow."

William Cecil gestured Walsingham to silence.

"I know what you are thinking, sir. It is unthinkable.."

277

Kit interrupted to say, "If you know what I am thinking, then you must be thinking, which suggests it is not unthinkable as we are apparently both thinking."

William Cecil cried angrily, "Enough of your tomfoolery! What you suggest is outrageous. I'll have no part in it."

"We have been accomplices on a number of occasions, sir. I would not account your sheet as stainless."

Kit paused to add, "Which of you will disclose to the household that the Queen is dead. Murdered by a Jesuit. When by ill chance we stand in danger of invasion by the Spanish."

Neither gentleman responded.

"Who will break the news to the Army tomorrow that their beloved Queen has been shot dead?"

Both gentlemen refused eye contact with Kit.

"It is a desperate gamble, but what remedy do you propose? I would gladly listen."

Lord Walsingham answered for both gentlemen.

"I will have no hand in this."

"But you have no solution?"

There was no response.

"So, you would announce the death of the Queen at this critical moment?"

He didn't expect an answer.

"It would be a terrible waste of one of the best speeches I have ever written."

Kit turned to Ralph to implore him, "Trust to me if you would save England. Ignore these old men. They are concerned more with their own positions. Find Ned and tell him to bring Matthew now."

Walsingham thumped his stick upon the floor and cried, "Do not listen to him, Sir Ralph. If you do, you will pay a sore price."

"What matters now, Ralph, is that all is well with England tomorrow. We must win time."

Reluctantly, a conflicted Ralph Boxborough quitted the Queen's chamber. Kit drew the curtains about the Queen's bed.

"Who is this Matthew, Kit?"

"Matthew Querrilon. Fifty two. Right height and size. A poor actor, but an astonishing mimic."

"You've lost your mind, Kit!"

"While you're looking for it, bring me Matthew Querrilon!"

*

"Guess who?" cried the unmistakeable voice from behind the impressive bouquet of flowers.

"Who else would it be," Anna responded, "Good to see you, Tammie. When you lower the flowers."

The familiar puckish face appeared and Anna laughed. The girl took the empty vase from the bedside cabinet and vanished.

"Two ticks! I promise."

Anna found her hairbrush and started untangling the brambles. Tammie appeared with the flowers in the vase.

"I want to do that!"

Anna surrendered. Tammie put down the flowers safely on the cabinet and took the hairbrush from reluctant fingers. She sat on the bed and began to brush Anna's hair.

"You look better than you did the last time I saw you."

"A madman was about to shoot me. I hadn't time for a facial." Tammie laughed.

"You don't have to worry about that madman any more."

"Let me guess. You killed him?"

"I did. But somehow it didn't stick. But I got arrested for murder. And I had handcuffs. It was the best thing ever! Now if I go for audition and they say, have you ever been arrested for murder I can say yes, definitely."

"Whoa, whoa! What's happened to Bryce?"

"Bryce is locked up in the loony bin. He wanted to be buried, but they wouldn't do it. I would've."

"So, same old, same old? Anything new at the Queen's?"

"Oh, yes! Close your eyes and I'll tell you."

Anna obeyed.

"Your suspension has been lifted."

Anna opened her eyes to smile.

"Tammie, I'm just glad to be alive. And do you know something?"

The girl shook her head.

"There's an awful lot I don't know."

"There's an old gospel song. *I have laid down my load, laid down my load, now I'm walking on freedom road, freedom road.* I feel I'm walking free."

"And our run ends Saturday."

"Tell Gillian to let Melanie finish the season."

"And we're booked into the Royal Theatre, Newcastle, October for Christmas. Will you come with us?"

*

"Lady Fielding, I know you are devoted to the Queen's service. Therefore, I'm going to ask for your trust in a more perilous situation than even Lord Fielding faced in battle. He gave his life for Her Majesty."

The woman looked to Walsingham and Cecil who offered no guidance.

"Who are you, sir?"

"My name is Christopher Marlowe. I hold the Queen's Commission. Presently I speak for Her Majesty."

Lord Walsingham couldn't restrain a snort that Kit ignored.

"I hold her authority."

Lady Fielding looked again to the august gentlemen. William Cecil gave the merest nod.

"The Army is prepared for a Great Parade tomorrow. The Queen had prepared a speech to embolden every heart."

Kit paused to assess the lady before him. He saw a strong face no longer young, but a woman confident in her loyalty.

"I very much need your help, Lady Fielding. In the cause of the Queen."

"Then it will be given gladly, sir."

"I have to bind you to a Great Secret. Because England is in peril. We need for her Majesty to attend the Great Parade."

The lady could not restrain herself.

"You seem to express doubt that Her Majesty will attend?"

Lady Fielding faltered to silence and then confusion.

"You have just announced to the Household that her Majesty is unhurt. Shocked and bruised by her fall. But in good spirits. Are you a liar, sir?"

"Her Majesty was shot dead this morning by a cowardly assassin."

Lady Fielding gave a heartfelt cry and half-rose from her chair.

"I knew. I knew before you brought me here. I knew something was wrong. You didn't deceive me, sir."

I should be a simple scribe and let others tell lies for me.

"But we have need of deception. We cannot have the Army and the country knowing the truth tomorrow. Not with twenty thousand Spanish soldiers breathing down our necks."

One day I will forgive myself. When the theatre trembles with applause for my greatest play, Elizabeth Regina.

"Will you help us, milady?"

The silence was too long. Kit fought to keep his composure. Lady Fielding looked again to the esteemed gentlemen who regarded their shoe buckles.

"You will parade the actor?"

Kit nodded.

"Yes."

"Very well. I will parade as her Majesty's attendant."

This woman is a better man than Her Majesty's Counsellors who will thrust me to the axe or rope if Matthew Querrilon should fail to win the day. Our island's future depends upon a mimic. What royal throne will this fuse destroy, Christopher?

*

The tension within the pavilion was not lightened by the insistence of Walsingham and Cecil that Kit sign a vellum confirming the two gentlemen attended the Great Parade under restraint & against their will. Kit signed it as Kit Marlon, but the tension was such that neither gentleman scrutinised the document. What cheered Kit most was that Matthew and Lady Fielding had achieved rapport.

Ralph said, "Perhaps she has found a child to mother?"

To which Kit replied cynically, "Perhaps she's thinking to save her neck."

"That's not worthy of you, Kit. That would be her last concern. She spent yesterday tutoring Matthew."

281

Matthew Querrilon had vanished when the company returned to the pavilion. There was no question of caricature. He had absorbed the Queen's anima. Before them stood Elizabeth Gloriana in all her power & majesty. Instinctively all stopped and bowed. In her shadow stood her faithful handmaiden.

The Queen startled the company with her first words.

"Who are you staring at, fools? Have you never seen a Queen before?"

Her Majesty laughed her crow call. Walsingham and Cecil laughed dutifully. Ralph and Kit were astonished at the transformation.

It was the moment in every theatre when disbelief falters and the audience believes. Every tone, every tiny movement, every breath shattered disbelief. Face, form, stature, voice declared here was the living Elizabeth. The hair stood up on the back of Kit's neck; as when he first saw Ned Alleyn play Tamburlaine.

Lord Cecil cried, "Your Majesty, I would never have" and stopped when he realised what he was saying.

"And you, Lord Walsingham, so long my dearest confidant, what would you never have?"

The icy amusement, the hands coming together to caress one another, the glance shared with Lady Fielding chilled the pavilion. Facing the image of his Sovereign there was little the old man might say except, "I wish your Majesty every success on this most important day."

"You were always a champion arse licker, milord. How tasted Philip's greasy arse?"

Aware of the rising clamour of the townspeople who had come to see their Queen, Kit said, "May your Master of Horse bring in your mount, your Majesty? Time presses."

The Master of Horse and a boy at the rein brought in the pure white gelding Her Majesty would ride to inspect the Army. The boy's eyes were wider than the horse's.

"I were told to mount a cavalry saddle, your Majesty," apologised the Master.

"You did right! If I need be a soldier I will not ride into battle side saddle! I won't appear pussywillow before my brave warriors. Perched on a side saddle? With my lord Walsingham fearing for his heart? Will the bitch fall off or won't she?"

Walsingham demurred at the language, but was ignored.

"Bravo the woman who sails over a hedge side saddle! But how foolish. Is her husband wishing to be rid of her?"

The pavilion was silent as no one wished to answer the last question. Elizabeth broke into corncrake laughter, but only the boy laughed.

"You see? A surprise fit for a Queen. We have in our company an honest lad. He laughed because something tickled his funny bone. What was it that tickled you?"

For a moment his courage failed and then he spoke up.

"The lady in the hedge, Your Majesty!"

"Excellent! He has the inner eye. Master Marlowe, give this lad a penny. Ask in a year if he has spent it."

"Yes, your Majesty."

Kit borrowed a silver penny from a reluctant Ralph to reward the boy.

"Master Sergeant, look to this lad. I shall ask of him."

"I will diligently, your Majesty!"

"Then let us to our business!"

*

"Ask Wendy."

Anna persisted, "I was asking you. Why haven't you been to visit me?"

Carole offered, "Wendy said you weren't allowed visitors."

"I'll wring her neck one day."

"No! Be grateful you have a fan. Besides you're a star. Malnourished. Dehydrated. Abused. Concussion. Enjoy being pampered for a few days. They'll throw you out soon enough."

"How'd'y'know all that?"

"It's on your chart. You were asleep when I came in. By the way I told them I'm your sister."

"Older sister would explain a lot."

"Not that much older."

"How are things on the Rialto?"

"We're walking a tight rope at work. My Dad relies too much on mates rates. If we can't finish Boxborough we'll be in trouble. So, don't ask."

"I wish I could help."

"I found out the 'transmitter' isn't Tammie. It's Gillian. That you are Annie and Annie is a girl called Hannah Cato who has been separated from Kit Marlowe for nefarious reasons. But you may know that."

"How'd you do that?"

"I was worried for you and I went looking for you. And Time'll toss you up on some shore you have a connection to. Oh, and I'm never going to take a bath again."

Anna laughed to say, "I don't like the sound of that."

"I was dumped starkers on a woodland path and I killed Queen Elizabeth."

"You're kidding!"

"I didn't mean to. Kit Marlowe was dead and I went to make sure he wasn't. And I threw the beer bottle at this frightful priest and he didn't shoot Kit. He shot the Queen. And it's all my fault."

Carole was close to tears. Anna sat up in bed.

"Oh, you poor lamb! You're the one needs looking after. Would you like a glass of Lucozade? Wendy brought six bottles."

*

Sir Ralph Boxborough walked ahead with the Sword of State. A page bearing her silver helmet on a cushion followed him. Then came the Queen herself in white, armoured with a silver cuirass. At her waist was a silver-buttoned belt supporting a sword sheathed in gold. In her hat she wore a fine plume. At her side walked Master Christopher Marlowe. A page led her charger, dressed for war. Behind rode Lords Walsingham & Cecil with attendant pages. Four mounted cavaliers followed behind at a discreet distance.

The appearance of Elizabeth aroused a great volume of applause from the camp followers, mothers, children, seamstresses, cooks, blacksmiths, armourers, stable boys,

284

doxies, wagon drivers, townspeople to whom she raised her sword arm in response. The ranks of soldiers were silent awaiting orders.

"Well done!" Kit noted, "The people are rarely acknowledged."

The Queen turned her horse towards the jostling crowd beyond the pale. Her Company stopped and Kit ran with Her Majesty.

The crowd cheered and fell silent as she drew close.

"Where would my brave soldiers be without you?" she shouted.

A brave voice shouted, "In raggy britches, your Majesty!"

"You're right! We'd be in a fair pickle without your duty. I thank you on my Army's behalf!"

There was an absolute silence as never before had the followhood of any Army been so acknowledged.

Elizabeth shouted in her loudest cracked tone, "Master Chandler, how many childer do we have in camp?"

The senior chandler shouted, "Two hundred and thirty seven, your Majesty! One babby born this morn!"

"Then I have a silver penny for two hundred and thirty seven!"

Kit passed up the soft leather bag and Elizabeth tossed it to the Master Chandler amid thunderous cheering. She raised her arm in salute again and turned to rejoin the Company in review of the Great Parade.

Cheap at twice the price, thought Kit.

*

Hannah stood by the front garden wall of 18, Springfield Park Avenue, Gilsford. The gate was newly painted and the small front garden was neatly trimmed. The centrepiece was a small spruce from Christmas past that would grow to swamp the house one day. At its foot stood three large plastic frogs smiling up at Hannah. It was raining. No sooner had she grasped where she was than her world shook and rearranged itself.

The front gate was missing. The garden was the home of an ancient motorcycle & sidecar standing on scrubby grass. A young man knelt at the combo, struggling to tighten a nut. He swore as the spanner slipped. Hannah knew if she looked at the front window she would find herself behind the net curtain watching the young man's struggle. He scowled skywards as the rainfall increased. As he tightened the nut, the heavens opened. Pulling the tarpaulin over the motorcycle and grabbing his toolbox, he went to the front door, only to find it closed.

"Hannah!" he shouted through the letterbox, kicking the door.

A voice answered from within.

"Who is it, please?"

The man smothered a curse, saying, "Hannah, it's raining!"

"Not in here it's not!"

"Open the door, Hannah!"

"Who is it, please?"

"Hannah! Don't be so silly!"

"Have you an appointment?"

"Stop acting the fool!"

"The voice is familiar. And the sentiment."

The man surrendered.

"It's me! Your father by adoption! If you wish to be so formal."

"The father by adoption that was so rude to me?"

The man struggled with his pride and then admitted.

"Yes. I'm sorry. But you started it."

"But I'm only a child. I'm allowed hissy fits. How old are you?"

The door remained closed. Rain was running down the man's neck.

"Hannah, I'm sorry. Very sorry! Please, open the door! I'm drowning out here!"

The door opened and an older woman appeared. Hannah was startled. There was no motorcycle combo and no young man. The Christmas tree glistened in the rain and the gate was secure.

"Can I help you, dear?"

"I don't think so."

"You've been standing out there nearly fifteen minutes."

"Sorry."

"Are you working up to burgling the house?"

Hannah laughed and wiped rain from her nose.

"We don't have much."

"I don't go about stealing anything. Not my style."

"You still haven't said why you're standing there. Are you feeling ill?"

"We used to live here."

"Who did?"

"Kit and me. Christopher on a Sunday."

"Would you like to come in out of the rain?"

"I'd love to. If I'm not a bother."

Hannah followed the older woman into the hallway and wiped her feet punctiliously on the mat that said THANK YOU. She turned to enter the sitting room and in that brief moment the past replayed. She saw Kit and herself attacked as they entered the room. The tray she was carrying clattered across the room to strike the paraffin heater. Her head exploded with pain and darkness fell.

Hannah pushed aside the bewildered older woman to flee from the house.

"I'm sorry! I can't!"

She ran until she could run no farther. Looking about she saw she was on the bypass. She gave in to her aching legs & lungs. Hannah sat down on the verge.

She cried to the rainy air, "Now I know!"

A man's voice said, "You look as though you need a lift."

An articulated lorry had stopped beside her. When she looked doubtful the driver said, "I don't bite."

Hannah stood up on creaky legs to say, "Yes, thank you."

As she climbed into the cab, the driver asked, "Where you heading, miss?"

"Wherever it's not raining."

*

The martial horns called & called again, resounding over the martial field where Elizabeth's Army came to attention as the

287

Queen and her Company rode between the regimental rows. Here & there the white gelding halted and Her Majesty spoke to a common soldier, asking about his family. To an officer she phrased the question differently, but as Kit had suggested always drawing the men close to her as family must be. The great leafless forest of the pikemen, weapons taller than saplings drew Elizabeth's interest. She rode among them, talking to the men, suggesting crudely what they might do with the pikes on the appearance of any Spanish conquistadors. This brought them all to laughter; Queen & commoners together. Kit noted the alarm of Walsingham & Cecil as the gelding vanished among the pikemen. He knew she was never in any danger; that these men adored their monarch and would die for her.

There was no battalion, no regiment that didn't feel the brush of her skirts and heard her voice talking in a fashion they understood. Cheering filled the air as Gloriana moved from regiment to regiment. They had seen her acknowledging their children & their wives. They had seen her laughing with their comrades. It was a peerless performance, an afternoon that old soldiers would recount to their grandchildren. Those who were present learnt this woman to be their Queen, not some idol barely glimpsed as she passed by, neither seeing nor hearing the people.

The climax of this astonishing afternoon was Elizabeth's speech. She did not take the general officers aside, but called upon the Army to come to her, frightening Lords Walsingham & Cecil. The Army came to her, but not pressing, holding back from crowding the solitary figure in white, cuirass glittering, standing in her stirrups, flanked by Kit & Ralph who both said silent prayers for success.

Master Marlowe was correct. It was one of his better pieces, but it was the heartfelt truth of the delivery that has sent its clarion call through the centuries. The silence deepened as the rough strong voice told of her dedication to and love of her country. She told the soldiers she was willing to stand and die with them if necessary, but surely to triumph over any enemy that came against them. To a man they believed her.

In the climax to her speech she won over every heart as she cried, "I know I have the body but of a weak and feeble woman."

She paused and dropped her head to cast a wink at Kit who nearly evacuated his bowel there & then. Elizabeth Gloriana drew her sword and thrust it skyward to cry, "But I have the heart and stomach of a king and of a King of England too, and think foul scorn that Parma or Spain or any prince of Europe, should dare to invade the borders of my realm!"

All the cannons of England had never made greater explosion than was heard on that fine afternoon at Tilbury when her Majesty spoke to her Army of the threat of a Spanish invasion. It was said the noise was heard in the Channel and even in the Spanish camps in the Netherlands.

The multitude parted as the Red Sea for Moses as the Queen of England withdrew from the happy clamour to the comparative calm of the pavilion where Kit was the first to address the Queen.

"You mad bugger! I thought you'd given the game away! Where'd you get *stomach and heart of a king*? I nearly shit meself!"

He turned to the astonished company to complain.

"That's the bliddy trouble with actors. They won't stick to the script! *Stomach and heart of a king?* And you winked at me, you bliddy madman!"

Kit sat down trembling.

"I'm done with you, Matthew. Take your gear and piss off!"

"But, Kit, I only..."

Lord Walsingham interrupted to say, "We are not done with him. That was a magnificent performance. I am sure her late Majesty would agree."

"Thank you, milord. It is a wonderful part to play."

"Indeed, indeed! Lord Cecil and I would have you remain in the role. With suitable remuneration, of course."

The Virgin Queen could not restrain his delight.

Matthew Querrilon cried, "You want me to continue? To play the Queen?"

"The arrangements will need to be carefully considered. Only a few may know this great secret."

His gaze rested casually upon Kit Marlowe whose heart paused beating to consider the implication.

"Those few whose tongues are silent. Or removed."

His intent was clear.

Matthew Querrilon turned to Lady Fielding.

"Thank you, milady. Without you I would never have succeeded."

Kit almost opened his mouth to speak, but desisted. He spoke instead to Walsingham.

"Who will be penning the scripts for Her Majesty, milord?"

Lord Walsingham didn't respond, but merely smiled.

Lord Cecil declared, "Master Marlowe, I will require an accounting of the large sum of money which Her Majesty entrusted to you as her Commissioner in the matter of the Scottish woman."

"With all possible speed," Kit Marlowe assured his Lordship. But did not enlarge on what might be accomplished with all possible speed.

*

It was almost midnight before Kit and Ralph watched from horseback the wagon driven by Jonard cross safely on the raft to bear the dead Elizabeth Gloriana onward to Canterbury. It seemed at moments a doomed journey as the wagon rolled awkwardly and the horses shifted & complained. The raft master and his mate poled steadily, seemingly undisturbed.

"Is this important enough to risk our necks, Kit?"

"Only once has the raft failed. January sixty-four. A gentleman had his man light a fire to warm him."

"You know what I mean."

"Those villains have the Queen they have long wanted. A sovereign eager to do their bidding. My Elizabeth deserves better. They have given her barely a thought."

"Have you? What is the charge for stealing a Royal corpse? Hanging, drawing and quartering? After torture? The axe would be a mercy."

"Ralph, dear friend, Walsingham has you and me on a very short list to be silenced. What we do now is of little consequence."

"You are such a comfort to me, dear friend."

"If I recollect truly you were the gentleman who was tired of the frivolity of life at Court."

"But not life itself!"

They rode silently back towards the festivity that was keeping Tilbury awake. The rejoicing at the Fort where the Queen's household was lodged was more discreet, but when our heroes gave the care of their horses to the stable boys, they found everyone in the Hall in various stages of drunkenness.

Walsingham, Cecil and Matthew Querrilon shared a table and urged the new Queen to call for more wine. They roared with drunken laughter when the mimic cried in Elizabeth's crowbird tones, "More wine for my friends, you leprous scabs! More wine! In fact, a cask of wine! And quickly afore I skin your filthy hides!"

There was little point in excusing themselves. Their Lordships & the Company were too intoxicated to be aware of their presence. As they quitted the Hall, Kit asked of Ralph, "How judge you now your gentlemen? How would you rate them against swine?"

Ralph made no answer.

In the first false light of dawn Kit & Ralph were standing by their agitated horses on the raft as nervous as their mounts.

"You're shivering, milord. Should I light a fire to warm your precious arse, sir?"

"Should we not end up on a bonfire and survive this mad caper, Kit, I have to tell you I am going at all speed to join Mary Stuart in France."

"You don't even know she survived the Wash."

"I do. I was surprised to be given a message from that scurvy little Frenchman who clerks for Norfolk."

"His Lordship wasn't here yesterday."

"But his spy was."

"But you thought best not to tell me."

"On such a day I thought the less you knew the better."

"Oh, ye of little faith! Are you to tell me what the message said?"

"Une colombe errante a atterri dans le nid de Guise. A stray dove..."

Kit interrupted to say, "One day we must drink to that gallant little fisherman, Ganda."

"And the honest Gilbert and his brave lady."

*

In midstream the wind blew cold and they stood close together between the uneasy horses, as the raft crew fought to thwart the tide.

"And you, Kit? They'll be hunting you. Discounting the Queen's money, they will need to silence you."

"Which is why I cannot go to London. Canterbury I know as I was born there. If your father will ignore my presence for a few days?"

He left the rest unspoken as the raft finally nudged the welcome shore. The pole man leapt ashore to secure rope to crude bollard. Ralph led the horses onto secure ground and Kit paid the ferryman in gold.

"You have never ever seen me or my friend, have you, master?"

"No, sir, never! I'd swear to that on the Holy Book. I have not seen you, sir. Not a hair of you ever. I'm not even seeing you now, sir."

Kit gave the man silver coins.

"Hide the gold. Spend the silver."

"That I will do, sir."

Kit clapped his shoulder and went to make the same bargain with his mate. His eyes widened as if he had never seen gold coins before. Kit warned him, "Don't spend this gold. Show it to no one. Keep it for a time of great need. Spend it now and his Lordship will want to know how you came by it. Then he will hang you and your family."

Kit pressed two silver coins into his leathery hand.

"Spend this, but no more. For your own safety."

Ralph had been listening and asked, "Will he heed you?"

"The longer they hold the gold the sooner they will become aware they are partners in this conspiracy. They will keep silent."

"You are sinful man, Master Marlowe. I pray for your soul."

"If I had such."

*

The sun was shining. It wasn't raining. The lorry came to a stop. The driver asked, "You're sure this is where you want to be?"

"Yes, thank you," Hannah responded, unclipping her safety belt.

The driver searched his windscreen for something more than unending road, trees, fields & sheep.

"There's nothing here."

"There used to be a burger van."

"Not for years. Are you meeting someone?"

Hannah seemed uncertain.

"I think so."

"Have I upset you?"

Hannah laughed.

"No! You've been very kind. Thanks for stopping for me."

Hannah climbed down and the driver called, "If he's any sort of a man he'll turn up."

She raised a hand in salute and watched the lorry drive away. The echo of the engine faded to the chattering of birds and the grumbling of sheep. Hannah went to sit under an oak tree at the edge of the copse. The sun was shining and it wasn't raining.

*

The horsemen caught up with the wagon as Canterbury towers came in sight. Jonard was pleased to see Ralph and Kit. There was little to report. The horses had kept a good pace and occasionally Jonard had urged them into a canter. But it was with a sense of relief that they entered the gates of Boxborough Manor to halt before the great door. The Queen's coffin was

293

lifted from the wagon. Jonard drove on to the stableyard. Kit and Ralph carried the coffin into the house and through passages, finally stopping outside an unpretentious smaller door. The coffin was lowered respectfully to the floor. Ralph reached for the latch and stopped. There was a rumble of voices within the chapel.

"They're celebrating Mass. If we join them, will you behave yourself, Kit?"

His friend was indignant.

"Why would you need to ask?"

"I have seen you unfrock a bishop."

Kit raised his hands in surrender.

"I will behave."

Ralph opened the chapel door and stooped to enter. The Mass was in progress. Kit followed quietly. The Earl Boxborough and four women of the household knelt to receive Communion. A tall priest in Roman dress stooped to offer the paten and an older priest followed with the chalice. Two acolytes stood either side of the small altar. The slight draught reached the priest who looked up. The shock was absolute. Kit knew the pig face.

Ralph cried, "It's him! He murdered..."

He didn't finish as the Inquisitor dropped the paten and drew a pistol from his robe. The women screamed and ran from the chapel, hindering each other in the small doorway. The older priest and the Earl stood frozen. Ralph saw both acolytes were seeking weapons.

"Father! To the floor I beg you!"

The old man began clumsily to descend to his knees, but the Inquisitor struggled to bring him upright. This hesitation was fatal. There was no surprise as had cost Elizabeth her life. Ralph shot the Inquisitor and the older priest. The explosions were deafening in the small chapel. Seeing movement in the smoke Kit shot both acolytes. The hands of a clock would have barely quivered, but four men lay dead.

The Earl Boxborough declared, "Do you understand what irredeemable sin you have committed here?"

"Yes, father. We have disposed of four of the Devil's apostles."

294

Ralph helped his father to a chair where he sat regarding the bloody ruin of his chapel. Kit found a chair and sat down shakily.

"As I said before. The future lies with the pistol."

"You have befouled the chapel, Ralph. It can never be restored."

"It'll make a very useful storeroom. But you and I, father, are journeying to France. Do we not have Boxboroughs under some Gallic name with a chateau near Lille?"

"My father's brother. But why would we…?"

"Because you'll be bankrupt within a year and I know a lady of high station who owes Kit and I her life."

When the Earl looked dubious, Kit nodded.

"A most gracious lady."

"And we are leaving because very powerful people will kill us both for something I know. But first we must bury these vile bodies."

"But before we do," suggested Kit.

The dry well in the garden was an ideal burial site. To be filled in and forgotten. The corpses were stripped and their clothes burnt. The Inquisitor was dressed in Ralph's best Court dress. The old priest was attired as the Earl Boxborough. The acolytes wore gardeners' smocks that the Earl promised to replace.

Kit contributed his sword.

"Here lie the Earl Boxborough and his son with their faithful housemen. Murdered by unknown villains."

"Must you always turn every circumstance to drama, Kit?"

The two friends worked steadily to fill the pit. The Earl returned from the nursery with a small tree. To be planted on the burial ground.

"And what would that tree be called, milord?"

"Cercis siliquastrum. The Judas tree. Appropriate, I suggest."

Kit held the small tree in his hands and in his head a voice spoke; a girl's voice that laughed and lifted the heart.

"When we live somewhere and you plant a tree. Then I'll know that's where we will forever be."

295

The girl laughed and Kit remembered. He laid down his spade and said to Ralph, "I have to go now."

His friend was both surprised & disappointed.

"You're not coming to France with us?"

Kit shook his head.

"There's somewhere I have to be."

"What somewhere?"

"I'll find it."

*

Carole stopped in the passage to turn to her guests. She had at first feared failure, but had found the Mayor and Councillors truly impressed with the reconstruction she had shown them. Their enthusiasm had grown as they progressed through the Manor. They had duly stepped aside to allow three Elizabethan gentlemen plus their clerks pass by. They were not acknowledged, but Carole saw the glances that passed between the visitors.

"Sorry about that," Carole apologised, "That wasn't on schedule."

The smiles signified disbelief.

Let's hope we don't walk into a murder. Although . . .

Carole stopped to say, "Please note this modest door. You'd pass it without a second glance. Which I did. The little room beyond I categorised as a store room. I was wrong. It was the Boxborough family chapel and being covert Catholics they would have suffered torture and execution had the presence of the chapel ever been betrayed."

All the party broached the same question.

"Is it still a store room?"

Carole smiled to say, "I learn from my mistakes."

She opened the simple door and stooped to enter the chapel. Her visitors were on her heels when she realised there was an elderly priest offering the Eucharist to the Earl and three members of his household staff. Carole and the Councillors stood frozen. The Mayor whispered to Carole.

"Is this real?"

There was no other answer she could give.

296

"Yes. Of course!"

She was astounded when the Mayor and three Councillors went forward to drop to their knees at the rail. With little more than a puzzled look the old priest offered both bread and wine to these supplicants. When they rejoined the visiting party Carole led the Councillors from the chapel and closed the door. The Mayor shook hands with Carole.

"I don't know what the others thought, but that was the most wonderful moment of my life. I'll be forever grateful."

The Catholic Councillors were unanimous in agreeing.

"And worship has been going on in that little chapel for some four hundred years?"

"There would have been some glitches, but yes, four hundred years."

The Mayor looked round upon his colleagues.

"I don't doubt you'll have our full support."

Some days you're lucky and other days luck falls on you.

*

Dawn on the fresh green trees beckoned a sweet Summer morning. The day was beginning and life was waking. The old man and the youth coaxing the sheep from the pasture to cross the ancient road onto the farther pasture at the woodland edge hesitated. The erratic grumble of an old engine announced the approach of an antique motorcycle combination. The motorcycle slowed to a halt and the rider raised a glove in salute. The old man signalled his thanks.

The sheep began to flow as a woolly brook across the road into the safety of the fresh pasture. The old man and the dogs had their eyes on the sheep, but the boy was more engaged with the motorcycle combo and its rider. The man at the handlebars was tall, dark-eyed with overlong midnight hair spurning a safety helmet. If asked to describe him the boy might've said pirate. The old man called to him.

"Are thee with uzz, John?"

The youth flushed as the dogs rebuked him too, recalling him to the last rebellious ewes that had turned back into the old pasture. If lost it would take the morning to catch them. With

Tess and Tops, the youth retrieved them, apologising to the rider on the motorcycle as the old man stood by to close the gate on the last lingerers. They stood together at the latched gate, watching the young man kick the engine into life and slowly move away, gathering speed until distance lent invisibility.

The young man rode slowly checking hedge, scrub, verge, copse, broken wall, hedge, weedy verge and copse. The motorbike combo's engine rattled & stopped. A girl rose up from where she had been sitting beneath an age-old oak. She came to the young man to smile and say, "I never believed you would ever leave me. But you're going to ask, why did I leave you? Don't pretend. I know you too well, Kit."

The young man stood up in invisible stirrups.

"There used to be a burger van here."

"He was a brave, kindly man."

"We busked in the market."

"Gilsford market."

"I knew you would never leave me."

The girl climbed into the sidecar. She gave a sigh of happiness.

"I hate this Thing. I still have the bruises."

"Where have you been?" asked the young man.

"I was a barmaid. And an actor. Don't laugh! I saw you once, but you were just angry. Did you do what they wanted you to do?"

"Yes and no."

"My God! A typical Kit Marlowe answer. Either you did or you didn't."

"I remember when I caught some fish and we ate it. You hated it, but you ate it. Then you were sick everywhere."

"I remember you were frightened of the cooker, but you love Hoola Hoops."

"I thought you were dying and I went to get a priest and when we came back you were cleaning up your vomit and he was very angry with me. I never knew why. Aren't they supposed to be kind and forgiving?"

"You threw his bicycle over the back hedge."

"Aren't they supposed to forgive you seventy times seventy?"

Kit started the engine and they rode away together into the bright sweet morning. Time has no custody of love.

"So what did you do for them this time?"

"I wrote a speech for a Queen."

"And that's all?"

"If I told you the Queen gave me a lot of money, would you stop asking questions which ought not to be answered?"

SECRET STUFF YOU MIGHT
LIKE TO KNOW

Mary Stuart, Queen of Scots was not grotesquely butchered at Fotheringhay Castle in 1587. She was rescued by Christopher Marlowe, the Queen's Commissioner, who refused to carry out the death warrant. Mary was smuggled to France by the gallant chevalier Captain Louis de Saint des Vosges and Ganda, a resourceful Kentish fisherman. She lived under the protection of the de Guise family until her death in January, 1603 when her son ascended the English throne as James I of England & James VI of Scotland.

Whatever you do, you must never read the contemporary report of the appalling murder at Fotheringhay of Mary Stuart, great granddaughter of Henry VII, true inheritor of the Throne of England. If you do read this disgusting document, your view of the Virgin Queen of Merrie England will be changed forever. Now you know the true history of this forgotten lady, Mary Stuart, Queen of Scots.

Elizabeth I was shot dead at Tilbury before the Great Parade by a Papist assassin. In a unique coup d'etat the Queen was replaced by the remarkably talented actor, Matthew Querrilon who gave a brilliant performance as Elizabeth that dazzled the assembled company. The actor played the part of the Queen with remarkable success thereafter and undertook every public & private occasion without any doubt of her authenticity. Matthew Querrilon 'ruled' England with the aid of his Counsellors until his death in 1603 when James I ascended the throne.

The only error on his part was when he adlibbed in the speech at Tilbury saying, 'the heart & stomach of a king.' An astute observer might have questioned these words.

There have been some questionable burials. The traitor, Sir Royan Armitage lay buried in Peterborough Cathedral as Mary Queen of Scots until he was moved to Westminster Abbey as the Scottish Queen. Elizabeth Regina lies under the altar in the little chapel of Boxborough Manor, Kent. Matthew Querrilon as Elizabeth the Virgin Queen lies in Westminster Abbey. One wonders what unfortunate surprises await discovery elsewhere.

Noah & Annie escaped to Exeter where they ran a successful boarding house. Their two daughters took over the house when their parents retired to Salcombe.

Anna and Tameeyah, under other names, enjoy successful careers in theatre, television and film. They are lifelong friends.

Dame Carole Truscott is best known internationally as the President of SAVING ENGLAND. The Boxborough Manor project is among the earliest of her reclamation successes. Thanks to Carole Truscott many fine historical gems have been saved from demolition & restored. Her earliest international successes were the New York brownstones & the Boston town houses. Her work is now recognised worldwide.

Christopher 'Kit' Marlowe escaped from the sixteenth century to be reunited with his adopted daughter Hannah Cato. They now live in an old Bristol bus KEL 407 in a disused quarry in the village of Craster, Northumberland. They still ride Apollo's Chariot whose engine resounds as Olympian thunder within the quarry walls. They eat kippers from Robson's smokehouse and fresh-boiled crabs from the old man with the hut on the harbour.

Kit fishes from the pier and Hannah watches him. He needs reassurance when he doesn't catch anything and a wild celebration when he does. There have been few such celebrations. Kit has made a friend, a quiet older man. They fish together. He is a retired police officer called Stanley Robertson. What Hannah savours most is the peace & quiet wherein her beloved Christopher Marlowe continues to create masterpieces of theatre such as his recent successes, *THE DOWNFALL OF THE TYRANT* and *ELIZABETH GLORIANA,* performed centuries-wide.

And in another place & time the satire, Good *Queen Bess & the Defeat of the Armada!* Devised by Christopher Marlowe. A Comic Conflict Enacted by the Queen's Company under the Direction of the esteemed Ned Alleyn.

One last warning! Stay well clear of the past. Be aware of what happened to Mr. George Bryce. A sad example to us all.

Alex Y. Ferguson

Printed in Great Britain
by Amazon